THE INCOMPLETE AMORIST

E. NESBIT

1st WORLD
LIBRARY
Literary Society

The Incomplete Amorist

E. Nesbit

© 1st World Library, 2007
PO Box 2211
Fairfield, IA 52556
www.1stworldlibrary.com
First Edition

LCCN: 2007920632

Softcover ISBN: 978-1-4218-3943-1
Hardcover ISBN: 978-1-4218-3843-4
eBook ISBN: 978-1-4218-4043-7

Purchase *"The Incomplete Amorist"*
as a traditional bound book at:
www.1stWorldLibrary.com/purchase.asp?ISBN=978-1-4218-3943-1

1st World Library is a literary, educational organization
dedicated to:

- Creating a free internet library of downloadable ebooks

- Hosting writing competitions and offering book
publishing scholarships.

Interested in more 1st World Library books?
contact: literacy@1stworldlibrary.com
Check us out at: www.1stworldlibrary.com

1ˢᵗ World Library Literary Society

Giving Back to the World

"If you want to work on the core problem, it's early school literacy."
- James Barksdale, former CEO of Netscape

"No skill is more crucial to the future of a child, or to a democratic and prosperous society, than literacy."

- Los Angeles Times

Literacy... means far more than learning how to read and write... The aim is to transmit... knowledge and promote social participation."

- UNESCO

"Literacy is not a luxury, it is a right and a responsibility. If our world is to meet the challenges of the twenty-first century we must harness the energy and creativity of all our citizens."

- President Bill Clinton

"Parents should be encouraged to read to their children, and teachers should be equipped with all available techniques for teaching literacy, so the varying needs and capacities of individual kids can be taken into account."

- Hugh Mackay

To

Richard Reynolds
and
Justus Miles Forman

"Faire naitre un desir, le nourrir, le developper, le grandir, le satisfaire, c'est un poeme tout entier."

—*Balzac*

CONTENTS

BOOK I - THE GIRL

BOOK II - THE MAN

BOOK III - THE OTHER WOMAN

BOOK IV - THE OTHER MAN

PEOPLE OF THE STORY

Eustace Vernon. - The Incomplete Amorist

Betty Desmond - The Girl

The Rev. Cecil Underwood - Her Step-Father

Miss Julia Desmond - Her Aunt

Robert Temple - The Other Man

Lady St. Craye - The Other Woman

Miss Voscoe - The Art Student

Madame Chevillon. - The Inn-Keeper at Crez

Paula Conway - A Soul in Hell

Mimi Chantal - A Model

Village Matrons, Concierges, Art Students, Etc.

BOOK 1

THE GIRL

CHAPTER I

THE INEVITABLE

"No. The chemises aren't cut out. I haven't had time. There are enough shirts to go on with, aren't there, Mrs. James?" said Betty.

"We can make do for this afternoon, Miss, but the men they're getting blowed out with shirts. It's the children's shifts as we can't make shift without much longer." Mrs. James, habitually doleful, punctuated her speech with sniffs.

"That's a joke, Mrs. James," said Betty. "How clever you are!"

"I try to be what's fitting," said Mrs. James, complacently.

"Talk of fitting," said Betty, "If you like I'll fit on that black bodice for you, Mrs. Symes. If the other ladies don't mind waiting for the reading a little bit."

"I'd as lief talk as read, myself," said a red-faced sandy-haired woman; "books ain't what they was in my young days."

"If it's the same to you, Miss," said Mrs. Symes in a thick rich voice, "I'll not be tried on afore a room full. If we are poor we can all be clean's what I say, and I keeps my unders as I keeps my outside. But not before persons as has real imitation lace on their petticoat bodies. I see them when I was a-nursing her with her fourth. No, Miss, and thanking you kindly, but begging your pardon all the same."

"Don't mention it," said Betty absently. "Oh, Mrs. Smith, you can't have lost your thimble already. Why what's that you've got in your mouth?"

"So it is!" Mrs. Smith's face beamed at the gratifying coincidence. "It always was my habit, from a child, to put things there for safety."

"These cheap thimbles ain't fit to put in your mouth, no more than coppers," said Mrs. James, her mouth full of pins.

"Oh, nothing hurts you if you like it," said Betty recklessly. She had been reading the works of Mr. G.K. Chesterton.

A shocked murmur arose.

"Oh, Miss, what about the publy kows?" said Mrs. Symes heavily. The others nodded acquiescence.

"Don't you think we might have a window open?" said Betty. The May sunshine beat on the schoolroom windows. The room, crowded with the stout members of the "Mother's Meeting and Mutual Clothing Club," was stuffy, unbearable.

A murmur arose far more shocked than the first.

"I was just a-goin' to say why not close the door, that being what doors is made for, after all," said Mrs. Symes. "I feel a sort ofdraught a-creeping up my legs as it is."

The door was shut.

"You can't be too careful," said the red-faced woman; "we never know what a chill mayn't bring forth. My cousin's sister-in-law, she had twins, and her aunt come in and says she, 'You're a bit stuffy here, ain't you?' and with that she opens the window a crack,—not meaning no harm, Miss,—as it might be you. And within a year that poor unfortunate woman she popped off, when least expected. Gas ulsters, the doctor said. Which it's what you call chills, if you're a doctor and can't speak plain."

"My poor grandmother come to her end the same way," said Mrs. Smith, "only with her it was the Bible reader as didn't shut the door through being so set on shewing off her reading. And my granny, a clot of blood went to her brain, and her brain went to her head and she was a corpse inside of fifty minutes."

Every woman in the room was waiting, feverishly alert, for the pause that should allow her to begin her own detailed narrative of disease.

Mrs. James was easily first in the competition.

"Them quick deaths," she said, "is sometimes a blessing in disguise to both parties concerned. My poor husband—years upon years he lingered, and he had a bad leg—talk of bad legs, I wish you could all have seen it," she added generously.

"Was it the kind that keeps all on a-breaking out?" asked Mrs. Symes hastily, "because my youngest brother had a leg that nothing couldn't stop. Break out it would do what they might. I'm sure the bandages I've took off him in a morning—"

Betty clapped her hands.

It was the signal that the reading was going to begin, and the matrons looked at her resentfully. What call had people to start reading when the talk was flowing so free and pleasant?

Betty, rather pale, began: "This is a story about a little boy called Wee Willie Winkie."

"I call that a silly sort of name," whispered Mrs. Smith.

"Did he make a good end, Miss?" asked Mrs. James plaintively.

"You'll see," said Betty.

"I like it best when they dies forgiving of everybody and singing hymns to the last."

"And when they says, 'Mother, I shall meet you 'ereafter in the better land'—that's what makes you cry so pleasant."

"Do you want me to read or not?" asked Betty in desperation.

"Yes, Miss, yes," hummed the voices heavy and shrill.

"It's her hobby, poor young thing," whispered Mrs. Smith, "we all 'as 'em. My own is a light cake to my tea, and always was. Ush."

Betty read.

When the mothers had wordily gone, she threw open the windows, propped the door wide with a chair, and went to tea. She had it alone.

"Your Pa's out a-parishing," said Letitia, bumping down the tray in front of her.

"That's a let-off anyhow," said Betty to herself, and she propped up a Stevenson against the tea-pot.

After tea parishioners strolled up by ones and twos and threes to change their books at the Vicarage lending library. The books were covered with black calico, and smelt of rooms whose windows were never opened.

When she had washed the smell of the books off, she did her hair very carefully in a new way that seemed becoming, and went down to supper.

E. Nesbit

Her step-father only spoke once during the meal; he was luxuriating in the thought of the *Summa Theologiae* of Aquinas in leather still brown and beautiful, which he had providentially discovered in the wash-house of an ailing Parishioner. When he did speak he said:

"How extremely untidy your hair is, Lizzie. I wish you would take more pains with your appearance."

When he had withdrawn to his books she covered three new volumes for the library: the black came off on her hands, but anyway it was cleandirt.

She went to bed early.

"And that's my life," she said as she blew out the candle.

Said Mrs. James to Mrs. Symes over the last and strongest cup of tea:

"Miss Betty's ailing a bit, I fancy. Looked a bit peaky, it seemed to me. I shouldn't wonder if she was to go off in a decline like her father did."

"It wasn't no decline," said Mrs. Symes, dropping her thick voice, "'e was cut off in the midst of his wicked courses. A judgment if ever there was one."

Betty's blameless father had been killed in the hunting field.

"I daresay she takes after him, only being a female it all turns to her being pernickety in her food and allus wanting the windows open. And mark my words, it may turn into a decline yet, Mrs. Symes, my dear."

Mrs. Symes laughed fatly. "That ain't no decline," she said, "you take it from me. What Miss Betty wants is a young man. It is but nature after all, and what we must all come to, gentle or simple. Give her a young man to walk out with and you'll see the difference. Decline indeed! A young man's what she wants. And if I know anything of gells and their ways she'll get one, no matter how close the old chap keeps her."

Mrs. Symes was not so wrong as the delicate minded may suppose.

Betty did indeed desire to fall in love. In all the story books the main interest of the heroine's career began with that event. Not that she voiced the desire to herself. Only once she voiced it in her prayers.

"Oh, God," she said, "do please let something happen!"

That was all. A girl had her little reticences, even with herself, even with her Creator.

Next morning she planned to go sketching; but no, there were three more detestable books to be put into nasty little black cotton coats, the drawing-room to be dusted—all the hateful china—the peas to be shelled for dinner.

She shelled the peas in the garden. It was a beautiful green garden, and lovers could have walked very happily down the lilac-bordered paths.

"Oh, how sick I am of it all!" said Betty. She would not say, even to herself, that what she hated was the frame without the picture.

As she carried in the peas she passed the open window of the study where, among shelves of dull books and dusty pamphlets, her step-father had as usual forgotten his sermon in a chain of references to the Fathers. Betty saw his thin white hairs, his hard narrow face and tight mouth, the hands yellow and claw-like that gripped the thin vellum folio.

"I suppose even he was young once," she said, "but I'm sure he doesn't remember it."

E. Nesbit

He saw her go by, young and alert in the sunshine, and the May air stirred the curtains. He looked vaguely about him, unlocked a drawer in his writing-table, and took out a leather case. He gazed long at the face within, a young bright face with long ringlets above the formal bodice and sloping shoulders of the sixties.

"Well, well," he said, "well, well," locked it away, and went back to *De Poenis Parvulorum.*

"I *will* go out," said Betty, as she parted with the peas. "I don't care!"

It was not worth while to change one's frock. Even when one was properly dressed, at rare local garden-party or flower-show, one never met anyone that mattered.

She fetched her sketching things. At eighteen one does so pathetically try to feed the burgeoning life with the husks of polite accomplishment. She insisted on withholding from the clutches of the Parish the time to practise Beethoven and Sullivan for an hour daily. Daily, for half an hour, she read an improving book. Just now it was The French Revolution, and Betty thought it would last till she was sixty. She tried to read French and German—Telemaque and Maria Stuart. She fully intended to become all that a cultured young woman should be. But self-improvement is a dull game when there is no one to applaud your score.

What the gardener called the gravel path was black earth, moss-grown. Very pretty, but Betty thought it shabby.

It was soft and cool, though, to the feet, and the dust of the white road sparkled like diamond dust in the sunlight.

She crossed the road and passed through the swing gate into the park, where the grass was up for hay, with red sorrel and buttercups and tall daisies and feathery flowered grasses, their colours all tangled and blended together like ravelled ends of silk on the wrong side of some great square of tapestry. Here and there in the wide sweep of tall growing things stood a tree—a may-tree shining like silver, a laburnum like fine gold. There were horse-chestnuts whose spires of blossom shewed like fat candles on a Christmas tree for giant children. And the sun was warm and the tree shadows black on the grass.

Betty told herself that she hated it all. She took the narrow path—the grasses met above her feet—crossed the park, and reached the rabbit warren, where the chalk breaks through the thin dry turf, and the wild thyme grows thick.

A may bush, overhanging a little precipice of chalk, caught her eye. A wild rose was tangled round it. It was, without doubt, the most difficult composition within sight.

"I will sketch that," said Eighteen, confidently.

For half an hour she busily blotted and washed and niggled. Then she became aware that she no longer had the rabbit warren to herself.

"And he's an artist, too!" said Betty. "How awfully interesting! I wish I could see his face."

But this his slouched Panama forbade. He was in white, the sleeve and breast of his painting jacket smeared with many colours; he had a camp-stool and an easel and looked, she could not help feeling, much more like a real artist than she did, hunched up as she was on a little mound of turf, in her shabby pink gown and that hateful garden hat with last year's dusty flattened roses in it.

She went on sketching with feverish unskilled fingers, and a pulse that had actually quickened its beat.

She cast little glances at him as often as she dared. He was certainly a real artist. She could tell that by the very way he held his palette. Was he staying with people about there?

E. Nesbit

Should she meet him? Would they ever be introduced to each other?

"Oh, what a pity," said Betty from the heart, "that we aren't introduced *now*!"

Her sketch grew worse and worse.

"It's no good," she said. "I can't do anything with it."

She glanced at him. He had pushed back the hat. She saw quite plainly that he was smiling—a very little, but he *was* smiling. Also he was looking at her, and across the fifteen yards of gray turf their eyes met. And she knew that he knew that this was not her first glance at him.

She paled with fury.

"He has been watching me all the time! He is making fun of me. He knows I can't sketch. Of course he can see it by the silly way I hold everything." She ran her knife around her sketch, detached it, and tore it across and across.

The stranger raised his hat and called eagerly.

"I say—please don't move for a minute. Do you mind? I've just got your pink gown. It's coming beautifully. Between brother artists—Do, please! Do sit still and go on sketching— Ah, do!"

Betty's attitude petrified instantly. She held a brush in her hand, and she looked down at her block. But she did not go on sketching. She sat rigid and three delicious words rang in her ears: "Between brother artists!" How very nice of him! He hadn't been making fun, after all. But wasn't it rather impertinent of him to put her in his picture without asking her? Well, it wasn't she but her pink gown he wanted. And "between brother artists!" Betty drew a long breath.

"It's no use," he called; "don't bother any more. The pose is gone."

She rose to her feet and he came towards her.

"Let me see the sketch," he said. "Why did you tear it up?" He fitted the pieces together. "Why, it's quite good. You ought to study in Paris," he added idly.

She took the torn papers from his hand with a bow, and turned to go.

"Don't go," he said. "You're not going? Don't you want to look at my picture?"

Now Betty knew as well as you do that you musn't speak to people unless you've been introduced to them. But the phrase "brother artists" had played ninepins with her little conventions.

"Thank you. I should like to very much," said Betty. "I don't care," she said to herself, "and besides, it's not as if he were a young man, or a tourist, or anything. He must be ever so old—thirty; I shouldn't wonder if he was thirty-five."

When she saw the picture she merely said, "Oh," and stood at gaze. For it *was* a picture—a picture that, seen in foreign lands, might well make one sick with longing for the dry turf and the pale dog violets that love the chalk, for the hum of the bees and the scent of the thyme. He had chosen the bold sweep of the brown upland against the sky, and low to the left, where the line broke, the dim violet of the Kentish hills. In the green foreground the pink figure, just roughly blocked in, was blocked in by a hand that knew its trade, and was artist to the tips of its fingers.

"Oh!" said Betty again.

"Yes," said he, "I think I've got it this time. I think it'll make a hole in the wall, eh? Yes; it is good!"

"Yes," said Betty; "oh, yes."

"Do you often go a-sketching?" he asked.

"How modest he is," thought Betty; "he changes the subject so as not to seem to want to be praised."

Aloud she answered with shy fluttered earnestness: "Yes—no. I don't know. Sometimes."

His lips were grave, but there was the light behind his eyes that goes with a smile.

"What unnecessary agitation!" he was thinking. "Poor little thing, I suppose she's never seen a man before. Oh, these country girls!" Aloud he was saying: "This is such a perfect country. You ought to sketch every day."

"I've no one to teach me," said Betty, innocently phrasing a long-felt want.

The man raised his eyebrows. "Well, after that, here goes!" he said to himself. "I wish you'd let *me* teach you," he said to her, beginning to put his traps together.

"Oh, I didn't mean that," said Betty in real distress. What would he think of her? How greedy and grasping she must seem! "I didn't mean that at all!"

"No; but I do," he said.

"But you're a great artist," said Betty, watching him with clasped hands. "I suppose it would be—I mean—don't you know, we're not rich, and I suppose your lessons are worth pounds and pounds."

"I don't give lessons for money," his lips tightened—"only

for love."

"That means nothing, doesn't it?" she said, and flushed to find herself on the defensive feebly against—nothing.

"At tennis, yes," he said, and to himself he added: "*Vieux jeu,* my dear, but you did it very prettily."

"But I couldn't let you give me lessons for nothing."

"Why not?" he asked. And his calmness made Betty feel ashamed and sordid.

"I don't know," she answered tremulously, but I don't think my step-father would want me to."

"You think it would annoy him?"

"I'm sure it would, if he knew about it."

Betty was thinking how little her step-father had ever cared to know of her and her interests. But the man caught the ball as he saw it.

"Then why let him know?" was the next move; and it seemed to him that Betty's move of rejoinder came with a readiness born of some practice at the game.

"Oh," she said innocently, "I never thought of that! But wouldn't it be wrong?"

"She's got the whole thing stereotyped. But it's dainty type anyhow," he thought. "Of course it wouldn't be wrong," he said. "It wouldn't hurt him. Don't you know that nothing's wrong unless it hurts somebody?"

"Yes," she said eagerly, "that's what I think. But all the same it doesn't seem fair that you should take all that trouble for me and get nothing in return."

"Well played! We're getting on!" he thought, and added aloud: "But perhaps I shan't get nothing in return?"

Her eyes dropped over the wonderful thought that perhaps she might do something for *him*. But what? She looked straight at him, and the innocent appeal sent a tiny thorn of doubt through his armour of complacency. Was she—after all? No, no novice could play the game so well. And yet—

"I would do anything I could, you know," she said eagerly, "because it is so awfully kind of you, and I do so want to be able to paint. What can I do?"

"What can you do?" he asked, and brought his face a little nearer to the pretty flushed freckled face under the shabby hat. Her eyes met his. He felt a quick relenting, and drew back.

"Well, for one thing you could let me paint your portrait."

Betty was silent.

"Come, play up, you little duffer," he urged inwardly.

When she spoke her voice trembled.

"I don't know how to thank you," she said.

"And you will?"

"Oh, I will; indeed I will!"

"How good and sweet you are," he said. Then there was a silence.

Betty tightened the strap of her sketching things and said:

"I think I ought to go home now."

He had the appropriate counter ready.

"Ah, don't go yet!" he said; "let us sit down; see, that bank is quite in the shade now, and tell me—"

"Tell you what?" she asked, for he had made the artistic pause.

"Oh, anything—anything about yourself."

Betty was as incapable of flight as any bird on a limed twig.

She walked beside him to the bank, and sat down at his bidding, and he lay at her feet, looking up into her eyes. He asked idle questions: she answered them with a conscientious tremulous truthfulness that showed to him as the most finished art. And it seemed to him a very fortunate accident that he should have found here, in this unlikely spot, so accomplished a player at his favorite game. Yet it was the variety of his game for which he cared least. He did not greatly relish a skilled adversary. Betty told him nervously and in words ill-chosen everything that he asked to know, but all the while the undercurrent of questions rang strong within her—"When is he to teach me? Where? How?"—so that when at last there was left but the bare fifteen minutes needed to get one home in time for the midday dinner she said abruptly:

"And when shall I see you again?"

"You take the words out of my mouth," said he. And indeed she had. "She has no *finesse* yet," he told himself. "She might have left that move to me."

"The lessons, you know," said Betty, "and, and the picture, if you really do want to do it."

"If I want to do it!—You know I want to do it. Yes. It's like the nursery game. How, when and where? Well, as to the how—I can paint and you can learn. The where—there's a circle of pines in the wood here. You know it? A sort of giant fairy ring?"

She did know it.

"Now for the when—and that's the most important. I should like to paint you in the early morning when the day is young and innocent and beautiful—like—like—" He was careful to break off in a most natural seeming embarrassment. "That's a bit thick, but she'll swallow it all right. Gone down? Right!" he told himself.

"I could come out at six if you liked, or—or five," said Betty, humbly anxious to do her part.

He was almost shocked. "My good child," he told her silently, "someone really ought to teach you not to do all the running. You don't give a man a chance."

"Then will you meet me here to-morrow at six?" he said. "You won't disappoint me, will you?" he added tenderly.

"No," said downright Betty, "I'll be sure to come. But not to-morrow," she added with undisguised regret; "to-morrow's Sunday."

"Monday then," said he, "and good-bye."

"Good-bye, and—oh, I don't know how to thank you!"

"I'm very much mistaken if you don't," he said as he stood bareheaded, watching the pink gown out of sight.

"Well, adventures to the adventurous! A clergyman's daughter, too! I might have known it."

CHAPTER II

THE IRRESISTIBLE

Betty had to run all the way home, and then she was late for dinner. Her step-father's dry face and dusty clothes, the solid comfort of the mahogany furnished dining room, the warm wet scent of mutton,—these seemed needed to wake her from what was, when she had awakened, a dream—the open sky, the sweet air of the May fields and *Him*. Already the stranger was Him to Betty. But, then, she did not know his name.

She slipped into her place at the foot of the long white dining table, a table built to serve a dozen guests, and where no guests ever sat, save rarely a curate or two, and more rarely even, an aunt.

"You are late again, Lizzie," said her step-father.

"Yes, Father," said she, trying to hide her hands and the fact that she had not had time to wash them. A long streak of burnt sienna marked one finger, and her nails had little slices of various colours in them. Her paint-box was always hard to open.

Usually Mr. Underwood saw nothing. But when he saw anything he saw everything. His eye was caught by the green smudge on her pink sleeve.

"I wish you would contrive to keep yourself clean, or else wear a pinafore," he said.

Betty flushed scarlet.

"I'm very sorry," she said, "but it's only water colour. It will wash out."

"You are nearly twenty, are you not?" the Vicar inquired with the dry smile that always infuriated his step-daughter. How was she to know that it was the only smile he knew, and that smiles of any sort had long grown difficult to him?

"Eighteen," she said.

"It is almost time you began to think about being a lady."

This was badinage. No failures had taught the Reverend Cecil that his step-daughter had an ideal of him in which badinage had no place. She merely supposed that he wished to be disagreeable.

She kept a mutinous silence. The old man sighed. It is one's duty to correct the faults of one's child, but it is not pleasant. The Reverend Cecil had not the habit of shirking any duty because he happened to dislike it.

The mutton was taken away.

Betty, her whole being transfigured by the emotions of the morning, stirred the stewed rhubarb on her plate. She felt rising in her a sort of wild forlorn courage. Why shouldn't she speak out? Her step-father couldn't hate her more than he did, whatever she said. He might even be glad to be rid of her. She spoke suddenly and rather loudly before she knew that she had meant to speak at all.

"Father," she said, "I wish you'd let me go to Paris and study art. Not now," she hurriedly explained with a sudden vision of being taken at her word and packed off to France before six o'clock on Monday morning, "not now, but later. In the autumn perhaps. I would work very hard. I wish you'd let me."

He put on his spectacles and looked at her with wistful kindness. She read in his glance only a frozen contempt.

"No, my child," he said. Paris is a sink of iniquity. I passed a week there once, many years ago. It was at the time of the Great Exhibition. You are growing discontented, Lizzie. Work is the cure for that. Mrs. Symes tells me that the chemises for the Mother's sewing meetings are not cut out yet."

"I'll cut them out to-day. They haven't finished the shirts yet, anyway," said Betty; "but I do wish you'd just think about Paris, or even London."

"You can have lessons at home if you like. I believe there are excellent drawing-mistresses in Sevenoaks. Mrs. Symes was recommending one of them to me only the other day. With certificates from the High School I seem to remember her saying."

"But that's not what I want," said Betty with a courage that surprised her as much as it surprised him. "Don't you see, Father? One gets older every day, and presently I shall be quite old, and I shan't have been anywhere or seen anything."

He thought he laughed indulgently at the folly of youth. She thought his laugh the most contemptuous, the cruelest sound in the world. "He doesn't deserve that I should tell him about Him," she thought, "and I won't. I don't care!"

"No, no," he said, "no, no, no. The home is the place for girls. The safe quiet shelter of the home. Perhaps some day your husband will take you abroad for a fortnight now and then. If you manage to get a husband, that is."

He had seen, through his spectacles, her flushed prettiness, and old as he was he remembered well enough how a face like hers would seem to a young man's eyes. Of course she would get a husband? So he spoke in kindly irony. And she hated him for a wanton insult.

"Try to do your duty in that state of life to which you are called," he went on: "occupy yourself with music and books and the details of housekeeping. No, don't have my study turned out," he added in haste, remembering how his advice about household details had been followed when last he gave it. "Don't be a discontented child. Go and cut out the nice little chemises." This seemed to him almost a touch of kindly humour, and he went back to Augustine, pleased with himself.

Betty set her teeth and went, black rage in her heart, to cut out the hateful little chemises.

She dragged the great roll of evil smelling grayish unbleached calico from the schoolroom cupboard and heaved it on to the table. It was very heavy. The scissors were blunt and left deep red-blue indentations on finger and thumb. She was rather pleased that the scissors hurt so much.

"Father doesn't care a single bit, he hates me," she said, "and I hate him. Oh, I do."

She would not think of the morning. Not now, with this fire of impotent resentment burning in her, would she take out those memories and look at them. Those were not thoughts to be dragged through the litter of unbleached cotton cuttings. She worked on doggedly, completed the tale of hot heavy little garments, gathered up the pieces into the waste-paper basket and put away the roll.

Not till the paint had been washed from her hands, and the crumbled print dress exchanged for a quite respectable muslin did she consciously allow the morning's memories to come out and meet her eyes. Then she went down to the arbour where she had shelled peas only that morning.

"It seems years and years ago," she said. And sitting there, she slowly and carefully went over everything. What he had said, what she had said. There were some things she could not quite remember. But she remembered enough. "Brother artists" were the words she said oftenest to herself, but the words that sank themselves were, "young and innocent and beautiful like—like—"

"But he couldn't have meant me, of course," she told herself.

And on Monday she would see him again,—and he would give her a lesson!

Sunday was incredibly wearisome. Her Sunday-school class had never been so tiresome nor so soaked in hair-oil. In church she was shocked to find herself watching, from her pew in the chancel, the entry of late comers—of whom He was not one. No afternoon had ever been half so long. She wrote up her diary. Thursday and Friday were quickly chronicled. At "Saturday" she paused long, pen in hand, and then wrote very quickly: "I went out sketching and met a gentleman, an artist. He was very kind and is going to teach me to paint and he is going to paint my portrait. I do not like him particularly. He is rather old, and not really good-looking. I shall not tell father, because he is simply hateful to me. I am going to meet this artist at 6 to-morrow. It will be dreadful having to get up so early. I almost wish I hadn't said I would go. It will be such a bother."

Then she hid the diary in a drawer, under her confirmation dress and veil, and locked the drawer carefully.

He was not at church in the evening either. He had thought of it, but decided that it was too much trouble to get into decent clothes.

"I shall see her soon enough," he thought, "curse my impulsive generosity! Six o'clock, forsooth, and all to please a clergyman's daughter."

E. Nesbit

She came back from church with tired steps.

"I do hope I'm not going to be ill," she said. "I feel so odd, just as if I hadn't had anything to eat for days,—and yet I'm not a bit hungry either. I daresay I shan't wake up in time to get there by six."

She was awake before five.

She woke with a flutter of the heart. What was it? Had anything happened? Was anyone ill? Then she recognized that she was not unhappy. And she felt more than ever as though it were days since she had had anything to eat.

"Oh, dear," said Betty, jumping out of bed. "I'm going out, to meet Him, and have a drawing-lesson!"

She dressed quickly. It was too soon to start. Not for anything must she be first at the rendezvous, even though it were only for a drawing-lesson. That "only" pulled her up sharply.

When she was dressed she dug out the diary and wrote:

"This is terrible. Is it possible that I have fallen in love with him? I don't know. 'Who ever loved that loved not at first sight?' It is a most frightful tragedy to happen to one, and at my age too. What a long life of loneliness stretches in front of me! For of course he could never care for me. And if this *is* love—well, it will be once and forever with me, I know.

"That's my nature, I'm afraid. But I'm not,—I can't be. But I never felt so unlike myself. I feel a sort of calm exultation, as if something very wonderful was very near me. Dear Diary, what a comfort it is to have you to tell everything to!"

It seemed to her that she must certainly be late. She had to creep down the front stairs so very slowly and softly in order that she might not awaken her step-father. She had so carefully and silently to unfasten a window and creep out, to close the window again, without noise, lest the maids should hear and come running to see why their young mistress was out of her bed at that hour. She had to go on tiptoe through the shrubbery and out through the church yard. One could climb its wall, and get into the Park that way, so as not to meet labourers on the road who would stare to see her alone so early and perhaps follow her.

Once in the park she was safe. Her shoes and her skirts were wet with dew. She made haste. She did not want to keep him waiting.

But she was first at the rendezvous, after all.

She sat down on the carpet of pine needles. How pretty the early morning was. The sunlight was quite different from the evening sunlight, so much lighter and brighter. And the shadows were different. She tried to settle on a point of view for her sketch, the sketch he was to help her with.

Her thoughts went back to what she had written in her diary. If that *should* be true she must be very, very careful. He must never guess it, never. She would be very cold and distant and polite. Not hail-fellow well-met with a "brother artist," like she had been yesterday. It was all very difficult indeed. Even if it really did turn out to be true, if the wonderful thing had happened to her, if she really was in love she would not try a bit to make him like her. That would be forward and "horrid." She would never try to attract any man. Those things must come of themselves or not at all.

She arranged her skirt in more effective folds, and wondered how it would look as one came up the woodland path. She thought it would look rather picturesque. It was a nice heliotrope colour. It would look like a giant Parma violet against the dark green background. She hoped her hair was tidy. And that her hat was not very crooked. However little one desires to attract, one may at least wish one's hat to be straight.

She looked for the twentieth time at her watch, the serviceable silver watch that had been her mother's. Half-past six, and he had not come.

Well, when he did come she would pretend she had only just got there. Or how would it be if she gave up being a Parma violet and went a little way down the path and then turned back when she heard him coming? She walked away a dozen yards and stood waiting. But he did not come. Was it possible that he was not coming? Was he ill—lying uncared for at the Peal of Bells in the village, with no one to smooth his pillow or put eau-de-cologne on his head?

She walked a hundred yards or so towards the village on the spur of this thought.

Or perhaps he had come by another way to the trysting place? That thought drove her back. He was not there.

Well, she would not stay any longer. She would just go away, and come back ever so much later, and let him have a taste of waiting. She had had her share, she told herself, as she almost ran from the spot. She stopped suddenly. But suppose he did *not* wait? She went slowly back.

She sat down again, schooled herself to patience.

What an idiot she had been! Like any school-girl. Of course he had never meant to come. Why should he? That page in her diary called out to her to come home and burn it. Care for him indeed! Not she! Why she hadn't exchanged ten words with the man!

"But I knew it was all nonsense when I wrote it," she said. "I only just put it down to see what it would look like."

*   *   *   *   *

Mr. Eustace Vernon roused himself, and yawned.

"It's got to be done, I suppose. Buck up,—you'll feel better after your bath! Jove! Seven o'clock. Will she have waited? She's a keen player if she has. It's just worth trying, I suppose."

The church clock struck the half-hour as he turned into the wood. Something palely violet came towards him.

"So you *are* here," he said. "Where's the pink frock?"

"It's—it's going to the wash," said a stiff and stifled voice. "I'm sorry I couldn't get here at six. I hope you didn't wait long?"

"Not very long," he said, smiling; "but—Great Heavens, what on earth is the matter?"

"Nothing," she said.

"But you've been—you are—"

"I'm not," she said defiantly,—"besides, I've got neuralgia. It always makes me look like that."

"My Aunt!" he thought. "Then she *was* here at six and—she's been crying because I wasn't and—oh, where are we?" "I'm so sorry you've got neuralgia," he said gently, "but I'm awfully glad you didn't get here at six. Because my watch was wrong and I've only just got here, and I should never have forgiven myself if you'd waited for me a single minute. Is the neuralgia better now?"

"Yes," she said, smiling faintly, "much better. It was rather sharp while it lasted, though."

"Yes," he said, "I see it was. I am so glad you did come. But I was so certain you wouldn't that I didn't bring any of my

E. Nesbit

traps. So we can't begin the picture to-day. Will you start a sketch, or is your neuralgia too bad?"

He knew it would be: and it was.

So they merely sat on the pine carpet and talked till it was time for her to go back to the late Rectory breakfast. They told each other their names that day. Betty talked very carefully. It was most important that he should think well of her. Her manner had changed, as she had promised herself it should do if she found she cared for him. Now she was with him she knew, of course, that she did not care at all. What had made her so wretched—no, so angry that she had actually cried, was simply the idea that she had been made a fool of. That she had kept the tryst and he hadn't. Now he had come she was quite calm. She did not care in the least.

He was saying to himself: "I'm not often wrong, but I was off the line yesterday. All that doesn't count. We take a fresh deal and start fair. She doesn't know the game, *mais elle a des moyens*. She's never played the game before. And she cried because I didn't turn up. And so I'm the first—think of it, if you please—absolutely the first one! Well: it doesn't detract from the interest of the game. It's quite a different game and requires more skill. But not more than I have, perhaps."

They parted with another tryst set for the next morning. The brother artist note had been skilfully kept vibrating.

Betty was sure that she should never have any feeling for him but mere friendliness. She was glad of that. It must be dreadful to be really in love. So unsettling.

CHAPTER III

VOLUNTARY

Mr. Eustace Vernon is not by any error to be imagined as a villain of the deepest dye, coldly planning to bring misery to a simple village maiden for his own selfish pleasure. Not at all. As he himself would have put it, he meant no harm to the girl. He was a master of two arts, and to these he had devoted himself wholly. One was the art of painting. But one cannot paint for all the hours there are. In the intervals of painting Vernon always sought to exercise his other art. One is limited, of course, by the possibilities, but he liked to have always at least one love affair on hand. And just now there were none—none at least possessing the one charm that irresistibly drew him—newness. The one or two affairs that dragged on merely meant letter writing, and he hated writing letters almost as much as he hated reading them.

The country had been unfortunately barren of interest until his eyes fell on that sketching figure in the pink dress. For he respected one of his arts no less than the other, and would as soon have thought of painting a vulgar picture as of undertaking a vulgar love-affair. He was no pavement artist. Nor did he degrade his art by caricatures drawn in hotel bars. Dairy maids did not delight him, and the mood was rare with him in which one finds anything to say to a little milliner. He wanted the means, not the end, and was at one with the unknown sage who said: "The love of pleasure spoils the pleasure of love."

E. Nesbit

There is a gift, less rare than is supposed, of wiping the slate clean of memories, and beginning all over again: a certain virginity of soul that makes each new kiss the first kiss, each new love the only love. This gift was Vernon's, and he had cultivated it so earnestly, so delicately, that except in certain moods when he lost his temper, and with it his control of his impulses, he was able to bring even to a conservatory flirtation something of the fresh emotion of a schoolboy in love.

Betty's awkwardnesses, which he took for advances, had chilled him a little, though less than they would have done had not one of the evil-tempered moods been on him.

He had dreaded lest the affair should advance too quickly. His own taste was for the first steps in an affair of the heart, the delicate doubts, the planned misunderstandings. He did not question his own ability to conduct the affair capably from start to finish, but he hated to skip the dainty preliminaries. He had feared that with Betty he should have to skip them, for he knew that it is only in their first love affairs that women have the patience to watch the flower unfold itself. He himself was of infinite patience in that pastime. He bit his lip and struck with his cane at the buttercup heads. He had made a wretched beginning, with his "good and sweet." his "young and innocent and beautiful like—like." If the girl had been a shade less innocent the whole business would have been muffed—muffed hopelessly.

To-morrow he would be there early. A ship of promise should be—not launched—that was weeks away. The first timbers should be felled to build a ship to carry him, and her too, of course, a little way towards the enchanted islands.

He knew the sea well, and it would be pleasant to steer on it one to whom it was all new—all, all.

"Dear little girl," he said, "I don't suppose she has ever even thought of love."

He was not in love with her, but he meant to be. He carefully thought of her all that day, of her hair, her eyes, her hands; her hands were really beautiful—small, dimpled and well-shaped —not the hands he loved best, those were long and very slender,—but still beautiful. And before he went to bed he wrote a little poem, to encourage himself:

Yes. I have loved before; I know
This longing that invades my days,
This shape that haunts life's busy ways
I know since long and long ago.

This starry mystery of delight
That floats across my eager eyes,
This pain that makes earth Paradise,
These magic songs of day and night,

I know them for the things they are:
A passing pain, a longing fleet,
A shape that soon I shall not meet,
A fading dream of veil and star.

Yet, even as my lips proclaim
The wisdom that the years have lent,
Your absence is joy's banishment
And life's one music is your name.

I love you to the heart's hid core:
Those other loves? How can one learn
From marshlights how the great fires burn?
Ah, no—I never loved before!

When he read it through he entitled it, "The Veil of Maya," so that it might pretend to have no personal application.

After that more than ever rankled the memory of that first morning.

"How could I?" he asked himself. "I must indeed have been in a gross mood. One seems sometimes to act outside oneself altogether. Temporary possession by some brutal ancestor perhaps. Well, it's not too late."

Next morning he worked at his picture, in the rabbit-warren, but his head found itself turning towards the way by which on that first day she had gone. She must know that on a day like this he would not be wasting the light,—that he would be working. She would be wanting to see him again. Would she come out? He wished she would. But he hoped she wouldn't. It would have meant another readjustment of ideas. He need not have been anxious. She did not come.

He worked steadily, masterfully. He always worked best at the beginning of a love affair. All of him seemed somehow more alive, more awake, more alert and competent. His mood was growing quickly to what he meant it to be. He was what actors call a quick study. Soon he would be able to play perfectly, without so much as a thought to the "book," the part of Paul to this child's Virginia.

Had Virginia, he wondered, any relations besides the step-father whom she so light-heartedly consented to hoodwink? Relations who might interfere and pray and meddle and spoil things?

However ashamed we may be of our relations they cannot forever be concealed. It must be owned that Betty was not the lonely orphan she sometimes pretended to herself to be. She had aunts—an accident that may happen to the best of us.

A year or two before Betty was born, a certain youth of good birth left Harrow and went to Ealing where he was received in a family in the capacity of Crammer's pup. The family was the Crammer and his daughter, a hard-headed, tight-mouthed, black-haired young woman who knew exactly what she wanted, and who meant to get it. Poverty had taught her to know what she wanted. Nature, and the folly of youth—not her own youth—taught her how to get it. There were several pups. She selected the most eligible, secretly married him, and to the day of her death spoke and thought of the marriage as a love-match. He was a dreamy youth, who wrote verses and called the Crammer's daughter his Egeria. She was too clever not to be kind to him, and he adored her and believed in her to the end, which came before his twenty-first birthday. He broke his neck out hunting, and died before Betty was born.

His people, exasperated at the news of the marriage, threatened to try to invalidate it on the score of the false swearing that had been needed to get the boy of nineteen married to the woman of twenty-four. Egeria was frightened. She compromised for an annuity of two hundred pounds, to be continued to her child.

The passion of this woman's life was power. One cannot be very powerful with just two hundred a year, and a doubtful position as the widow of a boy whose relations are prepared to dispute one's marriage. Mrs. Desmond spent three years in thought, and in caring severely for the wants of her child. Then she bought four handsome dresses, and some impressive bonnets, went to a Hydropathic Establishment, and looked about her. Of the eligible men there Mr. Cecil Underwood seemed, on enquiry, to be the most eligible. So she married him. He resisted but little, for his parish needed a clergy-woman sadly. The two hundred pounds was a welcome addition to an income depleted by the purchase of rare editions, and at the moment crippled by his recent acquisition of the Omiliac of Vincentius in its original oak boards and leather strings; and, above all, he saw in the three-year-old Betty the child he might have had if things had gone otherwise with him and another when they both were young.

Mrs. Desmond had felt certain she could rule a parish. Mrs. Cecil Underwood did rule it—as she had known she could. She ruled her husband too. And Betty. When she caught cold from working all day among damp evergreens for the Christmas decorations, and, developing pneumonia, died, she died resentfully, thanking God that she had always done her duty, and quite unable to imagine how the world would go on without her. She felt almost sure that in cutting short her career of usefulness her Creator was guilty of an error of judgment which He would sooner or later find reason to regret.

Her husband mourned her. He had the habit of her, of her strong capable ways, the clockwork precision of her household and parish arrangements. But as time went on he saw that perhaps he was more comfortable without her: as a reformed drunkard sees that it is better not to rely on brandy for one's courage. He saw it, but of course he never owned it to himself.

Betty was heart-broken, quite sincerely heart-broken. She forgot all the mother's hard tyrannies, her cramping rules, her narrow bitter creed, and remembered only the calm competence, amounting to genius, with which her mother had ruled the village world, her unflagging energy and patience, and her rare moments of tenderness. She remembered too all her own lapses from filial duty, and those memories were not comfortable.

Yet Betty too, when the self-tormenting remorseful stage had worn itself out, found life fuller, freer without her mother. Her step-father she hated—had always hated. But he could be avoided. She went to a boarding-school at Torquay, and some of her holidays were spent with her aunts, the sisters of the boy-father who had not lived to see Betty.

She adored the aunts. They lived in a world of which her village world did not so much as dream; they spoke of things which folks at home neither knew of nor cared for; and they spoke a language that was not spoken at Long Barton. Of course, everyone who was anyone at Long Barton spoke in careful and correct English, but no one ever troubled to turn a phrase. And irony would have been considered very bad form indeed. Aunt Nina wore lovely clothes and powdered her still pretty face; Aunt Julia smoked cigarettes and used words that ladies at Long Barton did not use. Betty was proud of them both.

It was Aunt Nina who taught Betty how to spend her allowance, how to buy pretty things, and, better still, tried to teach her how to wear them. Aunt Julia it was who brought her the Indian necklaces, and promised to take her to Italy some day if she was good. Aunt Nina lived in Grosvenor Square and Aunt Julia's address was most often, vaguely, the Continent of Europe. Sometimes a letter addressed to some odd place in Asia or America would find her.

But when Betty had left school her visits to Aunt Nina ceased. Mr. Underwood feared that she was now of an age to be influenced by trifles, and that London society would make her frivolous. Besides he had missed her horribly, all through her school-days, though he had yielded to the insistence of the aunts. But he had wanted Betty badly. Only of course it never occurred to him to tell her so.

So Betty had lived on at the Rectory carrying on, with more or less of success, such of her Mother's Parish workings as had managed to outlive their author, and writing to the aunts to tell them how bored she was and how she hated to be called "Lizzie."

She could not be expected to know that her stepfather had known as "Lizzie" the girl who, if Fate had been kind, would have been his wife or the mother of his child. Betty's letters breathed contempt of Parish matters, weariness of the dulness of the country, and exasperation at the hardness of a lot where "nothing ever happened."

Well, something had happened now.

The tremendous nature of the secret she was keeping against the world almost took Betty's breath away. It was to the adventure, far more than to the man, that her heart's beat quickened. Something had happened.

Long Barton was no longer the dullest place in the world. It was the centre of the universe. See her diary, an entry following a gap where a page had been torn out:

"Mr. V. is very kind. He is teaching me to sketch. He says I shall do very well when I have forgotten what I learned at school. It is so nice of him to be so straightforward. I hate flattery. He has begun my portrait. It is beautiful, but he says it is exactly like me. Of course it is his painting that makes it beautiful, and not anything to do with me. That is not flattery. I do not think he could say anything unless he really thought it. He is that sort of man, I think. I am so glad he is so good. If he were a different sort of person perhaps it would not be quite nice for me to go and meet him without any one knowing. But there is nothing *of that sort*. He was quite different the first day. But I think then he was off his guard and could not help himself. I don't know quite what I meant by that. But, anyway, I am sure he is as good as gold, and that is such a comfort. I revere him. I believe he is really noble and unselfish, and so few men are, alas!"

The noble and unselfish Vernon meanwhile was quite happy. His picture was going splendidly, and every morning he woke to the knowledge that his image filled all the thoughts of a good little girl with gray dark charming eyes and a face that reminded one of a pretty kitten. Her drawing was not half bad either. He was spared the mortifying labour of trying to make a silk purse out of a sow's ear. In one of his arts as in the other he decided that she had talent. And it was pleasant that to him should have fallen the task of teacher in both departments. Those who hunt the fox will tell you that Reynard enjoys, equally with the hounds and their masters, the pleasures of the chase. Vernon was quite of this opinion in regard to his favourite sport. He really felt that he gave as much pleasure as he took. And his own forgettings were so easy that the easy forgetting of others seemed a foregone conclusion. His forgetting always came first, that was all. But now, the Spring, her charm and his own firm *parti pris* working together, it seemed to him that he could never forget Betty, could never wish to forget her.

Her pretty conscious dignity charmed him. He stood still to look at it. He took no step forward. His role was that of the deeply respectful "brother artist." If his hand touched hers as he corrected her drawing, that was accident. If, as he leaned over her, criticising her work, the wind sent the end of her hair against his ear, that could hardly be avoided in a breezy English spring. It was not his fault that the little thrill it gave him was intensified a hundred-fold when, glancing at her, he perceived that her own ears had grown scarlet.

Betty went through her days in a dream. There were all the duties she hated—the Mothers' meetings, the Parish visits when she tried to adjust the quarrels and calm the jealousies of the stout aggressive Mothers, the carrying round the Parish Magazine. There were no long hours, now. In every spare moment she worked at her drawing to please him. It was the least she could do, after all his kindness.

Her step-father surprised her once hard at work with charcoal and board and plumb-line, a house-maid posing for her with a broom. He congratulated himself that his little sermon on the advantages of occupation as a cure for discontent had borne fruit so speedy and so sound.

"Dear child, she only wanted a word in season," he thought. And he said:

"I am glad to see that you have put away vain dreams, Lizzie. And your labours will not be thrown away, either. If you go on taking pains I daresay you will be able to paint some nice blotting-books and screens for the School Bazaar."

"I daresay," said Betty, adding between her teeth, "If you only knew!"

"But we mustn't keep Letitia from her work," he added, vaguely conscientious. Letitia flounced off, and Betty, his back turned, tore up the drawing.

And, as a beautiful background to the gross realism of Mothers' meetings and Parish tiresomenesses, was always the atmosphere of the golden mornings, the dew and the stillness, the gleam of his white coat among the pine-trees. For he was always first at the tryst now.

Betty was drunk; and she was too young to distinguish between vintages. When she had been sober she had feared intoxication. Now she was drunk, she thanked Heaven that she was sober.

CHAPTER IV

INVOLUNTARY

Six days of sunlight and clear air, of mornings as enchanting as dreams, of dreams as full of magic as May mornings. Then an interminable Sunday hot and sultry, with rolling purple clouds and an evening of thunder and heavy showers. A magenta sunset, a night working, hidden in its own darkness, its own secret purposes, and a Monday morning gray beyond belief, with a soft steady rain.

Betty stood for full five minutes looking out at the straight fine fall, at the white mist spread on the lawn, the blue mist twined round the trees, listening to the plash of the drops that gathered and fell from the big wet ivy leaves, to the guggle of the water-spout, the hiss of smitten gravel.

"He'll never go," she thought, and her heart sank.

He, shaving, in the chill damp air by his open dimity-draped window, was saying:

"She'll be there, of course. Women are all perfectly insensible to weather."

Two mackintoshed figures met in the circle of pines.

"You have come," he said. "I never dreamed you would. How cold your hand is!"

E. Nesbit

He held it for a moment warmly clasped.

"I thought it might stop any minute," said Betty; "it seemed a pity to waste a morning."

"Yes," he said musingly, "it would be a pity to waste a morning. I would not waste one of these mornings for a kingdom."

Betty fumbled with her sketching things as a sort of guarantee of good faith.

"But it's too wet to work," said she. "I suppose I'd better go home again."

"That seems a dull idea—for me," he said; "it's very selfish, of course, but I'm rather sad this morning. Won't you stay a little and cheer me up?"

Betty asked nothing better. But even to her a tete-a-tete in a wood, with rain pattering and splashing on leaves and path and resonant mackintoshes, seemed to demand some excuse.

"I should think breakfast and being dry would cheer you up better than anything," said she. "And it's very wet here."

"Hang breakfast! But you're right about the wetness. There's a shed in the field yonder. A harrow and a plough live there; they're sure to be at home on a day like this. Let's go and ask for their hospitality."

"I hope they'll be nice to us," laughed Betty; "it's dreadful to go where you're not wanted."

"How do you know?" he asked, laughing too. "Come, give me your hand and let's run for it."

They ran, hand in hand, the wet mackintoshes flapping and slapping about their knees, and drew up laughing and breathless in the dry quiet of the shed. Vernon thought of Love and Mr. Lewisham, but it was not the moment to say so.

"See, they are quite pleased to see us," said he, "they don't say a word against our sheltering here. The plough looks a bit glum, but she'll grow to like us presently. As for harrow, look how he's smiling welcome at you with all his teeth."

"I'm glad he can't come forward to welcome us," said Betty. "His teeth look very fierce."

"He could, of course, only he's enchanted. He used to be able to move about, but now he's condemned to sit still and only smile till—till he sees two perfectly happy people. Are you perfectly happy?" he asked anxiously.

"I don't know," said Betty truly. "Are you?"

"No—not quite perfectly."

"I'm so glad," said Betty. "I shouldn't like the harrow to begin to move while we're here. I'm sure it would bite us."

He sighed and looked grave. "So you don't want me to be perfectly happy?"

She looked at him with her head on one side.

"Not here," she said. "I can't trust that harrow."

His eyelids narrowed over his eyes—then relaxed. No, she was merely playing at enchanted harrows.

"Are you cold still?" he asked, and reached for her hand. She gave it frankly.

"Not a bit," she said, and took it away again. "The run warmed me. In fact—"

She unbuttoned the mackintosh and spread it on the bar of the plough and sat down. Her white dress lighted up the shadows of the shed. Outside the rain fell steadily.

"May I sit down too? Can Mrs. Plough find room for two children on her lap?"

She drew aside the folds of her dress, but even then only a little space was left. The plough had been carelessly housed and nearly half of it was where the rain drove in on it. So that they were very close together.

So close that he had to throw his head back to see clearly how the rain had made the short hair curl round her forehead and ears, and how fresh were the tints of face and lips. Also he had to support himself by an arm stretched out behind her. His arm was not round her, but it might just as well have been, as far as the look of the thing went. He thought of the arm of Mr. Lewisham.

"Did you ever have your fortune told?" he asked.

"No, never. I've always wanted to, but Father hates gipsies. When I was a little girl I used to put on my best clothes, and go out into the lanes and sit about and hope the gipsies would steal me, but they never did."

"They're a degenerate race, blind to their own interests. But they haven't a monopoly of chances—fortunately." His eyes were on her face.

"I never had my fortune told," said Betty. "I'd love it, but I think I should be afraid, all the same. Something might come true."

Vernon was more surprised than he had ever been in his life at the sudden involuntary movement in his right arm. It cost him a conscious effort not to let the arm follow its inclination and fall across her slender shoulders, while he should say:

"Your fortune is that I love you. Is it good or bad fortune?"

He braced the muscles of his arm, and kept it where it was. That sudden unreasonable impulse was a mortification, an insult to the man whose pride it was to believe that his impulses were always planned.

"I can tell fortunes," he said. "When I was a boy I spent a couple of months with some gipsies. They taught me lots of things."

His memory, excellently trained, did not allow itself to dwell for an instant on his reason for following those gipsies, on the dark-eyed black-haired girl with the skin like pale amber, who had taught him, by the flicker of the camp-fire, the lines of head and heart and life, and other things beside. Oh, but many other things! That was before he became an artist. He was only an amateur in those days.

"Did they teach you how to tell fortunes—really and truly?" asked Betty. "We had a fortune-teller's tent at the School Bazaar last year, and the youngest Smithson girl dressed up in spangles and a red dress and said she was Zara, the Eastern Mystic Hand-Reader, and Foreteller of the Future. But she got it all out of Napoleon's Book of Fate."

"I don't get my fortune-telling out of anybody's book of anything," he said. "I get it out of people's hands, and their faces. Some people's faces are their fortunes, you know."

"I know they are," she said a little sadly, "but everybody's got a hand and a fortune, whether they've got that sort of fortune-face or not."

"But the fortunes of the fortune-faced people are the ones one likes best to tell."

"Of course," she admitted wistfully, "but what's going to happen to you is just as interesting to *you*, even if your face

E. Nesbit

isn't interesting to anybody. Do you always tell fortunes quite truly; I mean do you follow the real rules? or do you make up pretty fortunes for the people with the pretty fortune-faces."

"There's no need to 'make up.' The pretty fortunes are always there for the pretty fortune-faces: unless of course the hand contradicts the face."

"But can it?"

"Can't it? There may be a face that all the beautiful things in the world are promised to: just by being so beautiful itself it draws beautiful happenings to it. But if the hand contradicts the face, if the hand is one of those narrow niggardly distrustful hands, one of the hands that will give nothing and take nothing, a hand without courage, without generosity—well then one might as well be born without a fortune-face, for any good it will ever do one."

"Then you don't care to tell fortunes for people who haven't fortune faces?"

"I should like to tell yours, if you would let me. Shall I?"

He held out his hand, but her hand was withheld.

"I ought to cross your hand with silver, oughtn't I?" she asked.

"It's considered correct—but—"

"Oh, don't let's neglect any proper precaution," she said. "I haven't got any money. Tell it me to-morrow, and I will bring a sixpence."

"You could cross my hand with your watch," he said, "and I could take the crossing as an I.O.U. of the sixpence."

She detached the old watch. He held out his hand and she gravely traced a cross on it.

"Now," he said, "all preliminary formalities being complied with, let the prophet do his work. Give me your hand, pretty lady, and the old gipsy will tell you your fortune true."

He held the hand in his, bending back the pink finger-tips with his thumb, and looked earnestly at its lines. Then he looked in her face, longer than he had ever permitted himself to look. He looked till her eyes fell. It was a charming picture. He was tall, strong, well-built and quite as good-looking as a clever man has any need to be. And she was as pretty as any oleograph of them all.

It seemed a thousand pities that there should be no witness to such a well-posed tableau, no audience to such a charming scene. The pity of it struck Destiny, and Destiny flashed the white of Betty's dress, a shrill point of light, into an eye a hundred yards away. The eye's owner, with true rustic finesse, drew back into the wood's shadow, shaded one eye with a brown rustic hand, looked again, and began a detour which landed the rustic boots, all silently, behind the shed, at a spot where a knot-hole served as frame for the little picture. The rustic eye was fitted to the knot-hole while Vernon holding Betty's hand gazed in Betty's face, and decided that this was no time to analyse his sensations.

Neither heard the furtive rustic tread, or noted the gleam of the pale rustic eye.

The labourer shook his head as he hurried quickly away. He had daughters of his own, and the Rector had been kind when one of those daughters had suddenly come home from service, ill, and with no prospect of another place.

"A-holdin' of hands and a-castin' of sheep's eyes," said he. "We knows what that's the beginnings of! Well, well, youth's the season for silliness, but there's bounds—there's bounds. And all of a mornin' so early too. Lord above knows what it wouldn't be like of a evenin'." He shook his head again, and made haste.

E. Nesbit

Vernon had forced his eyes to leave the face of Betty.

"Your fortune," he was saying, "is, curiously enough, just one of those fortunes I was speaking of. You will have great chances of happiness, if you have the courage to take them. You will cross the sea. You've never travelled, have you?"

"No,—never further than Torquay; I was at school there, you know; and London, of course. But I should love it. Isn't it horrid to think that one might grow quite old and never have been anywhere or done anything?"

"That depends on oneself, doesn't it? Adventures are to the adventurous."

"Yes, that's all very well—girls can't be adventurous."

"Yes,—it's the Prince who sets out to seek his fortune, isn't it? The Princess has to sit at home and wait for hers to come to her. It generally does if she's a real Princess."

"But half the fun must be the seeking for it," said Betty.

"You're right," said he, "it is."

The labourer had reached the park-gate. His pace had quickened to the quickening remembrance of his own daughter, sitting at home silent and sullen.

"Do you really see it in my hand?" asked Betty,—"about my crossing the sea, I mean."

"It's there; but it depends on yourself, like everything else."

"I did ask my step-father to let me go," she said, "after that first day, you know, when you said I ought to study in Paris."

"And he wouldn't, of course?"

"No; he said Paris was a wicked place. It isn't really, is it?"

"Every place is wicked," said he, "and every place is good. It's all as one takes things."

The Rectory gate clicked sharply as it swung to behind the labourer. The Rectory gravel scrunched beneath the labourer's boots.

Yes, the Master was up; he could be seen.

The heavy boots were being rubbed against the birch broom that, rooted at Kentish back doors, stands to receive on its purple twigs the scrapings of Kentish clay from rustic feet.

"You have the artistic lines very strongly marked," Vernon was saying. "One, two, three—yes, painting—music perhaps?"

"I am very fond of music," said Betty, thinking of the hour's daily struggle with the Mikado and the Moonlight Sonata. "But three arts. What could the third one be?" Her thoughts played for an instant with unheard-of triumphs achieved behind footlights—rapturous applause, showers of bouquets.

"Whatever it is, you've enormous talent for it," he said; "you'll find out what it is in good time. Perhaps it'll be something much more important than the other two put together, and perhaps you've got even more talent for it than you have for others."

"But there isn't any other talent that I can think of."

"I can think of a few. There's the stage,—but it's not that, I fancy, or not exactly that. There's literature—confess now, don't you write poetry sometimes when you're all alone at night? Then there's the art of being amusing, and the art of being—of being liked."

"Shall I be successful in any of the arts?"

"In one, certainly."

"Ah," said Betty, "if I could only go to Paris!"

"It's not always necessary to go to Paris for success in one's art," he said.

"But I want to go. I'm sure I could do better there."

"Aren't you satisfied with your present Master?"

"Oh!"—It was a cry of genuine distress, of heartfelt disclaim. "You *know* I didn't mean that! But you won't always be here, and when you've gone—why then—"

Again he had to control the involuntary movement of his left arm.

"But I'm not going for months yet. Don't let us cross a bridge till we come to it. Your head-line promises all sorts of wonderful things. And your heart-line—" he turned her hand more fully to the light.

In the Rector's study the labourer was speaking, standing shufflingly on the margin of the Turkey carpet. The Rector listened, his hand on an open folio where fat infants peered through the ornamental initials.

"And so I come straight up to you, Sir, me being a father and you the same, Sir, for all the difference betwixt our ways in life. Says I to myself, says I, and bitter hard I feels it too, I says: 'George,' says I, 'you've got a daughter as begun that way, not a doubt of it—holdin' of hands and sittin' close alongside, and you know what's come to her!'"

The Rector shivered at the implication.

"Then I says, says I: 'Like as not the Rector won't thank you for interferin'. Least said soonest mended,' says I."

"I'm very much obliged to you," said the Rector difficultly, and his hand shook on Ambrosius's yellow page.

"You see, Sir," the man's tone held all that deferent apology that truth telling demands, "gells is gells, be they never so up in the world, all the world over, bless their hearts; and young men is young men, d—n them, asking your pardon, Sir, I'm sure, but the word slipped out. And I shouldn't ha' been easy if anything had have gone wrong with Miss, God bless her, all along of the want of a word in season. Asking your pardon, Sir, but even young ladies is flesh and blood, when it comes to the point. Ain't they now?" he ended appealingly.

The Rector spoke with an obvious effort, got his hand off the page and closed the folio.

"You've done quite right, George," he said, "and I'm greatly obliged to you. Only I do ask you to keep this to yourself. You wouldn't have liked it if people had heard a thing like that about your Ruby before—I mean when she was at home."

He replaced the two folios on the shelf.

"Not me, Sir," George answered. "I'm mum, I do assure you, Sir. And if I might make so bold, you just pop on your hat and step acrost directly minute. There's that little hole back of the shed what I told you of. You ain't only got to pop your reverend eye to that there, and you'll see for yourself as I ain't give tongue for no dragged scent."

"Thank you, George," said the Rector, "I will. Good morning. God bless you."

The formula came glibly, but it was from the lips only that it came.

Lizzie—his white innocent Lily-girl! In a shed—a man, a stranger, holding her hand, his arm around her, his eyes—his lips perhaps, daring—

E. Nesbit

The Rector was half way down his garden drive.

"Your heart-line," Vernon was saying, "it's a little difficult. You will be deeply beloved."

To have one's fortune told is disquieting. To keep silence during the telling deepens the disquiet curiously. It seemed good to Betty to laugh.

"Soldier, sailor, tinker, tailor," she said, "which am I going to marry, kind gipsy?"

"I don't believe the gipsies who say they can see marriage in a hand," he answered gravely, and Betty feared he had thought her flippant, or even vulgar; "what one sees are not the shadows of coming conventions. One sees the great emotional events, the things that change and mould and develop character. Yes, you will be greatly beloved, and you will love deeply."

"I'm not to be happy in my affairs of the heart then." Still a careful flippancy seemed best to Betty.

"Did I say so? Do you really think that there are no happy love affairs but those that end in a wedding breakfast and brides-maids, with a Bazaar show of hideous silver and still more hideous crockery, and all one's relations assembled to dissect one's most sacred secrets?"

Betty had thought so, but it seemed coarse to own it.

"Can't you imagine," he went on dreamily, "a love affair so perfect that it could not but lose its finest fragrance if the world were called to watch the plucking of love's flower? Can't you imagine a love so great, so deep, so tender, so absolutely possessing the whole life of the lover that he would almost grudge any manifestation of it? Because such a manifestation must necessarily be a repetition of some of the ways in which unworthy loves have been manifested, by less happy lovers? I can seem to see that one might love the one love of a life-time, and be content to hold the treasure in one's heart, a treasure such as no other man ever had, and grudge even a word or a look that might make it less the single perfect rose of the world."

"Oh, dear!" said Betty to herself.

"But I'm talking like a book," he said, and laughed. "I always get dreamy and absurd when I tell fortunes. Anyway, as I said before, you will be greatly beloved. Indeed, unless your hand is very untruthful, which I'm sure it never could be, you are beloved now, far more than you can possibly guess."

Betty caught at her flippancy but it evaded her, and all she found to say was, "Oh," and her eyes fell.

There was a silence. Vernon still held her hand, but he was no longer looking at it.

A black figure darkened the daylight.

The two on the plough started up—started apart. Nothing more was wanted to convince the Rector of all that he least wished to believe.

"Go home, Lizzie," he said, "go to your room," and to her his face looked the face of a fiend. It is hard to control the muscles under a sudden emotion compounded of sorrow, sympathy and an immeasurable pity. "Go to your room and stay there till I send for you."

Betty went, like a beaten dog.

The Rector turned to the young man.

"Now, Sir," he said.

CHAPTER V

THE PRISONER

When Vernon looked back on that interview he was honestly pleased with himself. He had been patient, he had been kind even. In the end he had been positively chivalrous. He had hardly allowed himself to be ruffled for an instant, but had met the bitter flow of Mr. Underwood's biblical language with perfect courtesy.

He regretted, of course, deeply, this unfortunate misunderstanding. Accident had made him acquainted with Miss Desmond's talent, he had merely offered her a little of that help which between brother artists—The well-worn phrase had not for the Rector the charm it had had for Betty.

The Rector spoke again, and Mr. Vernon listened, bareheaded, in deepest deference.

No, he had not been holding Miss Desmond's hand—he had merely been telling her fortune. No one could regret more profoundly than he,—and so on. He was much wounded by Mr. Underwood's unworthy suspicions.

The Rector ran through a few texts. His pulpit denunciations of iniquity, though always earnest, had lacked this eloquence.

Vernon listened quietly.

"I can only express my regret that my thoughtlessness should have annoyed you, and beg you not to blame Miss Desmond. It was perhaps a little unconventional, but—"

"Unconventional—to try to ruin—"

Mr. Vernon held up his hand: he was genuinely shocked.

"Forgive me," he said, "but I can't hear such words in connection with—with a lady for whom I have the deepest respect. You are heated now, Sir, and I can make every allowance for your natural vexation. But I must ask you not to overstep the bounds of decency."

The Rector bit his lip, and Vernon went on:

"I have listened to your abuse—yes, your abuse—without defending myself, but I can't allow anyone, even her father, to say a word against her."

"I am not her father," said the old man bitterly. And on the instant Vernon understood him as Betty had never done. The young man's tone changed instantly.

"Look here," he said, and his face grew almost boyish, "I am really most awfully sorry. The whole thing—what there is of it, and it's very little—was entirely my doing. It was inexcusably thoughtless. Miss Desmond is very young and very innocent. It is I who ought to have known better,—and perhaps I did. But the country is very dull, and it was a real pleasure to teach so apt a pupil."

He spoke eagerly, and the ring of truth was in his voice. But the Rector felt that he was listening to the excuses of a serpent.

"Then you'd have me believe that you don't even love her?"

"No more than she does me," said Vernon very truly. "I've never breathed a word of love to her," he went on; "such an

E. Nesbit

idea never entered our heads. She's a charming girl, and I admire her immensely, but—" he sought hastily for a weapon, and defended Betty with the first that came to hand, "I am already engaged to another lady. It is entirely as an artist that I am interested in Miss Betty."

"Serpent," said the Rector within himself, "Lying serpent!"

Vernon was addressing himself silently in terms not more flattering. "Fool, idiot, brute to let the child in for this!—for it's going to be a hell of a time for her, anyhow. And as for me—well, the game is up, absolutely up!"

"I am really most awfully sorry," he said again.

"I find it difficult to believe in the sincerity of your repentance," said the Rector frowning.

"My regret you may believe in," said Vernon stiffly. "There is no ground for even the mention of such a word as repentance."

"If your repentance is sincere"—he underlined the word—"you will leave Long Barton to-day."

Leave without a word, a sign from Betty—a word or a sign to her? It might be best—if—

"I will go, Sir, if you will let me have your assurance that you will say nothing to Miss Desmond, that you won't make her unhappy, that you'll let the whole matter drop."

"I will make no bargains with you!" cried the Rector. "Do your worst! Thank God I can defend her from you!"

"She needs no defence. It's not I who am lacking in respect and consideration for her," said Vernon a little hotly, "but, as I say, I'll go—if you'll just promise to be gentle with her."

"I do not need to be taught my duty by a villain, Sir!—" The old clergyman was trembling with rage. "I wish to God I were a younger man, that I might chastise you for the hound you are." His upraised cane shook in his hand. "Words are thrown away on you! I'm sorry I can't use the only arguments that can come home to a puppy!"

"If you were a younger man," said Vernon slowly, "your words would not have been thrown away on me. They would have had the answer they deserved. I shall not leave Long Barton, and I shall see Miss Desmond when and how I choose."

"Long Barton shall know you in your true character, Sir, I promise you."

"So you would blacken her to blacken me? One sees how it is that she does not love her father."

He meant to be cruel, but it was not till he saw the green shadows round the old man's lips that he knew just how cruel he had been. The quivering old mouth opened and closed and opened, the cold eyes gleamed. And the trembling hand in one nervous movement raised the cane and struck the other man sharply across the face. It was a hysterical blow, like a woman's, and with it the tears sprang to the faded eyes.

Then it was that Vernon behaved well. When he thought of it afterwards he decided that he had behaved astonishingly well.

With the smart of that cut stinging on his flesh, the mark of it rising red and angry across his cheek, he stepped back a pace, and without a word, without a retaliatory movement, without even a change of facial expression he executed the most elaborately courteous bow, as of one treading a minuet, recovered the upright and walked away bareheaded. The old clergyman was left planted there, the cane still jigging up and down in his shaking hand.

"A little theatrical, perhaps," mused Vernon, when the cover of the wood gave him leave to lay his fingers to his throbbing cheek, "but nothing could have annoyed the old chap more."

However effective it may be to turn the other cheek, the turning of it does not cool one's passions, and he walked through the wood angrier than he ever remembered being. But the cool rain dripping from the hazel and sweet chestnut leaves fell pleasantly on his uncovered head and flushed face. Before he was through the wood he was able to laugh, and the laugh was a real laugh, if rather a rueful one. Vernon could never keep angry very long.

"Poor old devil!" he said. "He'll have to put a special clause in the general confession next Sunday. Poor old devil! And poor little Betty! And poorest me! Because, however, we look at it, and however we may have damn well bluffed over it, the game *is* up—absolutely up."

When one has a definite end in view—marriage, let us say, or an elopement,—secret correspondences, the surmounting of garden walls, the bribery of servants, are in the picture. But in a small sweet idyll, with no backbone of intention to it, these things are inartistic. And Vernon was, above and before all, an artist. He must go away and he knew it. And his picture was not finished. Could he possibly leave that incomplete? The thought pricked sharply. He had not made much progress with the picture in these last days. It had been pleasanter to work at the portrait of Betty. If he moved to the next village? Yes, that must be thought over.

He spent the day thinking of that and of other things.

The Reverend Cecil Underwood stood where he was left till the man he had struck had passed out of sight. Then the cane slipped through his hand and fell rattling to the ground. He looked down at it curiously. Then he reached out both hands vaguely and touched the shaft of the plough. He felt his way along it, and sat down, where they had sat, staring dully before him at the shadows in the shed, and at the steady fall of the rain outside. Betty's mackintosh was lying on the floor. He picked it up presently and smoothed out the creases. Then he watched the rain again.

An hour had passed before he got stiffly up and went home, with her cloak on his arm.

Yes, Miss Lizzie was in her room—had a headache. He sent up her breakfast, arranging the food himself, and calling back the maid because the tray lacked marmalade.

Then he poured out his own tea, and sat stirring it till it was cold.

She was in her room, waiting for him to send for her. He must send for her. He must speak to her. But what could he say? What was there to say that would not be a cruelty? What was there to ask that would not be a challenge to her to lie, as the serpent had lied?

"I am glad I struck him," the Reverend Cecil told himself again and again; "*that* brought it home to him. He was quite cowed. He could do nothing but bow and cringe away. Yes, I am glad."

But the girl? The serpent had asked him to be gentle with her—had dared to ask him. He could think of no way gentle enough for dealing with this crisis. The habit of prayer caught him. He prayed for guidance.

Then quite suddenly he saw what to do.

"That will be best," he said; "she will feel that less."

He rang and ordered the fly from the Peal of Bells, went to his room to change his old coat for a better one, since appearances must be kept up, even if the heart be breaking. His thin hair was disordered, and his tie, he noticed, was oddly crumpled, as though strange hands had been busy with his throat. He put on a fresh tie, smoothed his hair, and went down again. As he

E. Nesbit

passed, he lingered a moment outside her door.

Betty watching with red eyes and swollen lips saw him enter the fly, saw him give an order, heard the door bang. The old coachman clambered clumsily to his place, and the carriage lumbered down the drive.

"Oh, how cruel he is! He might have spoken to me *now*! I suppose he's going to keep me waiting for days, as a penance. And I haven't really done anything wrong. It's a shame! I've a good mind to run away!"

Running away required consideration. In the meantime, since he was out of the house, there was no reason why she should not go downstairs. She was not a child to be kept to her room in disgrace. She bathed her distorted face, powdered it, and tried to think that the servants, should they see her, would notice nothing.

Where had he gone? For no goal within his parish would a hired carriage be needed. He had gone to Sevenoaks or to the station. Perhaps he had gone to Westerham—there was a convent there, a Protestant sisterhood. Perhaps he was going to make arrangements for shutting her up there! Never!—Betty would die first. At least she would run away first. But where could one run to?

The aunts? Betty loved the aunts, but she distrusted their age. They were too old to sympathise really with her. They would most likely understand as little as her step-father had done. An Inward Monitor told Betty that the story of the fortune-telling, of the seven stolen meetings with no love-making in them, would sound very unconvincing to any ears but those of the one person already convinced. But she would not be shut up in a convent—no, not by fifty aunts and a hundred step-fathers!

She would go to Him. He would understand. He was the only person who ever had understood. She would go straight to him and ask him what to do. He would advise her. He was so clever, so good, so noble. Whatever he advised would be *right*.

Trembling and in a cold white rage of determination, Betty fastened on her hat, found her gloves and purse. The mackintosh she remembered had been left in the shed. She pictured her step-father trampling fiercely upon it as he told Mr. Vernon what he thought of him. She took her golf cape.

At the last moment she hesitated. Mr. Vernon would not be idle. What would he be doing? Suppose he should send a note? Suppose he had watched Mr. Underwood drive away and should come boldly up and ask for her? Was it wise to leave the house? But perhaps he would be hanging about the church yard, or watching from the park for a glimpse of her. She would at least go out and see.

"I'll leave a farewell letter," she said, "in case I never come back."

She found her little blotting-book—envelopes, but no paper. Of course! One can't with dignity write cutting farewells on envelopes. She tore a page from her diary.

"You have driven me to this," she wrote. "I am going away, and in time I shall try to forgive you all the petty meannesses and cruelties of all these years. I know you always hated me, but you might have had some pity. All my life I shall bear the marks on my soul of the bitter tyranny I have endured here. Now I am going away out into the world, and God knows what will become of me."

She folded, enveloped, and addressed the note, stuck a long hat-pin fiercely through it, and left it, patent, speared to her pin-cushion, with her step-father's name uppermost.

"Good-bye, little room," she said. "I feel I shall never see you again."

Slowly and sadly she crossed the room and turned the handle

E. Nesbit

of the door. The door was locked.

Once, years ago, a happier man than the Reverend Cecil had been Rector of Long Barton. And in the room that now was Betty's he had had iron bars fixed to the two windows, because that room was the nursery.

*   *   *   *   *

That evening, after dinner, Mr. Vernon sat at his parlour window looking idly along the wet bowling-green to the belt of lilacs and the pale gleams of watery sunset behind them. He had passed a disquieting day. He hated to leave things unfinished. And now the idyll was ruined and the picture threatened,—and Betty's portrait was not finished, and never would be.

"Come in," he said; and his landlady heavily followed up her tap on his door.

"A lady to see you, Sir," said she with a look that seemed to him to be almost a wink.

"A lady? To see me? Good Lord!" said Vernon. Among all the thoughts of the day this was the one thought that had not come to him.

"Shall I show her in?" the woman asked, and she eyed him curiously.

"A lady," he repeated. "Did she give her name?"

"Yes, Sir. Miss Desmond, Sir. Shall I shew her in?"

"Yes; shew her in, of course," he answered irritably.

And to himself he said:

"The Devil!"

CHAPTER VI

THE CRIMINAL

If you have found yourself, at the age of eighteen, a prisoner in your own bedroom you will be able to feel with Betty. Not otherwise. Even your highly strung imagination will be impotent to present to you the ecstasy of rage, terror, resentment that fills the soul when locked door and barred windows say, quite quietly, but beyond appeal: "Here you are, and here, my good child, you stay."

All the little familiar objects, the intimate associations of the furniture of a room that has been for years your boudoir as well as your sleeping room, all the decorations that you fondly dreamed gave to your room a *cachet*—the mark of a distinctive personality,—these are of no more comfort to you than would be strange bare stone walls and a close unfamiliar iron grating.

Betty tried to shake the window bars, but they were immovable. She tried to force the door open, but her silver buttonhook was an insufficient lever, and her tooth-brush handle broke when she pitted it in conflict against the heavy, old-fashioned lock. We have all read how prisoners, outwitting their gaolers, have filed bars with their pocket nail-scissors, and cut the locks out of old oak doors with the small blade of a penknife. Betty's door was only of pine, but her knife broke off short; and the file on her little scissors wore itself smooth against the first unmoved bar.

She paced the room like a caged lioness. We read that did the lioness but know her strength her bars were easily shattered by one blow of her powerful paw. Betty's little pink paws were not powerful like the lioness's, and when she tried to make them help her, she broke her nails and hurt herself.

It was this moment that Letitia chose for rapping at the door.

"You can't come in. What is it?" Betty was prompt to say.

"Mrs. Edwardes's Albert, Miss, come for the Maternity bag."

"It's all ready in the school-room cupboard," Betty called through the door. "Number three."

She resisted an impulse to say that she had broken the key in the lock and to send for the locksmith. No: there should be no scandal at Long Barton,—at least not while she had to stay in it.

She did not cry. She was sick with fury, and anger made her heart beat as Vernon had never had power to make it.

"I will be calm. I won't lose my head," she told herself again and again. She drank some water. She made herself eat the neglected breakfast. She got out her diary and wrote in it, in a handwriting that was not Betty's, and with a hand that shook like totter-grass.

"What will become of me? What has become of *him*? My step-father must have done something horrible to him. Perhaps he has had him put in prison; of course he couldn't do that in these modern times, like in the French revolution, just for talking to some one he hadn't been introduced to, but he may have done it for trespassing, or damage to the crops, or something. I feel quite certain something has happened to him. He would never have deserted me like this in my misery if he were free. And I can do nothing to help him—nothing. How shall I live through the day? How can I bear it? And this awful trouble has come upon him just because he was kind to another artist. The world is very, very, very cruel. I wish I were dead!" She blotted the words and locked away the book. Then she burnt that farewell note and went and sat in the window-seat to watch for her step-father's return.

The time was long. At last he came. She saw him open the carriage door and reach out a flat foot, feeling for the carriage step. He stepped out, turned and thrust a hand back into the cab. Was he about to hand out a stern-faced Protestant sister, who would take her to Westerham, and she would never be heard of again? Betty set her teeth and waited anxiously to see if the sister seemed strong. Betty was, and she would fight for her liberty. With teeth and nails if need were.

It was no Protestant sister to whom the Reverend Cecil had reached his hand. It was only his umbrella. Betty breathed again.

Well, now at least he'll come and speak to me: he must come himself; even *he* couldn't give the key to the servants and say: "Please go and unlock Miss Lizzie and bring her down!"

Betty would not move. "I shall just stay here and pretend I didn't know the door was locked," said she.

But her impatience drove her back to the caged-lioness walk and when at last she heard the key turn in the door she had only just time to spring to the window-seat and compose herself in an attitude of graceful defiance.

It was thrown away.

The door only opened wide enough to admit a dinner tray pushed in by a hand she knew. Then the door closed again.

The same thing happened with tea and supper.

It was not till after supper that Betty, gazing out on the pale watery sunset, found it blurred to her eyes. There was no more hope now. She was a prisoner. If He was not a prisoner he ought to be. It was the only thing that could excuse his silence. He might at least have gone by the gate or waved a hand-kerchief. Well, all was over between them, and Betty was alone in the world. She had not cried all day, but now she did cry.

*   *   *   *   *

Vernon always prided himself on having a heart for any fate, but this was one of the interviews that one would rather have avoided. All day he had schooled himself to resignation, had almost reconciled himself to the spoiling of what had promised to be a masterpiece. Explications with Betty would brush the bloom off everything. Yet he must play the part well. But what part? Oh, hang all meddlers!

"Miss Desmond," said the landlady; and he braced his nerves to meet a tearful, an indignant or a desperate Betty.

But there was no Betty to be met; no Betty of any kind.

Instead, a short squarely-built middle-aged lady walked briskly into the room, and turned to see the door well closed before she advanced towards him.

He bowed with indescribable emotions.

"Mr. Eustace Vernon?" said the lady. She wore a sensible short skirt and square-toed brown boots. Her hat was boat-shaped and her abundant hair was screwed up so as to be well out of her way. Her face was square and sensible like her shoulders, and her boots. Her eyes dark, clear and near sighted. She wore gold-rimmed spectacles and carried a crutch-handled cane. No vision could have been less like Betty.

Vernon bowed, and moved a chair towards her.

"Thank you," she said, and took it. "Now, Mr. Vernon, sit

down too, and let's talk this over like reasonable beings. You may smoke if you like. It clears the brain."

Vernon sat down and mechanically took out a cigarette, but he held it unlighted.

"Now," said the square lady, leaning her elbows on the table and her chin on her hands, "I am Betty's aunt."

"It is very good of you to come," said Vernon helplessly.

"Not at all," she briskly answered. "Now tell me all about it."

"There's nothing to tell," said Vernon.

"Perhaps it will clear the ground a little if I say at once that I haven't come to ask your intentions, because of course you haven't any. My reverend brother-in-law, on the other hand, insists that you have, and that they are strictly dishonourable."

Vernon laughed, and drew a breath of relief.

"I fear Mr. Underwood misunderstood,—" he said, "and—"

"He is a born misunderstander," said Miss Julia Desmond. "Now, I'm not. Light your cigarette, man; you can give me one if you like, to keep you in countenance. A light—thanks. Now will you speak, or shall I?"

"You seem to have more to say than I, Miss Desmond."

"Ah, that's because you don't trust me. In other words, you don't know me. That's one of the most annoying things in life: to be really an excellent sort, and to be quite unable to make people see it at the first go-off. Well, here goes. My worthy brother-in-law finds you and my niece holding hands in a shed."

"We were not," said Vernon. "I was telling her fortune—"

E. Nesbit

"It's my lead now," interrupted the lady. "Your turn next. He being what he is—to the pure all things are impure, you know—instantly draws the most harrowing conclusions, hits you with a stick.—By the way, you behaved uncommonly well about that."

"Thank you," said Vernon, smiling a little. It is pleasant to be appreciated.

"Yes, really very decently, indeed. I daresay it wouldn't have hurt a fly, but if you'd been the sort of man he thinks you are—However that's neither here nor there. He hits you with a stick, locks the child into her room—What did you say?"

"Nothing," said Vernon.

"All right. I didn't hear it. Locks her in her room, and wires to my sister. Takes a carriage to Sevenoaks to do it too, to avoid scandal. I happen to be at my sister's, on my way from Cairo to Norway, so I undertake to run down. He meets me at the station, and wants me to go straight home and blackguard Betty. But I prefer to deal with principals."

"You mean—"

"I mean that I know as well as you do that whatever has happened has been your doing and not that dear little idiot's. Now, are you going to tell me about it?"

He had rehearsed already a form of words in which "Brother artists" should have loomed large. But now that he rose, shrugged his shoulders and spoke, it was in words that had not been rehearsed.

"Look here, Miss Desmond," said he, "the fact is, you're right. I haven't any intentions—certainly not dishonourable ones. But I was frightfully bored in the country, and your niece is bored, too—more bored than I am. No one ever understands or pities the boredom of the very young," he added pensively.

"Well?"

"Well, that's all there is to it. I liked meeting her, and she liked meeting me."

"And the fortune-telling? Do you mean to tell me you didn't enjoy holding the child's hand and putting her in a silly flutter?"

"I deny the flutter," he said, "but—Well, yes, of course I enjoyed it. You wouldn't believe me if I said I didn't."

"No," said she.

"I enjoyed it more than I expected to," he added with a frankness that he had not meant to use, "much more. But I didn't say a word of love——only perhaps—"

"Only perhaps you made the idea of it underlie every word you did speak. Don't I know?" said Miss Desmond. "Bless the man, I've been young myself!"

"Miss Betty is very charming," said he, "and—and if I hadn't met her—"

"If you hadn't met her some other man would. True; but I fancy her father would rather it had been some other man."

"I didn't mean that in the least," said Vernon with some heat. "I meant that if I hadn't met her she would have gone on being bored, and so should I. Don't think me a humbug, Miss Desmond. I am more sorry than I can say that I should have been the means of causing her any unhappiness."

"'Causing her unhappiness,'—poor little Betty, poor little trusting innocent silly little girl! That's about it, isn't it?"

It was so like it that he hotly answered:

"Not in the least."

"Well, well," said Miss Desmond, "there's no great harm done. She'll get over it, and more's been lost on market days. Thanks."

She lighted a second cigarette and sat very upright, the cigarette in her mouth and her hands on the handle of her stick.

"You can't help it, of course. Men with your coloured eyes never can. That green hazel—girls ought to be taught at school that it's a danger-signal. Only, since your heart's not in the business any more than her's is—as you say, you were both bored to death—I want to ask you, as a personal favour to me, just to let the whole thing drop. Let the girl alone. Go right away."

"It's an unimportant detail, and I'm ashamed to mention it," said Vernon, "but I've got a picture on hand—I'm painting a bit of the Warren."

"Well, go to Low Barton and put up there and finish your precious picture. You won't see Betty again unless you run after her."

"To tell the truth," said Vernon, "I had already decided to let the whole thing drop. I'm ashamed of the trouble I've caused her and—and I've taken rooms at Low Barton."

"Upon my word," said Miss Desmond, "you are the coldest lover I've ever set eyes on."

"I'm not a lover," he answered swiftly. "Do you wish I were?"

"For Betty's sake, I'm glad you aren't. But I think I should respect you more if you weren't quite so arctic."

"I'm not an incendiary, at any rate," said he, "and that's

something, with my coloured eyes, isn't it?"

"Well," she said, "whatever your temperature is, I rather like you. I don't wonder at Betty in the least."

Vernon bowed.

"All I ask is your promise that you'll not speak to her again."

"I can't promise that, you know. I can't be rude to her. But I'll promise not to go out of my way to meet her again." He sighed.

"As, yes—it is sad—all that time wasted and no rabbits caught." Again Miss Desmond had gone unpleasantly near his thought. Of course he said:

"You don't understand me."

"Near enough," said Miss Desmond; "and now I'll go."

"Let me thank you for coming," said Vernon eagerly; "it was more than good of you. I must own that my heart sank when I knew it was Miss Betty's aunt who honoured me with a visit. But I am most glad you came. I never would have believed that a lady could be so reasonable and—and—"

"And gentlemanly?" said the lady. "Yes,—it's my brother-in-law who is the old woman, poor dear! You see, Mr. Vernon, I've been running round the world for five and twenty years, and I've kept my eyes open. And when I was of an age to be silly, the man I was silly about had your coloured eyes. He married an actress, poor fellow,—or rather, she married him, before he could say 'knife.' That's the sort of thing that'll happen to you, unless you're uncommonly careful. So that's settled. You give me your word not to try to see Betty?"

"I give you my word. You won't believe in my regret—"

E. Nesbit

"I believe in that right enough. It must be simply sickening to have the whole show given away like this. Oh, I believe in your regret!"

"My regret," said Vernon steadily, "for any pain I may have caused your niece. Do please see how grateful I am to you for having seen at once that it was not her fault at all, but wholly mine."

"Very nicely said: good boy!" said Betty's aunt. "Well, my excellent brother-in-law is waiting outside in the fly, gnashing his respectable teeth, no doubt, and inferring all sorts of complications from the length of our interview. Good-bye. You're just the sort of young man I like, and I'm sorry we haven't met on a happier footing. I'm sure we should have got on together. Don't you think so?"

"I'm sure we should," said he truly. "Mayn't I hope—"

She laughed outright.

"You have indeed the passion for acquaintance without introduction," she said. "No, you may *not* call on me in town. Besides, I'm never there. Good-bye. And take care of yourself. You're bound to be bitten some day you know, and bitten badly."

"I wish I thought you forgave me."

"Forgive you? Of course I forgive you! You can no more help making love, I suppose—no, don't interrupt: the thing's the same whatever you call it—you can no more help making love than a cat can help stealing cream. Only one day the cat gets caught, and badly beaten, and one day you'll get caught, and the beating will be a bad one, unless I'm a greater fool than I take myself for. And now I'll go and unlock Betty's prison and console her. Don't worry about her. I'll see that she's not put upon. Good night. No, in the circumstances you'd better *not* see me to my carriage!"

She shook hands cordially, and left Vernon to his thoughts.

Miss Desmond had done what she came to do, and he knew it. It was almost a relief to feel that now he could not try to see Betty however much he wished it,—however much he might know her to wish it. He shrugged his shoulders and lighted another cigarette.

* * * * *

Betty, worn out with crying, had fallen asleep. The sound of wheels roused her. It seemed to rain cabs at the Rectory to-day.

There were voices in the hall, steps on the stairs. Her door was unlocked and there entered no tray of prisoner's fare, no reproachful step-father, no Protestant sister, but a brisk and well-loved aunt, who shut the door, and spoke.

"All in the dark?" she said. "Where are you, child?"

"Here," said Betty.

"Let me strike a light. Oh, yes, there you are!"

"Oh, aunt,—has he sent for you?" said Betty fearfully. "Oh, don't scold me, auntie! I am so tired. I don't think I can bear any more."

"I'm not going to scold you, you silly little kitten," said the aunt cheerfully. "Come, buck up! It's nothing so very awful, after all. You'll be laughing at it all before a fortnight's over."

"Then he hasn't told you?"

"Oh, yes, he has; he's told me everything there was to tell, and a lot more, too. Don't worry, child. You just go straight to bed and I'll tuck you up, and we'll talk it all over in the morning."

"Aunty," said Betty, obediently beginning to unfasten her

dress, "did he say anything about *Him*?"

"Well, yes—a little."

"He hasn't—hasn't done anything to him, has he?"

"What could he do? Giving drawing lessons isn't a hanging matter, Bet."

"I haven't heard anything from him all day,—and I thought—"

"You won't hear anything more of him, Betty, my dear. I've seen your Mr. Vernon, and a very nice young man he is, too. He's frightfully cut up about having got you into a row, and he sees that the only thing he can do is to go quietly away. I needn't tell you, Betty, though I shall have to explain it very thoroughly to your father, that Mr. Vernon is no more in love with you than you are with him. In fact he's engaged to another girl. He's just interested in you as a promising pupil."

"Yes," said Betty, "of course I know that."

CHAPTER VII

THE ESCAPE

"It's all turned out exactly like what I said it was going to, exactly to a T," said Mrs. Symes, wrapping her wet arms in her apron and leaning them on the fence; "if it wasn't that it's Tuesday and me behindhand as it is, I'd tell you all about it."

"Do the things good to lay a bit in the rinse-water," said Mrs. James, also leaning on the fence, "sorter whitens them's what I always say. I don't mind if I lend you a hand with the wringing after. What's turned out like you said it was going to?"

"Miss Betty's decline." Mrs. Symes laughed low and huskily. "What did I tell you, Mrs. James?"

"I don't quite remember not just at the minute," said Mrs. James; "you tells so many things."

"And well for some people I do. Else they wouldn't never know nothing. I told you as it wasn't no decline Miss Betty was setting down under. I said it was only what's natural, her being the age she is. I said what she wanted was a young man, and I said she'd get one. And what do you think?"

"I don't know, I'm sure."

"She did get one," said Mrs. Symes impressively, "that same week, just as if she'd been a-listening to my very words. It was

E. Nesbit

as it might be Friday you and me had that little talk. Well, as it might be the Saturday, she meets the young man, a-painting pictures in the Warren—my Ernest's youngest saw 'em a-talking, and told his mother when he come home to his dinner."

"To think of that, and me never hearing a word!" said Mrs. James with frank regret.

"I knew it ud be 'Whistle and I'll come to you, my lad,'" Mrs. Symes went on with cumbrous enjoyment, "and so it was. They used to keep their rondyvoos in the wood—six o'clock in the morning. Mrs. Wilson's Tom used to see 'em reg'lar every day as he went by to his work."

"Lor," said Mrs. James feebly.

"Of course Tom he never said nothing, except to a few friends of his over a glass. They enjoyed the joke, I promise you. But old George Marbould—he ain't never been quite right in his head, I don't think, since his Ruby went wrong. Pity, I always think. A great clumsy plain-faced girl like her might a kept herself respectable. She hadn't the temptation some of us might have had in our young days."

"No indeed," said Mrs. James, smoothing her hair, "and old George—what silliness was he up to this time?"

"Why he sees the two of 'em together one fine morning and 'stead of doing like he'd be done by he ups to the Vicarage and tells the old man. 'You come alonger me, Sir,' says he, 'and have a look at your daughter a-kissin' and huggin' up in Beale's shed, along of a perfect stranger.' So the old man he says, 'God bless you,'—George is proud of him saying that—and off he goes, in a regular fanteague, beats the young master to a jelly, for all he's an old man and feeble, and shuts Miss up in her room. Now that wouldn't a been *my* way."

"No, indeed," said Mrs. James.

"I should a asked him in," said Mrs. Symes, "if it had been a gell of mine, and give him a good meal with a glass of ale to it, and a tiddy drop of something to top up with, and I'd a let him light his nasty pipe,—and then when he was full and contented I'd a up and said, 'Now my man, you've 'ad time to think it over, and no one can't say as I've hurried you nor flurried you. But it's time as we began talking. So just you tell me what you're a-goin to do about it. If you 'ave the feelings of a man,' I'd a said 'you'll marry the girl.'"

"Yes, indeed," said Mrs. James with emotion.

"Instead of which, bless your 'art, he beats the young man off with a stick, like as if he was a mad dog; and young Miss is a goin' to be sent to furrin parts to a strick boardin' school, to learn her not to have any truck with young chaps."

"'Ard, I call it," said Mrs. James.

"An' well you may—crooil 'ard. How's he expect the girl to get a husband if he drives the young fellers away with walking-sticks? Pore gell! I shouldn't wonder but what she lives and dies a maid, after this set-out."

"We shall miss 'er when she goes," said Mrs. James.

"I don't say we shan't. But there ain't no one as you can't get on without if you're put to it And whether or not, she's going to far foreign parts where there ain't no young chaps."

"Poor young thing," said Mrs. James, very sympathetic. "I think I'll drop in as I'm passing, and see how she takes it"

"If you do," said Mrs. Symes, unrolling her arms, white and wrinkled with washing, to set them aggressively on her lips, "it's the last word as passes between us, Mrs. James, so now you know."

"Lord, Maria, don't fly out at me that way." Mrs. James

E. Nesbit

shrank back: "How was I to know you'd take it like that?"

"Do you suppose," asked Mrs. Symes, "as no one ain't got no legs except you? *I'm* a going up, soon as I've got the things on the line and cleaned myself. I only heard it after I'd got every blessed rag in soak, or I'd a gone up afore."

"Mightn't I step up with you for company?" Mrs. James asked.

"No, you mightn't. But I don't mind dropping in as I come home, to tell you about it. One of them Catholic Nunnery schools, I expect, which it's sudden death to a man but to set his foot into."

"Poor young thing," said Mrs. James again.

*   *   *   *   *

Betty was going to Paris.

There had been "much talk about and about" the project. Now it was to be.

There had been interviews.

There was the first in which the elder Miss Desmond told her brother-in-law in the plain speech she loved exactly what sort of a fool he had made of himself in the matter of Betty and the fortune-telling.

When he was convinced of error—it was not easily done—he would have liked to tell Betty that he was sorry, but he belonged to a generation that does not apologise to the next.

The second interview was between the aunt and Betty. That was the one in which so much good advice was given.

"You know," the aunt wound up, "all young women want to be in love, and all young men too. I don't mean that there was anything of that sort between you and your artist friend. But there might have been. Now look here,—I'm going to speak quite straight to you. Don't you ever let young men get monkeying about with your hands; whether they call it fortune-telling or whether they don't, their reason for doing so is always the same—or likely to be. And you want to keep your hand—as well as your lips—for the man you're going to marry. That's all, but don't you forget it. Now what's this I hear about your wanting to go to Paris?"

"I did want to go," said Betty, "but I don't care about anything now. Everything's hateful."

"It always is," said the aunt, "but it won't always be."

"Don't think I care a straw about not seeing Mr. Vernon again," said Betty hastily. "It's not that."

"Of course not," said the aunt sympathetically.

"No,—but Father was so hateful—you've no idea. If I'd—if I'd run away and got married secretly he couldn't have made more fuss."

"You're a little harsh—just a little. Of course you and I know exactly how it was, but remember how it looked to him. Why, it couldn't have looked worse if you really *had* been arranging an elopement."

"He *hadn't* got his arm around me," insisted Betty; "it was somewhere right away in the background. He was holding himself up with it."

"Don't I tell you I understand all that perfectly? What I want to understand is how you feel about Paris. Are you absolutely off the idea?"

"I couldn't go if I wasn't."

"I wonder what you think Paris is like," mused the aunt. "I suppose you think it's all one wild razzle-dazzle—one delirious round of—of museums and picture galleries."

"No, I don't," said Betty rather shortly.

"If you went you'd have to work."

"There's no chance of my going."

"Then we'll put the idea away and say no more about it. Get me my Continental Bradshaw out of my dressing-bag: I'm no use here. Nobody loves me, and I'll go to Norway by the first omnibus to-morrow morning."

"Don't," said Betty; "how can you say nobody loves you?"

"Your step-father doesn't, anyway. That's why I can make him do what I like when I take the trouble. When people love you they'll never do anything for you,—not even answer a plain question with a plain yes or no. Go and get the Bradshaw. You'll be sorry when I'm gone."

"Aunt Julia, you don't really mean it."

"Of course not. I never mean anything except the things I don't say. The Bradshaw!"

Betty came and sat on the arm of her aunt's chair.

"It's not fair to tease me," she said, "and tantalise me. You know how mizzy I am."

"No. I don't know anything. You won't tell me anything. Go and get—"

"Dear, darling, pretty, kind, clever Aunt," cried Betty, "I'd give my ears to go."

"Then borrow a large knife from cook, and sharpen it on the front door-step! No—I don't mean to use it on your step-father. I'll have your pretty ears mummified and wear them on my watch-chain. No—mind my spectacles! Let me go. I daresay it won't come to anything."

"Do you really mean you'd take me?"

"I'd take you fast enough, but I wouldn't keep you. We must find a dragon to guard the Princess. Oh, we'll get a nice tame kind puss-cat of a dragon,—but that dragon will not be your Aunt Julia! Let me go, I say. I thought you didn't care about anything any more?"

"I didn't know there could be anything to care for," said Betty honestly, "especially Paris. Well, I won't if you hate it so, but oh, aunt—" She still sat on the floor by the chair her aunt had left, and thought and thought. The aunt went straight down to the study.

"Now, Cecil," she said, coming briskly in and shutting the door, "you've made that poor child hate the thought of you and you've only yourself to thank."

"I know you think so," said he, closing the heavy book over which he had been stooping.

"I don't mean," she added hastily, for she was not a cruel woman, "that she really hates you, of course. But you've frightened her, and shaken her nerves, locking her up in her room like that. Upon my word, you are old enough to know better!"

"I was so alarmed, so shaken myself—" he began, but she interrupted him.

"I didn't come in and disturb your work just to say all that, of course," she said, "but really, Cecil, I understand things better than you think. I know how fond you really are of Betty."

The Reverend Cecil doubted this; but he said nothing.

"And you know that I'm fond enough of the child myself. Now, all this has upset you both tremendously. What do you propose to do?"

"I—I—nothing I thought. The less said about these deplorable affairs the better. Lizzie will soon recover her natural tone, and forget all about the matter."

"Then you mean to let everything go on in the old way?"

"Why, of course," said he uneasily.

"Well, it's your own affair, naturally," she spoke with a studied air of detachment which worried him exactly as it was meant to do.

"What do you mean?" he asked anxiously. He had never been able wholly to approve Miss Julia Desmond. She smoked cigarettes, and he could not think that this would have been respectable in any other woman. Of course, she was different from any other woman, but still—. Then the Reverend Cecil could not deem it womanly to explore, unchaperoned, the less well-known quarters of four continents, to penetrate even to regions where skirts were considered improper and side-saddles were unknown. Even the nearness of Miss Desmond's fiftieth birthday hardly lessened at all the poignancy of his disapproval. Besides, she had not always been fifty, and she had always, in his recollection of her, smoked cigarettes, and travelled alone. Yet he had a certain well-founded respect for her judgment, and for that fine luminous common-sense of hers which had more than once shewn him his own mistakes. On the rare occasions when he and she had differed he had always realized, later, that she had been in the right. And she was "gentle-manly" enough never once to have said: "I told you so!"

"What do you mean?" he asked again, for she was silent, her hands in the pockets of her long coat, her sensible brown shoes sticking straight out in front of her chair.

"If you really want to know, I'll tell you," she said, "but I hate to interfere in other people's business. You see, I know how deeply she has felt this, and of course I know you have too, so I wondered whether you hadn't thought of some little plan for—for altering the circumstances a little, so that everything will blow over and settle down, so that when you and she come together again you'll be better friends than ever."

"Come together again," he repeated, and the paper-knife was still restless, "do you want me to let her go away? To London?"

Visions of Lizzie, in unseemly low-necked dresses surrounded by crowds of young men—all possible Vernons—lent a sudden firmness to his voice, a sudden alertness to his manner."

"No, certainly not," she answered the voice and the manner as much as the words. "I shouldn't dream of such a thing. Then it hadn't occurred to you?"

"It certainly had not."

"You see," she said earnestly, "it's like this—at least this is how I see it: She's all shaken and upset, and so are you, and when I've gone—and I must go in a very little time—you'll both of you simply settle down to thinking over it all, and you'll grow farther and farther apart!"

"I don't think so," said he; "things like this always right them-selves if one leaves them alone. Lizzie and I have always got on very well together, in a quiet way. We are neither of us demonstrative."

"Now Heaven help the man!" was the woman's thought. She remembered Betty's clinging arms, her heartfelt kisses, the fervency of the voice that said, "Dear darling, pretty, kind, clever Aunt! I'd give my ears to go." Betty not demonstrative! Heaven help the man!

E. Nesbit

"No," she said, "I know. But when people are young these thinks rankle."

"They won't with her," he said. "She has a singularly noble nature, under that quiet exterior."

Miss Desmond drew a long breath and began afresh.

"Then there's another thing. She's fretting over this—thinks now that it was something to be ashamed of; she didn't think so at the time, of course."

"You mean that it was I who—"

This was thin ice again. Miss Desmond skated quickly away from it with, "Well, you see, I've been talking to her. She really *is* fretting. Why she's got ever so much thinner in the last week."

"I could get a locum," he said slowly, "and take her to a Hydropathic Establishment for a fortnight."

"Oh dear, oh dear!" said Miss Desmond to herself. Aloud she said: "That *would* be delightful, later. But just now—well, of course it's for you to decide,—but it seems to me that it would be better for you two to be apart for a while. If you're here alone together—well, the very sight of you will remind each other—That's not grammar, as you say, but—"

He had not said anything. He was thinking, fingering the brass bosses on the corners of the divine Augustine, and tracing the pattern on the stamped pigskin.

"Of course if you care to risk it," she went on still with that fine air of detachment,—"but I have seen breaches that nothing could heal arise in just that way."

Two people sitting down together and thinking over everything they had against each other."

"But I've nothing against Lizzie."

"I daresay not," Miss Desmond lost patience at last, "but she has against you, or will have if you let her stay here brooding over it. However if you like to risk it—I'm sorry I spoke." She got up and moved to the door.

"No, no," he said hastily, "do not be sorry you spoke. You have given me food for reflection. I will think it all over quietly and—and—" he did not like to talk about prayers to Miss Desmond somehow, "and—calmly and if I see that you are right—I am sure you mean most kindly by me."

"Indeed I do," she said heartily, and gave him her hand in the manly way he hated. He took it, held it limply an instant, and repeated:

"Most kindly."

He thought it over for so long that the aunt almost lost hope.

"I have to hold my tongue with both hands to keep it quiet. And if I say another word I shall spoil the song," she told Betty. "I've done my absolute best. If that doesn't fetch him, nothing will!"

It had "fetched him." At the end of two interminable days he sent to ask Miss Desmond to speak to him in the study. She went.

"I have been thinking carefully," he said, "most carefully. And I feel that you are right. Perhaps I owe her some amends. Do you know of any quiet country place?"

Miss Desmond thought Betty had perhaps for the moment had almost enough of quiet country places.

"She is very anxious to learn drawing," he said, "and perhaps if I permitted her to do so she might understand it as a sign that

E. Nesbit

I cherish no resentment on account of what has passed. But—"

"I know the very thing," said the Aunt, and went on to tell of Madame Gautier, of her cloistral home in Paris where she received a few favoured young girls, of the vigilant maid who conducted them to and from their studies, of the quiet villa on the Marne where in the summer an able master—at least 60 or 65 years of age—conducted sketching parties, to which the students were accompanied either by Madame herself, or by the dragon-maid.

"I'll stand the child six months with her," she said, "or a year even. So it won't cost you anything. And Madame Gautier is in London now. You could run up and talk to her yourself."

"Does she speak English?" he asked, anxiously, and being reassured questioned further.

"And you?" he asked. And when he heard that Norway for a month and then America en route for Japan formed Miss Desmond's programme for the next year he was only just able to mask, with a cough, his deep sigh of relief. For, however much he might respect her judgment, he was always easier when Lizzie and her Aunt Julia were not together.

He went up to town, and found Madame Gautier, the widow of a French pastor, established in a Bloomsbury boarding-house. She was a woman after his own heart—severe, simple, earnest. If he had to part with his Lizzie, he told himself in the returning train, it could be to no better keeper than this.

He himself announced his decision to Betty.

"I have decided," he said, and he spoke very coldly because it was so very difficult to speak at all, "to grant you the wish you expressed some time ago. You shall go to Paris and learn drawing."

"Do you really mean it?" said Betty, as coldly as he.

"I am not in the habit of saying things which I do not mean."

"Thank you very much," said Betty. "I will work hard, and try that the money shan't be wasted."

"Your aunt has kindly offered to pay your expenses."

"When do I go?" asked Betty.

"As soon as your garments can be prepared. I trust that I shall not have cause to regret the confidence I have decided to place in you."

His phrasing was seldom well-inspired. Had he said, "I trust you, my child, and I know I shan't regret it," which was what he meant, she would have come to meet him more than half-way. As it was she said, "Thank you!" again, and left him without more words. He sighed.

"I don't believe she is pleased after all; but she sees I am doing it for her good. Now it comes to the point her heart sinks at the idea of leaving home. But she will understand my motives."

The one thought Betty gave him was:

"He can't bear the sight of me at all now! He's longing to be rid of me! Well, thank Heaven I'm going to Paris! I will have a grass-lawn dress over green, with three rows of narrow lace insertion, and a hat with yellow roses and—oh, it can't be true. It's too good to be true. Well, it's a good thing to be hated sometimes, by some people, if they only hate you enough!"

*   *   *   *   *

"'So you're going to foreign parts, Miss,' says I."

Mrs. Symes had flung back her bonnet strings and was holding a saucerful of boiling tea skilfully poised on the fingers of one

E. Nesbit

hand. "'Yes, Mrs. Symes,' says she, 'don't you wish you was going too?' she says. And she laughed, but I'm not easy blinded, and well I see as she only laughed to 'ide a bleedin' 'art. 'Not me, Miss,' says I; 'nice figure I should look a-goin' to a furrin' boardin' school at my time of life.'

"'It ain't boardin' school,' says she. 'I'm a-going to learn to paint pictures. I'll paint your portrait when I come home,' says she, and laughs again—I could see she done it to keep the tears back.

"'I'm sorry for you, Miss, I'm sure,' I says, not to lose the chance of a word in season, 'but I hope it'll prove a blessing to you—I do that.'"

"'Oh, it'll be a blessing right enough,' says she, and keeps on laughing a bit wild like. When the art's full you can't always stop yourself. She'd a done better to 'ave a good cry and tell me 'er troubles. I could a cheered her up a bit p'raps. You know whether I'm considered a comfort at funerals and christenings, Mrs. James."

"I do," said Mrs. James sadly; "none don't know it better."

"You'd a thought she'd a bin glad of a friend in need. But no. She just goes on a-laughing fit to bring tears to your eyes to hear her, and says she, 'I hope you'll all get on all right without me.'"

"I hope you said as how we should miss her something dreadful," said Mrs. James anxiously, "Have another cup."

"Thank you, my dear. Do you take me for a born loony? Course I did. Said the parish wouldn't be the same without her, and about her pretty reading and all. See here what she give me."

Mrs. James unrolled a violet petticoat.

"Good as new, almost," she said, looking critically at the hem. "Specially her being taller'n me. So what's not can be cut away, and no loss. She kep' on a-laughing an' a-smiling till the old man he come in and he says in his mimicking way, 'Lizzie,' says 'e, 'they're a-waitin' to fit on your new walkin' costoom,' he says. So I come away, she a-smiling to the last something awful to see."

"Dear, dear," said Mrs. James.

"But you mark my words—she don't deceive *me*. If ever I see a bruised reed and a broken 'art on a young gell's face I see it on hers this day. She may laugh herself black in the face, but she won't laugh me into thinking what I knows to be far otherwise."

"Ah," said Mrs. James resignedly, "we all 'as it to bear one time or another. Young gells is very deceitful though, in their ways, ain't they?"

E. Nesbit

BOOK 2

THE MAN

CHAPTER VIII

THE ONE AND THE OTHER

"Some idiot," remarked Eustace Vernon, sipping Vermouth at a little table, "insists that, if you sit long enough outside the Cafe de la Paix, you will see everyone you have ever known or ever wanted to know pass by. I have sat here for half-an-hour—and—*voila*."

"You met me, half an hour ago," said the other man.

"Oh, *you*!" said Vernon affectionately.

"And your hat has gone off every half minute ever since," said the other man.

"Ah, that's to the people I've known. It's the people I've wanted to know that are the rarity."

"Do you mean people you have wanted to know and not known?"

"There aren't many of those," said Vernon; "no it's—Jove, that's a sweet woman!"

"I hate the type," said the other man briefly: "all clothes—no real human being."

The woman was beautifully dressed, in the key whose

harmonies are only mastered by Frenchwomen and Americans. She turned her head as her carriage passed, and Vernon's hat went off once more.

"I'd forgotten her profile," said Vernon, "and she's learned how to dress since I saw her last. She's quite human, really, and as charming as anyone ought to be."

"So I should think," said the other man. "I'm sorry I said that, but I didn't know you knew her. How's trade?"

"Oh, I did a picture—well, but a picture! I did it in England in the Spring. Best thing I've done yet. Come and see it."

"I should like to look you up. Where do you hang out?"

"Eighty-six bis Rue Notre Dame des Champs," said Vernon. "Everyone in fiction lives there. It's the only street on the other side that authors seem ever to have dreamed of. Still, it's convenient, so I herd there with all sorts of blackguards, heroes and villains and what not. Eighty-six bis."

"I'll come," said the other man, slowly. "Do you know, Vernon, I'd like awfully to get at your point of view—your philosophy of life?"

"Haven't you got one, my dear chap!—'sufficient unto' is my motto."

"You paint pictures,", the other went on, "so very much too good for the sort of life you lead."

Vernon laughed.

"My dear Temple," he said, "I live, mostly, the life of a vestal virgin."

"You know well enough I'm not quarrelling with the way you spend your evenings," said his dear Temple; "it's your whole

E. Nesbit

outlook that doesn't match your work. Yet there must be some relation between the two, that's what I'd like to get at."

There is a bond stronger than friendship, stronger than love—a bond that cannot be forged in any other shop than the one—the bond between old schoolfellows. Vernon had sometimes wondered why he "stood so much" from Temple. It is a wonder that old schoolfellows often feel, mutually.

"The subject you've started," said he, "is of course, to me, the most interesting. Please develop your thesis."

"Well then, your pictures are good, strong, thorough stuff, with sentiment—yes, just enough sentiment to keep them from the brutality of Degas or the sensualism of Latouche. Whereas you, yourself, seem to have no sentiment."

"I? No sentiment! Oh, Bobby, this is too much! Why, I'm a mass of it! Ask—"

"Yes, ask any woman of your acquaintance. That's just it—or just part of it. You fool them into thinking—oh, I don't know what; but you don't fool me."

"I haven't tried."

"Then you're not brutal, except half a dozen times in the year when you—And I've noticed that when your temper goes smash your morals go at the same time. Is that cause or effect? What's the real you like, and where do you keep it?"

"The real me," said Vernon, "is seen in my pictures, and—and appreciated by my friends; you for instance, are, I believe, genuinely attached to me."

"Oh, rot!" said Bobby.

"I don't see," said Vernon, moving his iron chair to make room for two people at the next table, "why you should expect my pictures to rhyme with my life. A man's art doesn't rhyme with his personality. Most often it contradicts flatly. Look at musicians—what a divine art, and what pigs of high priests! And look at actors—but no, one can't; the spectacle is too sickening."

"I sometimes think," said Temple, emptying his glass, "that the real you isn't made yet. It's waiting for—"

"For the refining touch of a woman's hand, eh? You think the real me is—Oh, Temple, Temple, I've no heart for these childish imaginings! The real me is the man that paints pictures, damn good pictures, too, though I say it."

"And is that what all the women think?

"Ask them, my dear chap; ask them. They won't tell you the truth."

"They're not the only ones who won't. I should like to know what you really think of women, Vernon."

"I don't think about them at all," lied Vernon equably. "They aren't subjects for thought but for emotion—and even of that as little as may be. It's impossible seriously to regard a woman as a human being; she's merely a dear, delightful, dainty—"

"Plaything?"

"Well, yes—or rather a very delicately tuned musical instrument. If you know the scales and the common chords, you can improvise nice little airs and charming variations. She's a sort of—well, a penny whistle, and the music you get depends not on her at all, but on your own technique."

"I've never been in love," said Temple; "not seriously, I mean," he hastened to add, for Vernon was smiling, "not a life or death matter, don't you know; but I do hate the way you talk, and one of these days you'll hate it too."

Miss Desmond's warning floated up through the dim waters of half a year.

"So a lady told me, only last Spring," he said. "Well, I'll take my chance. Going? Well, I'm glad we ran across each other. Don't forget to look me up."

Temple moved off, and Vernon was left alone. He sat idly smoking cigarette after cigarette, and watched the shifting crowd. It was a bright October day, and the crowd was a gay one.

Suddenly his fingers tightened on his cigarette,—but he kept the hand that held it before his face, and he bent his head forward.

Two ladies were passing, on foot. One was the elder Miss Desmond—she who had warned him that one of these days he would be caught—and the other, hanging lovingly on her aunt's arm, was, of course, Betty. But a smart, changed, awakened Betty! She was dressed almost as beautifully as the lady whose profile he had failed to recognise, but much more simply. Her eyes were alight, and she was babbling away to her aunt. She was even gesticulating a little, for all the world like a French girl. He noted the well-gloved hand with which she emphasized some point in her talk.

"That's the hand," he said, "that I held when we sat on the plough in the shed and I told her fortune."

He had risen, and his feet led him along the road they had taken. Ten yards ahead of him he saw the swing of the aunt's serviceable brown skirt and beside it Betty's green and gray.

"I am not breaking my word," he replied to the Inward Monitor. "Who's going out of his way to speak to the girl?"

He watched the brown gown and the green all the way down the Boulevard des Capucines, saw them cross the road and go up the steps of the Madeleine. He paused at the corner. It was hard, certainly, to keep his promise; yet so far it was easy, because he could not well recall himself to the Misses Desmond on the ground of his having six months ago involved the one in a row with her relations, and discussed the situation afterwards with the other.

"I do wonder where they're staying, though," he told himself. "If one were properly introduced—?" But he knew that the aunt would consider no introduction a proper one that should renew his acquaintance with Betty.

"Wolf, wolf," he said, "let the fold alone! There's no door for you, and you've pledged your sacred word as an honourable wolf not to jump any more hurdles."

And as he stood musing, the elder Miss Desmond came down the church steps and walked briskly away.

Some men would, doubtless, have followed her example, if not her direction. Vernon was not one of these. He found himself going up the steps of the great church. He had as good a right to go into the Madeleine as the next man. He would probably not see the girl If he did he would not speak. Almost certainly he would not even see her. But Destiny had remembered Mr. Vernon once more. Betty was standing just inside the door, her face upturned, and all her soul in her eyes. The mutterings of the organ and the voices of boys filled the great dark building.

He went and stood close by her. He would not speak. He would keep his word. But she should have a chance of speaking. His eyes were on her face. The hymn ended. She exhaled a held breath, started and spoke.

"You?" she said, "*you*?" The two words are spelled alike. Spoken, they are capable of infinite variations. The first "you" sent Vernon's blood leaping. The second froze it to what it had been before he met her. For indeed that little unfinished idyll had been almost forgotten by the man who sat drinking Vermouth outside the Cafe de la Paix.

"How are you?" he whispered. "Won't you shake hands?"

She gave him a limp and unresponsive glove.

"I had almost forgotten you," she said, "but I am glad to see you—because—Come to the door. I don't like talking in churches."

They stood on the steps behind one of the great pillars.

"Do you think it is wise to stand here?" he said. "Your aunt might see us."

"So you followed us in?" said Betty with perfect self-possession. "That was very kind. I have often wished to see you, to tell you how much obliged I am for all your kindness in the Spring. I was only a child then, and I didn't understand, but now I quite see how good it was of you."

"Why do you talk like that?" he said. "You don't think—you can't think it was my fault?"

"Your fault! What?"

"Why, your father finding us and—"

"Oh, *that*!" she said lightly. "Oh, I had forgotten that! Ridiculous, wasn't it? No, I mean your kindness in giving so many hours to teaching a perfect duffer. Well, now I've seen you and said what I had to say, I think I'll go back."

"No, don't go," he said. "I want to know—oh, all sorts of things! I can see your aunt from afar, and fly if she approaches."

"You don't suppose," said Betty, opening her eyes at him,

"that I shan't tell her I've seen you?"

He had supposed it, and cursed his clumsiness.

"Ah, I see," she went on, "you think I should deceive my aunt now because I deceived my step-father in the Spring. But I was a child then,—and besides, I'm fond of my aunt."

"Did you know that she came to see me?"

"Of course. You seem to think we live in an atmosphere of deceit, Mr. Vernon."

"What's the matter with you?" he said bluntly, for finer weapons seemed useless. "What have I done to make you hate me?"

"I hate you? Oh, no—not in the least," said Betty spitefully. I am very grateful to you for all your kindness."

"Where are you staying?" he asked.

"Hotel Bete," said Betty, off her guard, "but—"

The "but" marked his first score.

"I wish I could have called to see your aunt," he said carelessly, "but I am off to Vienna to-morrow."

Betty believed that she did not change countenance by a hair's breadth.

"I hope you'll have a delightful time," she said politely.

"Thanks. I am sure I shall. The only consolation for leaving Paris is that one is going to Vienna. Are you here for long?"

"I don't know." Betty was on her guard again.

"Paris is a delightful city, isn't it?"

"Most charming."

"Have you been here long?"

"No, not very long."

"Are you still working at your painting? It would be a pity to give that up."

"I am not working just now."

"I see your aunt," he said hurriedly. "Are you going to send me away like this? Don't be so unjust, so ungenerous. It's not like you—my pupil of last Spring was not unjust."

"Your pupil of last Spring was a child and a duffer, Mr. Vernon, as I said before. But she is grateful to you for one thing—no, two."

"What's the other?" he asked swiftly.

"Your drawing-lessons," she demurely answered.

"Then what's the one?"

"Good-bye," she said, and went down the steps to meet her aunt. He effaced himself behind a pillar. In spite of her new coldness, he could not believe that she would tell her aunt of the meeting. And he was right, though Betty's reasons were not his reasons.

"What's the good?" she asked herself as she and her aunt walked across to their hotel. "He's going away to-morrow, and I shall never see him again. Well, I behaved beautifully, that's one thing. He must simply loathe me. So that's all right! If he were staying on in Paris, of course I would tell her."

She believed this fully.

He waited five minutes behind that pillar, and then had himself driven to the Rue Notre Dame des Champs, choosing as driver a man with a white hat, in strict accordance with the advice in Baedeker, though he had never read any of the works of that author.

This new Betty, with the smart gown and the distant manner, awoke at the same time that she contradicted his memories of the Betty of Long Barton. And he should not see her again. Of course he was not going to Vienna, but neither was he going to hang round the Hotel Bete, or to bribe Franz or Elise to smuggle notes to Miss Betty.

"It's never any use trying to join things on again," he told himself. "As well try to mend a spider's web when you have put your boot through it."

'No diver brings up love again
Dropped once
In such cold seas!'

"But what has happened? Why does she hate me so? You acted very nicely, dear, but that wasn't indifference. It was hatred, if ever I've seen it. I wonder what it means? Another lover? No— then she'd be sorry for me. It's something that belongs to me—not another man's shadow. But what I shall never know. And she's prettier than ever, too. Oh, hang it!"

His key turned in the lock, and on the door-mat shewed the white square of an envelope—a note from the other woman, the one whose profile he had not remembered. She was in Paris for a time. She had seen him at the Paix, had wondered whether he had his old rooms, had driven straight up on the chance of being able to leave this—wasn't that devotion?—and would he care to call for her at eight and they could dine somewhere and talk over old times? One familiar initial, that of her first name, curled in the corner and the card smelt of

E. Nesbit

jasmine—not of jasmine-scent in bottles, but of the real flower. He had never known how she managed it.

Vernon was not fond of talking over old times, but Betty would be dining at the Hotel Bete—some dull hole, no doubt; he had never heard of it. Well, he could not dine at the Bete, and after all one must dine somewhere. And the other woman had never bored him. That is a terrible weapon in the hands of a rival. And Betty had been most unjust. And what was Betty to him, anyway? His thoughts turned to the American girl who had sketched with him in Brittany that Summer. Ah, if she had not been whisked back to New York by her people, it would not now be a question of Betty or of the Jasmine lady. He took out Miss Van Tromp's portrait and sat looking at it: it was admirable, the fearless poise of the head, the laughing eyes, the full pouting lips. Then Betty's face and the face of the Jasmine lady came between him and Miss Van Tromp.

"Bah," he said, "smell, kiss, wear—at last throw away. Never keep a rose till it's faded." A little tide of Breton memories swept through him.

"Bah," he said again, "she was perfectly charming, but what is the use of charm, half the world away?"

He pulled his trunk from the front of the fire-place, pushed up the iron damper, and made a little fire. He burned all Miss Van Tromp's letters, and her photograph—but, from habit, or from gratitude, he kissed it before he burned it.

"Now," said he as the last sparks died redly on the black embers, "the decks are cleared for action. Shall I sentimentalise about Betty—cold, cruel, changed Betty—or shall I call for the Jasmine lady?"

He did both, and the Jasmine lady might have found him dull. As it happened, she only found him *distrait*, and that interested her.

"When we parted," she said, "it was I who was in tears. Now it's you. What is it?"

"If I am in tears," he roused himself to say, "it is only because everything passes, 'tout lasse, tout passe, tout casse.'"

"What's broken now?" she asked; "another heart? Oh, yes! you broke mine all to little, little bits. But I've mended it. I wanted frightfully to see you to thank you!

"This is a grateful day for women," thought Vernon, looking the interrogatory.

"Why, for showing me how hearts are broken," she explained; "it's quite easy when you know how, and it's a perfectly delightful game. I play it myself now, and I can't imagine how I ever got on before I learned the rules."

"You forget," he said, smiling. "It was you who broke my heart. And it's not mended yet."

"That's very sweet of you. But really, you know, I'm very glad it was you who broke my heart, and not anyone else. Because, now it's mended, that gives us something to talk about. We have a past. That's really what I wanted to tell you. And that's such a bond, isn't it? When it really *is* past—dead, you know, no nonsense about cataleptic trances, but stone dead."

"Yes," he said, "it is a link. But it isn't the past for me, you know. It can never—"

She held up a pretty jewelled hand.

"Now, don't," she said. "That's just what you don't understand. All that's out of the picture. I know you too well. Just realize that I'm the only nice woman you know who doesn't either expect you to make love to her in the future or hate you for having done it in the past, and you'll want to see me every day. Think of the novelty of it."

E. Nesbit

"I do and I do," said he, "and I won't protest any more while you're in this mood. Bear with me if I seem idiotic to-night— I've been burning old letters, and that always makes me like a funeral."

"Old letters—mine?"

"I burned yours long ago."

"And it isn't two years since we parted! How many have there been since?"

"Is this the Inquisition or is it Durand's?"

"It's somewhere where we both are," she said, without a trace of sentiment; "that's good enough for me. Do you know I've been married since I saw you last? *And* left a widow—in a short three months it all happened. And—well I'm not very clever, as you know, but—can you imagine what it is like to be married to a man who doesn't understand a single word you say, unless it's about the weather or things to eat? No, don't look shocked. He was a good fellow, and very happy till the motor accident took him and left me this."

She shewed a scar on her smooth arm.

"What a woman it is for surprises! So he was very happy? But of course he was."

"Yes, of course, as you say. I was a model wife. I wore black for a whole year too!"

"Why did you marry him?"

"Well, at the time I thought you might hear of it and be disappointed, or hurt, or something."

"So I am," said Vernon with truth.

"You needn't be," said she. "You'll find me much nicer now I don't want to disappoint you or hurt you, but only to have a good time, and there's no nonsense about love to get in the way, and spoil everything."

"So you're—But this isn't proper! Here am I dining with a lady and I don't even know her name!"

"I know—I wouldn't put it to the note. Didn't that single initial arouse your suspicions? Her name? Her title if you please! I married Harry St. Craye. You remember how we used to laugh at him together."

"That little—I beg your pardon, Lady St. Craye."

"Yes," she said, "De mortuis nil nisi bonum: of the dead nothing but the bones. If he had lived he would certainly have beaten me. Here's to our new friendship!"

"Our new friendship!" he repeated, raising his glass and looking in her eyes. Lady St. Craye looked very beautiful, and Betty was not there. In fact, just now there was no Betty.

He went back to his room humming a song of Yvette Guilbert's. There might have been no flowering May, no buttercup meadows in all the world, for any thought of memory that he had of them. And Betty was a thousand miles away.

That was at night. In the morning Betty was at the Hotel Bete, and the Hotel Bete was no longer a petty little hotel which he did not know and never should know. For the early post brought him a letter which said:

"I am in Paris for a few days and should like to see you if you can make it convenient to call at my hotel on Thursday."

This was Tuesday.

The letter was signed with the name of the uncle from whom Vernon had expectations, and at the head of the letter was the address:

"Hotel Bete,
Cite de Retraite,
Rue Boissy d'Anglais."

"Now bear witness!" cried Vernon, appealing to the Universe, "bear witness that this is *not* my fault!"

CHAPTER IX

THE OPPORTUNITY

Vernon in those two days decided that he did not wish to see Betty again. She was angry with him, and, though he never for an instant distrusted his power to dissipate the cloud, he felt that the lifting of it would leave him and her in that strong light wherein the frail flower of sentiment must wither and perish. Explications were fatal to the delicate mystery, the ethereal half-lights, that Vernon loved. Above all things he detested the *trop dit*.

Already a mood of much daylight was making him blink and shrink. He saw himself as he was—or nearly—and the spectacle did not please him. The thought of Lady St. Craye was the only one that seemed to make for any sort of complacency. The thought of Temple rankled oddly.

"He likes me, and he dislikes himself for liking me. Why does he like me? Why does anyone like me? I'm hanged if I know!"

This was the other side of his mood of most days, when the wonder seemed that everyone should not like him. Why shouldn't they? Ordinarily he was hanged if he knew that.

He had expected a note from Lady St. Craye to follow up his dinner with her. He knew how a woman rarely resists the temptation to write to the man in whom she is interested, even while his last words are still ringing in her ears. But no note came, and he concluded that Lady St. Craye was not interested. This reassured while it piqued.

The Hotel Bete is very near the Madeleine, and very near the heart of Paris—of gay Paris, that is,—yet it might have been a hundred miles from anywhere. You go along the Rue Boissy, and stopping at a gateway you turn into a dreary paved court, which is the Cite de la Retraite. Here the doors of the Hotel Bete open before you like the portals of a mausoleum. There is no greeting from the Patronne; your arrival gives rise to no pleasant welcoming bustle. The concierge receives you, and you see at once that her cheerful smile is assumed. No one could really be cheerful at the Hotel Bete.

Vernon felt as though he was entering a family vault of the highest respectability when he passed through its silent hall and enquired for Mr. James Vernon.

Monsieur Vernon was out. No, he had charged no one with a billet for monsieur. Monsieur Vernon would doubtless return for the dejeuner; it was certain that he would return for the diner. Would Monsieur wait?

Monsieur waited, in a little stiff salon with glass doors, prim furniture, and an elaborately ornamental French clock. It was silent, of course. One wonders sometimes whether ornamental French Ormolu clocks have any works, or are solid through-out. For no one has ever seen one of them going.

There were day-old English papers on the table, and the New York Herald. Through the glass doors he could see everyone who came in or went out. And he saw no one. There was a stillness as of the tomb.

Even the waiter, now laying covers for the dejeuner, wore list slippers and his movements were silent as a heron's ghost-gray flight.

He came to the glass door presently.

"Did Monsieur breakfast?"

Vernon was not minded to waste two days in the pursuit of uncles. Here he was, and here he stayed, till Uncle James should appear.

Yes, decidedly, Monsieur breakfasted.

He wondered where the clients of the hotel had hidden themselves. Were they all dead, or merely sight-seeing? As his watch shewed him the approach of half-past twelve he found himself listening for the tramp of approaching feet, the rustle of returning skirts. And still all was silent as the grave.

The sudden summoning sound of a bell roused him from a dreamy wonder as to whether Betty and her aunt had already left. If not, should he meet them at dejeuner? The idea of the possible meeting amused more than it interested him. He crossed the hall and entered the long bare salle a manger.

By Heaven—he was the only guest! A cover was laid for him only—no, at a distance of half the table for another. Then Betty and her aunt had gone. Well, so much the better.

He unfolded his table-napkin. In another moment, doubtless, Uncle James would appear to fill the vacant place.

But in another moment the vacant place was filled—and by Betty—Betty alone, unchaperoned, and bristling with hostility. She bowed very coldly, but she was crimson to the ears. He rose and came to her holding out his hand.

With the waiter looking on, Betty had to give hers, but she gave it in a way that said very plainly:

"I am very surprised and not at all pleased to see you here."

"This is a most unexpected pleasure," he said very distinctly, and added the truth about his uncle.

"Has Monsieur Vernon yet returned?" he asked the waiter who hovered anxiously near.

"No, Monsieur was not yet of return."

"So you see," his look answered the speech of her hand, "it is not my doing in the least."

"I hope your aunt is well," he went on, the waiter handing baked eggs the while.

"Quite well, thank you," said Betty. "And how is your wife? I ought to have asked yesterday, but I forgot."

"My wife?"

"Oh, perhaps you aren't married yet. Of course my father told me of your engagement."

She crumbled bread and smiled pleasantly.

"So *that's* it," thought Vernon. "Fool that I was to forget it!"

"I am not married," he said coldly, "nor have I ever been engaged to be married."

And he ate eggs stolidly wondering what her next move would be. It was one that surprised him. For she leaned towards him and said in a perfectly new voice:

"Couldn't you get Franz to move you a little more this way? One can't shout across these acres of tablecloth, and I've heaps of things to tell you."

He moved nearer, and once again he wronged Betty by a mental shrinking. Was she really going to own that she had resented the news of his engagement? She was really hopeless. He began to bristle defensively.

"Anything you care to tell me will of course be of the greatest possible interest," he was beginning, but Betty interrupted him.

"*Ah, don't be cross!*" she said. "I know I was perfectly horrid yesterday, but I own I was rather hurt."

"Hold back," he adjured her, inwardly, "for Heaven's sake, hold back!"

"You see," she went on, "you and I were such good friends—you'd been so kind—and you told me—you talked to me about things you didn't talk of to other people,—and when I thought you'd told my step-father a secret of yours that you'd never told me, of course I felt hurt—anyone would have."

"I see," said he, beginning to.

"Of course I never dreamed that he'd lied, and even now I don't see—" Then suddenly she did see and crimsoned again.

"He didn't lie," said Vernon carefully, "it was I. But I would never have told him anything that I wouldn't have told you—nor half that I did tell you."

The waiter handed pale meat.

"Yes, the scenery in Brittany is most charming; I did some good work there. The people are so primitive and delightful too."

The waiter withdrew, and Betty said:

"How do you mean—he didn't lie?"

"The fact is," said Vernon, "he—he did not understand our friendship in the least. I imagine friendship was not invented when he was young. It's a tiresome subject, Miss Desmond; let's drop it—shall we?"

"If you like," said she, chilly as December.

"Oh, well then, just let me say it was done for your sake, Miss Desmond. He had no idea that two people should have any interests in common except—except matters of the heart, and the shortest way to convince him was to tell him that my heart was elsewhere. I don't like lies, but there are some people who insist on lies—nothing else will convince them of the truth. Here comes some abhorrent preparation of rice. How goes it with art?"

"I have been working very hard," she said, "but every day I seem to know less and less."

"Oh, that's all right! It's only that every day one knows more and more—of how little one does know. You'll have to pass many milestones before you pass out of that state. Do they always feed you like this here?"

"Some days it's custard," said Betty, "but we've only been here a week."

"We're friends again now, aren't we?" he questioned suddenly.

"Yes—oh, yes!"

"Then I may ask questions. I want to hear what you've been doing since we parted, and where you've been, and how you come to Paris—and where your aunt is, and what she'll say to me when she comes in."

"She likes you," said Betty, "and she won't come in, but Madame Gautier will. Aunt Julia went off this morning—she couldn't delay any longer because of catching the P. & O. at Brindisi; and I'm to wait here till Madame Gautier comes at three. Auntie came all the way back from America to see whether I was happy here. She *is* a dear!"

"And who is Madame Gautier? Is she also a dear? But let's have our coffee in the salon—and tell me everything from the beginning."

"Yes," said Betty, "oh, yes!"

But the salon window was darkened by a passing shape.

"My uncle, bless him!" said Vernon. "I must go. See, here's my card! Won't you write and tell me all about everything? You will, won't you?"

"Yes, but you musn't write to me. Madame Gautier opens all our letters, and friendships weren't invented when she was young either. Good-bye."

Vernon had to go towards the strong English voice that was filling the hall with its inquiries for "Ung Mossoo—ung mossoo Anglay qui avoir certainmong etty icy ce mattan."

Five minutes later Betty saw two figures go along the pavement on the other side of the decorous embroidered muslin blinds which, in the unlikely event of any happening in the Cite de la Retraite, ensure its not being distinctly seen by those who sojourn at the Hotel Bete.

Betty instantly experienced that feminine longing which makes women write to lovers or friends from whom they have but now parted, and she was weaker than Lady St. Craye. There was nothing to do. Her trunks were packed. She had before her two hours, or nearly, of waiting for Madame Gautier. So she wrote, and this is the letter, erasures and all. Vernon, when he got it, was most interested in the erasures here given in italics.

Dear Mr. Vernon:

I am very glad we are good friends again, and I should like to tell you everything that has happened. (*After you, after he—when my step-father*). After the last time I saw you (*I was very unhappy because I wanted to go to Paris*) I was very anxious to go to Paris because of what you had said. My aunt came down and was very kind. (*She told me*) She persuaded my step-father to let me go. I think (*we*) he was glad to get rid of me, for (*somehow*) he never did care about me, any more than I did about him. There are a great many (*other*) things that he does not understand. Of course I was wild with joy and thought of nothing but (*what you*) work, and my aunt brought me over. But I did not see anything of Paris then. We went straight on to Joinville where Madame Gautier has a villa, and (*we*) my aunt left me there, and went to Norway. It was all very strange at first, but I liked it. Madame Gautier is very strict; it was like being at school. Sometimes I almost (*forgot*) fancied that I as at school again. There were three other girls besides me, and we had great fun. The Professor was very nice and encouraging. He is very old. So is everybody who comes to the house—(*but*) it (*was*) is jolly, because when there are four of you everything is so interesting. We used to have picnics in the woods, and take it in turn to ride in the donkey-cart. And there were musical evenings with the Pastor and the Avocat and their wives. It was very amusing sometimes. Madame Gautier had let her Paris flat, so we stayed at Joinville till a week ago, and then my Aunt walked in one day and took me to Paris for a week. I did enjoy that. And now aunt has gone, and Madame Gautier is taking the inventory and getting the keys, and presently she will come for me, I shall go with her to the Rue Vaugirard, Number 62. It will be very nice seeing the other girls again and telling them all about (*everything*) my week in Paris. I am so sorry that I shall not have the pleasure of seeing you again, but I am glad we met—because I do not like to think my friends do not trust me.

Yours sincerely,

Betty Desmond.

That was the letter which Betty posted. But the first letter she wrote was quite different. It began:

> "You don't know, you never will know what it is to me to
> know that you did not deceive me. My dear friend, my only
> friend! And how I treated you yesterday! And how nobly
> you forgave me. I shall see you again. I must see you again.
> No one else has ever understood me." And so on to the
> "True and constant friend Betty."

She burned this letter.

"The other must go," she said, "that's the worst of life. If I sent
the one that's really written as I feel he'd think I was in love
with him or some nonsense. But a child who was just in two
syllables might have written the other. So *that's* all right."

She looked at her watch. The same silver watch with which she
had once crossed the hand of one who told her fortune.

"How silly all that was!" she said. "I have learned wisdom now.
Nearly half-past three. I never knew Madame late before."

And now Betty began to watch the windows for the arrival of
her chaperone; and four o'clock came, and five, but no
Madame Gautier.

She went out at last and asked to see the Patronne, and to her
she explained in a French whose fluency out-ran its correct-
ness, that a lady was to have called for her at three. It was now
a quarter past five. What did Madame think she should do?

Madame was lethargic and uninterested. She had no idea. She
could not advise. Probably Mademoiselle would do well to
wait always.

The concierge was less aloof.

But without doubt Madame, Mademoiselle's friend had
forgotten the hour. She would arrive later, certainly. If not,

Mademoiselle could stay the night at the hotel, where a young lady would be perfectly well, and go to Madame her friend in the morning.

But Betty was not minded to stay the night alone at the Hotel Bete. For one thing she had very little money,—save that in the fat envelope addressed to Madame Gautier which her aunt had given her. It contained, she knew, the money to pay for her board and lessons during the next six months,—for the elder Miss Desmond was off to India, Japan and Thibet, and her horror of banks and cheques made her very downright in the matter of money. That in the envelope was all Betty had, and that was Madame Gautier's. But the other part of the advice—to go to Madame Gautier's in the morning? If in the morning, why not now?

She decided to go now. No one opposed the idea much. Only Franz seemed a little disturbed and the concierge tepidly urged patience.

But Betty was fretted by waiting. Also she knew that Vernon and his uncle might return at any moment. And it would perhaps be awkward for him to find her there—she would not for the world cause him a moment's annoyance. Besides he might think she had waited on the chance of seeing him again. That was not to be borne.

"I will return and take my trunks," she said; and a carriage was called.

There was something very exhilarating in driving through the streets of Paris, alone, in a nice little carriage with fat pneumatic tires. The street lamps were alight, and the shops not yet closed. Almost every house seemed to be a shop.

"I wonder where all the people live," said Betty.

The Place de la Concorde delighted her with its many lamps and its splendid space.

"How glorious it would be to live alone in Paris," she thought, "be driven about in cabs just when one liked and where one liked! Oh, I am tired of being a school-girl! I suppose they won't let me be grown up till I'm so old I shall wish I was a school-girl again."

She loved the river with its reflected lights,—but it made her shudder, too.

"Of course I shall never be allowed to see the Morgue," she said; "they won't let me see anything real. Even this little teeny tiny bit of a drive, I daresay it's not comme il faut! I do hope Madame won't be furious. She couldn't expect me to wait forever. Perhaps, too, she's ill, and no one to look after her. Oh, I'm sure I'm right to go."

The doubt, however, grew as the carriage jolted through narrower streets, and when it drew up at an open carriage-door, Betty jumped out, paid the coachman, and went in quite prepared to be scolded.

She went through the doorway and stood looking for the list of names such as are set at the foot of the stairs leading to flats in London. There was no such list. From a lighted doorway on the right came a babel of shrill, high-pitched voices. Betty looked in at the door and the voices ceased.

"Pardon, Madame," said Betty. "I seek Madame Gautier."

Everyone in the crowded stuffy lamplit little room drew a deep breath.

"Mademoiselle is without doubt one of Madame's young ladies?"

Perhaps it was the sudden hushing of the raised voices, perhaps it was something in the flushed faces that all turned towards her. To her dying day Betty will never know why she did not say "Yes." What she did say was:

"I am a friend of Madame's. Is she at home?"

"No, Mademoiselle,—she is not at home; she will never be at home more, the poor lady. She is dead, Mademoiselle—an accident, one of those cursed automobiles ran over her at her very door, Mademoiselle, before our eyes."

Betty felt sick.

"Thank you," she said, "it is very sudden."

"Will Mademoiselle leave her name?" the concierge asked curiously. "The brother of Madame, he is in the commerce at Nantes. A telegramme has been sent—he arrives to-morrow morning. He will give Mademoiselle details."

Again Betty said what she had not intended to say. She said:

"Miss Brown." Perhaps the brother in the commerce vaguely suggested the addition, "of Manchester."

Then she turned away, and got out of the light into the friendly dusk of the street.

"Tiens, but it is droll," said the concierge's friend, "a young girl, and all alone like that."

"Oh, it is nothing," said the concierge; "the English are mad—all! Their young girls run the streets at all hours, and the Devil guards them."

Betty stood in the street. She could not go back to that circle of harpy faces, all eagerly tearing to pieces the details of poor old Madame Gautier's death. She must be alone—think. She would have to write home. Her father would come to fetch her. Her aunt was beyond the reach of appeal. Her artist-life would be over. Everything would be over. She would be dragged back to the Parishing and the Mothers' meetings and the black-cotton-covered books and the Sunday School.

And she would never have lived in Paris at all!

She walked down the street.

"I can't think—I *must* think! I'll have this night to myself to think in, anyway. I'll go to some cheap hotel. I have enough for that."

She hailed a passing carriage, drove to the Hotel Bete, took her luggage to the Gare du Nord, and left it there.

Then as she stood on the station step, she felt something in her hand. It was the fat letter addressed to Madame Gautier. And she knew it was fat with bank notes.

She unfastened her dress and thrust the letter into her bosom, buttoning the dress carefully over it.

"But I won't go to my hotel yet," she said. "I won't even look for one. I'll see Paris a bit first."

She hailed a coachman.

"Go," she said, "to some restaurant in the Latin Quarter— where the art students eat."

"And I'm alone in Paris, and perfectly free," said Betty, leaning back on the cushions. "No, I won't tell my coachman to drive along the Rue Notre Dame des Champs, wherever that is. Oh, it is glorious to be perfectly free. Oh, poor Madame Gautier! Oh dear, oh dear!" She held her breath and wondered why she could feel sorry.

"You are a wretch," she said, "poor Madame was kind to you in her hard narrow way, and now is she lying cold and dead, all broken up by that cruel motor car."

The horror of the picture helped by Betty's excitement brought the tears and she encouraged them.

E. Nesbit

"It is something to find one is not entirely heartless," she said at last, drying her eyes, as the carriage drew up at a place where there were people and voices and many lights.

CHAPTER X

SEEING LIFE

The thoughts of the two who loved her were with Betty that night. The aunt, shaken, jolted, enduring much in the Paris, Lyons and Mediterranean express thought fondly of her.

"She's a nice little thing. I must take her about a bit," she mused, and even encouraged her fancy to play with the idea of a London season—a thing it had not done for years.

The Reverend Cecil, curtains drawn and lamp alight, paused to think of her even in the midst of his first thorough examination of his newest treasure in Seventeenth Century Tracts, "The Man Mouse baited and trapped for nibbling the margins of Eugenius Philalethes, being an assault on Henry Moore." It was bound up with, "The Second Wash, or the Moore scoured again," and a dozen others. A dumpy octavo, in brown leather, he had found it propping a beer barrel in the next village.

"Dear Lizzie!—I wonder if she will ever care for really important things. There must be treasures upon treasures in those boxes on the French quays that one reads about. But she never would learn to know one type from another."

He studied the fire thoughtfully.

"I wonder if she does understand how much she is to me," he thought.

E. Nesbit

"Those are the things that are better unsaid. At least I always think so when she's here. But all these months—I wonder whether girls like you to *say things*, or to leave them to be understood. It is more delicate not to say them, perhaps."

Then his thoughts went back to the other Lizzie, about whom he had never felt these doubts. He had loved her, and had told her so. And she had told him her half of the story in very simple words—and most simply, and without at all "leaving things to be understood" they had planned the future that never was to be. He remembered the day when sitting over the drawing-room fire, and holding her dear hand he had said:

"This is how we shall sit when we are old and gray, dearest." It had seemed so impossibly far-off then.

And she had said:

"I hope we shall die the same day, Cec."

But this had not happened.

And he had said:

"And we shall have such a beautiful life—doing good, and working for God, and bringing up our children in the right way. Oh, Lizzie, it's very wonderful to think of that happiness, isn't it?"

And she had laid her head on his shoulder and whispered:

"I hope we shall have a little girl, dear."

And he had said:

"I shall call her Elizabeth, after my dear wife."

"She must have eyes like yours though."

"She will be exactly like both of us," he had said, and they sat hand in hand, and talked innocently, like two children, of the little child that was never to be.

He had wanted them to put on her tombstone, Lizzie daughter of—and affianced wife of Cecil Underwood, but her mother had said that *there* there was no marrying or giving in marriage. In his heart the Reverend Cecil had sometimes dared to hope that that text had been misunderstood. To him his Lizzie had always been "as the angels of God in Heaven."

Then came the long broken years, and then the little girl— Elizabeth, his step-child.

The pent-up love of all his life spent itself on her: a love so fond, so tender, so sacred that it seemed only self-respecting to hide it a little from the world by a mask of coldness. And Betty had never seen anything but the mask.

"I think, when I see her, I will tell her all about my Lizzie," he said. "I wonder if she knows what the house is like without her. But of course she doesn't, or she would have asked to come home, long ago. I wonder whether she misses me very much. Madame Gautier is kind, she says; but no stranger can make a home, as love can make it."

Meanwhile Betty dining alone at a restaurant in the Boulevard St. Michel, within a mile of the Serpent, ordered what she called a nice dinner—it was mostly vegetables and sweet things—and ate it with appetite, looking about her. The long mirrors, the waiters were like the ones in London restaurants, but the people who ate there they were different. Everything was much shabbier, yet much gayer. Shopkeeping-looking men were dining with their wives; some of them had a child, napkin under chin, solemnly struggling with a big soup spoon or upturning on its little nose a tumbler of weak red wine and water. There were students—she knew them by their slouched hats and beards a day old—dining by twos and threes and fours. No one took any more notice of Betty than was shewn by a careless glance or two. She was very quietly dressed. Her hat even was rather an unbecoming brown thing. When she had eaten, she ordered coffee, and began to try to think, but thinking was difficult with the loud voices and the laughter, and the clink of glasses and the waiters' hurrying transits. And at the back of her mind was a thought waiting for her to think it. And she was afraid.

So presently she paid her bill, and went out, and found a tram, and rode on the top of it through the lighted streets, on the level of the first floor windows and the brown leaves of the trees in the Boulevards, and went away and away through the heart of Paris; and still all her mind could do nothing but thrust off, with both hands, the thought that was pushing forward towards her thinking. When the tram stopped at its journey's end she did not alight, but paid for, and made, the return journey, and found her feet again in the Boulevard St. Michel.

Of course, she had read her Trilby, and other works dealing with the Latin Quarter. She knew that in that quarter everyone is not respectable, but everyone is kind. It seemed good to her to go to a cafe, to sit at a marble topped table, and drink—not the strange liqueurs which men drink in books, but homely hot milk, such as some of the other girls there had before them. It would be perfectly simple, as well as interesting, to watch the faces of the students, boys and girls, and when she found a nice girl-face, to speak to it, asking for the address of a respectable hotel.

So she walked up the wide, tree-planted street feeling very Parisian indeed, as she called it the "Boule Miche" to herself. And she stopped at the first Cafe she came to, which happened to be the Cafe d'Harcourt.

She did not see its name, and if she had it would naturally not have conveyed any idea to her. The hour was not yet ten, and the Cafe d'Harcourt was very quiet. There were not a dozen people at the little tables. Most of them were women. It would be easy to ask her little questions, with so few people to stare and wonder if she addressed a stranger.

She sat down, and ordered her hot milk and, with a flutter, awaited it. This was life. And to-morrow she must telegraph to her step-father, and everything would end in the old round of parish duties; all her hopes and dreams would be submerged in the heavy morass of meeting mothers. The thought leapt up.— Betty hid her eyes and would not look at it. Instead, she looked at the other people seated at the tables—the women. They were laughing and talking among themselves. One or two looked at Betty and smiled with frank friendliness. Betty smiled back, but with embarrassment. She had heard that French ladies of rank and fashion would as soon go out without their stockings as without their paint, but she had not supposed that the practice extended to art students. And all these ladies were boldly painted—no mere soupçon of carmine and pearl powder, but good solid masterpieces in body colour, black, white and red. She smiled in answer to their obvious friendliness, but she did not ask them for addresses. A handsome black-browed scowling woman sitting alone frowned at her. She felt quite hurt. Why should anyone want to be unkind?

Men selling flowers, toy rabbits, rattling cardboard balls, offered their wares up and down the row of tables. Betty bought a bunch of fading late roses and thought, with a sudden sentimentality that shocked her, of the monthly rose below the window at home. It always bloomed well up to Christmas. Well, in two days she would see that rose-bush.

The trams rattled down the Boulevard, carriages rolled by. Every now and then one of these would stop, and a couple would alight. And people came on foot. The cafe was filling up. But still none of the women seemed to Betty exactly the right sort of person to know exactly the right sort of hotel.

Of course she knew from books that Hotels keep open all night,—but she did not happen to have read any book which told of the reluctance of respectable hotels to receive young women without luggage, late in the evening. So it seemed to her that there was plenty of time.

A blonde girl with jet black brows and eyes like big black beads was leaning her elbows on her table and talking to her companions, two tourist-looking Germans in loud checks. They kept glancing at Betty, and it made her nervous to know that they were talking about her. At last her eyes met the eyes of the girl, who smiled at her and made a little gesture of invitation to her, to come and sit at their table. Betty out of sheer embarrassment might have gone, but just at that moment the handsome scowling woman rose, rustled quickly to Betty, knocking over a chair in her passage, held out a hand, and said in excellent English:

"How do you do?"

Betty gave her hand, but "I don't remember you," said she.

"May I join you?" said the woman sitting down. She wore black and white and red, and she was frightfully smart, Betty thought. She glanced at the others—the tourists and the blonde; they were no longer looking at her.

"Look here," said the woman, speaking low, "I don't know you from Adam, of course, but I know you're a decent girl. For God's sake go home to your friends! I don't know what they're about to let you out alone like this."

"I'm alone in Paris just now," said Betty.

"Good God in Heaven, you little fool! Get back to your lodging. You've no business here."

"I've as much business as anyone else," said Betty. "I'm an artist, too, and I want to see life."

"You've not seen much yet," said the woman with a, laugh that

Betty hated to hear. "Have you been brought up in a convent? You an artist! Look at all of us! Do you need to be told what *our* trade is?"

"Don't," said Betty; "oh, don't."

"Go home," said the woman, "and say your prayers—I suppose you *do* say your prayers?—and thank God that it isn't your trade too."

"I don't know what you mean," said Betty.

"Well then, go home and read your Bible. That'll tell you the sort of woman it is that stands about the corners of streets, or sits at the Cafe d'Harcourt. What are your people about?"

"My father's in England," said Betty; "he's a clergyman."

"I generally say mine was," said the other, "but I won't to you, because you'd believe me. My father was church organist, though. And the Vicarage people were rather fond of me. I used to do a lot of Parish work." She laughed again.

Betty laid a hand on the other woman's.

"Couldn't you go home to your father—or—something?" she asked feebly.

"He's cursed me forever—Put it all down in black and white— a regular commination service. It's you that have got to go home, and do it *now*, too." She shook off Betty's hand and waved her own to a man who was passing.

"Here, Mr. Temple—"

The man halted, hesitated and came up to them.

"Look here," said the black-browed woman, "look what a pretty flower I've found,—and here of all places!"

E. Nesbit

She indicated Betty by a look. The man looked too, and took the third chair at their table. Betty wished that the ground might open and cover her, but the Boule Miche asphalt is solid. The new-comer was tall and broad-shouldered, with a handsome, serious, boyish face, and fair hair.

"She won't listen to me—"

"Oh, I did!" Betty put in reproachfully.

"You talk to her like a father. Tell her where naughty little girls go who stay out late at the Cafe d'Harcourt—fire and brimstone, you know. She'll understand, she's a clergyman's daughter."

"I really do think you'd better go home," said the new-comer to Betty with gentle politeness.

"I would, directly," said Betty, almost in tears, "but—the fact is I haven't settled on a hotel, and I came to this cafe. I thought I could ask one of these art students to tell me a good hotel, but—so that's how it is."

"I should think not," Temple answered the hiatus. Then he looked at the black-browed, scowling woman, and his look was very kind.

"Nini and her German swine were beginning to be amiable," said the woman in an aside which Betty did not hear. "For Christ's sake take the child away, and put her safely for the night somewhere, if you have to ring up a Mother Superior or a Governesses' Aid Society."

"Right. I will." He turned to Betty.

"Will you allow me," he said, "to find a carriage for you, and see you to a hotel?"

"Thank you," said Betty.

He went out to the curbstone and scanned the road for a passing carriage.

"Look here," said the black-browed woman, turning suddenly on Betty; "I daresay you'll think it's not my place to speak—oh, if you don't think so you will some day, when you're grown up,—but look here. I'm not chaffing. It's deadly earnest. You be good. See? There's nothing else that's any good really."

"Yes," said Betty, "I know. If you're not good you won't be happy."

"There you go," the other answered almost fiercely; "it's always the way. Everyone says it—copybooks and Bible and everything—and no one believes it till they've tried the other way, and then it's no use believing anything."

"Oh, yes, it is," said Betty comfortingly, "and you're so kind. I don't know how to thank you. Being kind *is* being good too, isn't it?"

"Well, you aren't always a devil, even if you are in hell. I wish I could make you understand all the things I didn't understand when I was like you. But nobody can. That's part of the hell. And you don't even understand half I'm saying."

"I think I do," said Betty.

"Keep straight," the other said earnestly; "never mind how dull it is. I used to think it must be dull in Heaven. God knows it's dull in the other place! Look, he's got a carriage. You can trust him just for once, but as a rule I'd say 'Don't you trust any of them—they're all of a piece.' Good-bye; you're a nice little thing."

"Good-bye," said Betty; "oh, good-bye! You *are* kind, and good! People can't all be good the same way," she added, vaguely and seeking to comfort.

E. Nesbit

"Women can," said the other, "don't you make any mistake. Good-bye."

She watched the carriage drive away, and turned to meet the spiteful chaff of Nini and her German friends.

"Now," said Mr. Temple, as soon as the wheels began to revolve, "perhaps you will tell me how you come to be out in Paris alone at this hour."

Betty stared at him coldly.

"I shall be greatly obliged if you can recommend me a good hotel," she said.

"I don't even know your name," said he.

"No," she answered briefly.

"I cannot advise you unless you will trust me a little," he said gently.

"You are very kind,—but I have not yet asked for anyone's advice."

"I am sorry if I have offended you," he said, "but I only wish to be of service to you."

"Thank you very much," said Betty: "the only service I want is the name of a good hotel."

"You are unwise to refuse my help," he said. "The place where I found you shews that you are not to be trusted about alone."

"Look here," said Betty, speaking very fast, "I dare say you mean well, but it isn't your business. The lady I was speaking to—"

"That just shews," he said.

"She was very kind, and I like her. But I don't intend to be interfered with by any strangers, however well they mean."

He laughed for the first time, and she liked him better when she had heard the note of his laughter.

"Please forgive me," he said. "You are quite right. Miss Conway is very kind. And I really do want to help you, and I don't want to be impertinent. May I speak plainly?"

"Of course."

"Well the Cafe d'Harcourt is not a place for a respectable girl to go to."

"I gathered that," she answered quietly. "I won't go there again."

"Have you quarreled with your friends?" he persisted; "have you run away?"

"No," said Betty, and on a sudden inspiration, added: "I'm very, very tired. You can ask me any questions you like in the morning. Now: will you please tell the man where to go?"

The dismissal was unanswerable.

He took out his card-case and scribbled on a card.

"Where is your luggage?" he asked.

"Not here," she said briefly.

"I thought not," he smiled again. "I am discerning, am I not? Well, perhaps you didn't know that respectable hotels prefer travellers who have luggage. But they know me at this place. I have said you are my cousin," he added apologetically.

He stopped the carriage. "Hotel de l'Unicorne," he told the

driver and stood bareheaded till she was out of sight.

The Thought came out and said: "There will be an end of Me if you see that well-meaning person again." Betty would not face the Thought, but she was roused to protect it.

She stood up and touched the coachman on the arm.

"Go back to the Cafe d'Harcourt," she said. "I have forgotten something."

That was why, when Temple called, very early, at the Hotel de l'Unicorne he heard that his cousin had not arrived there the night before—Had not, indeed, arrived at all.

He shrugged his shoulders.

"It's a pity," he said. "Certainly she had run away from home. I suppose I frightened her. I was always a clumsy brute with women."

CHAPTER XI

THE THOUGHT

The dark-haired woman was still ably answering the chaff of Nini and the Germans. And her face was not the face she had shewn to Betty. Betty came quietly behind her and touched her shoulder. She leapt in her chair and turned white under the rouge.

"What the devil!—You shouldn't do that!" she said roughly; "You frightened me out of my wits."

"I'm so sorry," said Betty, who was pale too. "Come away, won't you? I want to talk to you."

"Your little friend is charming," said one of the men in thick German-French. "May I order for her a bock or a cerises?"

"Do come," she urged.

"Let's walk," she said. "What's the matter? Where's young Temple? Don't tell me he's like all the others."

"He meant to be kind," said Betty, "but he asked a lot of questions, and I don't want to know him. I like you better. Isn't there anywhere we can be quiet, and talk? I'm all alone here in Paris, and I do want help. And I'd rather you'd help me than anyone else. Can't I come home with you?"

E. Nesbit

"No you can't."

"Well then, will you come with me?—not to the hotel he told me of, but to some other—you must know of one."

"What will you do if I don't?"

"I don't know," said Betty very forlornly, "but you *will*, won't you. You don't know how tired I am. Come with me, and then in the morning we can talk. Do—do."

The other woman took some thirty or forty steps in silence. Then she asked abruptly:

"Have you plenty of money?"

"Yes, lots."

"And you're an artist?"

"Yes—at least I'm a student."

Again the woman reflected. At last she shrugged her shoulders and laughed. "Set a thief to catch a thief," she said. "I shall make a dragon of a chaperon, I warn you. Yes, I'll come, just for this one night, but you'll have to pay the hotel bill."

"Of course," said Betty.

"This *is* an adventure! Where's your luggage?"

"It's at the station, but I want you to promise not to tell that Temple man a word about me. I don't want to see him again. Promise."

"Queer child. But I'll promise. Now look here: if I go into a thing at all I go into it heart and soul; so let's do the thing properly. We must have some luggage. I've got an old portmanteau knocking about. Will you wait for me somewhere while I get it?"

"I'd rather not," said Betty, remembering the Germans and Nini.

"Well then,—there'd be no harm for a few minutes. You can come with me. This is really rather a lark!"

Five minutes' walking brought the two to a dark house. The woman rang a bell; a latch clicked and a big door swung open. She grasped Betty's hand.

"Don't say a word," she said, and pulled her through.

It was very dark.

The other woman called out a name as they passed the door of the concierge, a name that was not Conway, and her hand pulled Betty up flight after flight of steep stairs. On the fifth floor she opened a door with a key, and left Betty standing at the threshold till she had lighted a lamp.

Then "Come in," she said, and shut the door and bolted it.

The room was small and smelt of white rose scent; the looking-glass had a lace drapery fastened up with crushed red roses; and there were voluminous lace and stuff curtains to bed and window.

"Sit down," said the hostess. She took off her hat and pulled the scarlet flowers from it. She washed her face till it shewed no rouge and no powder, and the brown of lashes and brows was free from the black water-paint. She raked under the bed with a faded sunshade till she found an old brown portmanteau. Her smart black and white dress was changed for a black one, of a mode passee these three years. A gray chequered golf cape and the dulled hat completed the transformation.

"How nice you look," said Betty.

E. Nesbit

The other bundled some linen and brushes into the portmanteau.

"The poor old Gladstone's very thin still," she said, and folded skirts; "we must plump it out somehow."

When the portmanteau was filled and strapped, they carried it down between them, in the dark, and got it out on to the pavement.

"I am Miss Conway now," said the woman, "and we will drive to the Hotel de Lille. I went there one Easter with my father."

With the change in her dress a change had come over Miss Conway's voice.

At the Hotel de Lille it was she who ordered the two rooms, communicating, for herself and her cousin, explained where the rest of the luggage was, and gave orders for the morning chocolate.

"This is very jolly," said Betty, when they were alone. "It's like an elopement."

"Exactly," said Miss Conway. "Good night."

"It's rather like a dream, though. I shan't wake up and find you gone, shall I?" Betty asked anxiously.

"No, no. We've all your affairs to settle in the morning."

"And yours?"

"Mine were settled long ago. Oh, I forgot—I'm Miss Conway, at the Hotel de Lille. Yes, we'll settle my affairs in the morning, too. Good night, little girl."

"Good night, Miss Conway."

"They call me Lotty."

"My name's Betty and—look here, I can't wait till the morning." Betty clasped her hands, and seemed to be holding her courage between them. "I've come to Paris to study art, and I want you to come and live with me. I know you'd like it, and I've got heaps of money—will you?"

She spoke quickly and softly, and her face was flushed and her eyes bright.

There was a pause.

"You silly little duffer—you silly dear little duffer."

The other woman had turned away and was fingering the chains of an ormolu candlestick on the mantelpiece.

Betty put an arm over her shoulders.

"Look here," she said, "I'm not such a duffer as you think. I know people do dreadful things—but they needn't go on doing them, need they?"

"Yes, they need," said the other; "that's just it."

Her fingers were still twisting the bronze chains.

"And the women you talked about—in the Bible—they weren't kind and good, like you; they were just only horrid and not anything else. You told *me* to be good. Won't you let me help you? Oh, it does seem such cheek of me, but I never knew anyone before who—I don't know how to say it. But I am so sorry, and I want you to be good, just as much as you want me to. Dear, dear Lotty!"

"My name's Paula."

"Paula dear, I wish I wasn't so stupid, but I know it's not your fault, and I know you aren't like that woman with the Germans."

"I should hope not indeed," Paula was roused to flash back; "dirty little French gutter-cat."

"I've never been a bit of good to anyone," said Betty, adding her other arm and making a necklace of the two round Paula's neck, "except to Parishioners perhaps. Do let me be a bit of good to you. Don't you think I could?"

"You dear little fool!" said Paula gruffly.

"Yes, but say yes—you must! I know you want to. I've got lots of money. Kiss me, Paula."

"I won't!—Don't kiss me!—I won't have it! Go away," said the woman, clinging to Betty and returning her kisses.

"Don't cry," said Betty gently. "We shall be ever so happy. You'll see. Good night, Paula. Do you know I've never had a friend—a girl-friend, I mean?"

"For God's sake hold your tongue, and go to bed! Good night."

Betty, alone, faced at last, and for the first time, The Thought. But it had changed its dress when Miss Conway changed hers. It was no longer a Thought: it was a Resolution.

Twin-born with her plan for saving her new friend was the plan for a life that should not be life at Long Barton.

All the evening she had refused to face The Thought. But it had been shaping itself to something more definite than thought. As a Resolution, a Plan, it now unrolled itself before her. She sat in the stiff arm-chair looking straight in front of her, and she saw what she meant to do. The Thought had been wise not to insist too much on recognition. Earlier in the evening it would have seemed merely a selfish temptation. Now it was an opportunity for a good and noble act. And Betty had always wanted so much to be noble and good.

Here she was in Paris, alone. Her aunt, train-borne, was every moment further and further away. As for her step-father:

"I hate him," said Betty, "and he hates me. He only let me come to get rid of me. And what good could I do at Long Barton compared with what I can do here? Any one can do Parish work. I've got the money Aunt left for Madame Gautier. Perhaps it's stealing. But is it? The money was meant to pay to keep me in Paris to study Art. And it's not as if I were staying altogether for selfish reasons—there's Paula. I'm sure she has really a noble nature. And it's not as if I were staying because He is in Paris. Of course, that would be *really wrong*. But he said he was going to Vienna. I suppose his uncle delayed him, but he'll certainly go. I'm sure it's right. I've learned a lot since I left home. I'm not a child now. I'm a woman, and I must do what I think is right. You know I must, mustn't I?"

She appealed to the Inward Monitor, but it refused to be propitiated.

"It only seems not quite right because it's so unusual," she went on; "that's because I've never been anywhere or done anything. After all, it's my own life, and I have a right to live it as I like. My step-father has never written to Madame Gautier all these months. He won't now. It's only to tell him she has changed her address—he only writes to me on Sunday nights. There's just time. And I'll keep the money, and when Aunt comes back I'll tell her everything. She'll understand."

"Do you think so?" said the Inward Monitor.

"Any way," said Betty, putting her foot down on the Inward Monitor, "I'm going to do it. If it's only for Paula's sake. We'll take rooms, and I'll go to a Studio, and work hard; and I won't make friends with gentlemen I don't know, or anything silly, so there," she added defiantly. "Auntie left the money for me to study in Paris. If I tell my step-father that Madame Gautier is dead, he'll just fetch me home, and what'll become of Paula then?"

Thus and thus, ringing the changes on resolve and explanation, her thoughts ran. A clock chimed midnight.

"Is it possible," she asked herself, "that it's not twelve hours since I was at the Hotel Bete—talking to Him? Well, I shall never see him again, I suppose. How odd that I don't feel as if I cared whether I did or not. I suppose what I felt about him wasn't real. It all seems so silly now. Paula is real, and all that I mean to do for her is real. He isn't."

She prayed that night as usual, but her mind was made up, and she prayed outside a closed door.

Next morning, when her chocolate came up, she carried it into the next room, and, sitting on the edge of her new friend's bed, breakfasted there.

Paula seemed dazed when she first woke, but soon she was smiling and listening to Betty's plans.

"How young you look," said Betty, "almost as young as me."

"I'm twenty-five."

"You don't look it—with your hair in those pretty plaits, and your nightie. You do have lovely nightgowns."

"I'll get up now," said Paula. "Look out—I nearly upset the tray."

Betty had carefully put away certain facts and labelled them: "Not to be told to anyone, even Paula." No one was to know anything about Vernon. "There is nothing to know really," she told herself. No one was to know that she was alone in Paris without the knowledge of her relations. Lots of girls came to Paris alone to study art. She was just one of these.

She found the lying wonderfully easy. It did not bring with it, either, any of the shame that lying should bring, but rather a sense of triumphant achievement, as from a difficult part played excellently.

She paid the hotel bill, and then the search for rooms began.

"We must be very economical, you know," she said, "but you won't mind that, will you? I think it will be rather fun."

"It would be awful fun," said the other. "You'll go and work at the studio, and when you come home after your work I shall have cooked the dejeuner, and we shall have it together on a little table with a nice white cloth and a bunch of flowers on it."

"Yes; and in the evening we'll go out, to concerts and things, and ride on the tops of trams. And on Sundays—what does one do on Sundays?"

"I suppose one goes to church," said Paula.

"Oh, I think not when we're working so hard all the week. We'll go into the country."

"We can take the river steamer and go to St. Cloud, or go out on the tram to Clamart—the woods there are just exactly like the woods at home. What part of England do you live in?"

"Kent," said Betty.

"My home's in Devonshire," said Paula.

It was a hard day: so many stairs to climb, so many apartments to see! And all of them either quite beyond Betty's means, or else little stuffy places, filled to choking point with the kind of furniture no one could bear to live with, and with no light, and no outlook except a blank wall a yard or two from the window.

They kept to the Montparnasse quarter, for there, Paula said, were the best ateliers for Betty. They found a little restaurant, where only art students ate, and where one could breakfast royally for about a shilling. Betty looked with interest at the faces of the students, and wondered whether she should ever know any of them. Some of them looked interesting. A few were English, and fully half American.

Then the weary hunt for rooms began again.

It was five o'clock before a *concierge, unexpected amiable* in face of their refusal of her rooms, asked whether they had tried Madame Bianchi's—Madame Bianchi where the atelier was, and the students' meetings on Sunday evenings,—Number 57 Boulevard Montparnasse.

They tried it. One passes through an archway into a yard where the machinery, of a great laundry pulses half the week, up some wide wooden stairs—shallow, easy stairs—and on the first floor are the two rooms. Betty drew a long breath when she saw them. They were lofty, they were airy, they were light. There was not much furniture, but what there was was good— old carved armoires, solid divans and—joy of joys—in each room a carved oak, Seventeenth Century mantelpiece eight feet high and four feet deep.

"I *must* have these rooms!" Betty whispered. "Oh, I could make them so pretty!"

The rent of the rooms was almost twice as much as the sum they fixed on, and Paula murmured caution.

"Its no use," said Betty. "We'll live on bread and water if you like, but we'll live on it *here*."

And she took the rooms.

"I'm sure we've done right," she said as they drove off to fetch her boxes: "the rooms will be like a home, you see if they aren't. And there's a piano too. And Madame Bianchi, isn't she a darling; Isn't she pretty and sweet and nice?"

"Yes," said Paula thoughtfully; "it certainly is something that you've got rooms in the house of a woman like that."

"And that ducky little kitchen! Oh, we shall have such fun, cooking our own meals! You shall get the dejeuner but I'll cook the dinner while you lie on the sofa and read novels 'like a real lady.'"

"Don't use that expression—I hate it," said Paula sharply. "But the rooms are lovely, aren't they?"

"Yes, it's a good place for you to be in—I'm sure of that," said the other, musing again.

When the boxes were unpacked, and Betty had pinned up a few prints and photographs and sketches and arranged some bright coloured Liberty scarves to cover the walls' more obvious defects—left by the removal of the last tenant's decorations—when flowers were on table and piano, the curtains drawn and the lamps lighted, the room did, indeed,look "like a home."

"We'll have dinner out to-night," said Paula, "and to-morrow we'll go marketing, and find you a studio to work at."

"Why not here?"

"That's an idea. Have you a lace collar you can lend me? This is not fit to be seen."

Betty pinned the collar on her friend.

"I believe you get prettier every minute," she said. "I must just write home and give them my address."

She fetched her embroidered blotting-book.

"It reminds one of bazaars," said Miss Conway.

*   *   *   *   *

57 Boulevard Montparnasse.

My dear Father:

This is our new address. Madame Gautier's tenant wanted to keep on her flat in the Rue de Vaugirard, so she has taken this one which is larger and very convenient, as it is close to many of the best studios. I think I shall like it very much. It is not decided yet where I am to study, but there is an Atelier in the House for ladies only, and I think it will be there, so that I shall not have to go out to my lessons. I will write again as soon as we are more settled. We only moved in late this afternoon, so there is a lot to do. I hope you are quite well, and that everything is going on well in the Parish. I will certainly send some sketches for the Christmas sale. Madame Gautier does not wish me to go home for Christmas; she thinks it would interrupt my work too much. There is a new girl, a Miss Conway. I like her very much. With love,

Yours affectionately,

E. Desmond.

She was glad when that letter was written. It is harder to lie in writing than in speech, and the use of the dead woman's name made her shiver.

"But I won't do things by halves," she said.

"What's this?" Paula asked sharply. She had stopped in front of one of Betty's water colours.

"That? Oh, I did it ages ago—before I learned anything. Don't look at it."

"But *what* is it?"

"Oh, only our house at home."

"I wonder," said Paula, "why all English Vicarages are exactly alike."

"It's a Rectory," said Betty absently.

"That ought to make a difference, but it doesn't. I haven't seen an English garden for four years."

"Four years is a long time," said Betty.

"You don't know how long," said the other. "And the garden's been going on just the same all the time. It seems odd, doesn't it? Those hollyhocks—the ones at the Vicarage at home are just like them. Come, let's go to dinner!"

E. Nesbit

CHAPTER XII

THE RESCUE

When Vernon had read Betty's letter—and holding it up to the light he was able to read the scratched-out words almost as easily as the others—he decided that he might as well know where she worked, and one day, after he had called on Lady St. Craye, he found himself walking along the Rue de Vaugirard. Lady St. Craye was charming. And she had been quite right when she had said that he would find a special charm in the companionship of one in whose heart his past love-making seemed to have planted no thorns. Yet her charm, by its very nature—its finished elegance, its conscious authority—made him think with the more interest of the unformed, immature grace of the other woman—Betty, in whose heart he had not had the chance to plant either thorns or roses.

How could he find out? Concierges are venal, but Vernon disliked base instruments. He would act boldly. It was always the best way. He would ask to see this Madame Gautier—if Betty were present he must take his chance. It would be interesting to see whether she would commit herself to his plot by not recognizing him. If she did that—Yet he hoped she wouldn't. If she did recognize him he would say that it was through Miss Desmond's relatives that he had heard of Madame Gautier. Betty could not contradict him. He would invent a niece whose parents wished to place her with Madame. Then he could ask as many questions as he liked, about hours and studios, and all the details of the life Betty led.

It was a simple straight-forward design, and one that carried success in its pocket. No one could suspect anything.

Yet at the very first step suspicion, or what looked like it, stared at him from the eyes of the concierge when he asked for Madame Gautier.

"Monsieur is not of the friends of Madame?" she asked curiously.

He knew better than to resent the curiosity. He explained that he desired to see Madame on business.

"You will see her never," the woman said dramatically; "she sees no one any more."

"Is it that she is ill?"

"It is that she is dead,—and the dead do not receive, Monsieur." She laughed, and told the tale of death circumstantially, with grim relish of detail.

"And the young ladies—they have returned to their parents?"

"Ah, it is in the young ladies that Monsieur interests himself? But yes. Madame's brother, who is in the Commerce of Nantes, he restored instantly the young ladies to their friends. One was already with her aunt."

Vernon had money ready in his hand.

"What was her name, Madame—the young lady with the aunt?"

"But I know not, Monsieur. She was a new young lady, who had been with Madame at her Villa—I have not seen her. At the time of the regrettable accident she was with her aunt, and doubtless remains there. Thank you, Monsieur. That is all I know."

"Thank you, Madame. I am desolated to have disturbed you. Good day."

And Vernon was in the street again.

So Betty had never come to the Rue Vaugirard! The aunt must somehow have heard the news—perhaps she had called on the way to the train—she had returned to the Bete and Betty now was Heaven alone knew where. Perhaps at Long Barton. Perhaps in Paris, with some other dragon.

Vernon for a day or two made a point of being near when the studios—Julien's, Carlorossi's, Delacluse's, disgorged their students. He did not see Betty, because she was not studying at any of these places, but at the Atelier Bianchi, of which he never thought. So he shrugged his shoulders, and dined again with Lady St. Craye, and began to have leisure to analyse the emotions with which she inspired him. He had not believed that he could be so attracted by a woman with whom he had played the entire comedy, from first glance to last tear—from meeting hands to severed hearts. Yet attracted he was, and strongly. He experienced a sort of resentment, a feeling that she had kept something from him, that she had reserves of which he knew nothing, that he, who in his blind complacency had imagined himself to have sucked the orange and thrown away the skin, had really, in point of fact, had a strange lovely fruit snatched from him before his blunt teeth had done more than nibble at its seemingly commonplace rind.

In the old days she had reared barriers of reserve, walls of reticence over which he could see so easily; now she posed as having no reserves, and he seemed to himself to be following her through a darkling wood, where the branches flew back and hit him in the face so that he could not see the path.

"You know," she said, "what makes it so delightful to talk to you is that I can say exactly what I like. You won't expect me to be clever, or shy, or any of those tiresome things. We can be perfectly frank with each other. And that's such a relief, isn't it?"

"I wonder whether it would be—supposing it could be?" said he.

They were driving in the Bois, among the autumn tinted trees where the pale mist wreaths wandered like ghosts in the late afternoon.

"Of course it could be; it is," she said, opening her eyes at him under the brim of her marvel of a hat: "at least it is for simple folk like me. Why don't you wear a window in your breast as I do?"

She laid her perfectly gloved hand on her sables.

"Is there really a window? Can one see into your heart?"

"*One* can—not the rest. Just the one from whom one feareth nothing, expecteth nothing, hopeth nothing. That's out of the Bible, isn't it?"

"It's near enough," said he. "Of course, to you it's a new sensation to have the window in your breast. Whereas I, from innocent childhood to earnest manhood, have ever been open as the day."

"Yes," she said, "you were always transparent enough. But one is so blind when one is in love."

Her calm references to the past always piqued him.

"I don't think Love is so blind as he's painted," he said: "always as soon as I begin to be in love with people I begin to see their faults."

"You may be transparent, but you haven't a good mirror," she laughed; "you don't see yourself as you are. It isn't when you begin to love people that you see their faults, is it? It's really when they begin to love you."

"But I never begin to love people till they begin to love me. I'm too modest."

"And I never love people after they've done loving me. I'm too—"

"Too what?"

"Too something—forgetful, is it? I mean it takes two to make a quarrel, and it certainly takes two to make a love affair."

"And what about all the broken hearts?"

"What broken hearts?"

"The ones you find in the poets and the story books."

"That's just where you do find them. Nowhere else.—Now, honestly, has your heart ever been broken?"

"Not yet: so be careful how you play with it. You don't often find such a perfect specimen—absolutely not a crack or a chip."

"The pitcher shouldn't crow too loud—can pitchers crow? They have ears, of course, but only the little pitchers. The ones that go to the well should go in modest silence."

"Dear Lady," he said almost impatiently, "what is there about me that drives my friends to stick up danger boards all along my path? 'This way to Destruction!' You all label them. I am always being solemnly warned that I shall get my heart broken one of these days, if I don't look out."

"I wish you wouldn't call me dear Lady," she said; "it's not the mode any more now."

"What may I call you?" he had to ask, turning to look in her eyes.

"You needn't call me anything. I hate being called names. That's a pretty girl—not the dark one, the one with the fur hat."

He turned to look.

Two girls were walking briskly under the falling leaves. And the one with the fur hat was Betty. But it was at the other that he gazed even as he returned Betty's prim little bow. He even turned a little as the carriage passed, to look more intently at the tall figure in shabby black whose arm Betty held.

"Well?" said Lady St. Craye, breaking the silence that followed.

"Well?" said he, rousing himself, but too late. "You were saying I might call you—"

"It's not what I was saying—it's what you were looking. Who is the girl, and why don't you approve of her companion?"

"Who says I don't wear a window in my breast?" he laughed. "The girl's a little country girl I knew in England—I didn't know she was in Paris. And I thought I knew the woman, too, but that's impossible: it's only a likeness."

"One nice thing about me is that I never ask impertinent questions—or hardly ever. That one slipped out and I withdraw it. I don't want to know anything about anything and I'm sorry I spoke. I see, of course, that she is a little country girl you knew in England, and that you are not at all interested in her. How fast the leaves fall now, don't they?"

"No question of your's could be im—could be anything but flattering. But since you *are* interested—"

"Not at all," she said politely.

"Oh, but do be interested," he urged, intent on checking her inconvenient interest, "because, really, it is rather interesting when you come to think of it. I was painting my big picture— I wish you'd come and see it, by the way. Will you some day, and have tea in my studio?"

"I should love it. When shall I come?"

"Whenever you will."

He wished she would ask another question about Betty, but she wouldn't. He had to go on, a little awkwardly.

"Well, I only knew them for a week—her and her aunt and her father—and she's a nice, quiet little thing. The father's a parson—all of them are all that there is of most respectable."

She listened but she did not speak.

"And I was rather surprised to see her here. And for the moment I thought the woman with her was—well, the last kind of woman who could have been with her, don't you know."

"I see," said Lady St. Craye. "Well, it's fortunate that the dark woman isn't that kind of woman. No doubt you'll be seeing your little friend. You might ask her to tea when I come to see your picture."

"I wish I could." Vernon's manner was never so frank as when he was most on his guard. "She'd love to know you. I wish I could ask them to tea, but I don't know them well enough. And their address I don't know at all. It's a pity; she's a nice little thing."

It was beautifully done. Lady St. Craye inwardly applauded Vernon's acting, and none the less that her own part had grown strangely difficult. She was suddenly conscious of a longing to be alone—to let her face go. She gave herself a moment's pause, caught at her fine courage and said:

"Yes, it is a pity. However, I daresay it's safer for her that you can't ask her to tea. She *is* a nice little thing, and she might fall in love with you, and then, your modesty appeased, you might follow suit! Isn't it annoying when one can't pick up the thread of a conversation? All the time you've been talking I've been wondering what we were talking about before I pointed out the fur hat to you. And I nearly remember, and I can't quite. That is always so worrying, isn't it?"

Her acting was as good as his. And his perception at the moment less clear than hers.

He gave a breath of relief. It would never have done to have Lady St. Craye spying on him and Betty; and now he knew that she was in Paris he knew too that it would be "him and Betty."

"We were talking," he said carefully, "about calling names."

"Oh, thank you!—When one can't remember those silly little things it's like wanting to sneeze and not being able to, isn't it? But we must turn back, or I shall be late for dinner, and I daren't think of the names my hostess will call me then. She has a vocabulary, you know." She named a name and Vernon thought it was he who kept the talk busy among acquaintances till the moment for parting. Lady St. Craye knew that it was she.

The moment Betty had bowed to Mr. Vernon she turned her head in answer to the pressure on her arm.

"Who's that?" her friend asked.

Betty named him, and in a voice genuinely unconcerned.

"How long have you known him?"

E. Nesbit

"I knew him for a week last Spring: he gave me a few lessons. He is a great favourite of my aunt's, but we don't know him much. And I thought he was in Vienna."

"Does he know where you are?"

"No."

"Then mind he doesn't."

"Why?"

"Because when girls are living alone they can't be too careful. Remember you're the person that's responsible for Betty Desmond now. You haven't your aunt and your father to take care of you."

"I've got you," said Betty affectionately.

"Yes, you've got me," said her friend.

Life in the new rooms was going very easily and pleasantly. Betty had covered some cushions with the soft green silk of an old evening dress Aunt Julia had given her; she had bought chrysanthemums in pots; and now all her little belongings, the same that had "given the *cachet*" to her boudoir bedroom at home lay about, and here, in this foreign setting, did really stamp the room with a pretty, delicate, conventional individuality. The embroidered blotting-book, the silver pen-tray, the wicker work-basket lined with blue satin, the long worked pin-cushion stuck with Betty's sparkling hat-pins,—all these, commonplace at Long Barton were here not commonplace. There was nothing of Paula's lying about. She had brought nothing with her, and had fetched nothing from her room save clothes—dresses and hats of the plainest.

The experiments in cooking were amusing; so were the marketings in odd little shops that sold what one wanted, and a great many things that one had never heard of. The round of concerts and theatres and tram-rides had not begun yet. In the evenings Betty drew, while Paula read aloud—from the library of stray Tauchnitz books Betty had gleaned from foreign bookstalls. It was a very busy, pleasant home-life. And the studio life did not lack interest.

Betty suffered a martyrdom of nervousness when first—a little late—she entered the Atelier. It is a large light room; a semi-circular alcove at one end, hung with pleasant-coloured drapery, holds a grand piano. All along one side are big windows that give on an old garden—once a convent garden where nuns used to walk, telling their beads. The walls are covered with sketches, posters, studies. Betty looked nervously round—the scene was agitatingly unfamiliar. The strange faces, the girls in many-hued painting pinafores, the little forest of easels, and on the square wooden platform the model—smooth, brown, with limbs set, moveless as a figure of wax.

Betty got to work, as soon as she knew how one began to get to work. It was her first attempt at a drawing from the life, saving certain not unsuccessful caricatures of her fellow pupils, her professor and her chaperon. So far she had only been set to do landscape, and laborious drawings of casts from the antique. The work was much harder than she had expected. And the heat was overpowering. She wondered how these other girls could stand it. Their amused, half-patronising, half-disdainful glances made her furious.

She rubbed out most of the lines she had put in and gasped for breath.

The room, the students, the naked brown girl on the model's throne, all swam before her eyes. She got to the door somehow, opened and shut it, and found herself sitting on the top stair with closed eyelids and heart beating heavily.

Some one held water to her lips. She was being fanned with a handkerchief.

E. Nesbit

"I'm all right," she said.

"Yes, it's hotter than usual to-day," said the handkerchief-holder, fanning vigorously.

"Why do they have it so hot?" asked poor Betty.

"Because of the model, of course. Poor thing! she hasn't got a nice blue gown and a pinky-greeny pinafore to keep her warm. We have to try to match the garden of Eden climate—when we're drawing from a girl who's only allowed to use Eve's fashion plates."

Betty laughed and opened her eyes.

"How jolly of you to come out after me," she said.

"Oh, I was just the same at first. All right now? I ought to get back. You just sit here till you feel fit again. So long!"

So Betty sat there on the bare wide brown stair, staring at the window, till things had steadied themselves, and then she went back to her work.

Her easel was there, and her half-rubbed out drawing—No, that was not her drawing. It was a head, vaguely but very competently sketched, a likeness—no, a caricature—of Betty herself.

She looked round—one quick but quite sufficient look. The girl next her, and the one to that girl's right, were exchanging glances, and the exchange ceased just too late. Betty saw.

From then till the rest Betty did not look at the model. She looked, but furtively, at those two girls. When, at the rest-time, the model stretched and yawned and got off her throne and into a striped petticoat, most of the students took their "easy" on the stairs: among these the two.

Betty, who never lacked courage, took charcoal in hand and advanced quite boldly to the easel next to her own.

How she envied the quality of the drawing she saw there. But envy does not teach mercy. The little sketch that Betty left on the corner of the drawing was quite as faithful, and far more cruel, than the one on her own paper. Then she went on to the next easel. The few students who were chatting to the model looked curiously at her and giggled among themselves.

When the rest was over and the model had reassumed, quite easily and certainly, that pose of the uplifted arms which looked so difficult, the students trooped back and the two girls—Betty's enemies, as she bitterly felt—returned to their easels. They looked at their drawings, they looked at each other, and they looked at Betty. And when they looked at her they smiled.

"Well done!" the girl next her said softly. "For a tenderfoot you hit back fairly straight. I guess you'll do!"

"You're very kind," said Betty haughtily.

"Don't you get your quills up," said the girl. "I hit first, but you hit hardest. I don't know you,—but I want to."

She smiled so queer yet friendly a smile that Betty's haughtiness had to dissolve in an answering smile.

"My name's Betty Desmond," she said. "I wonder why you wanted to hit a man when he was down."

"My!" said the girl, "how was I to surmise about you being down? You looked dandy enough—fit to lick all creation."

"I've never been in a studio before," said Betty, fixing fresh paper.

"My!" said the girl again. "Turn the faucet off now. The model don't like us to whisper. Can't stand the draught."

So Betty was silent, working busily. But next day she was greeted with friendly nods and she had some one to speak to in the rest-intervals.

On the third day she was asked to a studio party by the girl who had fanned her on the stairs. "And bring your friend with you," she said.

But Betty's friend had a headache that day. Betty went alone and came home full of the party.

"She's got such a jolly studio," she said; "ever so high up,—and busts and casts and things. Everyone was so nice to me you can't think: it was just like what one hears of Girton Cocoa parties. We had tea—such weak tea, Paula, it could hardly crawl out of the teapot! We had it out of green basins. And the loveliest cakes! There were only two chairs, so some of us sat on the sommier and the rest on the floor."

"Were there any young men?" asked Paula.

"Two or three very, very young ones—they came late. But they might as well have been girls; there wasn't any flirting or nonsense of that sort, Paula. Don't you think *we* might give a party—not now, but presently, when we know some more people? Do you think they'd like it? Or would they think it a bore?"

"They'd love it, I should think." Paula looked round the room which already she loved. "And what did you all talk about?"

"Work," said Betty, "work and work and work and work and work: everyone talked about their work, and everyone else listened and watched for the chance to begin to talk about theirs. This is real life, my dear. I am so glad I'm beginning to know people. Miss Voscoe is very queer, but she's a dear. She's the one who caricatured me the first day. Oh, we shall do now, shan't we?"

"Yes," said the other, "you'll do now."

"I said 'we,'" Betty corrected softly.

"I meant we, of course," said Miss Conway.

E. Nesbit

CHAPTER XIII

CONTRASTS

Vernon's idea of a studio was a place to work in, a place where there should be room for all the tools of one's trade, and besides, a great space to walk up and down in those moods that seize on all artists when their work will not come as they want it.

But when he gave tea-parties he had store of draperies to pull out from his carved cupboard, deeply coloured things embroidered in rich silk and heavy gold—Chinese, Burmese, Japanese, Russian.

He came in to-day with an armful of fair chrysanthemums, deftly set them in tall brazen jars, pulled out his draperies and arranged them swiftly. There was a screen to be hung with a Chinese mandarin's dress, where, on black, gold dragons writhed squarely among blue roses; the couch was covered by a red burnous with a gold border. There were Persian praying mats to lay on the bare floor, kakemonos to be fastened with drawing pins on the bare walls. A tea cloth worked by Russian peasants lay under the tea-cups—two only—of yellow Chinese egg-shell ware. His tea-pot and cream-jug were Queen Anne silver, heirlooms at which he mocked. But he saw to it that they were kept bright.

He lighted the spirit-lamp.

"She was always confoundedly punctual," he said.

But to-day Lady St. Craye was not punctual. She arrived half an hour late, and the delay had given her host time to think about her.

He heard her voice in the courtyard at last—but the only window that looked that way was set high in the wall of the little corridor, and he could not see who it was to whom she was talking. And he wondered, because the inflection of her voice was English—not the exquisite imitation of the French inflexion which he had so often admired in her.

He opened the door and went to the stair head. The voices were coming up the steps.

"A caller," said Vernon, and added a word or two. However little you may be in love with a woman, two is better company than three.

The voices came up. He saw the golden brown shimmer of Lady St. Craye's hat, and knew that it matched her hair and that there would be violets somewhere under the brim of it— violets that would make her eyes look violet too. She was coming up—a man just behind her. She came round the last turn, and the man was Temple.

"What an Alpine ascent!" she exclaimed, reaching up her hand so that Vernon drew her up the last three steps. "We have been hunting you together, on both the other staircases. Now that the chase is ended, won't you present your friend? And I'll bow to him as soon as I'm on firm ground!"

Vernon made the presentation and held the door open for Lady St. Craye to pass. As she did so Temple behind her raised eyebrows which said:

"Am I inconvenient? Shall I borrow a book or something and go?"

Vernon shook his head. It was annoying, but inevitable. He could only hope that Lady St. Craye also was disappointed.

"How punctual you are," he said. "Sit here, won't you?—I hadn't finished laying the table." He deliberately brought out four more cups. "What unnatural penetration you have, Temple! How did you find out that this is the day when I sit 'at home' and wait for people to come and buy my pictures?"

"And no one's come?" Lady St. Craye had sunk into the chair and was pulling off her gloves. "That's very disappointing. I thought I should meet dozens of clever and interesting people, and I only meet two."

Her brilliant smile made the words seem neither banal nor impertinent.

Vernon was pleased to note that he was not the only one who was disappointed.

"You are too kind," he said gravely.

Temple was looking around the room.

"Jolly place you've got here," he said, "but it's hard to find. I should have gone off in despair if I hadn't met Lady St. Craye."

"We kept each other's courage up, didn't we, Mr. Temple? It was like arctic explorers. I was beginning to think we should have to make a camp and cook my muff for tea."

She held out the sable and Vernon laid it on the couch when he had held it to his face for a moment.

"I love the touch of fur," he said; "and your fur is scented with the scent of summer gardens, 'open jasmine muffled lattices,'" he quoted softly. Temple had wandered to the window.

"What ripping roofs!" he said. "Can one get out on them?"

"Now what," demanded Vernon, "*is* the hidden mainspring that impels every man who comes into these rooms to ask, instantly, whether one can get out on to the roof? It's only Englishmen, by the way; Americans never ask it, nor Frenchmen."

"It's the exploring spirit, I suppose," said Temple idly; "the spirit that has made England the Empire which—et cetera."

"On which the sun never sets. Yes—but I think the sunset would be one of the attractions of your roof, Mr. Vernon."

"Sunset is never attractive to me," said he, "nor Autumn. Give me sunrise, and Spring."

"Ah, yes," said Lady St. Craye, "you only like beginnings. Even Summer—"

"Even Summer, as you say," he answered equably. "The sketch is always so much better than the picture."

"I believe that is your philosophy of life," said Temple.

"This man," Vernon explained, "spends his days in doing ripping etchings and black and white stuff and looking for my philosophy of life."

"One would like to see that in black and white. Will you etch it for me, Mr. Temple, when you find it?"

"I don't think the medium would be adequate," Temple said. "I haven't found it yet, but I should fancy it would be rather highly coloured."

"Iridescent, perhaps. Did you ever speculate as to the colour of people's souls? I'm quite sure every soul has a colour."

E. Nesbit

"What is yours?" asked Vernon of course.

"I'm too humble to tell you. But some souls are thick—body-colour, don't you know—and some are clear like jewels."

"And mine's an opal, is it?"

"With more green in it, perhaps; you know the lovely colour on the dykes in the marshes?"

"Stagnant water? Thank you!"

"I don't know what it is. It has some hateful chemical name, I daresay. They have vases the colour I mean, mounted in silver, at the Army and Navy Stores."

"And your soul—it is a pearl, isn't it?"

"Never! Nothing opaque. If you will force my modesty to the confession I believe in my heart that it is a sapphire. True blue, don't you know!"

"And Temple's—but you've not known him long enough to judge."

"So it's no use my saying that I am sure his soul is a dewdrop."

"To be dried up by the sun of life?" Temple questioned.

"No—to be hardened into a diamond—by the fire of life. No, don't explain that dewdrops don't harden Into diamonds. I know I'm not scientific, but I honestly did mean to be complimentary. Isn't your kettle boiling over, Mr. Vernon?"

Lady St. Craye's eyes, while they delicately condoled with Vernon on the spoiling of his tete-a-tete with her, were also made to indicate a certain interest in the spoiler. Temple was more than six feet high, well built. He had regular features and clear gray eyes, with well-cut cases and very long dark lashes.

His mouth was firm and its lines were good. But for his close-cropped hair and for a bearing at once frank, assured, and modest, he would have been much handsomer than a man has any need to be. But his expression saved him: No one had ever called him a barber's block or a hairdresser's apprentice.

To Temple Lady St. Craye appeared the most charming woman he had ever seen. It was an effect which she had the habit of producing. He had said of her in his haste that she was all clothes and no woman, now he saw that on the contrary the clothes were quite intimately part of the woman, and took such value as they had, from her.

She carried her head with the dainty alertness of a beautiful bird. She had a gift denied to most Englishwomen—the genius for wearing clothes. No one had ever seen her dress dusty or crushed, her hat crooked. No uncomfortable accidents ever happened to her. Blacks never settled on her face, the buttons never came off her gloves, she never lost her umbrella, and in the windiest weather no loose untidy wisps escaped from her thick heavy shining hair to wander unbecomingly round the ears that were pearly and pink like the little shells of Vanessae. Some of the women who hated her used to say that she dyed her hair. It was certainly very much lighter than her brows and lashes. To-day she was wearing a corduroy dress of a gold some shades grayer than the gold of her hair. Sable trimmed it, and violet silk lined the loose sleeves and the coat, now unfastened and thrown back. There were, as Vernon had known there would be, violets under the brim of the hat that matched her hair.

The chair in which she sat wore a Chinese blue drapery. The yellow tea-cups gave the highest note in the picture.

"If I were Whistler, I should ask you to let me paint your portrait like that—yes, with my despicable yellow tea-cup in your honourable hand."

"If you were Mr. Whistler—or anything in the least like Mr.

Whistler—I shouldn't be drinking tea out of your honourable tea-cup," she said. "Do you really think, Mr. Temple, that one ought not to say one doesn't like people just because they're dead?"

He had been thinking something a little like it.

"Well," he said rather awkwardly, "you see dead people can't hit back."

"No more can live ones when you don't hit them, but only stick pins in their effigies. I'd rather speak ill of the dead than the living."

"Yet it doesn't seem fair, somehow," Temple insisted.

"But why? No one can go and tell the poor things what people are saying of them. You don't go and unfold a shroud just to whisper in a corpse's ear: 'It was horrid of her to say it, but I thought you ought to know, dear.'—And if you did, they wouldn't lie awake at night worrying over it as the poor live people do.—No more tea, thank you."

"Do you really think anyone worries about what anyone says?"

"Don't you, Mr. Temple?"

He reflected.

"He never has anything to worry about," Vernon put in; "no one ever says anything unkind about him. The cruelest thing anyone ever said of him was that he would make as excellent a husband as Albert the Good."

"The white flower of a blameless life? My felicitations," Lady St. Craye smiled them.

Temple flushed.

"Now isn't it odd," Vernon asked, "that however much one plumes oneself on one's blamelessness, one hates to hear it attributed to one by others? One is good by stealth and blushes to find it fame. I myself—"

"Yes!" said Lady St. Craye with an accent of finality.

"What a man really likes is to be saint with the reputation of being a bit of a devil."

"And a woman likes, you think, to be a bit of a devil, with the reputation of a saint?"

"Or a bit of a saint with a reputation that rhymes to the reality. It's the reputation that's important, isn't it?"

"Isn't the inward truth the really important thing?" said Temple rather heavily.

Lady St. Craye looked at him in such a way as to make him understand that she understood. Vernon looked at them both, and turning to the window looked out on his admired roofs.

"Yes," she said very softly, "but one doesn't talk about that, any more than one does of one's prayers or one's love affairs."

The plural vexed Temple, and he told himself how unreasonable the vexation was.

Lady St. Craye turned her charming head to look at him, to look at Vernon. One had been in love with her. The other might be. There is in the world no better company than this.

Temple, always deeply uninterested in women's clothes, was noting the long, firm folds of her skirt. Vernon had turned from the window to approve the loving closeness of those violets against her hair. Lady St. Craye in her graceful attitude of conscious unconsciousness was the focus of their eyes.

"Here comes a millionaire, to buy your pictures," she said suddenly,—"no—a millionairess, by the sound of her high-heeled shoes. How beautiful are the feet—"

The men had heard nothing, but following hard on her words came the sound of footsteps along the little corridor, an agitated knock on the door.

Vernon opened the door—to Betty.

"Oh—come in," he said cordially, and his pause of absolute astonishment was brief as an eye-flash. "This is delightful—"

And as she passed into the room he caught her eyes and, looking a warning, said: "I am so glad to see you. I began to be afraid you wouldn't be able to come."

"I saw you in the Bois the other day," said Lady St. Craye, "and I have been wanting to know you ever since."

"You are very kind," said Betty. Her hat was on one side, her hair was very untidy, and it was not a becoming untidiness either. She had no gloves, and a bit of the velvet binding of her skirt was loose. Her eyes were red and swollen with crying. There was a black smudge on her cheek.

"Take this chair," said Vernon, and moved a comfortable one with its back to the light.

"Temple—let me present you to Miss Desmond."

Temple bowed, with no flicker of recognition visible in his face. But Betty, flushing scarlet, said:

"Mr. Temple and I have met before."

There was the tiniest pause. Then Temple said: "I am so glad to meet you again. I thought you had perhaps left Paris."

"Let me give you some tea," said Vernon.

Tea was made for her,—and conversation. She drank the tea, but she seemed not to know what to do with the conversation.

It fluttered, aimlessly, like a bird with a broken wing. Lady St. Craye did her best, but talk is not easy when each one of a party has its own secret pre-occupying interest, and an over-lapping interest in the preoccupation of the others. The air was too electric.

Lady St. Craye had it on her lips that she must go—when Betty rose suddenly.

"Good-bye," she said generally, looking round with miserable eyes that tried to look merely polite.

"Must you go?" asked Vernon, furious with the complicated emotions that, warring in him, left him just as helpless as anyone else.

"I do hope we shall meet again," said Lady St. Craye.

"Mayn't I see you home?" asked Temple unexpectedly, even to himself.

Betty's "No, thank you," was most definite.

She went. Vernon had to let her go. He had guests. He could not leave them. He had lost wholly his ordinary control of circumstances. All through the petrifying awkwardness of the late talk he had been seeking an excuse to go with Betty—to find out what was the matter.

He closed the door and came back. There was no help for it.

But there was help. Lady St. Craye gave it. She rose as Vernon came back.

E. Nesbit

"Quick!" she said, "Shall we go? Hadn't you better bring her back here? Go after her at once."

"You're an angel," said Vernon. "No, don't go. Temple, look after Lady St. Craye. If you'll not think me rude?—Miss Desmond is in trouble, I'm afraid."

"Of course she is—poor little thing. Oh, Mr. Vernon, do run! She looks quite despairing. There's your hat. Go—go!"

The door banged behind her.

The other two, left alone, looked at each other.

"I wonder—" said she.

"Yes," said he, "it's certainly mysterious."

"We ought to have gone at once," said she. "I should have done, of course, only Mr. Vernon so elaborately explained that he expected her. One had to play up. And so she's a friend of yours?"

"She's not a friend of mine," said Temple rather ruefully, "and I didn't know Vernon was a friend of hers. You saw that she wouldn't have my company at any price."

"Mr. Vernon's a friend of her people, I believe. We saw her the other day in the Bois, and he told me he knew them in England. Did you know them there too? Poor child, what a woe-begone little face it was!"

"No, not in England. I met her in Paris about a fortnight ago, but she didn't like me, from the first, and our acquaintance broke off short."

There was a silence. Lady St. Craye perceived a ring-fence of reticence round the subject that interested her, and knew that she had no art strong enough to break it down.

She spoke again suddenly:

"Do you know you're not a bit the kind of man I expected you to be, Mr. Temple? I've heard so much of you from Mr. Vernon. We're such old friends, you know."

"Apparently he can't paint so well with words as he does with oils. May I ask exactly how flattering the portrait was?"

"It wasn't flattering at all.—In fact it wasn't a portrait."

"A caricature?"

"But you don't mind what people say of you, do you?"

"You are trying to frighten me."

"No, really," she said with pretty earnestness; "it's only that he has always talked about you as his best friend, and I imagined you would be like him."

Temple's uneasy wonderings about Betty's trouble, her acquaintance with Vernon, the meaning of her visit to him, were pushed to the back of his mind.

"I wish I were like him," said he,—"at any rate, in his paintings."

"At any rate—yes. But one can't have everything, you know. You have qualities which he hasn't—qualities that you wouldn't exchange for any qualities of his."

"That wasn't what I meant; I—the fact is, I like old Vernon, but I can't understand him."

"That philosophy of life eludes you still? Now, I understand him, but I don't always like him—not all of him."

"I wonder whether anyone understands him?"

"He's not such a sphinx as he looks!" Her tone betrayed a slight pique—"Now, your character would be much harder to read. That's one of the differences."

"We are all transparent enough—to those who look through the right glasses," said Temple. "And part of my character is my inability to find any glass through which I could see him clearly."

This comparison of his character and Vernon's, with its sudden assumption of intimacy, charmed yet embarrassed him.

She saw both emotions and pitied him a little. But it was necessary to interest this young man enough to keep him there till Vernon should return. Then Vernon would see her home, and she might find out something, however little, about Betty. But if this young man went she too must go. She could not outstay him in the rooms of his friend. So she talked on, and Temple was just as much at her mercy as Betty had been at the mercy of the brother artist in the rabbit warren at Long Barton.

But at seven o'clock Vernon had not returned, and it was, after all, Temple who saw her home.

Temple, free from the immediate enchantment of her presence, felt the revival of a resentful curiosity.

Why had Betty refused his help? Why had she sought Vernon's? Why did women treat him as though he were a curate and Vernon as though he were a god? Well—Lady St. Craye at least had not treated him as curates are treated.

CHAPTER XIV

RENUNCIATION

Vernon tore down the stairs three and four at a time, and caught Betty as she was stepping into a hired carriage.

"What is it?" he asked. "What's the matter?"

"Oh, go back to your friends!" said Betty angrily.

"My friends are all right. They'll amuse each other. Tell me."

"Then you must come with me," said she. "If I try to tell you here I shall begin to cry again. Don't speak to me. I can't bear it."

He got into the carriage. It was not until Betty had let herself into her room and he had followed her in—not till they stood face to face in the middle of the carpet that he spoke again.

"Now," he said, "what is it? Where's your aunt, and—"

"Sit down, won't you?" she said, pulling off her hat and throwing it on the couch; "it'll take rather a long time to tell, but I must tell you all about it, or else you can't help me. And if you don't help me I don't know what I shall do."

Despair was in her voice.

E. Nesbit

He sat down. Betty, in the chair opposite his, sat with hands nervously locked together.

"Look here," she said abruptly, "you're sure to think that everything I've done is wrong, but it's no use your saying so."

"I won't say so."

"Well, then—that day, you know, after I saw you at the Bete—Madame Gautier didn't come to fetch me, and I waited, and waited, and at last I went to her flat, and she was dead,—and I ought to have telegraphed to my step-father to fetch me, but I thought I would like to have one night in Paris first—you know I hadn't seen Paris at all, really."

"Yes," he said, trying not to let any anxiety into his voice. "Yes—go on."

"And I went to the Cafe d'Harcourt—What did you say?"

"Nothing."

"I thought it was where the art students went. And I met a girl there, and she was kind to me."

"What sort of a girl? Not an art student?"

"No," said Betty hardly, "she wasn't an art student. She told me what she was."

"Yes?"

"And I—I don't think I should have done it just for me alone, but—I did want to stay in Paris and work—and I wanted to help her to be good—she *is* good really, in spite of everything. Oh, I know you're horribly shocked, but I can't help it! And now she's gone,—and I can't find her."

"I'm not shocked," he said deliberately, "but I'm extremely

stupid. How gone?"

"She was living with me here.—Oh, she found the rooms and showed me where to go for meals and gave me good advice— oh, she did everything for me! And now she's gone. And I don't know what to do. Paris is such a horrible place. Perhaps she's been kidnapped or something. And I don't know even how to tell the police. And all this time I'm talking to you is wasted time."

"It isn't wasted. But I must understand. You met this girl and she—"

"She asked your friend Mr. Temple—he was passing and she called out to him—to tell me of a decent hotel, but he asked so many questions. He gave me an address and I didn't go. I went back to her, and we went to a hotel and I persuaded her to come and live with me."

"But your aunt?"

Betty explained about her aunt.

"And your father?"

She explained about her father.

"And now she has gone, and you want to find her?"

"Want to find her?"—Betty started up and began to walk up and down the room.—"I don't care about anything else in the world! She's a dear; you don't know what a dear she is—and I know she was happy here—and now she's gone! I never had a girl friend before—what?"

Vernon had winced, just as Paula had winced, and at the same words.

"You've looked for her at the Cafe d'Harcourt?"

"No; I promised her that I'd never go there again."

"She seems to have given you some good advice."

"She advised me not to have anything to do with *you*" said Betty, suddenly spiteful.

"That was good advice—when she gave it," said Vernon, quietly; "but now it's different."

He was silent a moment, realising with a wonder beyond words how different it was. Every word, every glance between him and Betty had, hitherto, been part of a play. She had been a charming figure in a charming comedy. He had known, as it were by rote, that she had feelings—a heart, affections—but they had seemed pale, dream-like, just a delightful background to his own sensations, strong and conscious and delicate. Now for the first time he perceived her as real, a human being in the stress of a real human emotion. And he was conscious of a feeling of protective tenderness, a real, open-air primitive sentiment, with no smell of the footlights about it. He was alone with Betty. He was the only person in Paris to whom she could turn for help. What an opportunity for a fine scene in his best manner! And he found that he did not want a scene: he wanted to help her.

"Why don't you say something?" she said impatiently. "What am I to do?"

"You can't do anything. I'll do everything. You say she knows Temple. Well, I'll find him, and we'll go to her lodgings and find out if she's there. You don't know the address?"

"No," said Betty. "I went there, but it was at night and I don't even know the street."

"Now look here." He took both her hands and held them firmly. "You aren't to worry. I'll do everything. Perhaps she has been taken ill. In that case, when we find her, she'll need you to look after her. You must rest. I'm certain to find her. You must eat something. I'll send you in some dinner. And then lie down."

"I couldn't sleep," said Betty, looking at him with the eyes of a child that has cried its heart out.

"Of course you couldn't. Lie down, and make yourself read. I'll get back as soon as I can. Good-bye." There was something further that wanted to get itself said, but the words that came nearest to expressing it were "God bless you,"—and he did not say them.

On the top of his staircase he found Temple lounging.

"Hullo—still here? I'm afraid I've been a devil of a time gone, but Miss Desmond's—"

"I don't want to shove my oar in," said Temple, "but I came back when I'd seen Lady St. Craye home. I hope there's nothing wrong with Miss Desmond."

"Come in," said Vernon. "I'll tell you the whole thing."

They went into the room desolate with the disorder of half empty cups and scattered plates with crumbs of cake on them.

"Miss Desmond told me about her meeting you. Well, she gave you the slip; she went back and got that woman—Lottie what's her name—and took her to live with her."

"Good God! She didn't know, of course?"

"But she did know—that's the knock-down blow. She knew, and she wanted to save her."

Temple was silent a moment.

E. Nesbit

"I say, you know, though—that's rather fine," he said presently.

"Oh, yes," said Vernon impatiently, "it's very romantic and all that. Well, the woman stayed a fortnight and disappeared to-day. Miss Desmond is breaking her heart about her."

"So she took her up, and—she's rather young for rescue work."

"Rescue work? Bah! She talks of the woman as the only girl friend she's ever had. And the woman's probably gone off with her watch and chain and a collection of light valuables. Only I couldn't tell Miss Desmond that. So I promised to try and find the woman. She's a thorough bad lot. I've run up against her once or twice with chaps I know."

"She's not *that* sort," said Temple. "I know her fairly well."

"What—Sir Galahad? Oh, I won't ask inconvenient questions." Vernon's sneer was not pretty.

"She used to live with de Villermay," said Temple steadily; "he was the first—the usual coffee maker business, you know, though God knows how an English girl got into it. When he went home to be married—It was rather beastly. The father came up—offered her a present. She threw it at him. Then Schauermacher wanted her to live with him. No. She'd go to the devil her own way. And she's gone."

"Can't something be done?" said Vernon.

"I've tried all I know. You can save a woman who doesn't know where she's going. Not one who knows and means to go. Besides, she's been at it six months; she's past reclaiming now."

"I wonder," said Vernon—and his sneer had gone and he looked ten years younger—"I wonder whether anybody's past reclaiming? Do you think I am? Or you?"

The other stared at him.

"Well," Vernon's face aged again instantly, "the thing is: we've got to find the woman."

"To get her to go back and live with that innocent girl?"

"Lord—no! To find her. To find out why she bolted, and to make certain that she won't go back and live with that innocent girl. Do you know her address?"

But she was not to be found at her address. She had come back, paid her bill, and taken away her effects.

It was at the Cafe d'Harcourt, after all, that they found her, one of a party of four. She nodded to them, and presently left her party and came to spread her black and white flounces at their table.

"What's the best news with you?" she asked gaily. "It's a hundred years since I saw you, Bobby, and at least a million since I saw your friend."

"The last time I saw you," Temple said, "was the night when you asked me to take care of a girl."

"So it was! And did you?"

"No," said Temple; "she wouldn't let me. She went back to you."

"So you've seen her again? Oh, I see—you've come to ask me what I meant by daring to contaminate an innocent girl by my society?—Well, you can go to Hell, and ask there."

She rose, knocking over a chair.

"Don't go," said Vernon. "That's not what we want to ask."

"'*We*' too," she turned fiercely on him: "as if you were a king or a deputation."

"One and one *are* two," said Vernon; "and I did very much want to talk to you."

"And two are company."

She had turned her head away.

"You aren't going to be cruel," Vernon asked.

"Well, send him off then. I won't be bullied by a crowd of you."

Temple took off his hat and went.

"I've got an appointment. I've no time for fool talk," she said.

"Sit down," said Vernon. "First I want to thank you for the care you've taken of Miss Desmond, and for all your kindness and goodness to her."

"Oh!" was all Paula could say. She had expected something so different. "I don't see what business it is of yours, though," she added next moment.

"Only that she's alone here, and I'm the only person she knows in Paris. And I know, much better than she does, all that you've done for her sake."

"I did it for my own sake. It was no end of a lark," said Paula eagerly, "that little dull pious life. And all the time I used to laugh inside to think what a sentimental fool she was."

"Yes," said Vernon slowly, "it must have been amusing for you."

"I just did it for the fun of the thing. But I couldn't stand it any longer, so I just came away. I was bored to death."

"Yes," he said, "you must have been. Just playing at cooking and housework, reading aloud to her while she drew—yes, she told me that. And the flowers and all her little trumpery odds and ends about. Awfully amusing it must have been."

"Don't," said Paula.

"And to have her loving you and trusting you as she did—awfully comic, wasn't it? Calling you her girl-friend—"

"Shut up, will you?"

"And thinking she had created a new heaven and a new earth for you. Silly sentimental little school-girl!"

"Will you hold your tongue?"

"So long, Lottie," cried the girl of her party; "we're off to the Bullier. You've got better fish to fry, I see."

"Yes," said Paula with sudden effrontery; "perhaps we'll look in later."

The others laughed and went.

"Now," she said, turning furiously on Vernon, "will you go? Or shall I? I don't want any more of you."

"Just one word more," he said with the odd change of expression that made him look young. "Tell me why you left her. She's crying her eyes out for you."

"Why I left her? Because I was sick of—"

"Don't. Let me tell you. You went with her because she was alone and friendless. You found her rooms, you set her in the way of making friends. And when you saw that she was in a fair way to be happy and comfortable, you came away, because—"

"Because?" she leaned forward eagerly.

"Because you were afraid."

"Afraid?"

"Afraid of handicapping her. You knew you would meet people who knew you. You gave it all up—all the new life, the new chances—for her sake, and came away. Do I understand? Is it fool-talk?"

Paula leaned her elbows on the table and her chin on her hands.

"You're not like most men," she said; "you make me out better than I am. That's not the usual mistake. Yes, it *was* all that, partly. And I should have liked to stay—for ever and ever—if I could. But suppose I couldn't? Suppose I'd begun to find myself wishing for—all sorts of things, longing for them. Suppose I'd stayed till I began to think of things that I *wouldn't* think of while *she* was with me. *That's* what I was afraid of."

"And you didn't long for the old life at all?"

She laughed. "Long for that? But I might have. I might have. It was safer.—Well, go back to her and tell her I've gone to the devil and it's not her fault. Tell her I wasn't worth saving. But I did try to save her. If you're half a man you won't undo my one little bit of work."

"What do you mean?"

"You know well enough what I mean. Let the girl alone."

He leaned forward, and spoke very earnestly. "Look here," he said, "I won't jaw. But this about you and her—well, it's made a difference to me that I can't explain. And I wouldn't own that to anyone but *her* friend. I mean to be a friend to her too, a good friend. No nonsense."

"Swear it by God in Heaven," she said fiercely.

"I do swear it," he said, "by God in Heaven. And I can't tell her you've gone to the devil. You must write to her. And you can't tell her that either."

"What's the good of writing?"

"A lie or two isn't much, when you've done all this for her. Come up to my place. You can write to her there."

This was the letter that Paula wrote in Vernon's studio, among the half-empty cups and the scattered plates with cake-crumbs on them.

"My Dear Little Betty:

"I must leave without saying good-bye, and I shall never see you again. My father has taken me back. I wrote to him and he came and found me. He has forgiven me everything, only I have had to promise never to speak to anyone I knew in Paris. It is all your doing, dear. God bless you. You have saved me. I shall pray for you every day as long as I live.

"Your poor

"Paula."

"Will that do?" she laughed as she held out the letter.

He read it. And he did not laugh.

"Yes—that'll do," he said. "I'll tell her you've gone to England, and I'll send the letter to London to be posted."

"Then that's all settled!"

"Can I do anything for *you*?" he asked.

"God Himself can't do anything for me," she said, biting the edge of her veil.

"Where are you going now?"

"Back to the d'Harcourt. It's early yet."

She stood defiantly smiling at him.

"What were you doing there—the night you met her?" he asked abruptly.

"What does one do?"

"What's become of de Villermay?" he asked.

"Gone home—got married."

"And so you thought—"

"Oh, if you want to know what I thought you're welcome! I thought I'd damn myself as deep as I could—to pile up the reckoning for him; and I've about done it. Good-bye. I must be getting on."

"I'll come a bit of the way with you," he said.

At the door he turned, took her hand and kissed it gently and reverently.

"That's very sweet of you." She opened astonished eyes at him. "I always used to think you an awful brute."

"It was very theatrical of me," he told himself later. "But it summed up the situation. Sentimental ass you're growing!"

Betty got her letter from England and cried over it and was glad over it.

"I have done one thing, anyway," she told herself, "one really truly good thing. I've saved my poor dear Paula. Oh, how right I was! How I knew her!"

E. Nesbit

BOOK 3

THE OTHER WOMAN

CHAPTER XV

ON MOUNT PARNASSUS

At Long Barton the Reverend Cecil had strayed into Betty's room, now no longer boudoir and bedchamber, but just a room, swept, dusted, tidy, with the horrible tidiness of a room that is not used. There were squares of bright yellow on the dull drab of the wall-paper, marking the old hanging places of the photographs and pictures that Betty had taken to Paris. He opened the cupboard door: one or two faded skirts, a flattened garden hat and a pair of Betty's old shoes. He shut the door again quickly, as though he had seen Betty's ghost.

The next time he went to Sevenoaks he looked in at the builders and decorators, gave an order, and chose a wall paper with little pink roses on it. When Betty came home for Christmas she should not find her room the faded desert it was now. He ordered pink curtains to match the rosebuds. And it was when he got home that he found the letter that told him she was not to come at Christmas.

But he did not countermand his order. If not at Christmas then at Easter; and whenever it was she should find her room a bower. Since she had been away he had felt more and more the need to express his affection. He had expressed it, he thought, to the uttermost, by letting her go at all. And now he wanted to express it in detail, by pink curtains, satin-faced wall-paper with pink roses. The paper cost two shillings a piece, and he gloated over the extravagance and over his pretty, poetic choice. Usually the wall-papers at the Rectory had been chosen by Betty, and the price limited to sixpence. He would refrain from buying that Fuller's Church History, the beautiful brown folio whose perfect boards and rich yellow paper had lived in his dreams for the last three weeks, ever since he came upon it in the rag and bone shop in the little back street in Maidstone. When the rosebud paper and the pink curtains were in their place, the shabby carpet was an insult to their bright prettiness. The Reverend Cecil bought an Oriental carpet—of the bright-patterned jute variety—and was relieved to find that it only cost a pound.

The leaves were falling in brown dry showers in the Rectory garden, the chrysanthemums were nearly over, the dahlias blackened and blighted by the first frosts. A few pale blooms still clung to the gaunt hollyhock stems; here and there camomile flowers, "medicine daisies" Betty used to call them when she was little, their whiteness tarnished, showed among bent dry stalks of flowers dead and forgotten. Round Betty's window the monthly rose bloomed pale and pink amid disheartened foliage. The damp began to shew on the North walls of the rooms. A fire in the study now daily, for the sake of the books: one in the drawing-room, weekly, for the sake of the piano and the furniture. And for Betty, in far-away Paris, a fire of crackling twigs and long logs in the rusty fire-basket, and blue and yellow flames leaping to lick the royal arms of France on the wrought-iron fire-back.

The rooms were lonely to Betty now that Paula was gone. She missed her inexpressibly. But the loneliness was lighted by a glow of pride, of triumph, of achievement. Her deception of her step-father was justified. She had been the means of saving Paula. But for her Paula would not have returned, like the Prodigal son, to the father's house. Betty pictured her there, subdued, saddened, but inexpressibly happy, warming her cramped heart in the sun of forgiveness and love.

"Thank God, I have done some good in the world," said Betty.

In the brief interview which Vernon took to tell her that Paula had gone to England with her father, Betty noticed no change in him. She had no thought for him then. And in the next weeks, when she had thoughts for him, she did not see him.

She could not but be glad that he was in Paris. In the midst of her new experiences he seemed to her like an old friend. Yet his being there put a different complexion on her act of mutiny. When she decided to deceive her step-father, and to stay on in Paris alone Paula had been to be saved, and *he* had been, to her thought, in Vienna, not to be met. Now Paula was gone—and he was here. In the night when Betty lay wakeful and heard the hours chimed by a convent bell whose voice was toneless and gray as an autumn sky it seemed to her that all was wrong, that she had committed a fault that was almost a crime, that there was nothing now to be done but to confess, to go home and to expiate, as the Prodigal Son doubtless did among the thorny roses of forgiveness, those days in the far country. But always with the morning light came the remembrance that it was not her father's house to which she must go to make submission. It was her step-father's. And after all, it was her own life—she had to live it. Once that confession and submission made she saw herself enslaved beyond hope of freedom. Meanwhile here was the glad, gay life of independence, new experiences, new sensations. And her step-father was doubtless glad to be rid of her.

"It isn't as though anyone wanted me at home," she said; "and everything here is so new and good, and I have quite a few friends already—and I shall have more. This is what they call seeing life."

Life as she saw it was good to see. The darker, grimmer side of the student life was wholly hidden from Betty. She saw only a colony of young artists of all nations—but most of England and America—all good friends and comrades, working and playing with an equal enthusiasm. She saw girls treated as equals and friends by the men students. If money were short it was borrowed from the first friend one met, and quite usually repaid when the home allowance arrived. A young man would borrow from a young woman or a young woman from a young man as freely as school-boys from each other. Most girls had a special friend among the boys. Betty thought at first that these must be betrothed lovers. Miss Voscoe, the American, stared when she put the question about a pair who had just left the restaurant together with the announcement that they were off to the Musee Cluny for the afternoon.

"Engaged?" Not that I know of. Why should they be?" she said in a tone that convicted Betty of a social lapse in the putting of the question. Yet she defended herself.

"Well, you know, in England people don't generally go about together like that unless they're engaged, or relations."

"Yes," said Miss Voscoe, filling her glass from the little bottle of weak white wine that costs threepence at Garnier's, "I've heard that is so in your country. Your girls always marry the wrong man, don't they, because he's the first and only one they've ever had the privilege of conversing with?"

"Not quite always, I hope," said Betty good humouredly.

"Now in our country," Miss Voscoe went on, "girls look around so as they can tell there's more different sorts of boys than there are of squashes. Then when they get married to a husband it's because they like him, or because they like his dollars, or for some reason that isn't just that he's the only one they've ever said five words on end to."

"There's something in that," Betty owned; "but my aunt says men never want to be friends with girls—they always want—"

"To flirt? May be they do, though I don't think so. Our men don't, any way. But if the girl doesn't want to flirt things won't get very tangled up."

"But suppose a man got really fond of you, then he might

E. Nesbit

think you liked him too, if you were always about with him—"

"Do him good to have his eyes opened then! Besides, who's always about with anyone? You have a special friend for a bit, and just walk around and see the sights,—and then change partners and have a turn with somebody else. It's just like at a dance. Nobody thinks you're in love because you dance three or four times running with one boy."

Betty reflected as she ate her *noix de veau.* It was certainly true that she had seen changes of partners. Milly St. Leger, the belle of the students' quarter, changed her partners every week.

"You see," the American went on, "We're not the stay-at-home-and-mind-Auntie kind that come here to study. What we want is to learn to paint and to have a good time in between. Don't you make any mistake, Miss Desmond. This time in Paris is *the* time of our lives to most of us. It's what we'll have to look back at and talk about. And suppose every time there was any fun going we had to send around to the nearest store for a chaperon how much fun would there be left by the time she toddled in? No—the folks at home who trust us to work trust us to play. And we have our little heads screwed on the right way."

Betty remembered that she had been trusted neither for play nor work. Yet, from the home standpoint she had been trustworthy, more trustworthy than most. She had not asked Vernon, her only friend, to come and see her, and when he had said, "When shall I see you again?" she had answered, "I don't know. Thank you very much. Good-bye."

"I don't know how *you* were raised," Miss Voscoe went on, "but I guess it was in the pretty sheltered home life. Now I'd bet you fell in love with the first man that said three polite words to you!"

"I'm not twenty yet," said Betty, with ears and face of scarlet.

"Oh, you mean I'm to think nobody's had time to say those three polite words yet? You come right along to my studio, I've got a tea on, and I'll see if I can't introduce my friends to you by threes, so as you get nine polite words at once. You can't fall in love with three boys a minute, can you?"

Betty went home and put on her prettiest frock. After all, one was risking a good deal for this Paris life, and one might as well get as much out of it as one could. And one always had a better time of it when one was decently dressed. Her gown was of dead-leaf velvet, with green undersleeves and touches of dull red and green embroidery at elbows and collar.

Miss Voscoe's studio was at the top of a hundred and seventeen polished wooden steps, and as Betty neared the top flight the sound of talking and laughter came down to her, mixed with the rattle of china and the subdued tinkle of a mandolin. She opened the door—the room seemed full of people, but she only saw two. One was Vernon and the other was Temple.

Betty furiously resented the blush that hotly covered neck, ears and face.

"Here you are!" cried Miss Voscoe. She was kind: she gave but one fleet glance at the blush and, linking her arm in Betty's, led her round the room. Betty heard her name and other names. People were being introduced to her. She heard:

"Pleased to know you,—"

"Pleased to make your acquaintance,—"

"Delighted to meet you—"

and realised that her circle of American acquaintances was widening. When Miss Voscoe paused with her before the group of which Temple and Vernon formed part Betty felt as though her face had swelled to that degree that her eyes must, with the next red wave, start out of her head. The two hands, held out in successive greeting, gave Miss Voscoe the key to Betty's flushed entrance.

She drew her quickly away, and led her up to a glaring poster where a young woman in a big red hat sat at a cafe table, and under cover of Betty's purely automatic recognition of the composition's talent, murmured:

"Which of them was it?"

"I beg your pardon?" Betty mechanically offered the deferent defence.

"Which was it that said the three polite words—before you'd ever met anyone else?"

"Ah!" said Betty, "you're so clever—"

"Too clever to live, yes," said Miss Voscoe; "but before I die— which was it?"

"I was going to say," said Betty, her face slowly drawing back into itself its natural colouring, "that you're so clever you don't want to be told things. If you're sure it's one of them, you ought to know which."

"Well," remarked Miss Voscoe, "I guess Mr. Temple."

"Didn't I say you were clever?" said Betty.

"Then it's the other one."

Before the studio tea was over, Vernon and Temple both had conveyed to Betty the information that it was the hope of meeting her that had drawn them to Miss Voscoe's studio that afternoon.

"Because, after all," said Vernon, "we *do* know each other

better than either of us knows anyone else in Paris. And, if you'd let me, I could put you to a thing or two in the matter of your work. After all, I've been through the mill."

"It's very kind of you," said Betty, "but I'm all alone now Paula's gone, and—"

"We'll respect the conventions," said Vernon gaily, "but the conventions of the Quartier Latin aren't the conventions of Clapham."

"No, I know," said she, "but there's a point of honour." She paused. "There are reasons," she added, "why I ought to be more conventional than Clapham. I should like to tell you, some time, only—But I haven't got anyone to tell anything to. I wonder—"

"What? What do you wonder?"

Betty spoke with effort.

"I know it sounds insane, but, you know my stepfather thought you—you wanted to marry me. You didn't ever, did you?"

Vernon was silent: none of his habitual defences served him in this hour.

"You see," Betty went on, "all that sort of thing is such nonsense. If I knew you cared about someone else everything would be so simple."

"Eliminate love," said Vernon, "and the world is a simple example in vulgar fractions."

"I want it to be simple addition," said Betty. "Lady St. Craye is very beautiful."

"Yes," said Vernon.

"Is she in love with you?"

"Ask her," said Vernon, feeling like a schoolboy in an examination.

"If she were—and you cared for her—then you and I could be friends: I should like to be real friends with you."

"Let us be friends," said he when he had paused a moment. He made the proposal with every possible reservation.

"Really?" she said. "I'm so glad."

If there was a pang, Betty pretended to herself that there was none. If Vernon's conscience fluttered him he was able to soothe it; it was an art that he had studied for years.

"Say, you two!"

The voice of Miss Voscoe fell like a pebble into the pool of silence that was slowly widening between them.

"Say—we're going to start a sketch-club for really reliable girls. We can have it here, and it'll only be one franc an hour for the model, and say six sous each for tea. Two afternoons a week. Three, five, nine of us—you'll join, Miss Desmond?"

"Yes—oh, yes!" said Betty, conscientiously delighted with the idea of more work.

"That makes—nine six sous and two hours model—how much is that, Mr. Temple?—I see it written on your speaking brow that you took the mathematical wranglership at Oxford College."

"Four francs seventy," said Temple through the shout of laughter.

"Have I said something comme il ne faut pas?" said Miss Voscoe.

"You couldn't," said Vernon: "every word leaves your lips without a stain upon its character."

"Won't you let us join?" asked an Irish student. "You'll be lost entirely without a Lord of Creation to sharpen your pencils."

"We mean to *work*," said Miss Voscoe; "if you want to work take a box of matches and a couple of sticks of brimstone and make a little sketch class of your own."

"I don't see what you want with models," said a very young and shy boy student. "Couldn't you pose for each other, and—"

A murmur of dissent from the others drove him back into shy silence.

"No amateur models in this Academy," said Miss Voscoe. "Oh, we'll make the time-honoured institutions sit up with the work we'll do. Let's all pledge ourselves to send in to the Salon—or anyway to the Independants! What we're suffering from in this quarter's git-up-and-git. Why should we be contented to be nobody?"

"On the contrary," said Vernon, "Miss Voscoe is everybody—almost!"

"I'm the nobody who can't get a word in edgeways anyhow," she said. "What I've been trying to say ever since I was born—pretty near—is that what this class wants is a competent Professor, some bully top-of-the-tree artist, to come and pull our work all to pieces and wipe his boots on the bits. Mr. Vernon, don't you know any one who's pining to give us free crits?"

"Temple is," said Vernon. "There's no mistaking that longing

E. Nesbit

glance of his."

"As a competent professor I make you my bow of gratitude," said Temple, "but I should never have the courage to criticise the work of nine fair ladies."

"You needn't criticise them all at once," said a large girl from Minneapolis, "nor yet all in the gaudy eye of heaven. We'll screen off a corner for our Professor—sort of confessional business. You sit there and we'll go to you one by one with our sins in our hand."

"*That* would scare him some I surmise," said Miss Voscoe.

"Not at all," said Temple, a little nettled, he hardly knew why.

"I didn't know you were so brave," said the Minneapolis girl.

"Perhaps he didn't want you to know," said Miss Voscoe; "perhaps that's his life's dark secret."

"People often pretend to a courage that they haven't," said Vernon. "A consistent pose of cowardice, that would be novel and—I see the idea developing—more than useful."

"Is that *your* pose?" asked Temple, still rather tartly, "because if it is, I beg to offer you, in the name of these ladies, the chair of Professor-behind-the-screen."

"I'm not afraid of the nine Muses," Vernon laughed back, "as long as they are nine. It's the light that lies in woman's eyes that I've always had such a nervous dread of."

"It does make you blink, bless it," said the Irish student, "but not from nine pairs at once, as you say. It's the light from one pair that turns your head."

"Mr. Vernon isn't weak in the head," said the shy boy suddenly.

"No," said Vernon, "it's the heart that's weak with me. I have to be very careful of it."

"Well, but will you?" said a downright girl.

"Will I what? I'm sorry, but I've lost my cue, I think. Where were we—at losing hearts, wasn't it?"

"No," said the downright girl, "I didn't mean that. I mean will you come and criticise our drawings?"

"Fiddle," said Miss Voscoe luminously. "Mr. Vernon's too big for that."

"Oh, well," said Vernon, "if you don't think I should be competent!"

"You don't mean to say you would?"

"Who wouldn't jump at the chance of playing Apollo to the fairest set of muses in the Quartier?" said Temple; "but after all, I had the refusal of the situation—I won't renounce—"

"Bobby, you unman me," interrupted Vernon, putting down his cup, "you shall *not* renounce the altruistic pleasure which you promise to yourself in yielding this professorship to me. I accept it."

"I'm hanged if you do!" said Temple. "You proposed me yourself, and I'm elected—aren't I, Miss Voscoe?"

"That's so," said she; "but Mr. Vernon's president too."

"I've long been struggling with the conviction that Temple and I were as brothers. Now I yield—Temple, to my arms!"

They embraced, elegantly, enthusiastically, almost as Frenchmen use; and the room applauded the faithful burlesque.

"What's come to me that I should play the goat like this?" Vernon asked himself, as he raised his head from Temple's broad shoulder. Then he met Betty's laughing eyes, and no longer regretted his assumption of that difficult role.

"It's settled then. Tuesdays and Fridays, four to six," he said. "At last I am to be—"

"The light of the harem," said Miss Voscoe.

"Can there be two lights?" asked Temple anxiously. "If not, consider the fraternal embrace withdrawn."

"No, you're *the* light, of course," said Betty. "Mr. Vernon's the Ancient Light. He's older than you are, isn't he?"

The roar of appreciation of her little joke surprised Betty, and, a little, pleased her—till Miss Voscoe whispered under cover of it:

"*Ancient* light? Then he *was* the three-polite-word man?"

Betty explained her little jest.

"All the same," said the other, "it wasn't any old blank walls you were thinking about. I believe he is the one."

"It's a great thing to be able to believe anything," said Betty; and the talk broke up into duets. She found that Temple was speaking to her.

"I came here to-day because I wanted to meet you, Miss Desmond," he was saying. "I hope you don't think it's cheek of me to say it, but there's something about you that reminds me of the country at home."

"That's a very pretty speech," said Betty. He reminded her of the Cafe d'Harcourt, but she did not say so.

"You remind me of a garden," he went on, "but I don't like to see a garden without a hedge round it."

"You think I ought to have a chaperon," said Betty bravely, "but chaperons aren't needed in this quarter."

"I wish I were your brother," said Temple.

"I'm so glad you're not," said Betty. She wanted no chaperonage, even fraternal. But the words made him shrink, and then sent a soft warmth through him. On the whole he was not sorry that he was not her brother.

At parting Vernon, at the foot of the staircase, said:

"And when may I see you again?"

"On Tuesday, when the class meets."

"But I didn't mean when shall I see the class. When shall I see Miss Desmond?"

"Oh, whenever you like," Betty answered gaily; "whenever Lady St. Craye can spare you."

He let her say it.

E. Nesbit

CHAPTER XVI

"LOVE AND TUPPER."

"Whenever Vernon liked" proved to be the very next day. He was waiting outside the door of the atelier when Betty, in charcoal-smeared pinafore, left the afternoon class.

"Won't you dine with me somewhere to-night?" said he.

"I am going to Garnier's," she said. Not even for him, friend of hers and affianced of another as he might be, would she yet break the rule of a life Paula had instituted.

"Fallen as I am," he answered gaily, "I am not yet so low as to be incapable of dining at Garnier's."

So when Betty passed through the outer room of the restaurant and along the narrow little passage where eyes and nose attest strongly the neighborhood of the kitchen, she was attended by a figure that aroused the spontaneous envy of all her acquaintances. In the inner room where they dined it was remarked that such a figure would be more at home at Durand's or the Cafe de Paris than at Garnier's. That night the first breath of criticism assailed Betty. To afficher oneself with a fellow-student—a "type," Polish or otherwise—that was all very well, but with an obvious Boulevardier, a creature from the other side, this dashed itself against the conventions of the Artistic Quartier. And conventions—even of such quarters—are iron-strong.

"Fiddle-de-dee," said Miss Voscoe to her companions' shocked comments, "they were raised in the same village, or something. He used to give her peanuts when he was in short jackets, and she used to halve her candies with him. Friend of childhood's hour, that's all. And besides he's one of the presidents of our Sketch Club."

But all Garnier's marked that whereas the habitues contented themselves with an omelette aux champignons, saute potatoes and a Petit Suisse, or the like modest menu, Betty's new friend ordered for himself, and for her, "a real regular dinner," beginning with hors d'oeuvre and ending with "mendiants." "Mendiants" are raisins and nuts, the nearest to dessert that at this season you could get at Garniers. Also he passed over with smiling disrelish the little carafons of weak wine for which one pays five sous if the wine be red, and six if it be white. He went out and interviewed Madame at her little desk among the flowers and nuts and special sweet dishes, and it was a bottle of real wine with a real cork to be drawn that adorned the table between him and Betty. To her the whole thing was of the nature of a festival. She enjoyed the little sensation created by her companion; and the knowledge which she thought she had of his relations to Lady St. Craye absolved her of any fear that in dining with him tete-a-tete she was doing anything "not quite nice." To her the thought of his engagement was as good or as bad as a chaperon. For Betty's innocence was deeply laid, and had survived the shock of all the waves that had beaten against it since her coming to Paris. It was more than innocence, it was a very honest, straightforward childish naivete.

"It's almost the same as if he was married," she said: "there can't be any harm in having dinner with a man who's married—or almostmarried."

So she enjoyed herself. Vernon exerted himself to amuse her. But he was surprised to find that he was not so happy as he had expected to be. It was good that Betty had permitted him to dine with her alone, but it was flat. After dinner he took her

E. Nesbit

to the Odeon, and she said good-night to him with a lighter heart than she had known since Paula left her.

In these rooms now sometimes it was hard to keep one's eyes shut. And to keep her eyes shut was now Betty's aim in life, even more than the art for which she pretended to herself that she lived. For now that Paula had gone the deception of her father would have seemed less justifiable, had she ever allowed herself to face the thought of it for more than a moment; but she used to fly the thought and go round to one of the girls' rooms to talk about Art with a big A, and forget how little she liked or admired Betty Desmond.

She was now one of a circle of English, American and German students. The Sketch Club had brought her eight new friends, and they went about in parties by twos and threes, or even sevens and eights, and Betty went with them, enjoying the fun of it all, which she liked, and missing all that she would not have liked if she had seen it. But Vernon was the only man with whom she dined tete-a-tete or went to the theatre alone.

To him the winter passed in a maze of doubt and self-contempt. He could not take what the gods held out: could not draw from his constant companionship of Betty the pleasure which his artistic principles, his trained instincts taught him to expect. He had now all the tete-a-tetes he cared to ask for, and he hated that it should be so. He almost wanted her to be in a position where such things should be impossible to her. He wanted her to be guarded, watched, sheltered. And he had never wanted that for any woman in his life before.

"I shall be wishing her in a convent next," he said, "with high walls with spikes on the top. Then I should walk round and round the outside of the walls and wish her out. But I should not be able to get at her. And nothing else would either."

Lady St. Craye was more charming than ever. Vernon knew it and sometimes he deliberately tried to let her charm him. But though he perceived her charm he could not feel it. Always before he had felt what he chose to feel. Or perhaps—he hated the thought and would not look at it—perhaps all his love affairs had been just pictures, perhaps he had never felt anything but an artistic pleasure in their grouping and lighting. Perhaps now he was really feeling natural human emotion, didn't they call it? But that was just it. He wasn't. What he felt was resentment, dissatisfaction, a growing inability to control events or to prearrange his sensations. He felt that he himself was controlled. He felt like a wild creature caught in a trap. The trap was not gilded, and he was very uncomfortable in it. Even the affairs of others almost ceased to amuse him. He could hardly call up a cynical smile at Lady St. Craye's evident misapprehension of those conscientious efforts of his to be charmed by her. He was only moved to a very faint amusement when one day Bobbie Temple, smoking in the studio, broke a long silence abruptly to say:

"Look here. Someone was saying the other day that a man can be in love with two women at a time. Do you think it's true?"

"Two? Yes. Or twenty."

"Then it's not love," said Temple wisely.

"They call it love," said Vernon. "*I* don't know what they mean by it. What do *you* mean?"

"By love?"

"Yes."

"I don't exactly know," said Temple slowly. "I suppose it's wanting to be with a person, and thinking about nothing else. And thinking they're the most beautiful and all that. And going over everything that they've ever said to you, and wanting—"

"Wanting?"

E. Nesbit

"Well, I suppose if it's really love you want to marry them."

"You can't marry *them*, you know," said Vernon; "at least not simultaneously. That's just it. Well?"

"Well that's all. If that's not love, what is?"

"I'm hanged if *I* know," said Vernon.

"I thought you knew all about those sort of things."

"So did I," said Vernon to himself. Aloud he said:

"If you want a philosophic definition: it's passion transfigured by tenderness—at least I've often said so."

"But can you feel that for two people at once?"

"Or," said Vernon, getting interested in his words, "it's tenderness intoxicated by passion, and not knowing that it's drunk—"

"But can you feel that for two—"

"Oh, bother," said Vernon, "every sort of fool-fancy calls itself love. There's the pleasure of pursuit—there's vanity, there's the satisfaction of your own amour-propre, there's desire, there's intellectual attraction, there's the love of beauty, there's the artist's joy in doing what you know you can do well, and getting a pretty woman for sole audience. You might feel one or two or twenty of these things for one woman, and one or two or twenty different ones for another. But if you mean do you love two women in the same way, I say no. Thank Heaven it's new every time."

"It mayn't be the same way," said Temple, "but it's the same thing to you—if you feel you can't bear to give either of them up."

"Well, then, you can marry one and keep on with the other. Or be 'friends' with both and marry neither. Or cut the whole show and go to the Colonies."

"Then you have to choose between being unhappy or being a blackguard."

"My good chap, that's the situation in which our emotions are always landing us—our confounded emotions and the conventions of Society."

"And how are you to know whether the thing's love—or—all those other things?"

"You don't know: you can't know till it's too late for your knowing to matter. Marriage is like spinach. You can't tell that you hate it till you've tried it. Only—"

"Well?"

"I think I've heard it said," Vernon voiced his own sudden conviction, very carelessly, "that love wants to give and passion wants to take. Love wants to possess the beloved object—and to make her happy. Desire wants possession too—but the happiness is to be for oneself; and if there's not enough happiness for both so much the worse. If I'm talking like a Sunday School book you've brought it on yourself."

"I like it," said Temple.

"Well, since the Dissenting surplice has fallen on me, I'll give you a test. I believe that the more you love a woman the less your thoughts will dwell on the physical side of the business. You want to take care of her."

"Yes," said Temple.

"And then often," Vernon went on, surprised to find that he wanted to help the other in his soul-searchings, "if a chap's not

E. Nesbit

had much to do with women—the women of our class, I mean—he gets a bit dazed with them. They're all so nice, confound them. If a man felt he was falling in love with two women at once, and he had the tiresome temperament that takes these things seriously, it wouldn't be a bad thing for him to go away into the country, and moon about for a few weeks, and see which was the one that bothered his brain most. Then he'd know where he was, and not be led like a lamb to the slaughter by the wrong one. They can't both get him, you know, unless his intentions are strictly dishonourable."

"I wasn't putting the case that either of them wished to get him," said Temple carefully.

Vernon nodded.

"Of course not. The thing simplifies itself wonderfully if neither of them wants to get him. Even if they both do, matters are less complicated. It's when only one of them wants him that it's the very devil for a man not to be sure what *he* wants. That's very clumsily put—what I mean is—"

"I see what you mean," said Temple impatiently.

"—It's the devil for him because then he lets himself drift and the one who wants him collars him and then of course she always turns out to be the one he didn't want. My observations are as full of wants as an advertisement column. But the thing to do in all relations of life is to make up your mind what it is that you *do* want, and then to jolly well see that you get it. What I want is a pipe."

He filled and lighted one.

"You talk," said Temple slowly, "as though a man could get anyone—I mean anything, he wanted."

"So he can, my dear chap, if he only wants her badly enough."

"Badly enough?"

"Badly enough to make the supreme sacrifice to get her."

"?" Temple enquired.

"Marriage," Vernon answered; "there's only one excuse for marriage."

"Excuse?"

"Excuse. And that excuse is that one couldn't help it. The only excuse one will have to offer, some day, to the recording angel, for all one's other faults and follies. A man who *can* help getting married, and doesn't, deserves all he gets."

"I don't agree with you in the least," said Temple,—"about marriage, I mean. A man *ought* to want to get married—"

"To anybody? Without its being anybody in particular?"

"Yes," said Temple stoutly. "If he gets to thirty without wanting to marry any one in particular, he ought to look about till he finds some one he does want. It's the right and proper thing to marry and have kiddies."

"Oh, if you're going to be Patriarchal," said Vernon. "What a symbolic dialogue! We begin with love and we end with marriage! There's the tragedy of romance, in a nut-shell. Yes, life's a beastly rotten show, and the light won't last more than another two hours."

"Your hints are always as delicate as gossamer," said Temple. "Don't throw anything at me. I'm going."

He went, leaving his secret in Vernon's hands.

"Poor old Temple! That's the worst of walking carefully all your days: you do come such an awful cropper when you do come one. Two women. The Jasmine lady must have been practising on his poor little heart. Heigh-ho, I wish she could do as much for me! And the other one? *Her*—I suppose."

The use of the pronoun, the disuse of the grammar pulled him up short.

"By Jove," he said, "that's what people say when—But I'm not in love—with anybody. I want to work."

But he didn't work. He seldom did now. And when he did the work was not good. His easel held most often the portrait of Betty that had been begun at Long Barton—unfinished, but a disquieting likeness. He walked up and down his room not thinking, but dreaming. His dreams took him to the warren, in the pure morning light; he saw Betty; he told himself what he had said, what she had said.

"And it was I who advised her to come to Paris. If only I'd known then—"

He stopped and asked himself what he knew now that he had not known then, refused himself the answer, and went to call on Lady St. Craye.

Christmas came and went; the black winds of January swept the Boulevards, and snow lay white on the walls of court and garden. Betty's life was full now.

The empty cage that had opened its door to love at Long Barton had now other occupants. Ambition was beginning to grow its wing feathers. She could draw—at least some day she would be able to draw. Already she had won a prize with a charcoal study of a bare back. But she did not dare to name this to her father, and when he wrote to ask what was the subject of her prize drawing she replied with misleading truth that it was a study from nature. His imagination pictured a rustic cottage, a water-wheel, a castle and mountains in the distance and cows and a peasant in the foreground.

But though her life was now crowded with new interests that first-comer was not ousted. Only he had changed his plumage and she called him Friendship. She blushed sometimes and stamped her foot when she remembered those meetings in the summer mornings, her tremors, her heart-beats. And oh, the "drivel" she had written in her diary!

"Girls ought never to be allowed to lead that 'sheltered home life,'" she said to Miss Voscoe, "with nothing real in it. It makes your mind all swept and garnished and then you hurry to fill it up with rubbish."

"That's so," said her friend.

"If ever *I* have a daughter," said Betty, "she shall set to work at *something* definite the very instant she leaves school—if it's only Hebrew or algebra. Not just Parish duties that she didn't begin, and doesn't want to go on with. But something that's her *own* work."

"You're beginning to see straight. I surmised you would by and by. But don't you go to the other end of the see-saw, Miss Daisy-Face!"

"What do you mean?" asked Betty. It was the morning interval when students eat patisserie out of folded papers. The two were on the window ledge of the Atelier, looking down on the convent garden where already the buds were breaking to green leaf.

"Why, there's room for the devil even if your flat ain't swept and garnished. He folds up mighty small, and gets into less space than a poppy-seed."

"What do you mean?" asked Betty again.

"I mean that Vernon chap," said Miss Voscoe down-rightly. "I told you to change partners every now and then. But with you it's that Vernon this week and last week and the week

E. Nesbit

after next."

"I've known him longer than I have the others, and I like him," said Betty.

"Oh, he's all right; fine and dandy!" replied Miss Voscoe. "He's a big man, too, in his own line. Not the kind you expect to see knocking about at a students' cremerie. Does he give you lessons?"

"He did at home," said Betty.

"Take care he doesn't teach you what's the easiest thing in creation to learn about a man."

"What's that?" Betty did not like to have to ask the question.

"Why, how not to be able to do without him, of course," said Miss Voscoe.

"You're quite mistaken," said Betty eagerly: "one of the reasons I don't mind going about with him so much is that he's engaged to be married."

"Acquainted with the lady?"

"Yes," said Betty, sheltering behind the convention that an introduction at a tea-party constitutes acquaintanceship. She was glad Miss Voscoe had not asked her if she *knew* Lady St. Craye.

"Oh, well"—Miss Voscoe jumped up and shook the flakes of pastry off her pinafore—"if she doesn't mind, I guess I've got no call to. But why don't you give that saint in the go-to-hell collar a turn?"

"Meaning?"

"Mr. Temple. He admires you no end. He'd be always in your

pocket if you'd let him. He's worth fifty of the other man *as* a man, if he isn't as an artist. I keep my eyes skinned—and the Sketch Club gives me a chance to tot them both up. I guess I can size up a man some. The other man isn't *fast*. That's how it strikes me."

"Fast?" echoed Betty, bewildered.

"Fast dye: fast colour. I suspicion he'd go wrong a bit in the wash. Temple's fast colour, warranted not to run."

"I know," said Betty, "but I don't care for the colour, and I'm rather tired of the pattern."

"I wish you'd tell me which of the two was the three-polite-word man."

"I know you do. But surely you see *now*?"

"You're too cute. Just as likely it's the Temple one, and that's why you're so sick of the pattern by now."

"Didn't I tell you you were clever?" laughed Betty.

But, all the same, next evening when Vernon called to take her to dinner, she said:

"Couldn't we go somewhere else? I'm tired of Garnier's."

Vernon was tired of Garnier's, too.

"Do you know Thirion's?" he said. "Thirion's in the Boulevard St. Germain, Thirion's where Du Maurier used to go, and Thackeray, and all sorts of celebrated people; and where the host treats you like a friend, and the waiter like a brother?"

"I should love to be treated like a waiter's brother. Do let's go," said Betty.

"He's a dream of a waiter," Vernon went on as they turned down the lighted slope of the Rue de Rennes, "has a voice like a trumpet, and takes a pride in calling twenty orders down the speaking-tube in one breath, ending up with a shout. He never makes a mistake either. Shall we walk, or take the tram, or a carriage?"

The Fate who was amusing herself by playing with Betty's destiny had sent Temple to call on Lady St. Craye that afternoon, and Lady St. Craye had seemed bored, so bored that she had hardly appeared to listen to Temple's talk, which, duly directed by her quite early into the channel she desired for it, flowed in a constant stream over the name, the history, the work, the personality of Vernon. When at last the stream ebbed Lady St. Craye made a pretty feint of stifling a yawn.

"Oh, how horrid I am!" she cried with instant penitence, "and how very rude you will think me! I think I have the blues to-day, or, to be more French and more poetic, the black butterflies. It *is* so sweet of you to have let me talk to you. I know I've been as stupid as an owl. Won't you stay and dine with me? I'll promise to cheer up if you will."

Mr. Temple would, more than gladly.

"Or no," Lady St. Craye went on, "that'll be dull for you, and perhaps even for me if I begin to think I'm boring you. Couldn't we do something desperate—dine at a Latin Quarter restaurant for instance? What was that place you were telling me of, where the waiter has a wonderful voice and makes the orders he shouts down the tube sound like the recitative of the basso at the Opera."

"Thirion's," said Temple; "but it wasn't I, it was Vernon."

"Thirion's, that's it!" Lady St. Craye broke in before Vernon's name left his lips. "Would you like to take me there to dine, Mr. Temple?"

It appeared that Mr. Temple would like it of all things.

"Then I'll go and put on my hat," said she and trailed her sea-green tea-gown across the room. At the door she turned to say: "It will be fun, won't it?"—and to laugh delightedly, like a child who is promised a treat.

That was how it happened that Lady St. Craye, brushing her dark furs against the wall of Thirion's staircase, came, followed by Temple, into the room where Betty and Vernon, their heads rather close together, were discussing the menu.

This was what Lady St. Craye had thought of more than a little. Yet it was not what she had expected. Vernon, perhaps, yes: or the girl. But not Vernon and the girl together. Not now. At her very first visit. It was not for a second that she hesitated. Temple had not even had time to see who it was to whom she spoke before she had walked over to the two, and greeted them.

"How perfectly delightful!" she said. "Miss Desmond, I've been meaning to call on you, but it's been so cold, and I've been so cross, I've called on nobody. Ah, Mr. Vernon, you too?"

She looked at the vacant chair near his, and Vernon had to say:

"You'll join us, of course?"

So the two little parties made one party, and one of the party was angry and annoyed, and no one of the party was quite pleased, and all four concealed what they felt, and affected what they did not feel, with as much of the tact of the truly well-bred as each could call up. In this polite exercise Lady St. Craye was easily first.

She was charming to Temple, she was very nice to Betty, and she spoke to Vernon with a delicate, subtle, faint suggestion of proprietorship in her tone. At least that was how it seemed to

E. Nesbit

Betty. To Temple it seemed that she was tacitly apologising to an old friend for having involuntarily broken up a dinner a deux. To Vernon her tone seemed to spell out an all but overmastering jealousy proudly overmastered. All that pretty fiction of there being now no possibility of sentiment between him and her flickered down and died. And with it the interest that he had felt in her. "*She* have unexplored reserves? Bah!" he told himself, "she is just like the rest." He felt that she had not come from the other side of the river just to dine with Temple. He knew she had been looking for him. And the temptation assailed him to reward her tender anxiety by devoting himself wholly to Betty. Then he remembered what he had let Betty believe, as to the relations in which he stood to this other woman.

His face lighted up with a smile of answering tenderness. Without neglecting Betty he seemed to lay the real homage of his heart at the feet of that heart's lady.

"By Jove," he thought, as the dark, beautiful eyes met his in a look of more tenderness than he had seen in them this many a day, "if only she knew how she's playing my game for me!"

Betty, for her part, refused to recognise a little pain that gnawed at her heart and stole all taste from the best dishes of Thirion's. She talked as much as possible to Temple, because it was the proper thing to do, she told herself, and she talked very badly. Lady St. Craye was transfigured by Vernon's unexpected acceptance of her delicate advances, intoxicated by the sudden flutter of a dream she had only known with wings in full flight, into the region where dreams, clasped to the heart, become realities. She grew momently more beautiful. The host, going from table to table, talking easily to his guests, could not keep his fascinated eyes from her face. The proprietor of Thirion's had good taste, and knew a beautiful woman when he saw her.

Betty's eyes, too, strayed more and more often from her plate, and from Temple to the efflorescence of this new beauty-light. She felt mean and poor, ill-dressed, shabby, dowdy, dull, weary and uninteresting. Her face felt tired. It was an effort to smile.

When the dinner was over she said abruptly:

"If you'll excuse me—I've got a dreadful headache—no, I don't want anyone to see me home. Just put me in a carriage."

She insisted, and it was done.

When the carriage drew up in front of the closed porte cochere of 57 Boulevard Montparnasse, Betty was surprised and wounded to discover that she was crying.

"Well, you *knew* they were engaged!" she said as she let herself into her room with her latchkey. "You knew they were engaged! What did you expect?"

Temple could not remember afterwards exactly how he got separated from the others. It just happened, as such unimortant things will. He missed them somehow, at a crossing, looked about him in vain, shrugged his shoulders and went home.

Lady St. Craye hesitated a moment with her latchkey in her hand. Then she threw open the door of her flat.

"Come in, won't you?" she said, and led the way into her fire-warm, flower-scented, lamplit room. Vernon also hesitated a moment. Then he followed. He stood on the hearth-rug with his back to the wood fire. He did not speak.

Somehow it was difficult for her to take up their talk at the place and in the strain where it had broken off when Betty proclaimed her headache.

Yet this was what she must do, it seemed to her, or lose all the round she had gained.

"You've been very charming to me this evening," she said at

last, and knew as she said it that it was the wrong thing to say.

"You flatter me," said Vernon.

"I was so surprised to see you there," she went on.

Vernon was surprised that she should say it. He had thought more highly of her powers.

"The pleasure was mine," he said in his most banal tones, "the surprise, alas, was all for you—and all you gained."

"Weren't *you* surprised?"—Lady St. Craye was angry and humiliated. That she—she—should find herself nervous, at fault, find herself playing the game as crudely as any shopgirl!

"No," said Vernon.

"But you couldn't have expected me?" She knew quite well what she was doing, but she was too nervous to stop herself.

"I've always expected you," he said deliberately, "ever since I told you that I often dined at Thirion's."

"You expected me to—"

"To run after me?" said Vernon with paraded ingenuousness; "yes, didn't you?"

"*I* run after *you*? You—" she stopped short, for she saw in his eyes that, if she let him quarrel with her now, it was forever.

He at the same moment awoke from the trance of anger that had come upon him when he found himself alone with her; anger at her, and at himself, fanned to fury by the thought of Betty and of what she, at this moment, must be thinking. He laughed:

"Ah, don't break my heart!" he said, "I've been so happy all the evening fancying that you had—you had—"

"Had what?" she asked with dry lips, for the caress in his tone was such as to deceive the very elect.

"Had felt just the faintest little touch of interest in me. Had cared to know how I spent my evenings, and with whom!"

"You thought I could stoop to spy on you?" she asked. "Monsieur flatters himself."

The anger in him was raising its head again.

"Monsieur very seldom does," he said.

She took that as she chose to take it.

"No, you're beautifully humble."

"And you're proudly beautiful."

She flushed and looked down.

"Don't you like to be told that you're beautiful?"

"Not by you. Not like that!"

"And so you didn't come to Thirion's to see me? How one may deceive oneself! The highest hopes we cherish here! Another beautiful illusion gone!"

She said to herself: "I can do nothing with him in this mood," and aloud she could not help saying: "Was it a beautiful one?"

"Very," he answered gaily. "Can you doubt it?"

She found nothing to say. And even as she fought for words she suddenly found that he had caught her in his arms, and kissed her, and that the sound of the door that had banged

E. Nesbit

behind him was echoing in her ears.

She put her hands to her head. She could not see clearly.

CHAPTER XVII

INTERVENTIONS

That kiss gave Lady St. Craye furiously to think, as they say in France.

Had it meant—? What had it meant? Was it the crown of her hopes, her dreams? Was it possible that now, at last, after all that had gone before, she might win him—had won him, even?

The sex-instinct said "No."

Then, if "No" were the answer to that question, the kiss had been mere brutality. It had meant just:

"You chose to follow me—to play the spy. What the deuce do you want? Is it this? God knows you're welcome," the kiss following.

The kiss stung. It was not the first. But the others—even the last of them, two years before, had not had that sting.

Lady St. Craye, biting her lips in lonely dissection of herself and of him, dared take no comfort. Also, she no longer dared to follow him, to watch him, to spy on him.

In her jasmine-scented leisure Lady St. Craye analysed herself, and him and Her. Above all Her—who was Betty. To find out how it all seemed to her—that, presently, seemed to Lady St. Craye the one possible, the one important thing. So after she had given a few days to the analysis of that kiss, had failed to reach certainty as to its elements, had writhed in her failure, and bitterly resented the mysteries constituent that falsified all her calculations, she dressed herself beautifully, and went to call on the constituent, Betty.

Betty was at home. She was drawing at a table, cunningly placed at right angles to the window. She rose with a grace that Lady St. Craye had not seen in her. She was dressed in a plain gown, that hung from the shoulders in long, straight, green folds. Her hair was down.—And Betty had beautiful hair. Lady St. Craye's hair had never been long. Betty's fell nearly to her knees.

"Oh, was the door open?" she said. "I didn't know, I've—I'm so sorry—I've been washing my hair."

"It's lovely," said the other woman, with an appreciation quite genuine. "What a pity you can't always wear it like that!"

"It's long," said Betty disparagingly, "but the colour's horrid. What Miss Voscoe calls Boy colour."

"Boy colour?"

"Oh, just nothing in particular. Mousy."

"If you had golden hair, or black, Miss Desmond, you'd have a quite unfair advantage over the rest of us."

"I don't think so," said Betty very simply; "you see, no one ever sees it down."

"What a charming place you've got here," Lady St. Craye went on.

"Yes," said Betty, "it is nice," and she thought of Paula.

"And do you live here all alone?"

"Yes: I had a friend with me at first, but she's gone back to England."

"Don't you find it very dull?"

"Oh, no! I know lots of people now."

"And they come to see you here?"

Lady St. Craye had decided that it was not necessary to go delicately. The girl was evidently stupid, and one need not pick one's words.

"Yes," said Betty.

"Mr. Vernon's a great friend of yours, isn't he?"

"Yes."

"I suppose you see a great deal of him?"

"Yes. Is there anything else you would like to know?"

The scratch was so sudden, so fierce, so feline that for a moment Lady St. Craye could only look blankly at her hostess. Then she recovered herself enough to say:

"Oh, I'm so sorry! Was I asking a lot of questions? It's a dreadful habit of mine, I'm afraid, when I'm interested in people."

Betty scratched again quite calmly and quite mercilessly.

"It's quite natural that Mr. Vernon should interest you. But I don't think I'm likely to be able to tell you anything about him that you don't know. May I get you some tea?"

E. Nesbit

It was impossible for Lady St. Craye to reply: "I meant that I was interested in *you*—not in Mr. Vernon;" so she said:

"Thank you—that will be delightful."

Betty went along the little passage to her kitchen, and her visitor was left to revise her impressions.

When Betty came back with the tea-tray, her hair was twisted up. The kettle could be heard hissing in the tiny kitchen.

"Can't I help you?" Lady St. Craye asked, leaning back indolently in the most comfortable chair.

"No, thank you: it's all done now."

Betty poured the tea for the other woman to drink. Her own remained untasted. She exerted herself to manufacture small-talk, was very amiable, very attentive. Lady St. Craye almost thought she must have dreamed those two sharp cat-scratches at the beginning of the interview. But presently Betty's polite remarks came less readily. There were longer intervals of silence. And Lady St. Craye for once was at a loss. Her nerve was gone. She dared not tempt the claws again. After the longest pause of all Betty said suddenly:

"I think I know why you came to-day."

"I came to see you, because you're a friend of Mr. Vernon's."

"You came to see me because you wanted to find out exactly how much I'm a friend of Mr. Vernon's. Didn't you?"

Candour is the most disconcerting of the virtues.

"Not in the least," Lady St. Craye found herself saying. "I came to see you—because—as I said."

"I don't think it is much use your coming to see me," Betty

went on, "though, if you meant it kindly—But you didn't—you didn't! If you had it wouldn't have made any difference. We should never get on with each other, never."

"Really, Miss Desmond"—Lady St. Craye clutched her card-case and half rose—"I begin to think we never should."

Betty's ignorance of the usages of good society stood her friend. She ignored, not consciously, but by the prompting of nature, the social law which decrees that one should not speak of things that really interest one.

"Do sit down," she said. "I'm glad you came—because I know exactly what you mean, now."

"If the knowledge were only mutual!" sighed Lady St. Craye, and found courage to raise eyebrows wearily.

"You don't like my going about with Mr. Vernon. Well, you've only to say so. Only when you're married you'll find you've got your work cut out to keep him from having any friends except you."

Lady St. Craye had the best of reasons for believing this likely to be the truth. She said:

"When I'm married?"

"Yes," said Betty firmly. "You're jealous; you've no cause to be—and I tell you that because I think being jealous must hurt. But it would have been nicer of you, if you'd come straight to me and said: 'Look here, I don't like you going about with the man I'm engaged to.' I should have understood then and respected you. But to come like a child's Guide to Knowledge—"

The other woman was not listening. "Engaged to him!"—The words sang deliciously, disquietingly in her ears.

"But who said I was engaged to him?"

"He did, of course. He isn't ashamed of it—if you are."

"He told you that!"

"Yes. Now aren't you ashamed of yourself?"

Country-bred Betty, braced by the straightforward directness of Miss Voscoe, and full of the nervous energy engendered by a half-understood trouble, had routed, for a moment, the woman of the world. But only for a moment. Then Lady St. Craye, unable to estimate the gain or loss of the encounter, pulled herself together to make good her retreat.

"Yes," she said, with her charming smile. "I am ashamed of myself. I *was* jealous—I own it. But I shouldn't have shown it as I did if I'd known the sort of girl you are. Come, forgive me! Can't you understand—and forgive?"

"It was all my fault." The generosity of Betty hastened to meet what it took to be the generosity of the other. "Forgive me. I won't see him again at all—if you don't want me to."

"No, no." Even at that moment, in one illuminating flash, Lady St. Craye saw the explications that must follow the announcement of that renunciatory decision. "No, no. If you do that I shall feel sure that you don't forgive me for being so silly. Just let everything go on—won't you? And please, please don't tell him anything about—about to-day."

"How could I?" asked Betty.

"But promise you won't. You know—men are so vain. I should hate him to know"—she hesitated and then finished the sentence with fine art—"to know—how much I care."

"Of course you care," said Betty downrightly. "You ought to care. It would be horrid of you if you didn't."

"But I don't, *now*. Now I *know* you, Miss Desmond. I understand so well—and I like to think of his being with you."

Even to Betty's ears this did not ring quite true.

"You like—?" she said.

"I mean I quite understand now. I thought—I don't know what I thought. You're so pretty, you know. And he has had so very many—love-affairs."

"He hasn't one with me," said Betty briefly.

"Ah, you're still angry. And no wonder. Do forgive me, Miss Desmond, and let's be friends."

Betty's look as she gave her hand was doubtful. But the hand was given.

"And you'll keep my poor little secret?"

"I should have thought you would have been proud for him to know how much you care."

"Ah, my dear," Lady St. Craye became natural for an instant under the transfiguring influence of her real thoughts as she spoke them, "my dear, don't believe it! When a man's sure of you he doesn't care any more. It's while he's not quite sure that he cares."

"I don't think that's so always," said Betty.

"Ah, believe me, there are 'more ways of killing a cat than choking it with butter.' Forgive the homely aphorism. When you have a lover of your own—or perhaps you have now?"

"Perhaps I have." Betty stood on guard with a steady face.

"Well, when you have—or if you have—remember never to let

E. Nesbit

him be quite sure. It's the only way."

The two parted, with a mutually kindly feeling that surprised one as much as the other. Lady St. Craye drove home contrasting bitterly the excellence of her maxims with the ineptitude of her practice. She had let him know that she cared. And he had left her. That was two years ago. And, now that she had met him again, when she might have played the part she had recommended to that chit with the long hair—the part she knew to be the wise one—she had once more suffered passion to overcome wisdom, and had shown him that she loved him. And he had kissed her.

She blushed in the dusk of her carriage for the shame of that kiss.

But he had told that girl that he was engaged to her.

A delicious other flush replaced the blush of shame. Why should he have done that unless he really meant—? In that case the kiss was nothing to blush about. And yet it was. She knew it.

She had time to think in the days that followed, days that brought Temple more than once to her doors, but Vernon never.

Betty left alone let down her damp hair and tried to resume her drawing. But it would not do. The emotion of the interview was too recent. Her heart was beating still with anger, and resentment, and other feelings less easily named.

Vernon was to come to fetch her at seven. She would not face him. Let him go and dine with the woman he belonged to!

Betty went out at half-past six. She would not go to Garnier's, nor to Thirion's. That was where he would look for her.

She walked steadily on, down the boulevard. She would dine

at some place she had never been to before. A sickening vision of that first night in Paris swam before her. She saw again the Cafe d'Harcourt, heard the voices of the women who had spoken to Paula, saw the eyes of the men who had been the companions of those women. In that rout the face of Temple shone—clear cut, severe. She remembered the instant resentment that had thrilled her at his protective attitude, remembered it and wondered at it a little. She would not have felt that now. She knew her Paris better than she had done then.

And with the thought, the face of Temple came towards her out of the crowd. He raised his hat in response to her frigid bow, and had almost passed her, when she spoke on an impulse that surprised herself.

"Oh—Mr. Temple!"

He stopped and turned.

"I was looking for a place to dine. I'm tired of Garnier's and Thirion's."

He hesitated. And he, too, remembered the night at the Cafe d'Harcourt, when she had disdained his advice and gone back to take the advice of Paula.

He caught himself assuring himself that a man need not be ashamed to risk being snubbed—making a fool of himself even—if he could do any good. So he said: "You know I have horrid old-fashioned ideas about women," and stopped short.

"Don't you know of any good quiet place near here?" said Betty.

"I think women ought to be taken care of. But some of them—Miss Desmond, I'm so afraid of you—I'm afraid of boring you—"

Remorse stirred her.

"You've always been most awfully kind," she said warmly. "I've often wanted to tell you that I'm sorry about that first time I saw you—I'm not sorry for what I *did*," she added in haste; "I can never be anything but glad for that. But I'm sorry I seemed ungrateful to you."

"Now you give me courage," he said. "I do know a quiet little place quite near here. And, as you haven't any of your friends with you, won't you take pity on me and let me dine with you?"

"You're sure you're not giving up some nice engagement—just to—to be kind to me?" she asked. And the forlornness of her tone made him almost forget that he had half promised to join a party of Lady St. Craye's.

"I should like to come with you—I should like it of all things," he said; and he said it convincingly.

They dined together, and the dinner was unexpectedly pleasant to both of them. They talked of England, of wood, field and meadow, and Betty found herself talking to him of the garden at home and of the things that grew there, as she had talked to Paula, and as she had never talked to Vernon.

"It's so lovely all the year," she said. "When the last mignonette's over, there are the chrysanthemums, and then the Christmas roses, and ever so early in January the winter aconite and the snow-drops, and the violets under the south wall. And then the little green daffodil leaves come up and the buds, though it's weeks before they turn into flowers. And if it's a mild winter the primroses—just little baby ones—seem to go on all the time."

"Yes," he said, "I know. And the wallflowers, they're green all the time.—And the monthly roses, they flower at Christmas. And then when the real roses begin to bud—and when June comes—and you're drunk with the scent of red roses—the kind you always long for at Christmas."

"Oh, yes," said Betty—"do you feel like that too? And if you get them, they're soft limp-stalked things, like caterpillars half disguised as roses by some incompetent fairy. Not like the stiff solid heavy velvet roses with thick green leaves and heaps of thorns. Those are the roses one longs for."

"Yes," he said. "Those are the roses one longs for." And an odd pause punctuated the sentence.

But the pause did not last. There was so much to talk of—now that barrier of resentment, wattled with remorse, was broken down. It was an odd revelation to each—the love of the other for certain authors, certain pictures, certain symphonies, certain dramas. The discovery of this sort of community of tastes is like the meeting in far foreign countries of a man who speaks the tongue of one's mother land. The two lingered long over their coffee, and the "Grand Marnier" which their liking for "The Garden of Lies" led to their ordering. Betty had forgotten Vernon, forgotten Lady St. Craye, in the delightful interchange of:

"Oh, I do like—"

"And don't you like—?"

"And isn't that splendid?"

These simple sentences, interchanged, took on the value of intimate confidences.

"I've had such a jolly time," Temple said. "I haven't had such a talk for ages."

And yet all the talk had been mere confessions of faith—in Ibsen, in Browning, in Maeterlinck, in English gardens, in Art for Art's sake, and in Whistler and Beethoven.

"I've liked it too," said Betty.

"And it's awfully jolly," he went on, "to feel that you've forgiven me"—the speech suddenly became difficult,—at least I mean to say—" he ended lamely.

"It's I who ought to be forgiven," said Betty. "I'm very glad I met you. I've enjoyed our talk ever so much."

Vernon spent an empty evening, and waylaid Betty as she left her class next day.

"I'm sorry," she said. "I couldn't help it. I suddenly felt I wanted something different. So I dined at a new place."

"Alone?" said Vernon.

"No," said Betty with her chin in the air.

Vernon digested, as best he might, his first mouthful of jealousy—real downright sickening jealousy. The sensation astonished him so much that he lacked the courage to dissect it.

"Will you dine with me to-night?" was all he found to say.

"With pleasure," said Betty. But it was not with pleasure that she dined. There was something between her and Vernon. Both felt it, and both attributed it to the same cause.

The three dinners that followed in the next fortnight brought none of that old lighthearted companionship which had been the gayest of table-decorations. Something was gone—lost—as though a royal rose had suddenly faded, a rainbow-coloured bubble had broken.

"I'm glad," said Betty; "if he's engaged, I don't want to feel happy with him."

She did not feel happy without him. The Inward Monitor grew more and more insistent. She caught herself wondering how Temple, with the serious face and the honest eyes, would regard the lies, the trickeries, the whole tissue of deceit that had won her her chance of following her own art, of living her own life.

Vernon understood, presently, that not even that evening at Thirion's could give the key to this uncomforting change. He had not seen Lady St. Craye since the night of the kiss.

It was after the fourth flat dinner with Betty that he said good-night to her early and abruptly, and drove to Lady St. Craye's.

She was alone. She rose to greet him, and he saw that her eyes were dark-rimmed, and her lips rough.

"This is very nice of you," she said. "It's nearly a month since I saw you."

"Yes," he said. "I know it is. Do you remember the last time? Hasn't that taught you not to play with me?"

The kiss was explained now. Lady St. Craye shivered.

"I don't know what you mean?" she said, feebly.

"Oh, yes, you do! You're much too clever not to understand. Come to think of it, you're much too everything—too clever, too beautiful, too charming, too everything."

"You overwhelm me," she made herself say.

"Not at all. You know your points. What I want to know is just one thing—and that's the thing you're going to tell me."

She drew her dry lips inward to moisten them.

"What do you want to know? Why do you speak to me like

E. Nesbit

that? What have I done?"

"That's what you're going to tell me."

"I shall tell you nothing—while you ask in that tone."

"Won't you? How can I persuade you?" his tone caressed and stung. "What arguments can I use? Must I kiss you again?"

She drew herself up, called wildly on all her powers to resent the insult. Nothing came at her call.

"What do you want me to tell you?" she asked, and her eyes implored the mercy she would not consciously have asked.

He saw, and he came a little nearer to her—looking down at her upturned face with eyes before which her own fell.

"You don't want another kiss?" he said. "Then tell me what you've been saying to Miss Desmond."

CHAPTER XVIII

THE TRUTH

There was a silence.

"Come, my pretty Jasmine lady, speak the truth."

"I will: What a brute you are!"

"So another lady told me a few months ago. Come, tell me."

"Why should I tell you anything?" She tried to touch her tone with scorn.

"Because I choose. You thought you could play with me and fool me and trick me out of what I mean to have—"

"What you mean to have?"

"Yes, what I mean to have. I mean to marry Miss Desmond—if she'll have me."

"*You*—mean to marry? Saul is among the prophets with a vengeance!" The scorn came naturally to her voice now.

Vernon stood as if turned to stone. Nothing had ever astonished him so much as those four words, spoken in his own voice, "I mean to marry." He repeated them. "I mean to marry Miss Desmond, if she'll have me. And it's your doing."

"Of course," she shrugged her shoulders. "Naturally it would be. Won't you sit down? You look so uncomfortable. Those French tragedy scenes with the hero hat in one hand and gloves in the other always seem to me so comic."

That was her score, the first. He put down the hat and gloves and came towards her. And as he came he hastily sketched his plan of action. When he reached her it was ready formed. His anger was always short lived. It had died down and left him competent as ever to handle the scene.

He took her hands, pushed her gently into a chair near the table, and sat down beside her with his elbows on the table and his head in his hands.

"Forgive me, dear," he said. "I was a brute. Forgive me—and help me. No one can help me but you."

It was a master-stroke: and he had staked a good deal on it. The stake was not lost. She found no words.

"My dear, sweet Jasmine lady," he said, "let me talk to you. Let me tell you everything. I can talk to you as I can talk to no one else, because I know you're fond of me. You are fond of me—a little, aren't you—for the sake of old times?"

"Yes," she said, "I am fond of you."

"And you forgive me—you do forgive me for being such a brute? I hardly knew what I was doing."

"Yes," she said, speaking as one speaks in dreams, "I forgive you."

"Thank you," he said humbly; "you were always generous. And you always understand."

"Wait—wait. I'll attend to you presently," she was saying to her heart. "Yes, I know it's all over. I know the game's up. Let me pull through this without disgracing myself, and I'll let you hurt me as much as you like afterwards."

"Tell me," she said gently to Vernon, "tell me everything."

He was silent, his face still hidden. He had cut the knot of an impossible situation and he was pausing to admire the cleverness of the stroke. In two minutes he had blotted out the last six months—months in which he and she had been adversaries. He had thrown himself on her mercy, and he had done wisely. Never, even in the days when he had carefully taught himself to be in love with her, had he liked her so well as now, when she got up from her chair to come and lay her hand softly on his shoulder and to say:

"My poor boy,—but there's nothing for you to be unhappy about. Tell me all about it—from the very beginning."

There was a luxurious temptation in the idea. It was not the first time, naturally, that Vernon had "told all about it" with a sympathetic woman-hand on his shoulder. He knew the strategic value of confidences. But always he had made the confidences fit the occasion—serve the end he had in view. Now, such end as had been in view was gained. He knew that it was only a matter of time now, before she should tell him of her own accord, what he could never by any brutality have forced her to tell. And the temptation to speak, for once, the truth about himself was overmastering. It is a luxury one can so very rarely afford. Most of us go the whole long life-way without tasting it. There was nothing to lose by speaking the truth. Moreover, he must say something, and why not the truth? So he said:

"It all comes of that confounded habit of mine of wanting to be in love."

"Yes," she said, "you were always so anxious to be—weren't you? And you never were—till now."

The echo of his hidden thought made it easier for him to go on.

"It was at Long Barton," he said,—"it's a little dead and alive place in Kent. I was painting that picture that you like—the one that's in the Salon, and I was bored to death, and she walked straight into the composition in a pink gown that made her look like a La France rose that has been rained on—you know the sort of pink-turning-to-mauve."

"And it was love at first sight?" said she, and took away her hand.

"Not it," said Vernon, catching the hand and holding it; "it was just the usual thing. I wanted it to be like all the others."

"Like mine," she said, looking down on him.

"Nothing could be like *that*," he had the grace to say, looking up at her: "that was only like the others in one thing—that it couldn't last.—What am I thinking of to let you stand there?"

He got up and led her to the divan. They sat down side by side. She wanted to laugh, to sing, to scream. Here was he sitting by her like a lover—holding her hand, the first time these two years, three years nearly—his voice tender as ever. And he was telling her about Her.

"No," he went on, burrowing his shoulder comfortably in the cushions, "it was just the ordinary outline sketch. But it was coming very nicely. She was beginning to be interested, and I had taught myself almost all that was needed—I didn't want to marry her; I didn't want anything except those delicate delightful emotions that come before one is quite, quite sure that she—But you know."

"Yes," she said. "I know."

"Then her father interfered, and vulgarized the whole thing.

He's a parson—a weak little rat, but I was sorry for him. Then an aunt came on the scene—a most gentlemanly lady,"—he laughed a little at the recollection,—"and I promised not to go out of my way to see Her again. It was quite easy. The bloom was already brushed from the adventure. I finished the picture, and went to Brittany and forgot the whole silly business."

"There was some one in Brittany, of course?"

"Of course," said he; "there always is. I had a delightful summer. Then in October, sitting at the Cafe de la Paix, I saw her pass. It was the same day I saw you."

"Before or after you saw me?"

"After."

"Then if I'd stopped—if I'd made you come for a drive then and there, you'd never have seen her?"

"That's so," said Vernon; "and by Heaven I almost wish you had!"

The wish was a serpent in her heart. She said: "Go on."

And he went on, and, warming to his subject, grew eloquent on the events of the winter, his emotions, his surmises as to Betty's emotions, his slow awakening to the knowledge that now, for the first time—and so on and so forth.

"You don't know how I tried to fall in love with you again," he said, and kissed her hand. "You're prettier than she is, and cleverer and a thousand times more adorable. But it's no good; it's a sort of madness."

"You never were in love with me."

"No: I don't think I was: but I was happier with you than I shall ever be with her for all that. Talk of the joy of love! Love

E. Nesbit

hurts—hurts damnably. I beg your pardon."

"Yes. I believe it's painful. Go on."

He went on. He was enjoying himself, now, thoroughly.

"And so," the long tale ended, "when I found she had scruples about going about with me alone—because her father had suggested that I was in love with her—I—I let her think that I was engaged to you."

"That is too much!" she cried and would have risen: but he kept her hand fast.

"Ah, don't be angry," he pleaded. "You see, I knew you didn't care about me a little bit: and I never thought you and she would come across each other."

"So you knew all the time that I didn't care?" her self-respect clutched at the spar he threw out.

"Of course. I'm not such a fool as to think—Ah, forgive me for letting her think that. It bought me all I cared to ask for of her time. She's so young, so innocent—she thought it was quite all right as long as I belonged to someone else, and couldn't make love to her."

"And haven't you?"

"Never—never once—since the days at Long Barton when it had to be 'made;' and even then I only made the very beginnings of it. Now—"

"I suppose you've been very, very happy?"

"Don't I tell you? I've never been so wretched in my life! I despise myself. I've always made everything go as I wanted it to go. Now I'm like a leaf in the wind—*Pauvre feuille desechee*, don't you know. And I hate it. And I hate her being here without anyone to look after her. A hundred times I've had it on the tip of my pen to send that doddering old Underwood an anonymous letter, telling him all about it."

"Underwood?"

"Her step-father.—Oh, I forgot—I didn't tell you." He proceeded to tell her Betty's secret, the death of Madame Gautier and Betty's bid for freedom.

"I see," she said slowly. "Well, there's no great harm done. But I wish you'd trusted me before. You wanted to know, at the beginning of this remarkable interview," she laughed rather forlornly, "what I had told Miss Desmond. Well, I went to see her, and when she told me that you'd told her you were engaged to me, I—I just acted the jealous a little bit. I thought I was helping you—playing up to you. I suppose I overdid it. I'm sorry."

"The question is," said he anxiously, "whether she'll forgive me for that lie. She's most awfully straight, you know."

"She seems to have lied herself," Lady St. Craye could not help saying.

"Ah, yes—but only to her father."

"That hardly counts, you think?"

"It's not the same thing as lying to the person you love. I wish—I wonder whether you'd mind if I never told her it was a lie? Couldn't I tell her that we were engaged but you've broken it off? That you found you liked Temple better, or something?"

She gasped before the sudden vision of the naked gigantic egotism of a man in love.

"You can tell her what you like," she said wearily: "a lie or two more or less—what does it matter?"

"I don't want to lie to her," said Vernon. "I hate to. But she'd never understand the truth."

"You think *I* understand? It *is* the truth you've been telling me?"

He laughed. "I don't think I ever told so much truth in all my life."

"And you've thoroughly enjoyed it! You alway did enjoy new sensations!"

"Ah, don't sneer at me. You don't understand—not quite. Everything's changed. I really do feel as though I'd been born again. The point of view has shifted—and so suddenly, so completely. It's a new Heaven and a new earth. But the new earth's not comfortable, and I don't suppose I shall ever get the new Heaven. But you'll help me—you'll advise me? Do you think I ought to tell her at once? You see, she's so different from other girls—she's—"

"She isn't," Lady St. Craye interrupted, "except that she's the one you love; she's not a bit different from other girls. No girl's different from other girls."

"Ah, you don't know her," he said. "You see, she's so young and brave and true and—what is it—Why—"

Lady St. Craye had rested her head against his coat-sleeve and he knew that she was crying.

"What is it? My dear, don't—you musn't cry."

"I'm not.—At least I'm very tired."

"Brute that I am!" he said with late compunction. "And I've been worrying you with all my silly affairs. Cheer up,—and smile at me before I go! Of course you're tired!"

His hand on her soft hair held her head against his arm.

"No," she said suddenly, "it isn't that I'm tired, really. You've told the truth,—why shouldn't I?" Vernon instantly and deeply regretted the lapse.

"You're really going to marry the girl? You mean it?"

"Yes."

"Then I'll help you. I'll do everything I can for you."

"You're a dear," he said kindly. "You always were."

"I'll be your true friend—oh, yes, I will! Because I love you, Eustace. I've always loved you—I always shall. It can't spoil anything now to tell you, because everything *is* spoilt. She'll never love you like I do. Nobody ever will."

"You're tired. I've bothered you. You're saying this just to—because—"

"I'm saying it because it's true. Why should you be the only one to speak the truth? Oh, Eustace—when you pretended to think I didn't care, two years ago, I was too proud to speak the truth then. I'm not proud now any more. Go away. I wish I'd never seen you; I wish I'd never been born."

"Yes, dear, yes. I'll go" he said, and rose. She buried her face in the cushion where his shoulder had been.

He was looking round for his hat and gloves—more uncomfortable than he ever remembered to have been.

As he reached the door she sprang up, and he heard the silken swish of her gray gown coming towards him.

"Say good-night," she pleaded. "Oh, Eustace, kiss me again—kindly, not like last time."

He met her half-way, took her in his arms and kissed her forehead very gently, very tenderly.

"My dearest Jasmine lady," he said, "it sounds an impertinence and I daresay you won't believe it, but I was never so sorry in my life as I am now. I'm a beast, and I don't deserve to live. Think what a beast I am—and try to hate me."

She, clung to him and laid her wet cheek against his. Then her lips implored his lips. There was a long silence. It was she—she was always glad of that—who at last found her courage, and drew back.

"Good-bye," she said. "I shall be quite sane to-morrow. And then I'll help you."

When he got out into the street he looked at his watch. It was not yet ten o'clock. He hailed a carriage.

"Fifty-seven Boulevard Montparnasse," he said.

He could still feel Lady St. Craye's wet cheek against his own. The despairing passion of her last kisses had thrilled him through and through.

He wanted to efface the mark of those kisses. He would not be haunted all night by any lips but Betty's.

He had never called at her rooms in the evening. He had been careful for her in that. Even now as he rang the bell he was careful, and when the latch clicked and the door was opened a cautious inch he was ready, as he entered, to call out, in passing the concierge's door not Miss Desmond's name, but the name of the Canadian artist who occupied the studio on the top floor.

He went softly up the stairs and stood listening outside Betty's door. Then he knocked gently. No one answered. Nothing stirred inside.

"She may be out," he told himself. "I'll wait a bit."

At the same time he tapped again; and this time beyond the door something did stir.

Then came Betty's voice:

"*Qui est là?*"

"It's me—Vernon. May I come in?"

A moment's pause. Then:

"No. You can't possibly. Is anything the matter?"

"No—oh, no, but I wanted so much to see you. May I come to-morrow early?"

"You're sure there's nothing wrong? At home or anything? You haven't come to break anything to me?"

"No—no; it's only something I wanted to tell you."

He began to feel a fool, with his guarded whispers through a locked door.

"Then come at twelve," said Betty in the tones of finality. "Good-night."

He heard an inner door close, and went slowly away. He walked a long way that night. It was not till he was back in his rooms and had lighted his candle and wound up his watch that Lady St. Craye's kisses began to haunt him in good earnest, as he had known they would.

*   *   *   *   *

Lady St. Craye, left alone, dried her eyes and set to work, with heart still beating wildly to look about her at the ruins of her world.

The room was quiet with the horrible quiet of a death chamber. And yet his voice still echoed in it. Only a moment ago she had been in his arms, as she had never hoped to be again—more—as she had never been before.

"He would have loved me now," she told herself, "if it hadn't been for that girl. He didn't love me before. He was only playing at love. He didn't know what love was. But he knows now. And it's all too late!"

But was it?

A word to Betty—and—

"But you promised to help him."

"That was before he kissed me."

"But a promise is a promise."

"Yes,—and your life's your life. You'll never have another."

She stood still, her hands hanging by her sides—clenched hands that the rings bit into.

"He will go to her early to-morrow. And she'll accept him, of course. She's never seen anyone else, the little fool."

She knew that she herself would have taken him, would have chosen him as the chief among ten thousand.

"She could have Temple. She'd be much happier with Temple. She and Eustace would make each other wretched. She'd never understand him, and he'd be tired of her in a week."

She had turned up the electric lights now, at her toilet table, and was pulling the pins out of her ruffled hair.

"And he'd never care about her children. And they'd be ugly little horrors."

She was twisting her hair up quickly and firmly.

"I *have* a right to live my own life," she said, just as Betty had said six months before. "Why am I to sacrifice everything to her—especially when I don't suppose she cares—and now that I know I could get him if she were out of the way?"

She looked at herself in the silver-framed mirror and laughed.

"And you always thought yourself a proud woman!"

Suddenly she dropped the brush; it rattled and spun on the polished floor.

She stamped her foot.

"That settles it!" she said. For in that instant she perceived quite clearly and without mistake that Vernon's attitude had been a parti-pris: that he had thrown, himself on her pity of set purpose, with an end to gain.

"Laughing at me all the time too, of course! And I thought I understood him. Well, I don't misunderstand him for long, anyway," she said, and picked up the hair brush.

"You silly fool," she said to the woman in the glass.

And now she was fully dressed—in long light coat and a hat with, as usual, violets in it. She paused a moment before her writing-table, turned up its light, turned it down again.

"No," she said, "one doesn't write anonymous letters. Besides it would be too late. He'll see her to-morrow early—early."

The door of the flat banged behind her as it had banged behind Vernon half an hour before. Like him, she called a carriage, and on her lips too, as the chill April air caressed them, was the sense of kisses.

And she, too, gave to the coachman the address:

Fifty-seven Boulevard Montparnasse.

CHAPTER XIX

THE TRUTH WITH A VENGEANCE

In those three weeks whose meetings with Vernon had been so lacking in charm there had been other meetings for Betty, and in these charm had not been to seek. But it was the charm of restful, pleasant companionship illuminated by a growing certainty that Mr. Temple admired her very much, that he liked her very much, that he did not think her untidy and countrified and ill-dressed, and all the things she had felt herself to be that night when Lady St. Craye and her furs had rustled up the staircase at Thirion's. And she had dined with Mr. Temple and lunched with Mr. Temple, and there had been an afternoon at St. Cloud, and a day at Versailles. Miss Voscoe and some of the other students had been in the party, but not of it as far as Betty was concerned. She had talked to Temple all the time.

"I'm glad to see you've taken my advice," said Miss Voscoe, "only you do go at things so—like a bull at a gate. A month ago it was all that ruffian Vernon. Now it's all Mr. Go-to-Hell. Why not have a change? Try a Pole or a German."

But Betty declined to try a Pole or a German.

What she wanted to do was to persuade herself that she liked Temple as much as she liked Vernon, and, further, that she did not care a straw for either.

Of course it is very wrong indeed to talk pleasantly with a young man when you think you know that he might, just possibly, be falling in love with you. But then it is very interesting, too. To be loved, even by the wrong person, seems in youth's selfish eyes to light up the world as the candle lights the Japanese lantern. And besides, after all, one can't be sure. And it is not maidenly to say "No," even by the vaguest movements of retreat, to a question that has not been asked and perhaps never will be.

And when she was talking to Temple she was not thinking so much of Vernon, and of her unselfish friendship for him, and the depth of her hope that he really *would* be happy with that woman.

So that it was with quite a sick feeling that her days had been robbed of something that made them easier to live, if not quite worth living, that she read and reread the letter that she found waiting for her after that last unsuccessful dinner with the man whom Temple helped her to forget.

You will see by the letter what progress friendship can make in a month between a young man and woman, even when each is half in love with some one else.

"Sweet friend," said the letter: "This is to say good-bye for a little while. But you will think of me when I am away, won't you? I am going into the country to make some sketches and to think. I don't believe it is possible for English people to think in Paris. And I have things to think over that won't let themselves be thought over quietly here. And I want to see the Spring. I won't ask you to write to me, because I want to be quite alone, and not to have even a word from my sweet and dear friend. I hope your work will go well.

"Yours,

"Robert Temple."

Betty, in bed, was re-reading this when Vernon's knock came at her door. She spoke to him through the door with the letter in her hand. And her real thought when she asked him if he had come to break bad news was that something had happened to Temple.

She went back to bed, but not to sleep. Try as she would, she could not keep away the wonder—what could Vernon have had to say that wanted so badly to get itself said? She hid her eyes and would not look in the face of her hope. There had been a tone in his voice as he whispered on the other side of that stupid door, a tone she had not heard since Long Barton.

Oh, why had she gone to bed early that night of all nights? She would never go to bed early again as long as she lived!

What?—No, impossible! Yes. Another knock at her door. She sprang out of bed, and stood listening. There was no doubt about it. Vernon had come back. After all what he had to say would not keep till morning. A wild idea of dressing and letting him in was sternly dismissed. For one thing, at topmost speed, it took twenty minutes to dress. He would not wait twenty minutes. Another knock.

She threw on her dressing gown and ran along her little passage—and stooped to the key-hole just as another tap, discreet but insistent, rang on the door panel.

"Go away," she said low and earnestly. "I can't talk to you to-night *whatever it is*. It must wait till the morning."

"It's I," said the very last voice in all Paris that she expected to hear, "it's Lady St. Craye.—Won't you let me in?"

"Are you alone?" said Betty.

"Of course I'm alone. It's most important. Do open the door."

The door was slowly opened. The visitor rustled through, and

Betty shut the door. Then she followed Lady St. Craye into the sitting-room, lighted the lamp, drew the curtain across the clear April night, and stood looking enquiry—and not looking it kindly. Her lips were set in a hard line and she was frowning.

She waited for the other to speak, but after all it was she who broke the silence.

"Well," she said, "what do you want now?"

"I hardly know how to begin," said Lady St. Craye with great truth.

"I should think not!" said Betty. "I don't want to be disagreeable, but I can't think of anything that gives you the right to come and knock me up like this in the middle of the night."

"It's only just past eleven," said Lady St. Craye. And there was another silence. She did not know what to say. A dozen openings suggested themselves, and were instantly rejected. Then, quite suddenly, she knew exactly what to say, what to do. That move of Vernon's—it was a good one, a move too often neglected in this cynical world, but always successful on the stage.

"May I sit down?" she asked forlornly.

Betty, rather roughly, pushed forward a chair.

Lady St. Craye sank into it, looked full at Betty for a long minute; and by the lamp's yellow light Betty saw the tears rise, brim over and fall from the other woman's lashes. Then Lady St. Craye pulled out her handkerchief and began to cry in good earnest.

It was quite easy.

At first Betty looked on in cold contempt. Lady St. Craye had counted on that: she let herself go, wholly. If it ended in hysterics so much the more impressive. She thought of Vernon, of all the hopes of these months, of the downfall of them—everything that should make it impossible for her to stop crying.

"Don't distress yourself," said Betty, very chill and distant.

"Can you—can you lend me a handkerchief?" said the other unexpectedly, screwing up her own drenched cambric in her hand.

Betty fetched a handkerchief.

"I haven't any scent," she said. "I'm sorry."

That nearly dried the tears—but not quite: Lady St. Craye was a persevering woman.

Betty watching her, slowly melted, just as the other knew she would. She put her hand at last on the shoulder of the light coat.

"Come," she said, "don't cry so. I'm sure there's nothing to be so upset about—"

Then came to her sharp as any knife, the thought of what there might be.

"There's nothing wrong with anyone? There hasn't been an accident or anything?"

The other, still speechless, conveyed "No."

"Don't," said Betty again. And slowly and very artistically the flood was abated. Lady St. Craye was almost calm, though still her breath caught now and then in little broken sighs.

"I *am* so sorry," she said, "so ashamed.—Breaking down like

E. Nesbit

this. You don't know what it is to be as unhappy as I am."

Betty thought she did. We all think we do, in the presence of any grief not our own.

"Can I do anything?" She spoke much more kindly than she had expected to speak.

"Will you let me tell you everything? The whole truth?"

"Of course if you want to, but—"

"Then do sit down—and oh, don't be angry with me, I am so wretched. Just now you thought something had happened to Mr. Vernon. Will you just tell me one thing?—Do you love him?"

"You've no right to ask me that."

"I know I haven't. Well, I'll trust you—though you don't trust me. I'll tell you everything. Two years ago Mr. Vernon and I were engaged."

This was not true; but it took less time to tell than the truth would have taken, and sounded better.

"We were engaged, and I was very fond of him. But he—you know what he is about Women?"

"No," said Betty steadily. "I don't want to hear anything about him."

"But you must.—He is—I don't know how to put it. There's always some woman besides the One with him. I understand that now; I didn't then. I don't think he can help it. It's his temperament."

"I see," said Betty evenly. Her hands and feet were very cold. She was astonished to find how little moved she was in this interview whose end she foresaw so very plainly.

"Yes, and there was a girl at that time—he was always about with her. And I made him scenes—always a most stupid thing to do with a man, you know; and at last I said he must give her up, or give me up. And he gave me up. And I was too proud to let him think I cared—and just to show him how little I cared I married Sir Harry St. Craye. I might just as well have let it alone. He never even heard I had been married till last October! And then it was I who told him. My husband was a brute, and I'm thankful to say he didn't live long. You're very much shocked, I'm afraid?"

"Not at all," said Betty, who was, rather.

"Well, then I met Him again, and we got engaged again, as he told you. And again there was a girl—oh, and another woman besides. But this time I tried to bear it—you know I did try not to be jealous of you."

"You had no cause," said Betty.

"Well, I thought I had. That hurts just as much. And what's the end of it all—all my patience and trying not to see things, and letting him have his own way? He came to me to-night and begged me to release him from his engagement, because— oh, he was beautifully candid—because he meant to marry you."

Betty's heart gave a jump.

"He seems to have been very sure of me," she said loftily.

"No, no; he's not a hairdresser's apprentice—to tell one woman that he's sure of another. He said: 'I mean to marry Miss Desmond if she'll have me.'"

"How kind of him!"

"I wish you'd heard the way he spoke of you."

"I don't want to hear."

"*I* had to. And I've released him. And now I've come to you. I was proud two years ago. I'm not proud now. I don't care what I do. I'll kneel down at your feet and pray to you as if you were God not to take him away from me. And if you love him it'll all be no good. I know that."

"But—supposing I weren't here—do you think you could get him back?"

"I know I could. Unless of course you were to tell him I'd been here to-night. I should have no chance after that—naturally. I wish I knew what to say to you. You're very young; you'll find someone else, a better man. He's not a good man. There's a girl at Montmartre at this very moment—a girl he's set up in a restaurant. He goes to see her. You'd never stand that sort of thing. I know the sort of girl you are. And you're quite right. But I've got beyond that. I don't care what he is, I don't care what he does. I understand him. I can make allowances for him. I'm his real mate. I could make him happy. You never would—you're too good. Ever since I first met him I've thought of nothing else, cared for nothing else. If he whistled to me I'd give up everything else, everything, and follow him barefoot round the world."

"I heard someone say that in a play once," said Betty musing.

"So did I," said Lady St. Craye very sharply—"but it's true for all that. Well—you can do as you like."

"Of course I can," said Betty.

"I've done all I can now. I've said everything there is to say. And if you love him as I love him every word I've said won't make a scrap of difference. I know that well enough. What I want to know is—*do* you love him?"

The scene had been set deliberately. But the passion that spoke in it was not assumed. Betty felt young, school-girlish, awkward in the presence of this love—so different from her own timid dreams. The emotion of the other woman had softened her.

"I don't know," she said.

"If you don't know, you don't love him.—At least don't see him till you're sure. You'll do that? As long as he's not married to anyone, there's just a chance that he may love me again. Won't you have pity? Won't you go away like that sensible young man Temple? Mr. Vernon told me he was going into the country to decide which of the two women he likes best is the one he really likes best! Won't you do that?"

"Yes," said Betty slowly, "I'll do that. *Look* here, I am most awfully sorry, but I don't know—I can't think to-night. I'll go right away—I won't see him to-morrow. Oh, no. I can't come between you and the man you're engaged to," her thoughts were clearing themselves as she spoke. "Of course I knew you were engaged to him. But I never thought. At least—Yes. I'll go away the first thing to-morrow."

"You are very, very good," said Lady St. Craye, and she meant it.

"But I don't know where to go. Tell me where to go."

"Can't you go home?"

"No: I won't. That's too much."

"Go somewhere and sketch."

"Yes,—but *where?*" said poor Betty impatiently.

"Go to Grez," said the other, not without second thoughts. "It's a lovely place—close to Fontainebleau—Hotel Chevillon.

I'll write it down for you.—Old Madame Chevillon's a darling. She'll look after you. It *is* good of you to forgive me for everything. I'm afraid I was a cat to you."

"No," said Betty, "it was right and brave of you to tell me the whole truth. Oh, truth's the only thing that's any good!"

Lady St. Craye also thought it a useful thing—in moderation. She rose.

"I'll never forget what you're doing for me," she said. "You're a girl in thousand. Look here, my dear: I'm not blind. Don't think I don't value what you're doing. You cared for him in England a little,—and you care a little now. And everything I've said tonight has hurt you hatefully. And you didn't know you cared. You thought it was friendship, didn't you—till you thought I'd come to tell you that something had happened to him. And then you *knew*. I'm going to accept your sacrifice. I've got to. I can't live if I don't. But I don't want you to think I don't know what a sacrifice it is. I know better than you do—at this moment. No—don't say anything. I don't want to force your confidence. But I do understand."

"I wish everything was different," said Betty.

"Yes. You're thinking, aren't you, that if it hadn't been for Mr. Vernon you'd rather have liked me? And I know now that if it hadn't been for him I should have been very fond of you. And even as it is—"

She put her arms round Betty and spoke close to her ear.

"You're doing more for me than anyone has ever done for me in my life," she said—"more than I'd do for you or any woman. And I love you for it. Dear brave little girl. I hope it isn't going to hurt very badly. I love you for it—and I'll never forget it to the day I die. Kiss me and try to forgive me."

The two clung together for an instant.

"Good-bye," said Lady St. Craye in quite a different voice. "I'm sorry I made a scene. But, really, sometimes I believe one isn't quite sane. Let me write the Grez address. I wish I could think of any set of circumstances in which you'd be pleased to see me again."

"I'll pack to-night," said Betty. "I hope *you'll* be happy anyway. Do you know I think I have been hating you rather badly without quite knowing it."

"Of course you have," said the other heartily, "but you don't now. Of course you won't leave your address here? If you do that you might as well not go away at all!"

"I'm not quite a fool," said Betty.

"No," said the other with a sigh, "it's I that am the fool. You're—No, I won't say what you are. But—Well. Good night, dear. Try not to hate me again when you come to think it all over quietly."

CHAPTER XX

WAKING-UP TIME

Dear Mr. Vernon. This is to thank you very much for all your help and criticism of my work, and to say good-bye. I am called away quite suddenly, so I can't thank you in person, but I shall never forget your kindness. Please remember me to Lady St. Craye. I suppose you will be married quite soon now. And I am sure you will both be very happy.

Yours very sincerely,

Elizabeth Desmond.

This was the letter that Vernon read standing in the shadow of the arch by the concierge's window. The concierge had hailed him as he hurried through to climb the wide shallow stairs and to keep his appointment with Betty when she should leave the atelier.

"But yes, Mademoiselle had departed this morning at nine o'clock. To which station? To the Gare St. Lazare. Yes—Mademoiselle had charged her to remit the billet to Monsieur. No, Mademoiselle had not left any address. But perhaps chez Madame Bianchi?"

But chez Madame Bianchi there was no further news. The so amiable Mademoiselle Desmond had paid her account, had embraced Madame, and—Voila! she was gone. One divined that she had been called suddenly to return to the family roof. A sudden illness of Monsieur her father without doubt.

Could some faint jasmine memory have lingered on the staircase? Or was it some subtler echo of Lady St. Craye's personality that clung there? Abruptly, as he passed Betty's door, the suspicion stung him. Had the Jasmine lady had any hand in this sudden departure?

"Pooh—nonsense!" he said. But all the same he paused at the concierge's window.

"I am desolated to have deranged Madame,"—gold coin changed hands.—"A lady came to see Mademoiselle this morning, is it not?"

"No, no lady had visited Mademoiselle to-day: no one at all in effect."

"Nor last night—very late?"

"No, monsieur," the woman answered meaningly; "no visitor came in last night except Monsieur himself and he came, not to see Mademoiselle, that understands itself, but to see Monsieur Beauchesne an troisieme. No—I am quite sure—I never deceive myself. And Mademoiselle has had no letters since three days. Thanks a thousand times, Monsieur. Good morning."

She locked up the gold piece in the little drawer where already lay the hundred franc note that Lady St. Craye had given her at six o'clock that morning.

"And there'll be another fifty from her next month," she chuckled. "The good God be blessed for intrigues! Without intrigues what would become of us poor concierges?"

For Vernon Paris was empty—the spring sunshine positively

distasteful. He did what he could; he enquired at the Gare St. Lazare, describing Betty with careful detail that brought smiles to the lips of the employes. He would not call on Miss Voscoe. He made himself wait till the Sketch Club afternoon—made himself wait, indeed, till all the sketches were criticised—till the last cup of tea was swallowed, or left to cool—the last cake munched—the last student's footfall had died away on the stairs, and he and Miss Voscoe were alone among the scattered tea-cups, blackened bread-crumbs and torn paper.

Then he put his question. Miss Voscoe knew nothing. Guessed Miss Desmond knew her own business best.

"But she's so young," said Vernon; "anything might have happened to her."

"I reckon she's safe enough—where she is," said Miss Voscoe with intention.

"But haven't you any idea why she's gone?" he asked, not at all expecting any answer but "Not the least."

But Miss Voscoe said:

"I have a quite first-class idea and so have you."

He could but beg her pardon interrogatively.

"Oh, you know well enough," said she. "She'd got to go. And it was up to her to do it right now, I guess."

Vernon had to ask why.

"Well, you being engaged to another girl, don't you surmise it might kind of come home to her there were healthier spots for you than the end of her apron strings? Maybe she thought the other lady's apron strings 'ud be suffering for a little show?"

"I'm not engaged," said Vernon shortly.

"Then it's time you were," the answer came with equal shortness. "You'll pardon me making this a heart-to-heart talk—and anyway it's no funeral of mine. But she's the loveliest girl and I right down like her. So you take it from me. That F.F.V. Lady with the violets—Oh, don't pretend you don't know who I mean—the one you're always about with when you aren't with Betty. *She's* your ticket. Betty's not. Your friend's her style. You pass, this hand, and give the girl a chance."

"I really don't understand—"

"I bet you do," she interrupted with conviction. "I've sized you up right enough, Mr. Vernon. You're no fool. If you've discontinued your engagement Betty doesn't know it. Nor she shan't from me. And one of these next days it'll be borne in on your friend that she's *the* girl of his life—and when he meets her again he'll get her to see it his way. Don't you spoil the day's fishing."

Vernon laughed.

"You have all the imagination of the greatest nation in the world, Miss Voscoe," he said. "Thank you. These straight talks to young men are the salt of life. Good-bye."

"You haven't all the obfuscation of the stupidest nation in the world," she retorted. "If you had had you'd have had a chance to find out what straight talking means—which it's my belief you never have yet. Good-bye. You take my tip. Either you go back to where you were before you sighted Betty, or if the other one's sick of you too, just shuffle the cards, take a fresh deal and start fair. You go home and spend a quiet evening and think it all over."

Vernon went off laughing, and wondering why he didn't hate Miss Voscoe. He did not laugh long. He sat in his studio, musing till it was too late to go out to dine. Then he found some biscuits and sherry—remnants of preparations for the

E. Nesbit

call of a picture dealer—ate and drank, and spent the evening in the way recommended by Miss Voscoe. He lay face downward on the divan, in the dark, and he did "think it all over."

But first there was the long time when he lay quite still—did not think at all, only remembered her hands and her eyes and her hair, and the pretty way her brows lifted when she was surprised or perplexed—and the four sudden sweet dimples that came near the corners of her mouth when she was amused, and the way her mouth drooped when she was tired.

"I want you. I want you. I want you," said the man who had been the Amorist. "I want you, dear!"

When he did begin to think, he moved uneasily in the dark as thought after thought crept out and stung him and slunk away. The verses he had written at Long Barton—ironic verses, written with the tongue in the cheek—came back with the force of iron truth:

"I love you to my heart's hid core:
Those other loves? How can one learn
From marshlights how the great fires burn?
Ah, no—I never loved before!"

He had smiled at Temple's confidences—when Betty was at hand—to be watched and guarded. Now Betty was away—anywhere. And Temple was deciding whether it was she whom he loved. Suppose he did decide that it was she, and, as Miss Voscoe had said, made her see it? "Damn," said Vernon, "Oh, damn!"

He was beginning to be a connoisseur in the fine flavours of the different brands of jealousy. Anyway there was food for thought.

There was food for little else, in the days that followed. Mr. Vernon's heart, hungry for the first time, had to starve. He

The Incomplete Amorist 269

went often to Lady St. Craye's. She was so gentle, sweet, yet not too sympathetic—bright, amusing even, but not too vivacious. He approved deeply the delicacy with which she ignored that last wild interview. She was sister, she was friend—and she had the rare merit of seeming to forget that she had been confidante.

It was he who re-opened the subject, after ten days. She had told herself that it was only a question of time. And it was.

"Do you know she's disappeared?" he said abruptly.

"*Disappeared?*" No one was ever more astonished than Lady St. Craye. Quite natural, the astonishment. Not overdone by so much as a hair's breadth.

So he told her all about it, and she twisted her long topaz chain and listened with exactly the right shade of interest. He told her what Miss Voscoe had said—at least most of it.

"And I worry about Temple," he said; "like any school boy, I worry. If he *does* decide that he loves her better than you—You said you'd help me. Can't you make sure that he won't love her better?"

"I could, I suppose," she admitted. To herself she said: "Temple's at Grez. *She's* at Grez. They've been there ten days."

"If only you would," he said. "It's too much to ask, I know. But I can't ask anything that isn't too much! And you're so much more noble and generous than other people—"

"No butter, thanks," she said.

"It's the best butter," he earnestly urged. "I mean that I mean it. Won't you?"

"When I see him again—but it's not very fair to him, is it?"

"He's an awfully good chap, you know," said Vernon innocently. And once more Lady St. Craye bowed before the sublime apparition of the Egoism of Man.

"Good enough for me, you think? Well, perhaps you're right. He's a dear boy. One would feel very safe if one loved a man like that."

"Yes—wouldn't one?" said Vernon.

She wondered whether Betty was feeling safe. No: ten days are a long time, especially in the country—but it would take longer than that to cure even a little imbecile like Betty of the Vernon habit. It was worse than opium. Who ought to know if not she who sat, calm and sympathetic, promising to entangle Temple so as to leave Betty free to become a hopeless prey to the fell disease?

Quite suddenly and to her own intense surprise, she laughed out loud.

"What is it?" his alert vanity bristled in the query.

"It's nothing—only everything! Life's so futile! We pat and pinch our little bit of clay, and look at it and love it and think it's going to be a masterpiece.—and then God glances at it—and He doesn't like the modelling, and He sticks his thumb down, and the whole thing's broken up, and there's nothing left to do but throw away the bits."

"Oh, no," said Vernon; "everything's bound to come right in the end. It all works out straight somehow."

She laughed again.

"Optimism—from you?"

"It's not optimism," he asserted eagerly, "it's only—well, if everything doesn't come right somehow, somewhere, some day, what did He bother to make the world for?"

"That's exactly what I said, my dear," said she. She permitted herself the little endearment now and then with an ironical inflection, as one fearful of being robbed might show a diamond pretending that it was paste.

"You think He made it for a joke?"

"If He did it's a joke in the worst possible taste," said she, "but I see your point of view. There can't be so very much wrong with a world that has Her in it,—and you—and possibilities."

"Do you know," he said slowly, "I'm not at all sure that—Do you remember the chap in Jane Eyre?—he knew quite well that that Rosamund girl wouldn't make him the wife he wanted. Yet he wanted nothing else. I don't want anything but her; and it doesn't make a scrap of difference that I know exactly what sort of fool I am."

"A knowledge of anatomy doesn't keep a broken bone from hurting," said she, "and all even you know about love won't keep off the heartache. I could have told you that long ago."

"I know I'm a fool," he said, "but I can't help it. Sometimes I think I wouldn't help it if I could."

"I know," she said, and something in her voice touched the trained sensibilities of the Amorist. He stooped to kiss the hand that teased the topazes.

"Dear Jasmine Lady," he said, "my optimism doesn't keep its colour long, does it? Give me some tea, won't you? There's nothing so wearing as emotion."

She gave him tea.

"It's a sort of judgment on you, though," was what she gave him with his first cup: "you've dealt out this very thing to so

E. Nesbit

many women,—and now it's come home to roost."

"I didn't know what a fearful wildfowl it was," he answered smiling. "I swear I didn't. I begin to think I never knew anything at all before."

"And yet they say Love's blind."

"And so he is! That's just it. My exotic flower of optimism withers at your feet. It's all exactly the muddle you say it is. Pray Heaven for a clear way out! Meantime thank whatever gods may be—I've got *you*."

"Monsieur's confidante is always at his distinguished service," she said. And thus sealed the fountain of confidences for that day.

But it broke forth again and again in the days that came after. For now he saw her almost every day. And for her, to be with him, to know that she had of him more of everything, save the heart, than any other woman, spelled something wonderfully like happiness. More like it than she had the art to spell in any other letters.

Vernon still went twice a week to the sketch-club. To have stayed away would have been to confess, to the whole alert and interested class, that he had only gone there for the sake of Betty.

Those afternoons were seasons of salutary torture.

He tried very hard to work, but, though he still remembered how a paint brush should be handled, there seemed no good reason for using one. He had always found his planned and cultivated emotions strongly useful in forwarding his work. This undesired unrest mocked at work, and at all the things that had made up the solid fabric of one's days. The ways of love—he had called it love; it was a name like another—had merely been a sort of dram-drinking. Such love was the intoxicant necessary to transfigure life to the point where all things, even work, look beautiful. Now he tasted the real draught. It flooded his veins like fire and stung like poison. And it made work, and all things else, look mean and poor and unimportant.

"I want you—I want you—I want you," said Vernon to the vision with the pretty kitten face, and the large gray eyes. "I want you more than everything in the world," he said, "everything in the world put together. Oh, come back to me—dear, dear, dear."

He was haunted without cease by the little poem he had written when he was training himself to be in love with Betty:

"I love you to my heart's hid core:
Those other loves? How should one learn
From marshlights how the great fires burn?
Ah, no—I never loved before!"

"Prophetic, I suppose," he said, "though God knows I never meant it. Any fool of a prophet must hit the bull's eye at least once in a life. But there was a curious unanimity of prophecy about this. The aunt warned me; that Conway woman warned me; the Jasmine Lady warned me. And now it's happened," he told himself. "And I who thought I knew all about everything!"

Miss Conway's name, moving through his thoughts, left the trail of a new hope.

Next day he breakfasted at Montmartre.

The neatest little Cremerie; white paint, green walls stenciled with fat white geraniums. On each small table a vase of green Bruges ware or Breton pottery holding not a crushed crowded bouquet, but one single flower—a pink tulip, a pink carnation, a pink rose. On the desk from behind which the Proprietress ruled her staff, enormous pink peonies in a tall pot of Grez de Flandre.

Behind the desk Paula Conway, incredibly neat and business-like, her black hair severely braided, her plain black gown fitting a figure grown lean as any grey-hound's, her lace collar a marvel of fine laundry work.

Dapper-waisted waitresses in black, with white aprons, served the customers. Vernon was served by Madame herself. The clientele formed its own opinion of the cause of this, her only such condescension.

"Well, and how's trade?" he asked over his asparagus.

"Trade's beautiful," Paula answered, with the frank smile that Betty had seen, only once or twice, and had loved very much: "if trade will only go on behaving like this for another six weeks my cruel creditor will be paid every penny of the money that launched me."

Her eyes dwelt on him with candid affection.

"Your cruel creditor's not in any hurry," he said. "By the way, I suppose you've not heard anything of Miss Desmond?"

"How could I? You know you made me write that she wasn't to write."

"I didn't *make* you write anything."

"You approved. But anyway she hasn't my address. Why?"

"She's gone away: and she also has left no address."

"You don't think?—Oh, no—nothing *could* have happened to her!"

"No, no," he hastened to say. "I expect her father sent for her, or fetched her."

"The best thing too," said Paula. "I always wondered he let her come."

"Yes,"—Vernon remembered how little Paula knew.

"Oh, yes, she's probably gone home."

"Look here," said Miss Conway very earnestly; "there wasn't any love business between you and her, was there?"

"No," he answered strongly.

"I was always afraid of that. Do you know—if you don't mind, when I've really paid my cruel creditor everything, I should like to write and tell her what he's done for me. I should like her to know that she really *did* save me—and how. Because if it hadn't been for her you'd never have thought of helping me. Do you think I might?"

"It could do no harm," said Vernon after a silent moment. "You'd really like her to know you're all right. You *are* all right?"

"I'm right; as I never thought I could be ever again."

"Well, you needn't exaggerate the little services of your cruel creditor. Come to think of it, you needn't name him. Just say it was a man you knew."

But when Paula came to write the letter that was not just what she said.

BOOK 4

THE OTHER MAN

CHAPTER XXI

THE FLIGHT

The full sunlight streamed into the room when Betty, her packing done, drew back the curtain. She looked out on the glazed roof of the laundry, the lead roof of the office, the blank wall of the new grocery establishment in the Rue de Rennes. Only a little blue sky shewed at the end of the lane, between roofs, by which the sun came in. Not a tree, not an inch of grass, in sight; only, in her room, half a dozen roses that Temple had left for her, and the white marguerite plant—tall, sturdy, a little tree almost—that Vernon had sent in from the florist's next door but two. Everything was packed. She would say good-bye to Madame Bianchi; and she would go, and leave no address, as she had promised last night.

"Why did you promise?" she asked herself. And herself replied:

"Don't you bother. We'll talk about all that when we've got away from Paris. He was quite right. You can't think here."

"You'd better tell the cabman some other station. That cat of a concierge is sure to be listening."

"Ah, right. I don't want to give him any chance of finding me, even if he did say he wanted to marry me."

A fleet lovely picture of herself in bridal smart travelling clothes arriving at the Rectory on Vernon's arm:

"Aren't you sorry you misjudged him so, Father?" Gentle accents refraining from reproach. A very pretty picture. Yes. Dismissed.

Now the carriage swaying under the mound of Betty's luggage starts for the Gare du Nord. In the Rue Notre Dame des Champs Betty opens her mouth to say, "Gare de Lyons." No: this is *his* street. Better cross it as quickly as may be. At the Church of St. Germain—yes.

The coachman smiles at the new order: like the concierge he scents an intrigue, whips up his horse, and swings round to the left along the prettiest of all the boulevards, between the full-leafed trees. Past Thirion's. Ah!

That thought, or pang, or nausea—Betty doesn't quite know what it is—keeps her eyes from the streets till the carriage is crossing the river. Why—there is Notre Dame! It ought to be miles away. Suppose Vernon should have been leaning out of his window when she passed across the street, seen her, divined her destination, followed her in the fleetest carriage accessible? The vision of a meeting at the station:

"Why are you going away? What have I done?" The secret of this, her great renunciation—the whole life's sacrifice to that life's idol—honor, wrung from her. A hand that would hold hers—under pretence of taking her bundle of rugs to carry.— She wished the outermost rug were less shabby! Vernon's voice.

"But I can't let you go. Why ruin two lives—nay, three? For it is you only that I—"

Dismissed.

It is very hot. Paris is the hottest place in the world. Betty is glad she brought lavender water in her bag. Wishes she had put on her other hat. This brown one is hot; and besides, if Vernon *were* to be at the station. Interval. Dismissed.

Betty has never before made a railway journey alone. This gives one a forlorn feeling. Suppose she has to pay excess on her luggage, or to wrangle about contraband? She has heard all about the Octroi. Is lavender water smuggling? And what can they do to you for it? Vernon would know all these things. And if he were going into the country he would be wearing that almost-white rough suit of his and the Panama hat. A rose—Madame Abel de Chatenay—would go well with that coat. Why didn't brides consult their bridegrooms before they bought their trousseaux? You should get your gowns to rhyme with your husband's suits. A dream of a dress that would be, with all the shades of Madame Abel cunningly blended. A honeymoon lasts at least a month. The roses would all be out at Long Barton by the time they walked up that moss-grown drive, and stood at the Rectory door, and she murmured in the ear of the Reverend Cecil: "Aren't you sorry you—"

Dismissed. And perforce, for the station was reached.

Betty, even in the brown hat, attracted the most attractive of the porters—also, of course, the most attractable. He thought he spoke English, and though this was not so, yet the friendly blink of his Breton-blue eyes and his encouraging smile gave to his:

"Bourron? Mais oui—dix heures vingt. Par ici, Meess. Je m'occuperai de vous. Et des bagages aussi—all right," quite the ring of one's mother tongue.

He made everything easy for Betty, found her a carriage without company ("I can cry here if I like," said the Betty that Betty liked least), arranged her small packages neatly in the rack, took her 50 centime piece as though it had been a priceless personal souvenir, and ran half the length of the platform to get a rose from another porter's button-hole. He handed it to her through the carriage window.

"*Pour egayer le voyage de Meess.* All right!" he smiled, and was gone.

She settled herself in the far corner, and took off her hat. The carriage was hot as any kitchen. With her teeth she drew the cork of the lavender water bottle, and with her handkerchief dabbed the perfume on forehead and ears.

"Ah, Mademoiselle—*De grace!*"—the voice came through the open window beside her. A train full of young soldiers was beside her train, and in the window opposite hers three boys' faces crowded to look at her. Three hands held out three handkerchiefs—not very white certainly, but—

Betty smiling reached out the bottle and poured lavender water on each outheld handkerchief.

"*Ah, le bon souvenir!*" said one.

"We shall think of the beauty of an angel of Mademoiselle very time we smell the perfume so delicious," said the second.

"And longer than that—oh, longer than that by all a life!" cried the third.

The train started. The honest, smiling boy faces disappeared. Instinctively she put her head out of the window to look back at them. All three threw kisses at her.

"I ought to be offended," said Betty, and instantly kissed her hand in return.

"How *nice* French people are!" she said as she sank back on the hot cushions.

And now there was leisure to think—real thoughts, not those broken, harassing dreamings that had buzzed about her between 57 Boulevard Montparnasse and the station. Also, as some one had suggested, one could cry.

She leaned back, eyes shut. Her next thought was:

"I have been to sleep."

She had. The train was moving out of a station labelled Fontainebleau.

"And oh, the trees!" said Betty, "the green thick trees! And the sky. You can see the sky."

Through the carriage window she drank delight from the far grandeur of green distances, the intimate beauty of green rides, green vistas, as a thirsty carter drinks beer from the cool lip of his can—a thirsty lover madness from the warm lips of his mistress.

"Oh, how good! How green and good!" she told herself over and over again till the words made a song with the rhythm of the blundering train and the humming metals.

"Bourron!"

Her station. Little, quiet, sunlit, like the station at Long Barton; a flaming broom bush and the white of May and acacia blossom beyond prim palings; no platform—a long leap to the dusty earth. The train went on, and Betty and her boxes seemed dropped suddenly at the world's end.

The air was fresh and still. A chestnut tree reared its white blossoms like the candles on a Christmas tree for giant children. The white dust of the platform sparkled like diamond dust. May trees and laburnums shone like silver and gold. And the sun was warm and the tree-shadows black on the grass. And Betty loved it all.

"*Oh!*" she said suddenly, "it's a year ago to-day since I met *him*—in the warren."

A shadow caressed and stung her. She would have liked it to wear the mask of love foregone—to have breathed plaintively of hopes defeated and a broken heart. Instead it shewed the candid face of a real homesickness, and it spoke with convincing and abominably aggravating plainness—of Long Barton.

The little hooded diligence was waiting in the hot white dust outside the station.

"But yes.—It is I who transport all the guests of Madame Chevillon," said the smiling brown-haired bonnetless woman who held the reins.

Betty climbed up beside her.

Along a straight road that tall ranks of trees guarded but did not shade, through the patchwork neatness of the little culture that makes the deep difference between peasant France and pastoral England, down a steep hill into a little white town, where vines grew out of the very street to cling against the faces of the houses and wistaria hung its mauve pendants from every arch and lintel.

The Hotel Chevillon is a white-faced house, with little unintelligent eyes of windows, burnt blind, it seems, in the sun—neat with the neatness of Provincial France.

Out shuffled an old peasant woman in short skirt, heavy shoes and big apron, her arms bared to the elbow, a saucepan in one hand, a ladle in the other. She beamed at Betty.

"I wish to see Madame Chevillon."

"You see her, *ma belle et bonne*," chuckled the old woman. "It is me, Madame Chevillon. You will rooms, is it not? You are artist? All who come to the Hotel are artist. Rooms? Marie shall show you the rooms, at the instant even. All the rooms—except one—that is the room of the English Artist—all that there is of most amiable, but quite mad. He wears no hat, and his brain boils in the sun. Mademoiselle can chat with him: it will prevent that she bores herself here in the Forest."

E. Nesbit

Betty disliked the picture.

"I think perhaps," she said, translating mentally as she spoke, "that I should do better to go to another hotel, if there is only one man here and he is—"

She saw days made tiresome by the dodging of a lunatic—nights made tremulous by a lunatic's yelling soliloquies.

"Ah," said Madame Chevillon comfortably, "I thought Mademoiselle was artist; and for the artists and the Spaniards the *convenances* exist not. But Mademoiselle is also English. They eat the convenances every day with the soup.—See then, my cherished. The English man, he is not a dangerous fool, only a beast of the good God; he has the atelier and the room at the end of the corridor. But there is, besides the Hotel, the Garden Pavilion, un appartement of two rooms, exquisite, on the first, and the garden room that opens big upon the terrace. It is there that Mademoiselle will be well!"

Betty thought so too, when she had seen the "rooms exquisite on the first"—neat, bare, well-scrubbed rooms with red-tiled floors, scanty rugs and Frenchly varnished furniture—the garden room too, with big open hearth and no furniture but wicker chairs and tables.

"Mademoiselle can eat all alone on the terrace. The English mad shall not approach. I will charge myself with that. Mademoiselle may repose herself here as on the bosom of the mother of Mademoiselle."

Betty had her dejeuner on the little stone terrace with rickety rustic railings. Below lay the garden, thick with trees.

Away among the trees to the left an arbour. She saw through the leaves the milk-white gleam of flannels, heard the chink of china and cutlery. There, no doubt, the mad Englishman was even now breakfasting. There was the width of the garden between them. She sat still till the flannel gleam had gone away among the trees. Then she went out and explored the little town. She bought a blue packet of cigarettes. Miss Voscoe had often tried to persuade her to smoke. Most of the girls did. Betty had not wanted to do it any more for that. She had had a feeling that Vernon would not like her to smoke.

And in Paris one had to be careful. But now—

"I am absolutely my own master," she said. "I am staying by myself at a hotel, exactly like a man. I shall feel more at home if I smoke. And besides, no one can see me. It's just for me. And it shows I don't care what *he* likes."

Lying in a long chair reading one of her Tauchnitz books and smoking, Betty felt very manly indeed.

The long afternoon wore on. The trees of the garden crowded round Betty with soft whispers in a language not known of the trees on the boulevards.

"I am very very unhappy," said Betty with a deep sigh of delight.

She went in, unpacked, arranged everything neatly. She always arranged everything neatly, but nothing ever would stay arranged. She wrote to her father, explaining that Madame Gautier had brought her and the other girls to Grez for the summer, and she gave as her address:

Chez Madame Chevillon, Pavilion du Jardin, Grez.

"I shall be very very unhappy to-morrow," said Betty that night, laying her face against the coarse cool linen of her pillow; "to-day I have been stunned—I haven't been able to feel anything. But to-morrow."

To-morrow, she knew, would be golden and green even as to-day. But she should not care. She did not want to be happy. How could she be happy now that she had of her own free will put away the love of her life? She called and beckoned to all the thoughts that the green world shut out, and they came at her call, fluttering black wings to hide the sights and sounds of field and wood and green garden, and making their nest in her heart.

"Yes," she said, turning the hot rough pillow, "now it begins to hurt again. I knew it would."

It hurt more than she had meant it to hurt, when she beckoned those black-winged thoughts. It hurt so much that she could not sleep. She got up and leaned from the window.

She wondered where Vernon was. It was quite early. Not eleven. Lady St. Craye had called that quite early.

"He's with *her*, of course," said Betty, "sitting at her feet, no doubt, and looking up at her hateful eyes, and holding her horrid hand, and forgetting that he ever knew a girl named Me."

Betty dressed and went out.

She crossed the garden. It was very dark among the trees. It would be lighter in the road.

The big yard door was ajar. She pushed it softly. It creaked and let her through into the silent street. There were no lights in the hotel, no lights in any of the houses.

She stood a moment, hesitating. A door creaked inside the hotel. She took the road to the river.

"I wonder if people ever *do* drown themselves for love," said Betty: "he'd be sorry then."

CHAPTER XXII

THE LUNATIC

The night kept its promise. Betty, slipping from the sleeping house into the quiet darkness, seemed to slip into a poppy-fringed pool of oblivion. The night laid fresh, cold hands on her tired eyes, and shut out many things. She paused for a minute on the bridge to listen to the restful restless whisper of the water against the rough stone.

Her eyes growing used to the darkness discerned the white ribbon of road unrolling before her. The trees were growing thicker. This must be the forest. Certainly it was the forest.

"How dark it is," she said, "how dear and dark! And how still! I suppose the trams are running just the same along the Boulevard Montparnasse,—and all the lights and people, and the noise. And I've been there all these months—and all the time this was here—this!"

Paris was going on—all that muddle and maze of worried people. And she was out of it all; here, alone.

Alone? A quick terror struck at the heart of her content. An abrupt horrible certainty froze her—the certainty that she was not alone. There was some living thing besides herself in the forest, quite near her—something other than the deer and the squirrels and the quiet dainty woodland people. She felt it in every fibre long before she heard that faint light sound that was

E. Nesbit

not one of the forest noises. She stood still and listened.

She had never been frightened of the dark—of the outdoor dark. At Long Barton she had never been afraid even to go past the church-yard in the dark night—the free night that had never held any terrors, only dreams.

But now: she quickened her pace, and—yes—footsteps came on behind her. And in front the long straight ribbon of the road unwound, gray now in the shadow. There seemed to be no road turning to right or left. She could not go on forever. She would have to turn, sometime—if not now, yet some-time—in this black darkness, and then she would meet this thing that trod so softly, so stealthily behind her.

Before she knew that she had ceased to walk, she was crouched in the black between two bushes. She had leapt as the deer leaps, and crouched, still as any deer.

Her dark blue linen gown was one with the forest shadows. She breathed noiselessly—her eyes were turned to the gray ribbon of road that had been behind her. She had heard. Now she would see.

She did see—something white and tall and straight. Oh, the relief of the tallness and straightness and whiteness! She had thought of something dwarfed and clumsy—dark, misshapen, slouching beast-like on two shapeless feet. Why were people afraid of tall white ghosts?

It passed. It was a man—in a white suit. Just an ordinary man. No, not ordinary. The ordinary man in France does not wear white. Nor in England, except for boating and tennis and—

Flannels. Yes. The lunatic who boiled his brains in the sun!

Betty's terror changed colour as the wave changes from green to white, but it lost not even so much of its force as the wave loses by the change. It held her moveless till the soft step of the tennis shoes died away. Then softly and hardly moving at all, moving so little that not a leaf of those friendly bushes rustled, she slipped off her shoes: took them in her hand, made one leap through the crackling, protesting undergrowth and fled back along the road, fleet as a greyhound.

She ran and she walked, very fast, and then she ran again and never once did she pause to look or listen. If the lunatic caught her—well, he would catch her, but it should not be *her* fault if he did.

The trees were thinner. Ahead she saw glimpses of a world that looked quite light, the bridge ahead. With one last spurt she ran across it, tore up the little bit of street, slipped through the door, and between the garden trees to her pavilion.

She looked very carefully in every corner—all was still and empty. She locked the door, and fell face downward on her bed.

Vernon in his studio was "thinking things over" after the advice of Miss Voscoe in much the same attitude.

"Oh," said Betty, "I will never go out at night again! And I will leave this horrible, horrible place the very first thing to-morrow morning!"

But to-morrow morning touched the night's events with new colours from its shining palette.

"After all, even a lunatic has a right to walk out in the forest if it wants to," she told herself, "and it didn't know I was there, I expect, really. But I think I'll go and stay at some other hotel."

She asked, when her "complete coffee" came to her, what the mad gentleman did all day.

"He is not so stupid as Mademoiselle supposes," said Marie. "All the artists are insane, and he, he is only a little more

E. Nesbit

insane than the others. He is not a real mad, all the same, see you. To-day he makes drawings at Montigny."

"Which way is Montigny?" asked Betty. And, learning, strolled, when her coffee was finished, by what looked like the other way.

It took her to the river.

"It's like the Medway," said Betty, stooping to the fat cowslips at her feet, "only prettier; and I never saw any cowslips here— You dears!"

Betty would not look at her sorrow in this gay, glad world. But she knew at last what her sorrow's name was. She saw now that it was love that had stood all the winter between her and Vernon, holding a hand of each. In her blindness she had called it friendship,—but now she knew its real, royal name.

She felt that her heart was broken. Even the fact that her grief was a thing to be indulged or denied at will brought her no doubts. She had always wanted to be brave and noble. Well, now she was being both.

A turn of the river brought to sight a wide reach dotted with green islands, each a tiny forest of willow saplings and young alders.

There was a boat moored under an aspen, a great clumsy boat, but it had sculls in it. It would be pleasant to go out to the islands.

She got into the boat, loosened the heavy rattling chain and flung it in board, took up the sculls and began to pull. It was easy work.

"I didn't know I was such a good oar," said Betty as the boat crept swiftly down the river.

As she stepped into the boat, she noticed the long river reeds straining down stream like the green hair of hidden water-nixies.

She would land at the big island—the boat steered easily and lightly enough for all its size—but before she could ship her oars and grasp at a willow root she shot past the island.

Then she remembered the streaming green weeds.

"Why, there must be a frightful current!" she said. What could make the river run at this pace—a weir—or a waterfall?

She turned the boat's nose up stream and pulled. Ah, this was work! Then her eyes, fixed in the exertion of pulling, found that they saw no moving banks, but just one picture: a willow, a clump of irises, three poplars in the distance—and the foreground of the picture did not move. All her pulling only sufficed to keep the boat from going with the stream. And now, as the effort relaxed a little it did not even do this. The foreground did move—the wrong way. The boat was slipping slowly down stream. She turned and made for the bank, but the stream caught her broadside on, whirled the boat round and swept it calmly and gently down—towards the weir—or the waterfall.

Betty pulled two strong strokes, driving the boat's nose straight for the nearest island, shipped the sculls with a jerk, stumbled forward and caught at an alder stump. She flung the chain round it and made fast. The boat's stern swung round—it was thrust in under the bank and held there close; the chain clicked loudly as it stretched taut.

"Well!" said Betty. The island was between her and the riverside path. No one would be able to see her. She must listen and call out when she heard anyone pass. Then they would get another boat and come and fetch her away. She would not tempt fate again alone in that boat. She was not going to be drowned in any silly French river.

She landed, pushed through the saplings, found a mossy willow stump and sat down to get her breath.

It was very hot on the island. It smelt damply of wet lily leaves and iris roots and mud. Flies buzzed and worried. The time was very long. And no one came by.

"I may have to spend the day here," she told herself. "It's not so safe in the boat, but it's not so fly-y either."

And still no one passed.

Suddenly the soft whistling of a tune came through the hot air. A tune she had learned in Paris.

"*C'etait deux amants.*"

"Hi!" cried Betty in a voice that was not at all like her voice. "Help!—*Au secours!*" she added on second thoughts.

"Where are you?" came a voice. How alike all Englishmen's voices seemed—in a foreign land!

"Here—on the island! Send someone out with a boat, will you? I can't work my boat a bit."

Through the twittering leaves she saw something white waving. Next moment a big splash. She could see, through a little gap, a white blazer thrown down on the bank—a pair of sprawling brown boots; in the water a sleek wet round head, an arm in a blue shirt sleeve swimming a strong side stroke. It was the lunatic; of course it was. And she had called to him, and he was coming. She pushed back to the boat, leaped in, and was fumbling with the chain when she heard the splash and the crack of broken twigs that marked the lunatic's landing.

She would rather chance the weir or the waterfall than be alone on that island with a maniac. But the chain was stretched straight and stiff as a lance,—she could not untwist it. She was still struggling, with pink fingers bruised and rust-stained, when something heavy crashed through the saplings and a voice cried close to her:

"Drop it! What are you doing?"—and a hand fell on the chain.

Betty, at bay, raised her head. Lunatics, she knew, could be quelled by the calm gaze of the sane human eye.

She gave one look, and held out both hands with a joyous cry.

"Oh,—it's *you*! I *am* so glad! Where did you come from? Oh, how wet you are!"

Then she sat down on the thwart and said no more, because of the choking feeling in her throat that told her very exactly just how frightened she had been.

"You!" Temple was saying very slowly. "How on earth? Where are you staying? Where's your party?"

He was squeezing the water out of sleeves and trouser legs.

"I haven't got a party. I'm staying alone at a hotel—just like a man. I know you're frightfully shocked. You always are."

"Where are you staying?" he asked, drawing the chain in hand over hand, till a loose loop of it dipped in the water.

"Hotel Chevillon. How dripping you are!"

"Hotel Chevillon," he repeated. "Never! Then it was *you*!"

"What was me?"

"That I was sheep-dog to last night in the forest."

"Then it was *you*? And I thought it was the lunatic! Oh, if I'd only known! But why did you come after me—if you didn't know it *was* me?"

Temple blushed through the runnels of water that trickled from his hair.

"I—well, Madame told me there was an English girl staying at the hotel—and I heard some one go out—and I looked out of the window and I thought it was the girl, and I just—well, if anything had gone wrong—a drunken man, or anything—it was just as well there should be someone there, don't you know."

"That's very, very nice of you," said Betty. "But oh!"—She told him about the lunatic.

"Oh, that's me!" said Temple. "I recognise the portrait, especially about the hat."

He had loosened the chain and was pulling with strong even strokes across the river towards the bank where his coat lay.

"We'll land here if you don't mind."

"Can't you pull up to the place where I stole the boat?"

He laughed:

"The man's not living who could pull against this stream when the mill's going and the lower sluice gates are open. How glad I am that I—And how plucky and splendid of you not to lose your head, but just to hang on. It takes a lot of courage to wait, doesn't it?"

Betty thought it did.

"Let me carry your coat," said Betty as they landed. "You'll make it so wet."

He stood still a moment and looked at her.

"Now we're on terra cotta," he said, "let me remind you that we've not shaken hands. Oh, but it's good to see you again!"

*   *   *   *   *

"Look well, my child," said Madame Chevillon, "and when you see approach the Meess, warn me, that I may make the little omelette at the instant."

"Oh, la, la, madame!" cried Marie five minutes later. "Here it is that she comes, and the mad with her. He talks with her, in laughing. She carries his coat, and neither the one nor the other has any hat."

"I will make a double omelette," said Madame. "Give me still more of the eggs. The English are all mad—the one like the other; but even mads must eat, my child. Is it not?"

E. Nesbit

CHAPTER XXIII

TEMPERATURES

"It isn't as though she were the sort of girl who can't take care of herself," said Lady St. Craye to the Inward Monitor who was buzzing its indiscreet common-places in her ear. "I've really done her a good turn by sending her to Grez. No—it's not in the least compromising for a girl to stay at the same hotel. And besides, there are lots of amusing people there, I expect. She'll have a delightful time, and get to know that Temple boy really well. I'm sure he'd repay investigation. If I weren't a besotted fool I could have pursued those researches myself. But it's not what's worth having that one wants; it's—it's what one *does* want. Yes. That's all."

Paris was growing intolerable. But for—well, a thousand reasons—Lady St. Craye would already have left it. The pavements were red-hot. When one drove it was through an air like the breath from the open mouth of a furnace.

She kept much within doors, filled her rooms with roses, and lived with every window open. Her balcony, too, was full of flowers, and the striped sun-blinds beyond each open window kept the rooms in pleasant shadow.

"But suppose something happens to her—all alone there," said the Inward Monitor.

"Nothing will. She's not that sort of girl." Her headache had been growing worse these three days. The Inward Monitor might have had pity, remembering that—but no.

"You told Him that all girls were the same sort of girls," said the pitiless voice.

"I didn't mean in that way. I suppose you'd have liked me to write that anonymous letter and restore her to the bosom of her furious family? I've done the girl a good turn—for what she did for me. She's a good little thing—too good for him, even if I didn't happen to—And Temple's her ideal mate. I wonder if he's found it out yet? He must have by now: three weeks in the same hotel."

Temple, however, was not in the same hotel. The very day of the river rescue and the double omelette he had moved his traps a couple of miles down the river to Montigny.

A couple of miles is a good distance. Also a very little way, as you choose to take it.

"You know it was a mean trick," said the Inward Monitor. "Why not have let the girl go away where she could be alone—and get over it?"

"Oh, be quiet!" said Lady St. Craye. "I never knew myself so tiresome before. I think I must be going to be ill. My head feels like an ice in an omelette."

Vernon, strolling in much later, found her with eyes closed, leaning back among her flowers as she had lain all that long afternoon.

"How pale you look," he said. "You ought to get away from here."

"Yes," she said, "I suppose I ought. It would be easier for you if you hadn't the awful responsibility of bringing me roses every other day. What beauty-darlings these are!" She dipped her face in the fresh pure whiteness of the ones he had laid on her knee. Their faces felt cold, like the faces of dead people. She shivered.

"Heaven knows what I should do without you to—to bring my—my roses to," he said.

"Do you bring me anything else to-day?" she roused herself to ask. "Any news, for instance?"

"No," he said. "There isn't any news—there never will be. She's gone home—I'm certain of it. Next week I shall go over to England and propose for her formally to her step-father."

"A very proper course!"

It was odd that talking to some one else should make one's head throb like this. And it was so difficult to know what to say. Very odd. It had been much easier to talk to the Inward Monitor.

She made herself say: "And suppose she isn't there?" She thought she said it rather well.

"Well, then there's no harm done."

"He doesn't like you." She was glad she had remembered that.

"He didn't—but the one little word 'marriage,' simply spoken, is a magic spell for taming savage relatives. They'll eat out of your hand after that—at least so I'm told."

It was awful that he should decide to do this—heart-breaking. But it did not seem to be hurting her heart. That felt as though it wasn't there. Could one feel emotion in one's hands and feet? Hers were ice cold—but inside they tingled and glowed, like a worm of fire in a chrysalis of ice. What a silly simile.

"Must you go?" was what she found herself saying. "Suppose

she isn't there at all? You'll simply be giving her away—all her secret—and he'll fetch her home."

That at least was quite clearly put.

"I'm certain she is at home," he said. "And I don't see why I am waiting till next week. I'll go to-morrow."

If you are pulling a rose to pieces it is very important to lay the petals in even rows on your lap, especially if the rose be white.

"Eustace," she said, suddenly feeling quite coherent, "I wish you wouldn't go away from Paris just now. I don't believe you'd find her. I have a feeling that she's not far away. I think that is quite sensible. I am not saying it because I—And—I feel very ill, Eustace. I think I am—Oh, I am going, to be ill, very ill, I think! Won't you wait a little? You'll have such years and years to be happy in. I don't want to be ill here in Paris with no one to care."

She was leaning forward, her hands on the arms of her chair, and for the first time that day, he saw her face plainly. He said: "I shall go out now, and wire for your sister."

"Not for worlds! I forbid it. She'd drive me mad. No—but my head's running round like a beetle on a pin. I think you'd better go now. But don't go to-morrow. I mean I think I'll go to sleep. I feel as if I'd tumbled off the Eiffel tower and been caught on a cloud—one side of it's cold and the other's blazing."

He took her hand, felt her pulse. Then he kissed the hand.

"My dear, tired Jasmine Lady," he said, "I'll send in a doctor. And don't worry. I won't go to-morrow. I'll write."

"Oh, very well," she said, "write then,—and it will all come out—about her being here alone. And she'll always hate you. *I* don't care what you do!"

E. Nesbit

"I suppose I can write a letter as though—as though I'd not seen her since Long Barton." He inwardly thanked her for that hint.

"A letter written from Paris? That's so likely, isn't it? But do what you like. *I* don't care what you do."

She was faintly, agreeably surprised to notice that she was speaking the truth. "It's rather pleasant, do you know," she went on dreamily, "when everything that matters suddenly goes flat, and you wonder what on earth you ever worried about. Why do people always talk about cold shivers? I think hot shivers are much more amusing. It's like a skylark singing up close to the sun, and doing the tremolo with its wings. I'm sorry you're going away, though."

"I'm not going away," he said. "I wouldn't leave you when you're ill for all the life's happinesses that ever were. Oh, why can't you cure me? I don't want to want her; I want to want you."

"I'm certain," said Lady St. Craye brightly, "that what you've just been saying's most awfully interesting, but I like to hear things said ever so many times. Then the seventh time you understand everything, and the coldness and the hotness turn into silver and gold and everything is quite beautiful, and I think I am not saying exactly what you expected.—Don't think I don't know that what I say sounds like nonsense. I know that quite well, only I can't stop talking. You know one is like that sometimes. It was like that the night you hit me."

"I? *Hit you?*"

He was kneeling by her low chair holding her hand, as she lay back talking quickly in low, even tones, her golden eyes shining wonderfully.

"No—you didn't call it hitting. But things aren't always what we call them, are they? You mustn't kiss me now, Eustace. I think I've got some horrid fever—I'm sure I have. Because of course nobody could be bewitched nowadays, and put into a body that feels thick and thin in the wrong places. And my head *isn't* too big to get through the door.—Of course I know it isn't. It would be funny if it were. I do love funny things.— So do you. I like to hear you laugh. I wish I could say something funny, so as to hear you laugh now."

She was holding his hand very tightly with one of hers. The other held the white roses. All her mind braced itself to a great exertion as the muscles do for a needed effort. She spoke very slowly.

"Listen, Eustace. I am going to be ill. Get a nurse and a doctor and go away. Perhaps it is catching. And if I fall through the floor," she added laughing, "it is so hard to stop!"

"Put your arms round my neck," he said, for she had risen and was swaying like a flame in the wind—the white rose leaves fell in showers.

"I don't think I want to, now," she said, astonished that it should be so.

"Oh, yes, you do!"—He spoke as one speaks to a child. "Put your arms round Eustace's neck,—your own Eustace that's so fond of you."

"Are you?" she said, and her arms fell across his shoulders.

"Of course I am," he said. "Hold tight."

He lifted her and carried her, not quite steadily, for carrying a full-grown woman is not the bagatelle novelists would have us believe it.

He opened her bedroom door, laid her on the white, lacy coverlet of her bed.

E. Nesbit

"Now," he said, "you are to lie quite still. You've been so good and dear and unselfish. You've always done everything I've asked, even difficult things. This is quite easy. Just lie and think about me till I come back."

He bent over the bed and kissed her gently.

"Ah!" she sighed. There was a flacon on the table by the bed. He expected it to be jasmine. It was lavender water; he drenched her hair and brow and hands.

"That's nice," said she. "I'm not really ill. I think it's nice to be ill. Quite still do you mean, like that?"

She folded her hands, the white roses still clasped. The white bed, the white dress, the white flowers. Horrible!

"Yes," he said firmly, "just like that. I shall be back in five minutes."

He was not gone three. He came back and—till the doctor came, summoned by the concierge—he sat by her, holding her hands, covering her with furs from the wardrobe when she shivered, bathing her wrists with perfumed water when she threw off the furs and spoke of the fire that burned in her secret heart of cold clouds.

When the doctor came he went out by that excellent Irishman's direction and telegraphed for a nurse.

Then he waited in the cool shaded sitting-room, among the flowers. This was where he had hit her—as she said. There on the divan she had cried, leaning her head against his sleeve. Here, half-way to the door, they had kissed each other. No, he would certainly not go to England while she was ill. He felt sufficiently like a murderer already. But he would write. He glanced at her writing-table.

A little pang pricked him, and drove him to the balcony.

"No," he said, "if we are to hit people, at least let us hit them fairly." But all the same he found himself playing with the word-puzzle whose solution was the absolutely right letter to Betty's father, asking her hand in marriage.

"Well," he asked the doctor who closed softly the door of the bedroom and came forward, "is it brain-fever?"

"Holy Ann, no! Brain fever's a fell disease invented by novelists—I never met it in all *my* experience. The doctors in novels have special advantages. No, it's influenza—pretty severe touch too. She ought to have been in bed days ago. She'll want careful looking after."

"I see," said Vernon. "Any danger?"

"There's always danger, Lord—Saint-Croix isn't it?"

"I have not the honour to be Lady St. Craye's husband," said Vernon equably. "I was merely calling, and she seemed so ill that I took upon myself to—"

"I see—I see. Well, if you don't mind taking on yourself to let her husband know? It's a nasty case. Temperature 104. Perhaps her husband 'ud be as well here as anywhere."

"He's dead," said Vernon.

"Oh!" said the doctor with careful absence of expression. "Get some woman to put her to bed and to stay with her till the nurse comes. She's in a very excitable state. Good afternoon. I'll look in after dinner."

When Vernon had won the concierge to the desired service, had seen the nurse installed, had dined, called for news of Lady St. Craye, learned that she was "*toujours tres souffrante*," he went home, pulled a table into the middle of his large, bare, hot studio, and sat down to write to the Reverend Cecil Underwood.

"I mean to do it," he told himself, "and it can't hurt *her* my doing it now instead of a month ahead, when she's well again. In fact, it's better for all of us to get it settled one way or another while she's not caring about anything."

So he wrote. And he wrote a great deal, though the letter that at last he signed was quite short:

My Dear Sir:

I have the honour to ask the hand of your daughter in marriage. When you asked me, most properly, my intentions, I told you that I was betrothed to another lady. This is not now the case. And I have found myself wholly unable to forget the impression made upon me last year by Miss Desmond. My income is about L1,700 a year, and increases yearly. I beg to apologise for anything which may have annoyed you in my conduct last year, and to assure you that my esteem and affection for Miss Desmond are lasting and profound, and that, should she do me the honour to accept my proposal, I shall devote my life's efforts to secure her happiness.

I am, my dear Sir, Your obedient servant,

Eustace Vernon.

"That ought to do the trick," he told himself. "Talk of old world courtesy and ceremonial! Anyhow, I shall know whether she's at Long Barton by the time it takes to get an answer. If it's two days, she's there. If it's longer she isn't. He'll send my letter on to her—unless he suppresses it. Your really pious people are so shockingly unscrupulous."

There is nothing so irretrievable as a posted letter. This came home to Vernon as the envelope dropped on the others in the box at the Cafe du Dome—came home to him rather forlornly.

Next morning he called with more roses for Lady St. Craye, pinky ones this time.

"Milady was toujours *tres souffrante*. It would be ten days, at the least, before Milady could receive, even a very old friend, like Monsieur."

The letter reached Long Barton between the Guardian and a catalogue of Some Rare Books. The Reverend Cecil read it four times. He was trying to be just. At first he thought he would write "No" and tell Betty years later. But the young man had seen the error of his ways. And L1,700 a year!—

The surprise visit with which the Reverend Cecil had always intended to charm his step-daughter suddenly found its date quite definitely fixed. This could not be written. He must go to the child and break it to her very gently, very tenderly—find out quite delicately and cleverly exactly what her real feelings were. Girls were so shy about those things.

Miss Julia Desmond had wired him from Suez that she would be in Paris next week—had astonishingly asked him to meet her there.

"Paris next Tuesday Gare St. Lazare 6:45. Come and see Betty via Dieppe," had been her odd message.

He had not meant to go—not next Tuesday. He was afraid of Miss Julia Desmond. He would rather have his Lizzie all to himself. But now—

He wrote a cablegram to Miss Julia Desmond: "Care Captain S.S. Urania, Brindisi: Will meet you in Paris." Then he thought that this might seem to the telegraph people not quite nice, so he changed it to: "Going to see Lizzie Tuesday."

The fates that had slept so long were indeed waking up and beginning to take notice of Betty. Destiny, like the most attractive of the porters at the Gare de Lyon, "*s'occupait d'elle*."

CHAPTER XXIV

THE CONFESSIONAL

The concierge sat at her window under the arch of the porte-cochere at 57 Boulevard Montparnasse. She sat gazing across its black shade to the sunny street. She was thinking. The last twenty-four hours had given food for thought.

The trams passed and repassed, people in carriages, people on foot—the usual crowd—not interesting.

But the open carriage suddenly drawn up at the other side of the broad pavement was interesting, very. For it contained the lady who had given the 100 francs, and had promised another fifty on the first of the month. She had never come with that fifty, and the concierge having given up all hope of seeing her again, had acted accordingly.

Lady St. Craye, pale as the laces of her sea-green cambric gown, came slowly up the cobble-paved way and halted at the window.

"Good morning, Madame," she said. "I bring you the little present."

The concierge was genuinely annoyed. Why had she not waited a little longer? Still, all was not yet lost.

"Come in, Madame," she said. "Madame has the air

very fatigued."

"I have been very ill," said Lady St. Craye.

"If Madame will give herself the trouble to go round by the other door—" The concierge went round and met her visitor in the hall, and brought her into the closely furnished little room with the high wooden bed, the round table, the rack for letters, and the big lamp.

"Will Madame give herself the trouble to sit down? Would it be permitted to offer Madame something—a little glass of sugared water? No? I regret infinitely not having known that Madame was suffering. I should have acted otherwise."

"What have you done?" she asked quickly. "You haven't told anyone that I was here that night?"

"Do not believe it for an instant," said the woman reassuringly. "'No—after Madame's goodness I held myself wholly at the disposition of Madame. But when the day appointed passed itself without your visit, I said to myself: 'The little affaire has ceased to interest this lady; she is weary of it!' My grateful heart found itself free to acknowledge the kindness of others."

"Tell me exactly," said Lady St. Craye, "what you have done."

"It was but last week," the concierge went on, rearranging a stiff bouquet in exactly the manner of an embarrassed ingenue on the stage, "but only last week that I received a letter from Mademoiselle Desmond. She sent me her address."

She paused. Lady St. Craye laid the bank note on the table.

"Madame wants the address?"

"I have the address. I want to know whether you have given it to anyone else."

"No, Madame," said the concierge with simple pride, "when you have given a thing you have it not any longer."

"Well—pardon me—have you sold it?"

"For the same good reason, no, Madame."

"Take the note," said Lady St. Craye, "and tell me what you have done with the address."

"This gentleman, whom Madame did not wish to know that she had been here that night—"

"I didn't wish *anyone* to know!"

"Perfectly: this gentleman comes without ceasing to ask of me news of Mademoiselle Desmond. And always I have no news. But when Mademoiselle writes me: 'I am at the hotel such and such—send to me, I pray you, letters if there are any of them,'—then when Monsieur makes his eternal demand I reply: 'I have now the address of Mademoiselle,—not to give, but to send her letters. If Monsieur had the idea to cause to be expedited a little billet? I am all at the service of Monsieur.'"

"So he wrote to her. Have you sent on the letter?"

"Alas, yes!" replied the concierge with heartfelt regret. "I kept it during a week, hoping always to see Madame—but yesterday, even, I put it at the post. Otherwise.... I beg Madame to have the goodness to understand that I attach myself entirely to her interests. You may rely on me."

"It is useless," said Lady St. Craye; "the affair *is* ceasing to interest me."

"Do not say that. Wait only a little till you have heard. It is not only Monsieur that occupies himself with Mademoiselle. Last night arrives an aunt; also a father. They ask for Mademoiselle, are consternated when they learn of her departing. They run all Paris at the research of her. The father lodges at the Haute Loire. He is a priest it appears. Madame the aunt occupies the ancient apartment of Mademoiselle Desmond."

"An instant," said Lady St. Craye; "let me reflect."

The concierge ostentatiously went back to her flowers.

"You have not given *them* Miss Desmond's address?"

"Madame forgets," said the concierge, wounded virtue bristling in her voice, "that I was, for the moment, devoted to the interest of Monsieur. No. I am a loyal soul. I have told *nothing*. Only to despatch the letter. Behold all!"

"I will give myself the pleasure of offering you a little present next week," said Lady St. Craye; "it is only that you should say nothing—nothing—and send no more letters. And—the address?"

"Madame knows it—by what she says."

"Yes, but I want to know if the address you have is the same that I have. Hotel Chevillon, Grez sur Loing. Is it so?"

"It is exact. I thank you, Madame. Madame would do well to return *chez elle* and to repose herself a little. Madame is all pale."

"Is the aunt in Miss Desmond's rooms now?"

"Yes; she writes letters without end, and telegrams; and the priest-father he runs with them like a sad old black dog that has not the habit of towns."

"I shall go up and see her," said Lady St. Craye, "and I shall most likely give her the address. But do not give yourself anxiety. You will gain more by me than by any of the others. They are not rich. Me, I am, Heaven be praised."

She went out and along the courtyard. At the foot of the wide shallow stairs she paused and leaned on the dusty banisters.

"I feel as weak as any rat," she said, "but I must go through with it—I must."

She climbed the stairs, and stood outside the brown door. The nails that had held the little card "Miss E. Desmond" still stuck there, but only four corners of the card remained.

The door was not shut—it always shut unwillingly. She tapped.

"Come in," said a clear, pleasant voice. And she went in.

The room was not as she had seen it on the two occasions when it had been the battle ground where she and Betty fought for a man. Plaid travelling-rugs covered the divans. A gold-faced watch in a leather bracelet ticked on the table among scattered stationery. A lady in a short sensible dress rose from the table, and the room was scented with the smell of Hungarian cigarettes.

"I beg your pardon. I thought it was my brother-in-law. Did you call to see Miss Desmond? She is away for a short time."

"Yes," said Lady St. Craye. "I know. I wanted to see you. The concierge told me—"

"Oh, these concierges! They tell everything! It's what they were invented for, I believe. And you wanted—" She stopped, looked hard at the young woman and went on: "What you want is a good stiff brandy and soda. Here, where's the head of the pin?—I always think it such a pity bonnets went out. One could undo strings. That's it. Now, put your feet up. That's right, I'll be back in half a minute."

Lady St. Craye found herself lying at full length on Betty's divan, her feet covered with a Tussore driving-rug, her violet-wreathed hat on a table at some distance.

She closed her eyes. It was just as well. She could get back a little strength—she could try to arrange coherently what she meant to say. No: it was not unfair to the girl. She ought to be taken care of. And, besides, there was no such thing as "unfair." All was fair in—Well, she was righting for her life. All was fair when one was fighting for one's life—that was what she meant. Meantime, to lie quite still and draw long, even breaths—telling oneself at each breath: "I am quite well, I am quite strong—" seemed best.

There was a sound, a dull plop, the hiss and fizzle of a spurting syphon, then:

"Drink this: that's right. I've got you."

A strong arm round her shoulders—something buzzing and spitting in a glass under her nose.

"Drink it up, there's a good child."

She drank. A long breath.

"Now the rest." She was obedient.

"Now shut your eyes and don't bother. When you're better we'll talk."

Silence—save for the fierce scratching of a pen.

"I'm better," announced Lady St. Craye as the pen paused for the folding of the third letter.

The short skirted woman came and sat on the edge of the divan, very upright.

"Well then. You oughtn't to be out, you poor little thing."

The words brought the tears to the eyes of one weak with the self-pitying weakness of convalescence.

"I wanted—"

"Are you a friend of Betty's?"

"Yes—no—I don't know."

"A hated rival perhaps," said the elder woman cheerfully. "You didn't come to do her a good turn, anyhow, did you?"

"I—I don't know." Again this was all that would come.

"I do, though. Well, which of us is to begin? You see, child, the difficulty is that we neither of us know how much the other knows and we don't want to give ourselves away. It's so awkward to talk when it's like that."

"I think I know more than you do. I—you needn't think I want to hurt her. I should have liked her awfully, if it hadn't been—"

"If it hadn't been for the man. Yes, I see. Who was he?"

Lady St. Craye felt absolutely defenceless. Besides, what did it matter?"

"Mr. Vernon," she said.

"Ah, now we're getting to the horses! My dear child, don't look so guilty. You're not the first; you won't be the last—especially with eyes the colour his are. And so you hate Betty?"

"No, I don't. I should like to tell you all about it—all the truth."

"You can't," said Miss Desmond, "no woman can. But I'll give you credit for trying to, if you'll go straight ahead. But first of all—how long is it since you saw her?"

"Nearly a month."

"Well; she's disappeared. Her father and I got here last night. She's gone away and left no address. She was living with a Madame Gautier and—"

"Madame Gautier died last October," said Lady St. Craye—"the twenty-fifth."

"I had a letter from her brother—it got me in Bombay. But I couldn't believe it. And who has Betty been living with?"

"Look here," said Lady St. Craye. "I came to give the whole thing away, and hand her over to you. I know where she is. But now I don't want to. Her father's a brute, I know."

"Not he," said Miss Desmond; "he's only a man and a very, very silly one. I'll pledge you my word he'll never approach her, whatever she's done. It's not anything too awful for words, I'm certain. Come, tell me."

Lady St. Craye told Betty's secret at some length.

"Did she tell you this?"

"No."

"He did then?"

"Yes."

"Oh, men are darlings! The soul of honour—unsullied blades! My word! Do you mind if I smoke?"

She lighted a cigarette.

"I suppose *I'm* very dishonourable too," said Lady St. Craye.

"You? Oh no, you're only a woman!—And then?"

"Well, at last I asked her to go away, and she went."

"Well, that was decent of her, wasn't it?"

"Yes."

"And now you're going to tell me where she is and I'm to take her home and keep her out of his way. Is that it?"

"I don't know," said Lady St. Craye very truly, "why I came to you at all. Because it's all no good. He's written and proposed for her to her father—and if she cares—"

"Well, if she cares—and he cares—Do you really mean that *you'd* care to marry a man who's in love with another woman?"

"I'd marry him if he was in love with fifty other women."

"In that case," said Miss Desmond, "I should say you were the very wife for him."

"*She* isn't," said Lady St. Craye sitting up. "I feel like a silly school-girl talking to you like this. I think I'll go now. I'm not really so silly as I seem. I've been ill—influenza, you know—and I got so frightfully tired. And I don't think I'm so strong as I used to be. I've always thought I was strong enough to play any part I wanted to play. But—you've been very kind. I'll go—" She lay back.

"Don't be silly," said Miss Desmond briskly. "You *are* a school-girl compared with me, you know. I suppose you've been trying to play the role of the designing heroine—to part true lovers and so on, and then you found you couldn't."

"They're *not* true lovers," said Lady St. Craye eagerly; "that's just it. She'd never make him happy. She's too young and too innocent. And when she found out what a man like him is like, she'd break her heart. And he told me he'd be happier with me than he ever had been with her."

"Was that true, or—?"

"Oh, yes, it was true enough, though he said it. You've met him—he told me. But you don't know him."

"I know his kind though," said Miss Desmond. "And so you love him very much indeed, and you don't care for anything else,—and you think you understand him,—and you could forgive him everything? Then you may get him yet, if you care so very much—that is, if Betty doesn't."

"She doesn't. She thinks she does, but she doesn't. If only he hadn't written to her—"

"My dear," said Miss Desmond, "I was a fool myself once, about a man with eyes his colour. You can't tell me anything that I don't know. Does he know how much you care?"

"Yes."

"Ah, that's a pity—still—Well, is there anything else you want to tell me?"

"I don't want to tell anyone anything. Only—when she said she'd go away, I advised her where to go—and I told her of a quiet place—and Mr. Temple's there. He's the other man who admires her."

"I see. How Machiavelian of you!"—Miss Desmond touched the younger woman's hand with brusque gentleness— "And—?"

"And I didn't quite tell her the truth about Mr. Vernon and me," said Lady St. Craye, wallowing in the abject joys of the confessional. "And I am a beast and not fit to live. But," she added with the true penitent's instinct of self-defence, "I *know* it's only—oh, I don't know what—not love, with her. And it's my life."

"Yes. And what about him?"

"It's not love with him. At least it is—but she'd bore him. It's really his waking-up time. He's been playing the game just for counters all the while. Now he's learning to play with gold."

"And it'll stay learnt. I see," said Miss Desmond. "Look here, I like you. I know we shouldn't have said all we have if you weren't ill, and I weren't anxious. But I'm with you in one thing. I don't want him to marry Betty. She wouldn't understand an artist in emotion. Is this Temple straight?"

"As a yardstick."

"And as wooden? Well, that's better. I'm on your side. But— we've been talking without the veils on—tell me one thing. Are you sure you could get him if Betty were out of the way?"

"He kissed me once—since he's loved her," said Lady St. Craye, "and then I knew I could. He liked me better than he liked her—in all the other ways—before. I'm a shameless idiot; it's really only because I'm so feeble."

She rose and stood before the glass, putting on her hat.

"I do respect a woman who has the courage to speak the truth to another woman," said Miss Desmond. "I hope you'll get him—though it's not a very kind wish."

Lady St. Craye let herself go completely in a phrase whose memory stung and rankled for many a long day.

"Ah," she said, "even if he gets tired of me, I shall have got his children. You don't know what it is to want a child.

Good-bye."

"Good-bye," said Miss Desmond. "No—of course I don't."

CHAPTER XXV

THE FOREST

Nothing lifts the heart like the sense of a great self-sacrifice nobly made. Betty was glad that she could feel so particularly noble. It was a great help.

"He was mine," she told herself; "he meant to be—And I have given him up to her. It hurts—yes—but I did the right thing."

She thought she hoped that he would soon forget her. And almost all that was Betty tried quite sincerely, snatching at every help, to forget him.

Sometimes the Betty that Betty did not want to be would, quite deliberately and of set purpose, take out the nest of hungry memories, look at them, play with them, and hand over her heart for them to feed on. But always when she had done this she felt, afterwards, a little sorry, a little ashamed. It was too like the diary at Long Barton.

Consciously or unconsciously one must make some concessions to every situation or every situation would be impossible. Temple was here—interested, pleased to see her, glad to talk to her. But he was not at all inclined to be in love with her: that had been only a silly fancy of hers—in Paris. He had made up his mind by now who it was that he cared for. And it wasn't Betty. Probably she hadn't even been one of the two he came to Grez to think about. He was only a good friend—and she wanted a good friend. If he were not just a good friend the situation would be impossible. And Betty chose that the situation should be possible. For it was pleasant. It was a shield and a shelter from all the thoughts that she wanted to hide from.

"If she thinks I'm going to break my heart about *him*, she's mistaken. And so's He. I must be miserable for a bit," said Betty bravely, "but I'll not be miserable forever, so he needn't think it. Of course, I shall never care for anyone ever again—unless he were to love me for years and years before he ever said a word, and then I might say I would try.—*And* try. But fall in love?—Never again! Oh, good gracious, there he is,—and I've not *begun* to get ready."

Temple was whistling *Deux Amants* very softly in the courtyard below. She put her head out of the window.

"I shan't be two minutes," she said, "You might get the basket from Madame; and my sketching things are on the terrace all ready strapped up."

The hoofs of the smart gray pony slipped and rattled on the cobble-stones of the hotel entry.

"Au revoir: amuse yourselves well, my children." Madame Chevillon stood, one hand on fat hip, the other shading old eyes that they might watch the progress of the cart up the blinding whiteness of the village street.

"To the forest, and yet again to the forest and to the forest always," she said, turning into the darkened billiard room. "Marie, beware, thou, of the forest. The good God created it express for the lovers,—but it is permitted to the devil to promenade himself there also."

"Those two there," said Marie—"it is very certain that they are in love?"

"How otherwise?" said Madame. "The good God made us women that the men should be in love with us—and afterwards, to take care of the children. There is no other use that a man has for a woman. Friendship? The Art?—Bah! When a man wants those he demands them of a man. Of a woman he demands but love, and one gives it to him—one gives it to him without question!"

The two who had departed for the forest drove on through the swimming, spinning heat, in silence.

It was not till they reached the little old well by Marlotte that Betty spoke.

"Don't let's work to-day, Mr. Temple," she said. "My hands are so hot I could never hold a brush. And your sketch is really finished, you know."

"What would you like to do?" asked Temple: "river?"

"Oh, no,—not now that we've started for the forest! Its feelings would be hurt if we turned back. I am sure it loves us to love it, although it is so big—Like God, you know."

"Yes: I'm sure it does. Do you really think God cares?"

"Of course," said Betty, "because everything would be so silly if He didn't, you know. I believe He likes us to love him, and what's more, I believe He likes us to love all the pretty things He's made—trees and rivers and sunsets and seas."

"And each other," said Temple, and flushed to the ears: "human beings, I mean, of course," he added hastily.

"Of course," said Betty, unconscious of the flush; "but religion tells you that—it doesn't tell you about the little things. It does say about herbs of the field and the floods clapping their hands and all that—but that's only His works praising Him, not us loving all His works. I think He's most awfully pleased when we love some little, nice, tiny thing that He never thought we'd notice."

"Did your father teach you to think like this?"

"Oh, dear no!" said Betty. "He doesn't like the little pretty things."

"It's odd," said Temple. "Look at those yellow roses all over that hideous villa."

"My step-father would only see the villa. Well, must we work to-day?"

"What would you like to do?"

"I should like to go to those big rocks—the Rochers des Demoiselles, aren't they?—and tie up the pony, and climb up, and sit in a black shadow and look out over the green tops of the trees. You see things when you're idle that you never see when you're working, even if you're trying to paint those very things."

So, by and by, the gray pony was unharnessed and tied to a tree in a cool, grassy place where he also could be happy, and the two others took the winding stony path.

A turn in the smooth-worn way brought them to a platform overhanging the precipice that fell a sheer thirty feet to the tops of the trees on the slope below. White, silvery sand carpeted the ledge, and on the sand the shadow of a leaning rock fell blue.

"Here" said Betty, and sank down. Her sketchbook scooped the sand with its cover. "Oh, I *am* hot!" She threw off her hat.

"You don't look it," said Temple, and pulled the big bottle of weak claret and water from the luncheon basket.

"Drink!" he said, offering the little glass when he had filled it.

Betty drank, in little sips.

"How extraordinarily nice it is to drink when you're thirsty," she said, "and how heavenly this shadow is."

A long silence. Temple filled and lighted a pipe. From a slope of dry grass a little below them came the dusty rattle of grasshoppers' talk.

"It is very good here," said Betty. "Oh, how glad I am I came away from Paris. Everything looks different here—I mean the things that look as if they mattered there don't matter here—and the things that didn't matter there—oh, here, they do!"

"Yes," said Temple, making little mounds of sand with the edge of his hand as he lay, "I never expected to have such days in this world as I've had here with you. We've grown to be very good friends here, haven't we?"

"We were very good friends in Paris," said Betty, remembering the letter that had announced his departure.

"But it wasn't the same," he persisted. "When did we talk in Paris as we've talked here?"

"I talked to you, even in Paris, more than I've ever talked to anyone else, all the same," said Betty.

"Thank you," he said; "that's the nicest thing you've ever said to me."

"It wasn't meant to be nice," said Betty; "it's true. Don't you know there are some people you never can talk to without wondering what they'll think of you, and whether you hadn't better have said something else? It's nothing to do with whether you like them or not," she went on, thinking of talks with Vernon, many talks—and in all of them she had been definitely and consciously on guard. "You may like people quite frightfully, and yet you can't talk to them."

"Yes," he said, "but you couldn't talk to a person you disliked, could you? Real talk, I mean?"

"Of course not," said Betty. "Do you know I'm dreadfully hungry!"

It was after lunch that Temple said:

"When are you going home, Miss Desmond?" She looked up, for his use of her name was rare.

"I don't know: some time," she answered absently. But the question ran through her mind like a needle drawing after it the thread on which were strung all the little longings for Long Barton—for the familiar fields and flowers, that had gathered there since she first saw the silver may and the golden broom at Bourron station. That was nearly a month ago. What a month it had been—the gleaming river, the neat intimate simplicity of the little culture, white roads, and roses and rocks, and more than all—trees, and trees and trees again.

And with all this—Temple. He lodged at Montigny, true. And she at Grez. But each day brought to her door the best companion in the world. He had never even asked how she came to be at Grez. After that first, "Where's your party?" he had guarded his lips. It had seemed so natural, and so extremely fortunate that he should be here. If she had been all alone she would have allowed herself to think too much of Vernon—of what might have been.

"I am going to England next week!" he said. Betty was shocked to perceive that this news hurt her. Well, why shouldn't it hurt her? She wasn't absolutely insensible to friendship, she supposed. And sensibility to friendship was nothing to be ashamed of. On the contrary.

"I shall miss you most awfully," said she with the air of one flaunting a flag.

"I wish you'd go home," he said. "Haven't you had enough of your experiment, or whatever it was, yet?"

"I thought you'd given up interfering," she said crossly. At least she meant to speak crossly.

"I thought I could say anything to you now without your—your not understanding."

"So you can." She was suddenly not cross again.

"Ah, no I can't," he said. "I want to say things to you that I can't say here. Won't you go home? Won't you let me come to see you there? Say I may. You will let me?"

If she said Yes—she refused to pursue that train of thought another inch. If she said No—then a sudden end—and forever an end—to this good companionship. "I wish I had never, never seen *Him*!" she told herself.

Then she found that she was speaking.

"The reason I was all alone in Paris," she was saying. The reason took a long time to expound.—The shadow withdrew itself and they had to shift the camp just when it came to the part about Betty's first meeting with Temple himself.

"And so," she said, "I've done what I meant to do—and I'm a hateful liar—and you'll never want to speak to me again."

She rooted up a fern and tore it into little ribbons.

"Why have you told me all this?" he said slowly.

"I don't know," said she.

"It is because you care, a little bit about—about my thinking well of you?"

"I can't care about that, or I shouldn't have told you, should I? Let's get back home. The pony's lost by this time, I expect."

"Is it because you don't want to have any—any secrets between us?"

"Not in the least," said Betty, chin in the air. "I shouldn't *dream* of telling you my secrets—or anyone else of course, I mean," she added politely.

He sighed. "Well," he said, "I wish you'd go home."

"Why don't you say you're disappointed in me, and that you despise me, and that you don't care about being friends any more, with a girl who's told lies and taken her aunt's money and done everything wrong you can think of? Let's go back. I don't want to stay here any more, with you being silently contemptuous as hard as ever you can. Why don't you say something?"

"I don't want to say the only thing I want to say. I don't want to say it here. Won't you go home and let me come and tell you at Long Barton?"

"You do think me horrid. Why don't you say so?"

"No. I don't."

"Then it's because you don't care what I am or what I do. I thought a man's friendship didn't mean much!" She crushed the fern into a rough ball and threw it over the edge of the rock.

"Oh, hang it all," said Temple. "Look here, Miss Desmond. I came away from Paris because I didn't know what was the matter with me. I didn't know who it was I really cared about.

And before I'd been here one single day, I knew. And then I met you. And I haven't said a word, because you're here alone—and besides I wanted you to get used to talking to me and all that. And now you say I don't care. No, confound it all, it's too much! I wanted to ask you to marry me. And I'd have waited any length of time till there was a chance for me." He had almost turned his back on her, and leaning his chin on his elbow was looking out over the tree-tops far below. "And now you've gone and rushed me into asking you *now*, when I know there isn't the least chance for me,—and anyhow I ought to have held my tongue! And now it's all no good, and it's your fault. Why did you say I didn't care?"

"You knew it was coming," Betty told herself, "when he asked if he might come to Long Barton to see you. You knew it. You might have stopped it. And you didn't. And now what are you going to do?"

What she did was to lean back to reach another fern—to pluck and smooth its fronds.

"Are you very angry?" asked Temple forlornly.

"No," said Betty; "how could I be? But I wish you hadn't. It's spoiled everything."

"Do you think I don't know all that?"

"I wish I could," said Betty very sincerely, "but—"

"Of course," he said bitterly. "I knew that."

"He doesn't care about me," said Betty: "he's engaged to someone else."

"And you care very much?" He kept his face turned away.

"I don't know," said Betty; "sometimes I think I'm getting not to care at all."

"Then—look here: may I ask you again some time, and we'll go on just like we have been?"

"No," said Betty. "I'm going back to England at the end of the week. Besides, you aren't quite sure it's me you care for.—At least you weren't when you came away from Paris. How can you be sure you're sure now?"

He turned and looked at her.

"I beg your pardon," she said instantly. "I think I didn't understand. Let's go back now, shall we?"

"For Heaven's sake," he said, "don't let this break up everything! Don't avoid me in the little time that's left. I won't talk about it any more—I won't worry you—"

"Don't be silly," she said, and she smiled at him a little sadly; "you talk as though I didn't know you."

CHAPTER XXVI

THE MIRACLE

It seemed quite dark down in the forest—or rather, it seemed, after the full good light that lay upon the summit of the rocks, like the gray dream-twilight under the eyelids of one who dozes in face of a dying fire.

"Don't let's go straight back to Grez," said Betty when the pony was harnessed, "let's go on to Fontainebleau and have dinner and drive back by moonlight. Don't you think it would be fun? We've never done that."

"Thank you," he said. "You *are* good."

His eyes met hers in the green shadow, and she was satisfied because he had understood that this was her reply to his appeal to her "not to avoid him in the little time there was left."

Both were gay as they drove along the golden roads, gayer than ever they had been. The nearness of a volcano has never been a bar to gaiety. Dinner was a joyous feast, and when it was over, and the other guests had strolled out, Temple sang all the songs Betty liked best. Betty played for him. It was all very pleasant, and both pretended, quite beautifully, that they were the best of friends, and that it had never, never been a question of anything else. The pretence lasted through all the moonlight of the home drive—lasted indeed till the pony was trotting along the straight avenue that leads down into Grez. And even then it was not Temple who broke it. It was Betty, and she laid her hand on his arm.

"Look here," she said. "I've been thinking about it ever since you said it. And I'm not going to let it spoil anything. Only I don't want you to think I don't understand. And I'm most awfully proud that you should.... I am really. And I'd rather be liked by you than by anyone—"

"Almost," said Temple a little bitterly.

"I don't feel sure about that part of it—really. One feels and thinks such a lot of different things—and they all contradict everything else, till one doesn't know what anything means, or what it is one really—I can't explain. But I don't want you to think your having talked about it makes any difference. At least I don't mean that at all. What I mean is that of course I like you ever so much better now I know that you like me, and—oh, I don't want to—I don't want you to think it's all no good, because really and truly I don't know."

All this time she had kept her hand on his wrist.

Now he laid his other hand over it.

"Dear," he said, "that's all I want, and more than I hoped for now. I won't say another word about it—ever, if you'd rather not,—only if ever you feel that it is me, and not that other chap, then you'll tell me, won't you?"

"I'll tell you now," said Betty, "that I wish with all my heart it *was* you, and not the other."

When he had said goodnight at the deserted door of the courtyard Betty slipped through the trees to her pavilion. The garden seemed more crowded with trees than it had ever been. It was almost as though new trees from the forest had stolen in while she was at Fontainebleau, and joined the ranks of those that stood sentinel round the pavilion. There was a lamp in the

E. Nesbit

garden room—as usual. Its light poured out and lay like a yellow carpet on the terrace, and lent to the foliage beyond that indescribable air of festivity, of light-heartedness that green leaves can always borrow from artificial light.

"I'll just see if there are any letters," she told herself. "There always might be: from Aunt Julia or Miss Voscoe or—someone."

She went along the little passage that led to the stairs. The door that opened from it into the garden room was narrowly ajar. A slice of light through the chink stood across the passage.

Oh!

There was someone in the room. Someone was speaking. She knew the voice. "She must be in soon," it said. It was her Aunt Julia's voice. She stopped dead. And there was silence in the room.

Oh! to be caught like this! In a trap. And just when she had decided to go home! She would not be caught. She would steal up to her room, get her money, leave enough on the table to pay her bill, and *go*. She could walk to Marlotte—and go off by train in the morning to Brittany—anywhere. She would not be dragged back like a prisoner to be all the rest of her life with a hateful old man who detested her. Aunt Julia thought she was very clever. Well, she would just find out that she wasn't. Who was she talking to? Not Madame, for she spoke in English. To some one from Paris? Who could have betrayed her? Only one person knew. Lady St. Craye. Well, Lady St. Craye should not betray her for nothing. She would not go to Brittany: she would go back to Paris. That woman should be taught what it costs to play the traitor.

All this in the quite small pause before her aunt's voice spoke again.

"Unless she's got wind of our coming and flown," it said.

"Our" coming? Who was the other?

Betty was eavesdropping then? How dishonourable! Well, it is. And she was.

"I hope to Heaven she's safe," said another voice. Oh—it was her step-father! He had come—Then he must know everything! She moved, quite without meaning to move; her knee touched the door and it creaked. Very very faintly, but it creaked. Would they hear? Had they heard? No—the aunt's voice again:

"The whole thing's inexplicable to me! I don't understand it. You let Betty go to Paris."

"By your advice."

"By my advice, but also because you wanted her to be happy."

"Yes—Heaven knows I wanted her to be happy." The old man's voice was sadder than Betty had ever heard it.

"So we found Madame Gautier for her—and when Madame Gautier dies, she doesn't write to you, or wire to you, to come and find her a new chaperone. Why?"

"I can't imagine why."

"Don't you think it may have been because she was afraid of you, thought you'd simply make her come back to Long Barton?"

"It would surely have been impossible for her to imagine that I should lessen the time which I had promised her, on account of an unfortunate accident. She knows the depth of my affection for her. No, no—depend upon it there must have been some other reason for the deceit. I almost fear to conjecture what the reason may have been. Do you think it possible that she has been seeing that man again?"

E. Nesbit

There was a sound as of a chair impatiently pushed back. Betty fled noiselessly to the stairs. No footstep followed the movement of the chair. She crept back.

"—when you do see her?" her aunt was asking, "I suppose you mean to heap reproaches on her, and take her home in disgrace?"

"I hope I shall have strength given me to do my duty," said the Reverend Cecil.

"Have you considered what your duty is?"

"It must be my duty to reprove, to show her her deceit in its full enormity."

"You'll enjoy that, won't you? It'll gratify your sense of power. You'll stand in the place of God to the child, and you'll be glad to see her humbled and ashamed."

"Because a thing is painful to me it is none the less my duty."

"Nor any the more," snapped Miss Desmond; "nor any the more! That's what you won't see. She knows you don't care about her, and that's why she kept away from you as long as she could."

"She can't know it. It isn't true."

"She thinks it is."

"Do *you* think so? Do *you* imagine I don't care for her? Have you been poisoning her mind and—"

"Oh, don't let's talk about poison!" said Miss Desmond. "If she's lost altogether it won't matter to you. You'll have done your duty."

"If she's lost I—if she were lost I should not care to be saved. I am aware that the thought is sinful. But I fear that it is so."

"Of course," said Miss Desmond. "She's not your child—why should you care? You never had a child."

"What have I done to you that you should try to torture me like this?" It was her step-father's voice, but Betty hardly knew it. "For pity's sake, woman, be quiet! Let me bear what I have to bear without your chatter."

"I'm sorry," said Miss Desmond very gently. "Forgive me if I didn't understand. And you do really care about her a little?"

"Care about her a little! She's the only living thing I do care for—or ever have cared for except one. Oh, it is like a woman to cast it up at me as a reproach that I have no child! Why have I no child? Because the woman whom Almighty God made for my child's mother was taken from me—in her youth—before she was mine. Her name was Lizzie. And my Lizzie, my little Lizzie that's lied and deceived us, she *is* my child—the one *we* should have had. She's my heart's blood. Do you think I want to scold her; do you think I want to humble her? Do you not perceive how my own heart will be torn? But it is my duty. I will not spare the rod. And she will understand as you never could. Oh, my little Lizzie!—Oh, pray God she is safe! If it please God to restore her safely to me, I will not yield to the wicked promptings of my own selfish affection. I will show her her sin, and we will pray for forgiveness together. Yes, I will not shrink, even if it break my heart—I will tell her—"

"I should tell her," said Miss Desmond, "just what you've told me."

The old man was walking up and down the room. Betty could hear every movement.

"It's been the struggle of my life not to spoil her—not to let my love for her lead me to neglect her eternal welfare—not to lessen her modesty by my praises—not to condone the sin because of my love for the sinner. My love has not been selfish.—It has been the struggle of my life not to let my affection be a snare to her."

"Then I must say," said Miss Desmond, "that you might have been better employed."

"Thank God I have done my duty! You don't understand. But my Lizzie will understand."

"Yes, she will understand," cried Betty, bursting open the door and standing between the two with cheeks that flamed. "I do understand, Father dear! Auntie, I don't understand *you*! You're cruel,—and it's not like you. Will you mind going away, please?"

The cruel aunt smiled, and moved towards the door. As she passed Betty she whispered: "I thought you were *never* going to come from behind that door. I couldn't have kept it up much longer."

Then she went out and closed the door firmly.

Betty went straight to her step-father and put her arms round his neck.

"You do forgive me—you will forgive me, won't you?" she said breathlessly.

He put an arm awkwardly round her.

"There's nothing you could do that I couldn't forgive," he said in a choked voice. "But it is my duty not to—"

She interrupted him by drawing back to look at him, but she kept his arm where it was, by her hand on his.

"Father," she said, "I've heard everything you've been saying. It's no use scolding me, because you can't possibly say anything that I haven't said to myself a thousand times. Sit down and let me tell you everything, every single thing! I *did* mean to come home this week, and tell you; I truly did. I wish I'd gone home before."

"Oh, Lizzie," said the old man, "how could you? How could you?"

"I didn't understand. I didn't know. I was a blind idiot. Oh, Father, you'll see how different I'll be now! Oh, if one of us had died—and I'd never known!"

"Known what, my child? Oh, thank God I have you safe! Known what?"

"Why, that you—how fond you are of me."

"You didn't know *that?*"

"I—I wasn't always sure," Betty hastened to say. A miracle had happened. She could read now in his eyes the appeal that she had always misread before. "But now I shall always be sure—always. And I'm going to be such a good daughter to you—you'll see—if you'll only forgive me. And you will forgive me. Oh, you don't know how I trust you now!"

"Didn't you always?"

"Not enough—not nearly enough. But I do now. Let me tell you—Don't let me ever be afraid of you—oh, don't let me!" She had pushed him gently into a chair and was half kneeling on the floor beside him.

"Have you ever been afraid of me?"

"Oh, I don't know; a little perhaps sometimes! You don't know how silly I am. But not now. You *are* glad to see me?"

"Lizzie," he said, "God knows how glad I am! But it's my duty to ask you at once whether you've done anything wrong."

"Everything wrong you can think of!" she answered enthusiastically, "only nothing really wicked, of course. I'll tell you all about it. And oh, do remember you can't think worse of me than I do! Oh, it's glorious not to be afraid!"

"Of me?" His tone pleaded again.

"No, no—of anything! Of being found out. I'm glad you've come for me.

I'm glad I've got to tell you everything—I did mean to go home next week, but I'm glad it's like this. Because now I know how much you care, and I might never have found that out if I hadn't listened at the door like a mean, disgraceful cat. I ought to be miserable because I've done wrong—but I'm not. I can't be. I'm really most frightfully happy."

"Thank God you can say that," he said, timidly stroking her hair with the hand that she was not holding. "Now I'm not afraid of anything you may have to tell me, my child—my dear child."

* * * * *

To four persons the next day was one of the oddest in their lives.

Arriving early to take Betty to finish her sketch, the stricken Temple was greeted on the doorstep by a manly looking lady in gold-rimmed spectacles, short skirts, serviceable brown boots and a mushroom hat.

"I know who you are," said she; "you're Mr. Temple. I'm Betty Desmond's aunt. Would you like to take me on the river? Betty is busy this morning making the acquaintance of her step-father. She's taken him out in the little cart."

"I see," said Temple. "I shall be delighted to take you on the river."

"Nice young man. You don't ask questions. An excellent trait."

"An acquired characteristic, I assure you," said Temple, remembering his first meeting with Betty.

"Then you won't be able to transmit it to your children. That's a pity. However, since you don't ask I'll tell you. The old man has 'persistently concealed his real nature' from Betty. You'd think it was impossible, living in the same house all these years. Last night she found him out. She's as charmed with the discovery as a girl child with a doll that opens and shuts its eyes—or a young man with the nonentity he calls his ideal. Come along. She'll spend the morning playing with her new toy. Cheer up. You shall see her at *dejeuner*."

"*I* do not need cheering," said the young man. And I don't want you to tell me things you'd rather not. On the contrary—"

"You want me not to tell you the things I'd rather tell you?"

"No: I should like to tell you all about—"

"All about yourself. My dear young man, there is nothing I enjoy more; the passion for confidences is my only vice. It was really to indulge that that I asked you to come on the river with me."

"I thought," said Temple as they reached the landing stage, "that perhaps you had asked me to console me for not seeing your niece this morning."

"Thank you kindly," Miss Desmond stepped lightly into the boat. "I rather like compliments, especially when you're solidly built—like myself. Oh, yes, I'll steer; pull hard, bow, she's got no way on her yet, and the stream's strong just here under the bridge. I gather that you've been proposing to my niece."

"I didn't mean to," said Temple, pulling a racing stroke in his agitation.

"Gently, gently! The Diamond Sculls aren't at stake. She led you on, you mean?"

He rested on his oars a moment and laughed.

"What is there about you that makes me feel that I've known you all my life?"

"Possibly it's my enormous age. Or it may be that I nursed you when you were a baby. I have nursed one or two in my time, though I mayn't look it.—So Betty entrapped you into a proposal?"

"Are you trying to make me angry? It's a dangerous river. Can you swim."

"Like any porpoise. But of course I misunderstand people if they won't explain themselves. You needn't tremble like that. I'll be gentle with you."

"If I tremble it's with pleasure," said Temple.

"Come, moderate your transports, and unfold your tale. My ears are red, I know, but they are small, well-shaped and sympathetic."

"Well then," said Temple; and the tale began. By the time it was ended the boat was at a standstill on the little backwater below the pretties of the sluices.

There was a silence.

"Well?" said Temple.

"Well," said Miss Desmond, dipping her hand in the water—"what a stream this is, to be sure!—Well, your means are satisfactory and you seem to me to have behaved quite beautifully. I don't think I ever heard of such profoundly correct conduct."

"If I've made myself out a prig," said Temple, "I'm sorry. I could tell you lots of things."

"Please spare me! Why are people always so frightfully ashamed of having behaved like decent human beings? I esteem you immensely."

"I'd rather you liked me."

"Well, so I do. But I like lots of people I don't esteem. If I'd married anyone it would probably have been some one like that. But for Betty it's different. I shouldn't have needed to esteem my own husband. But I must esteem hers."

"I'll try not to deserve your esteem more than I'm obliged," said Temple, "but your liking—what can I do to deserve that—?"

"Go on as you've begun, my dear young man, and you'll be Aunt Julia's favourite nephew. No—don't blush. It's an acknowledgement of a tender speech that I always dispense with."

"Advise me," said he, red to the ears and hands. "She doesn't care for me, at present. What can I do?"

"What most of us have to do—when we want anything worth wanting. Wait. We're going home the day after to-morrow. If you turn up at Long Barton about the middle of September—you might come down for the Harvest Festival; it's the yearly excitement. That's what I should do."

"Must I wait so long as that?" he asked. "Why?"

E. Nesbit

"Let me whisper in your ear," said Miss Desmond, loud above the chatter of the weir. "Long Barton is very dull! Now let's go back."

"I don't want her to accept me because she's bored."

"No more do I. But one sees the proportions of things better when one's dull. And—yes. I esteem you; I like you. You are ingenuous, and innocuous.—No, really that was a yielding to the devil of alliteration. I mean you are a real good sort. The other man has the harmlessness of the serpent. As for me, I have the wisdom of the dove. You profit by it and come to Long Barton in September."

"It seems like a plot to catch her," said Temple.

"A friend of yours told me you were straight. And you are. I thought perhaps she flattered you."

"Who?—No, I'm not to ask questions."

"Lady St. Craye."

"Do you know," he said, slowly pulling downstream, "there's one thing I didn't tell you. I came away from Paris because I wasn't quite sure that I wasn't in love with *her*."

"Not you," said Miss Desmond. "She'd never have suited you. And now she'll throw herself away on the man with the green eyes and the past. I mean Pasts. And it's a pity. She's a woman after my own heart."

"She's extraordinarily charming," said Temple with a very small sigh.

"Yes extraordinarily, as you say. And so you came away from Paris! I begin to think *you* have a little of the wisdom of the dove too. Pull now—or we shall be late for breakfast."

He pulled.

*   *   *   *   *

"Now *that*," said the Reverend Cecil that evening to his sister-in-law, "that is the kind of youth I should wish to see my Lizzie select for her help-mate."

"Well," said Miss Desmond, "if you keep that wish strictly to yourself, I should think it had a better chance than most wishes of being gratified."

          E. Nesbit

CHAPTER XXVII

THE PINK SILK STORY

To call on the concierge at Betty's old address, and to ask for news of her had come to seem to Vernon the unbroken habit of a life-time. There never was any news: there never would be any news. But there always might be.

The days went by, days occupied in these fruitless gold-edged enquiries, in the other rose-accompanied enquiries after the health of Lady St. Craye, and in watching for the postman who should bring the answer to his formal proposal of marriage.

To his deep surprise and increasing disquietude, no answer came. Was the Reverend Cecil dead, or merely inabordable? Had Betty despised his offer too deeply to answer it? The lore learned in, as it seemed, another life assured him that a woman never despises an offer too much to say "No" to it.

Watch for the postman. Look at Betty's portrait. Call on the concierge. (He had been used to dislike the employment of dirty instruments.) Call on the florist. (There was a decency in things, even if all one's being were contemptibly parched for the sight of another woman.) Call and enquire for the poor Jasmine Lady. Studio—think of Betty—look at her portrait— pretend to work. Meals at fairly correct intervals. Call on the concierge. Look at the portrait again. Such were the recurrent incidents of Vernon's life. Between the incidents came a padding of futile endeavour. Work, he had always asserted, was the cure for inconvenient emotions. Only now the cure was not available.

And the postman brought nothing interesting, except a letter, post-mark Denver, Col., a letter of tender remonstrance from the Brittany girl, Miss Van Tromp.

Then came the morning when the concierge, demurely assuring him of her devotion to his interests, offered to post a letter. No bribe—and he was shameless in his offers—could wring more than that from her. And even the posting of the letter cost a sum that the woman chuckled over through all the days during which the letter lay in her locked drawer, under Lady St. Craye's bank note and the divers tokens of "*ce monsieur's*" interest in the intrigue—whatever the intrigue might be—its details were not what interested.

Vernon went home, pulled the table into the middle of the bare studio and wrote. This letter wrote itself without revision.

"Why did you go away?" it said. "Where are you? where can I see you? What has happened? Have your people found out?"

A long pause—the end of the pen bitten.

"I want to have no lies or deceit any more between us. I must tell you the truth. I have never been engaged to anyone. But you would not let me see you without that, so I let you think it. Will you forgive me? Can you? For lying to you? If you can't I shall know that nothing matters at all. But if you can forgive me—then I shall let myself hope for impossible things.

"Dear, whether it's all to end here or not, let me write this once without thinking of anything but you and me. I have written to your father asking his permission to ask you to marry me. To you I want to say that I love you, love you, love you—and I have never loved anyone else. That's part of my punishment for—I don't know what exactly. Playing with fire, I suppose. Dear—can you love me? Ever since I met you at Long Barton" (Pause: what about Miss Van Tromp? Nothing, nothing, nothing!) "I've not thought of anything but you. I want you for my very own. There is no one like you, my love, my Princess.

"You'll write to me. Even if you don't care a little bit you'll write. Dear, I hardly dare hope that you care, but I daren't fear that you don't. I shall count the minutes till I get your answer. I feel like a schoolboy.

"Dear it's my very heart I'm sending you here. If I didn't love you, love you, love you I could write a better letter, tell you better how I love you. Write now. You will write?

"Did someone tell you something or write you something that made you go away? It's not true, whatever it is. Nothing's true, but that I want you. As I've never wanted anything. Let me see you. Let me tell you. I'll explain everything—if anyone *has* been telling lies.

"If you don't care enough to write, I don't care enough to go on living. Oh, my dear Dear, all the words and phrases have been used up before. There's nothing new to *say*, I know. But what's in my heart for you—that's new, that's all that matters—that and what your heart might hold for me. Does it? Tell me. If I can't have your love, I can't bear my life. And I won't.—You'll think this letter isn't like me. It isn't, I know. But I can't help it. I am a new man: and you have made me. Dear,—can't you love the man you've made? Write, write, write!

"Yours—as I never thought I could be anyone's,

"Eustace Vernon."

"It's too long," he said, "most inartistic, but I won't re-write it.

Contemptible ass! If she cares it won't matter. If she doesn't, it won't matter either."

And that was the letter that lay in the locked drawer for a week. And through that week the watching for the postman went on—went on. And the enquiries, mechanically.

And no answer came at all, to either of his letters. Had the Concierge deceived him? Had she really no address to which to send the letter?

"Are you sure that you posted the letter?"

"Altogether, monsieur," said the concierge, fingering the key of the drawer that held it.

And the hot ferment of Paris life seethed and fretted all around him. If Betty were at Long Barton—oh, the dewy gray grass in the warren—and the long shadows on the grass!

Three days more went by.

"You have posted the letter?"

"But yes, Monsieur. Be tranquil. Without doubt it was a letter that should exact time for the response."

It was on the fifth day that he met Mimi Chantal, the prettiest model on the left bank.

"Is monsieur by chance painting the great picture which shall put him between Velasquez and Caran d'Ache on the last day?"

"I am painting nothing," said Vernon. "And why is the prettiest model in Paris not at work?"

"I was in lateness but a little quarter of an hour, Monsieur. And behold me—chucked."

"It wasn't for the first time, then?"

"A nothing one or two days last week. Monsieur had better begin to paint that *chef d'oeuvre*—to-day even. It isn't often that the prettiest model in Paris is free to sit at a moment's notice."

"But," said Vernon, "I haven't an idea for a picture even. It is too hot for ideas. I'm going into the country at the end of the month, to do landscape."

"To paint a picture it is then absolutely necessary to have an idea?"

"An idea—or a commission."

"There is always something that lacks! With me it is the technique that is to seek; with you the ideas! Otherwise we should both be masters. For you have technique both hands full; I have ideas, me."

"Tell me some of them," said Vernon, strolling along by her side. It was not his habit to stroll along beside models. But to-day he was fretted and chafed by long waiting for that answer to his letter. Anything seemed better than the empty studio where one waited.

"Here is one! I have the idea that artists have no eyes. How they pose me ever as l'Ete or La Source or Leda, or that clumsy Suzanne with her eternal old men. As if they knew better than I do how a woman holds herself up or sits herself down, or nurses a duck, or defends herself!"

"Your idea is probably correct. I understand you to propose that I should paint a picture called The Blind Artist?"

"Don't do the imbecile. I propose for subject Me—not posed; me as I am in the Rest. Is it not that it is then that I am the most pretty, the most chic?"

"It certainly is," said he. "And you propose that I should paint you as you appear in the Rest?"

"Perfectly," she interrupted. "Tender rose colour—it goes to a marvel with my Cleo de Merode hair. And if you want a contrast—or one of those little tricks to make people say: 'What does it mean?'"

"I don't, thank you," he laughed.

"Paint that white drowned girl's face that hangs behind your stove. Paint her and me looking at each other. She has the air of felicitating herself that she is dead. Me, I will have the air of felicitating myself that I am alive. You will see, Monsieur. Essay but one sole little sketch, and you will think of nothing else. One might entitle it 'The Rivals.'"

"Or 'The Rest,'" said Vernon, a little interested. "Oh, well, I'm not doing anything.—I'll make a sketch and give it you as a present. Come in an hour."

* * * * *

"Auntie, wake up, wake up!" Betty, white-faced and determined, was pulling back the curtain with fingers that rigidly would not tremble.

"Shut the door and spare my blushes," said her aunt. "What's up now?" She looked at the watch on the bed-table. "Why its only just six."

"I can't help it," said Betty; "you've had all the night to sleep in. I haven't. I want you to get up and dress and come to Paris with me by the early train."

"Sit down," said the aunt. "No, not on the bed. I hate that. In this chair. Now remember that we all parted last night in the best of spirits, and that as far as I know nothing has happened since."

"Oh, no—nothing of course!" said Betty.

"Don't be ironical," said Miss Desmond; "at six in the morning it's positively immoral. Tell me all—let me hear the sad sweet story of your life."

"Very well," said Betty, "if you're only going to gibe I'll go alone. Or I'll get Mr. Temple to take me."

"To see the other man? That *will* be nice."

"Who said anything about—?"

"You did, the moment you came in. Come child; sit down and tell me. I'm not unsympathetic. I'm only very, very sleepy. And I *did* think everything was arranged. I was dreaming of orange blossoms and The Voice That Breathed. And the most beautiful trousseau marked E.T. And silver fish-knives, and salt-cellars in a case lined with purple velvet."

"Go on," said Betty, "if it amuses you."

"No, no. I'm sorry. Forgive the ravings of delirium. Go on. Poor little Betty! Don't worry. Tell its own aunt."

"It's not a joke," said Betty.

"So I more and more perceive, now that I'm really waking up," said the aunt, sitting up and throwing back her thick blond hair. "Come, I'll get up now. Give me my stockings—and tell me—"

"They were under my big hat," said Betty, doing as she was told; "the one I wore the night you came. And I'd thrown it down on the chest of drawers—and they were underneath."

"My stockings?"

"No—my letters. Two of them. And one of them's from Him.

It's a week old. And he says he won't live if I don't love him."

"They always do," said Miss Desmond, pouring water into the basin. "Well?"

"And he wants me to marry him, and he was never engaged to Lady St. Craye; and it was a lie. I've had a letter from *her*."

"I can't understand a word you say," said Miss Desmond through splashings.

"My friend Paula, that I told you about. She never went home to her father. Mr. Vernon set her up in a restaurant! Oh, how good and noble he is! Here are your shoes—and he says he won't live without me; and I'm going straight off to him, and I wouldn't go without telling you. It's no use telling father yet, but I did think *you'd* understand."

"Hand me that green silk petticoat. Thank you. *What* did you think I'd understand?"

"Why that I—that it's him I love."

"You do, do you?"

"Yes, always, always! And I must go to him. But I won't go and leave Bobbie to think I'm going to marry him some day. I must tell him first, and then I'm going straight to Paris to find him, and give him the answer to his letter."

"You must do as you like. It's your life, not mine. But it's a pity," said her aunt, "and I should send a telegram to prepare him."

"The office won't be open. There's a train at seven forty-five. Oh, do hurry. I've ordered the pony. We'll call and tell Mr. Temple."

It was not the 7:45 that was caught, however, but the 10:15,

E. Nesbit

because Temple was, naturally, in bed. When he had been roused, and had dressed and come out to them, in the gay terrace overhanging the river where the little tables are and the flowers in pots and the vine-covered trellis, Miss Desmond turned and positively fled before the gay radiance of his face.

"This is dear and sweet of you," he said to Betty.

"What lovely scheme have you come to break to me? But what's the matter? You're not ill?"

"Oh, don't," said Betty; "don't look like that! I couldn't go without telling you. It's all over, Bobbie."

She had never before called him by that name, and now she did not know what she had called him.

"What's all over?" he asked mechanically.

"Everything," she said; "your thinking I was going to, perhaps, some time—and all that. Because now I never shall. O, Bobbie, I do hate hurting you, and I do like you so frightfully much! But he's written to me: the letter's been delayed. And it's all a mistake. And I'm going to him now. Oh,—I hope you'll be able to forgive me!"

"It's not your fault," he said. "Wait a minute. It's so sudden. Yes, I see. Don't you worry about me, dearest, I shall be all right. May I know who it is?"

"It's Mr. Vernon," said Betty.

"Oh, my God!" Temple's hand clenched. "No, no, no, no!"

"I am so very, very sorry," said Betty in the tone one uses who has trodden on another's foot in an omnibus.

He had sat down at one of the little tables, and was looking out over the shining river with eyes half shut.

"But it's not true," he said. "It can't be true! He's going to marry Lady St. Craye."

"That's all a mistake," said Betty eagerly; "he only said that because—I haven't time to tell you all about it now. But it was all a mistake."

"Betty, dear," he said, using in his turn, for the first time, her Christian name, "don't do it. Don't marry him. You don't know."

"I thought you were his friend."

"So I am," said Temple. "I like him right enough. But what's all the friendship in the world compared with your happiness? Don't marry him—dear. Don't."

"I shall marry whom I choose," said Betty, chin in air, "and it won't be you." ("I don't care if I am vulgar and brutal," she told herself, "it serves him right")

"It's not for me, dear. It's not for me—it's for you. I'll go right away and never see you again. Marry some straight chap— anyone—But not Vernon."

"I am going to marry Mr. Vernon," said Betty with lofty calm, "and I am very sorry for any annoyance I may have caused you. Of course, I see now that I could never—I mean," she added angrily, "I hate people who are false to their friends. Yes—and now I've missed my train."

She had.

"Forgive me," said Temple when the fact was substantiated, and the gray pony put up, "after all, I was your friend before I—before you—before all this that can't come to anything. Let me give you both some coffee and see you to the station. And Betty, don't you go and be sorry about me afterwards. Because, really, it's not your fault and," he laughed and was silent a

E. Nesbit

moment, "and I'd rather have loved you and have it end like this, dear, than never have known you. I truly would."

The journey to Paris was interminable. Betty had decided not to think of Temple, yet that happy morning face of his would come between her and the things she wanted to think of. To have hurt him like that!—It hurt her horribly; much more than she would have believed possible. And she had been cruel. "Of course it's natural that he should say things about Him. He must hate anyone that—He nearly cried when he said that about rather have loved me than not—Yes—" A lump came in Betty's own throat, and her eyes pricked.

"Come, don't cry," said her aunt briskly; "you've made your choice, and you're going to your lover. Don't be like Lot's wife. You can't eat your cake and have it too."

Vernon's concierge assured these ladies that Monsieur was at home.

"He makes the painting in this moment," she said. "Mount then, my ladies."

They mounted.

Betty remembered her last—her first—visit to his studio: when Paula had disappeared and she had gone to him for help. She remembered how the velvet had come off her dress, and how awful her hair had been when she had looked in the glass afterwards. And Lady St. Craye—how beautifully dressed, how smiling and superior!

"Hateful cat!" said Betty on the stairs.

"Eh?" said her aunt.

Now there would be no one in the studio but Vernon. He would be reading over her letters—nothing in them—only little notes about whether she would or wouldn't be free on

Tuesday—whether she could or couldn't dine with him on Wednesday. But he would be reading them over—perhaps—

The key was in the door.

"Do you mind waiting on the stairs, Auntie dear," said Betty in a voice of honey; "just the first minute?—I would like to have it for us two—alone. You don't mind?"

"Do as you like," said the aunt rather sadly. "I should knock if I were you."

Betty did not knock. She opened the studio door softly. She would like to see him before he saw her.

She had her wish.

A big canvas stood on the easel, a stool in front of it. The table was in the middle of the room, a yellow embroidered cloth on it. There was food on the cloth—little breads, pretty cakes and strawberries and cherries, and wine in tall, beautiful, topaz-coloured glasses.

Vernon sat in his big chair. Betty could see his profile. He sat there, laughing. On the further arm of the chair sat, laughing also, a very pretty young woman. Her black hair was piled high on her head and fastened with a jewelled pin. The sunlight played in the jewels. She wore a pink silk garment. She held cherries in her hand.

"*V'la cheri!*" she said, and put one of the twin cherries in her mouth; then she leant over him laughing, and Vernon reached his head forward to take in his mouth the second cherry that dangled below her chin. His mouth was on the cherry, and his eyes in the black eyes of the girl in pink.

Betty banged the door.

"Come away!" she said to Miss Desmond. And she, who had

354   E. Nesbit

seen, too, the pink picture, came away, holding Betty's arm tight.

"I wonder," she said as they reached the bottom of the staircase, "I wonder he didn't come after us to—to—try to explain."

"I locked the door," said Betty. "Don't speak to me, please."

They were in the train before either broke silence. Betty's face was white and she looked old—thirty almost her aunt thought.

It was Miss Desmond who spoke.

"Betty," she said, "I know how you feel. But you're very young. I think I ought to say that that girl—"

"*Don't!*" said Betty.

"I mean what we saw doesn't necessarily mean that he doesn't love you."

"Perhaps not," said Betty, fierce as a white flame. "Anyhow, it means that I don't love him."

Miss Desmond's tact, worn by three days of anxiety and agitation, broke suddenly, and she said what she regretted for some months:

"Oh, you don't love *him* now? Well, the other man will console you."

"I hate you," said Betty, "and I hate him; and I hope I shall never see a man again as long as I live!"

CHAPTER XXVIII

"AND SO—"

The banging of his door, the locking of it, annoyed Vernon, yet interested him but little. One's acquaintances have such queer notions of humour. He had the excuse—and by good luck the rope—to explore his celebrated roofs. Mimi was more agitated than he, so he dismissed her for the day with many compliments and a bunch of roses, and spent what was left of the light in painting in a background to the sketch of Betty—the warren as his sketch-book helped him to remember it. Perhaps he and she would go there together some day.

He looked with extreme content at the picture on the easel.

He had worked quickly and well. The thing was coming splendidly. Mimi had been right. She could pose herself as no artist had ever posed her. He would make a picture of the thing after all.

The next morning brought him a letter. That he, who had hated letters, should have come to care for a letter more than for anything that could have come to him except a girl. He kissed the letter before he opened it.

"At last," he said. "Oh, this minute was worth waiting for!"

He opened the envelope with a smile mingled of triumph and something better than triumph—and read:

E. Nesbit

"Dear Mr. Vernon:

"I hope that nothing in my manner has led you to expect any other answer than the one I must give. That answer is, of course, *no*. Although thanking you sincerely for your flattering offer, I am obliged to say that I have never thought of you except as a friend. I was extremely surprised by your letter. I hope I have not been in any way to blame. With every wish for your happiness, and regrets that this should have happened, I am yours faithfully,

"Elizabeth Desmond."

He read the letter, re-read it, raised his eyebrows. Then he took two turns across the studio, shrugged his shoulders impatiently, lit a match and watched the letter burn. As the last yellow moving sparks died in the black of its ash, he bit his lip.

"Damn," he said, "oh, damn!"

Next day he went to Spain. A bunch of roses bigger and redder than any roses he had ever sent her came to Lady St. Craye with his card—p.d.a. in the corner.

She, too, shrugged her shoulders, bit her lip and—arranged the roses in water. Presently she tried to take up her life at the point where she had laid it down when, last October, Vernon had taken it into his hands. Succeeding as one does succeed in such enterprises.

It was May again when Vernon found himself once more sitting at one of the little tables in front of the Cafe de la Paix.

"Sit here long enough," he said, "and you see every one you have ever known or ever wanted to know. Last year it was the jasmine lady—and that girl—on the same one and wonderful day. This year it's—by Jove!"

He rose and moved among the closely set chairs and tables to the pavement. The sightless stare of light-blanched spectacles met his eyes. A gentlemanly-looking lady in short skirts stood awaiting him.

"How are you?" she said. "Yes, I know you didn't see me, but I thought you'd like to."

"I do like to, indeed. May I walk with you—or—" he glanced back at the table where his Vermouth stood untasted.

"The impertinence of it! Frightfully improper to sit outside cafes, isn't it?—for women, I mean—and this Cafe in particular. Yes, I'll join you with the greatest pleasure. Coffee please."

"It's ages since I saw you," he said amiably, "not since—"

"Since I called on you at your hotel. How frightened you were!"

"Not for long," he answered, looking at her with the eyes she loved, the eyes of someone who was not Vernon—"Ah, me, a lot of water has run—"

"Not under the bridges," she pleaded: "say off the umbrellas."

"Since," he pursued, "we had that good talk. You remember, I wanted to call on you in London and you wouldn't let me. You might let me now."

"I will," she said. "97 Curzon Street. Your eyes haven't changed colour a bit. Nor your nature, I suppose. Yet something about you's changed. Got over Betty yet?"

"Quite, thanks," he said tranquilly. "But last time we met, you remember we agreed that I had no intentions."

"Wrong lead," she said, smiling frankly at him; "and besides I hold all the trumps. Ace, King, Queen; and Ace, Knave and

E. Nesbit

Queen of another suit."

"Expound, I implore."

"Aces equal general definite and decisive information. King and Queen of hearts equal Betty and the other man."

"There was another man then?"

"There always is, isn't there? Knave—your honoured self. Queen—where is the Queen, by the way,—the beautiful Queen with the sad eyes, blind, poor dear, quite blind to everything but the abominable Knave?"

"Meaning me?"

"It's not an unbecoming cap," she said, stirring her coffee, "and you wear it with an air. Where's the Queen of your suit?"

"I confess I'm at fault."

"The odd trick is mine. And the honours. You may as well throw down your hand. Yes. I play whist. Not bridge. Where is your Queen—Lady St.—what is it?"

"I haven't seen her," he said steadily, "since last June. I left Paris on a sudden impulse, and I hadn't time to say good-bye to her."

"Didn't you even leave a card? That's not like your eyes."

"I think I sent a tub of hydrangeas or something, *pour dire adieu.*"

"That was definite. Remember the date?"

"No," he said, remembering perfectly.

"Not the eleventh, was it? That was the day when you would

get Betty's letter of rejection."

"It may have been the eleventh.—In fact it *was*."

"Ah, that's better! And the tenth—who let you out of your studio on the tenth? I've often wondered."

"I've often wondered who locked me in. It couldn't have been you, of course?"

"As you say. But I was there."

"It wasn't—?"

"But it was. I thought you'd guess that. She got your letter and came up ready to fall into your arms—opened the door softly like any heroine of fiction—I told her to knock—but no: beheld the pink silk picture and fled the happy shore forever."

"Damn!" he said. "I do beg your pardon, but really—"

"Don't waste those really convincing damns on ancient history. I told her it didn't mean that you didn't love her."

"That was clear-sighted of you."

"It was also quite futile. She said it means *she* didn't love *you* at any rate. I suppose she wrote and told you so."

A long pause. Then:

"As you say," said Vernon, "it's ancient history. But you said something about another man."

"Oh, yes—your friend Temple.—Say 'damn' again if it's the slightest comfort to you—I've heard worse words."

"When?" asked Vernon, and he sipped his Vermouth; "not straight away?"

"Bless me, no! Months and months. That picture in your studio gave her the distaste for all men for quite a long time. We took her home, her father and me: by the way, he and she are tremendous chums now."

"Well?"

"You don't want me to tell you the sweet secret tale of their betrothal? He just came down—at Christmas it was. She was decorating the church. Her father had a transient gleam of common sense and sent him down to her. 'Is it you?' 'Is it you?'—All was over! They returned to that Rectory an engaged couple. They were made for each other.—Same tastes, same sentiments. They love the same things—gardens scenery, the simple life, lofty ideals, cathedrals and Walt Whitman."

"And when are they to be married?"

"They are married. 'What are we waiting for, you and I?' No, I don't know which of them said it. They were married at Easter: Sunday-school children throwing cowslips—quite idyllic. All the old ladies from the Mother's Mutual Twaddle Club came and shed fat tears. They presented a tea-set; maroon with blue roses—most 'igh class and select."

"Easter?" said Vernon, refusing interest to the maroon and blue tea-cups. "She must indeed have been extravagantly fond of me."

"Not she! She wanted to be in love. We all do, you know. And you were the first. But she'd never have suited you. I've never known but two women who would."

"Two?" he said. "Which?"

"Myself for one, saving your presence." She laughed and finished her coffee. "If I'd happened to meet you when I was young—and not bad-looking. It's only my age that keeps you from falling in love with me. The other one's the Queen of your suit, poor lady, that you sent the haystack of sunflowers to. Well—Good-bye. Come and see me when you're in town—97 Curzon Street; don't forget."

"I shan't forget," he said; "and if I thought you would condescend to look at me, it isn't what you call your age that would keep me from falling in love with you."

"Heaven defend me!" she cried. "*Au revoir.*"

* * * * *

When Vernon had finished his Vermouth, he strolled along to the street where last year Lady St. Craye had had a flat.

Yes—Madame retained still the apartment. It was to-day that Madame received. But the last of the friends of Madame had departed. Monsieur would find Madame alone.

Monsieur found Madame alone, and reading. She laid the book face downwards on the table and held out the hand he had always loved—slender, and loosely made, that one felt one could so easily crush in one's own.

"How time flies," she said. "It seems only yesterday that you were here. How sweet you were to me when I had influenza. How are you? You look very tired."

"I am tired," he said. "I have been in Spain. And in Italy. And in Algiers."

"Very fatiguing countries, I understand. And what is your best news?"

He stood on the hearth-rug, looking down at her.

"Betty Desmond's married," he said.

"Yes," she answered, "to that nice boy Temple, too. I saw it in the paper. Dreadful isn't it? Here to-day and gone to-morrow!"

"I'll tell you why she married him," said Vernon, letting himself down into a chair, "if you'd like me to. At least I'll tell you why she didn't marry me. But perhaps the subject has ceased to interest you?"

"Not at all," she answered with extreme politeness.

So he told her.

"Yes, I suppose it would be like that. It must have annoyed you very much. It's left marks on your face, Eustace. You look tired to death."

"That sort of thing does leave marks."

"That girl taught you something, Eustace; something that's stuck."

"It is not impossible, I suppose," he said and then very carelessly, as one leading the talk to lighter things, he added: "I suppose you wouldn't care to marry me?"

"Candidly," she answered, calling all her powers of deception to her aid, "candidly, I don't think I should."

"I knew it," said Vernon, smiling; "my heart told me so."

"She," said Lady St. Craye, "was frightened away from her life's happiness, as they call it, by seeing you rather near to a pink silk model. I suppose you think *I* shouldn't mind such things?"

"You forget," said Vernon demurely. "Such things never happen after one is married."

"No," she said, "of course they don't. I forgot that."

"You might as well marry me," he said, and the look of youth had come back suddenly, as it's way was, to his face.

"I might very much better not."

They looked at each other steadily. She saw in his eyes a little of what it was that Betty had taught him.

She never knew what he saw in hers, for all in a moment he was kneeling beside her; his arm was across the back of her chair, his head was on her shoulder and his face was laid against her neck, as the face of a child, tired with a long play-day, is laid against the neck of its mother.

"Ah, be nice to me!" he said. "I am very tired."

Her arm went round his shoulders as the mother's arm goes round the shoulders of the child.

E. Nesbit

ABOUT THE AUTHOR

 **Edith Nesbit** (married name Edith Bland; August 15, 1858 - May 4, 1924) was an English author and poet whose children's works were published under the androgynous name of E. Nesbit. She wrote or collaborated on over 60 books of fiction for children, several of which have been adapted for film and television. She started a new genre, of magical adventures arising from everyday settings, and has been much imitated. She was also a political activist and co-founded the Fabian Society, a precursor to the modern Labour Party.

She was born in 1858 at 38, Lower Kennington Lane in Kennington, Surrey (now part of Greater London), the daughter of a schoolteacher, John Collis Nesbit, who died in March 1862, before her fourth birthday. Her sister Mary's ill health meant that the family moved around constantly for some years, living variously in Brighton, Buckinghamshire, France (Dieppe, Rouen, Paris, Tours, Poitiers, Angouleme, Bordeaux, Arcachon, Pau, Bagneres de Bigorre, and Dinan in Brittany), Spain and Germany, before settling for three years at Halstead Hall in Halstead in north-west Kent, a location which later inspired The Railway Children.

Nesbit and Bland were among the founders of the Fabian Society (a precursor to the Labour Party) in 1884.

Choose from Thousands of 1stWorldLibrary Classics By

A. M. Barnard
Ada Leverson
Adolphus William Ward
Aesop
Agatha Christie
Alexander Aaronsohn
Alexander Kielland
Alexandre Dumas
Alfred Gatty
Alfred Ollivant
Alice Duer Miller
Alice Turner Curtis
Alice Dunbar
Allen Chapman
Alleyne Ireland
Ambrose Bierce
Amelia E. Barr
Amory H. Bradford
Andrew Lang
Andrew McFarland Davis
Andy Adams
Angela Brazil
Anna Alice Chapin
Anna Sewell
Annie Besant
Annie Hamilton Donnell
Annie Payson Call
Annie Roe Carr
Annonaymous
Anton Chekhov
Archibald Lee Fletcher
Arnold Bennett
Arthur C. Benson
Arthur Conan Doyle
Arthur M. Winfield
Arthur Ransome
Arthur Schnitzler
Arthur Train
Atticus
B.H. Baden-Powell
B. M. Bower
B. C. Chatterjee
Baroness Emmuska Orczy
Baroness Orczy
Basil King
Bayard Taylor
Ben Macomber
Bertha Muzzy Bower
Bjornstjerne Bjornson

Booth Tarkington
Boyd Cable
Bram Stoker
C. Collodi
C. E. Orr
C. M. Ingleby
Carolyn Wells
Catherine Parr Traill
Charles A. Eastman
Charles Amory Beach
Charles Dickens
Charles Dudley Warner
Charles Farrar Browne
Charles Ives
Charles Kingsley
Charles Klein
Charles Hanson Towne
Charles Lathrop Pack
Charles Romyn Dake
Charles Whibley
Charles Willing Beale
Charlotte M. Braeme
Charlotte M. Yonge
Charlotte Perkins Stetson
Clair W. Hayes
Clarence Day Jr.
Clarence E. Mulford
Clemence Housman
Confucius
Coningsby Dawson
Cornelis DeWitt Wilcox
Cyril Burleigh
D. H. Lawrence
Daniel Defoe
David Garnett
Dinah Craik
Don Carlos Janes
Donald Keyhoe
Dorothy Kilner
Dougan Clark
Douglas Fairbanks
E. Nesbit
E. P. Roe
E. Phillips Oppenheim
E. S. Brooks
Earl Barnes
Edgar Rice Burroughs
Edith Van Dyne
Edith Wharton

Edward Everett Hale
Edward J. O'Biren
Edward S. Ellis
Edwin L. Arnold
Eleanor Atkins
Eleanor Hallowell Abbott
Eliot Gregory
Elizabeth Gaskell
Elizabeth McCracken
Elizabeth Von Arnim
Ellem Key
Emerson Hough
Emilie F. Carlen
Emily Bronte
Emily Dickinson
Enid Bagnold
Enilor Macartney Lane
Erasmus W. Jones
Ernie Howard Pie
Ethel May Dell
Ethel Turner
Ethel Watts Mumford
Eugene Sue
Eugenie Foa
Eugene Wood
Eustace Hale Ball
Evelyn Everett-green
Everard Cotes
F. H. Cheley
F. J. Cross
F. Marion Crawford
Fannie E. Newberry
Federick Austin Ogg
Ferdinand Ossendowski
Fergus Hume
Florence A. Kilpatrick
Fremont B. Deering
Francis Bacon
Francis Darwin
Frances Hodgson Burnett
Frances Parkinson Keyes
Frank Gee Patchin
Frank Harris
Frank Jewett Mather
Frank L. Packard
Frank V. Webster
Frederic Stewart Isham
Frederick Trevor Hill
Frederick Winslow Taylor

Friedrich Kerst
Friedrich Nietzsche
Fyodor Dostoyevsky
G.A. Henty
G.K. Chesterton
Gabrielle E. Jackson
Garrett P. Serviss
Gaston Leroux
George A. Warren
George Ade
Geroge Bernard Shaw
George Cary Eggleston
George Durston
George Ebers
George Eliot
George Gissing
George MacDonald
George Meredith
George Orwell
George Sylvester Viereck
George Tucker
George W. Cable
George Wharton James
Gertrude Atherton
Gordon Casserly
Grace E. King
Grace Gallatin
Grace Greenwood
Grant Allen
Guillermo A. Sherwell
Gulielma Zollinger
Gustav Flaubert
H. A. Cody
H. B. Irving
H.C. Bailey
H. G. Wells
H. H. Munro
H. Irving Hancock
H. R. Naylor
H. Rider Haggard
H. W. C. Davis
Haldeman Julius
Hall Caine
Hamilton Wright Mabie
Hans Christian Andersen
Harold Avery
Harold McGrath
Harriet Beecher Stowe
Harry Castlemon
Harry Coghill
Harry Houidini

Hayden Carruth
Helent Hunt Jackson
Helen Nicolay
Hendrik Conscience
Hendy David Thoreau
Henri Barbusse
Henrik Ibsen
Henry Adams
Henry Ford
Henry Frost
Henry James
Henry Jones Ford
Henry Seton Merriman
Henry W Longfellow
Herbert A. Giles
Herbert Carter
Herbert N. Casson
Herman Hesse
Hildegard G. Frey
Homer
Honore De Balzac
Horace B. Day
Horace Walpole
Horatio Alger Jr.
Howard Pyle
Howard R. Garis
Hugh Lofting
Hugh Walpole
Humphry Ward
Ian Maclaren
Inez Haynes Gillmore
Irving Bacheller
Isabel Cecilia Williams
Isabel Hornibrook
Israel Abrahams
Ivan Turgenev
J.G.Austin
J. Henri Fabre
J. M. Barrie
J. M. Walsh
J. Macdonald Oxley
J. R. Miller
J. S. Fletcher
J. S. Knowles
J. Storer Clouston
J. W. Duffield
Jack London
Jacob Abbott
James Allen
James Andrews
James Baldwin

James Branch Cabell
James DeMille
James Joyce
James Lane Allen
James Lane Allen
James Oliver Curwood
James Oppenheim
James Otis
James R. Driscoll
Jane Abbott
Jane Austen
Jane L. Stewart
Janet Aldridge
Jens Peter Jacobsen
Jerome K. Jerome
Jessie Graham Flower
John Buchan
John Burroughs
John Cournos
John F. Kennedy
John Gay
John Glasworthy
John Habberton
John Joy Bell
John Kendrick Bangs
John Milton
John Philip Sousa
John Taintor Foote
Jonas Lauritz Idemil Lie
Jonathan Swift
Joseph A. Altsheler
Joseph Carey
Joseph Conrad
Joseph E. Badger Jr
Joseph Hergesheimer
Joseph Jacobs
Jules Vernes
Julian Hawthrone
Julie A Lippmann
Justin Huntly McCarthy
Kakuzo Okakura
Karle Wilson Baker
Kate Chopin
Kenneth Grahame
Kenneth McGaffey
Kate Langley Bosher
Kate Langley Bosher
Katherine Cecil Thurston
Katherine Stokes
L. A. Abbot
L. T. Meade

L. Frank Baum
Latta Griswold
Laura Dent Crane
Laura Lee Hope
Laurence Housman
Lawrence Beasley
Leo Tolstoy
Leonid Andreyev
Lewis Carroll
Lewis Sperry Chafer
Lilian Bell
Lloyd Osbourne
Louis Hughes
Louis Joseph Vance
Louis Tracy
Louisa May Alcott
Lucy Fitch Perkins
Lucy Maud Montgomery
Luther Benson
Lydia Miller Middleton
Lyndon Orr
M. Corvus
M. H. Adams
Margaret E. Sangster
Margret Howth
Margaret Vandercook
Margaret W. Hungerford
Margret Penrose
Maria Edgeworth
Maria Thompson Daviess
Mariano Azuela
Marion Polk Angellotti
Mark Overton
Mark Twain
Mary Austin
Mary Catherine Crowley
Mary Cole
Mary Hastings Bradley
Mary Roberts Rinehart
Mary Rowlandson
M. Wollstonecraft Shelley
Maud Lindsay
Max Beerbohm
Myra Kelly
Nathaniel Hawthrone
Nicolo Machiavelli
O. F. Walton
Oscar Wilde

Owen Johnson
P.G. Wodehouse
Paul and Mabel Thorne
Paul G. Tomlinson
Paul Severing
Percy Brebner
Percy Keese Fitzhugh
Peter B. Kyne
Plato
Quincy Allen
R. Derby Holmes
R. L. Stevenson
R. S. Ball
Rabindranath Tagore
Rahul Alvares
Ralph Bonehill
Ralph Henry Barbour
Ralph Victor
Ralph Waldo Emmerson
Rene Descartes
Ray Cummings
Rex Beach
Rex E. Beach
Richard Harding Davis
Richard Jefferies
Richard Le Gallienne
Robert Barr
Robert Frost
Robert Gordon Anderson
Robert L. Drake
Robert Lansing
Robert Lynd
Robert Michael Ballantyne
Robert W. Chambers
Rosa Nouchette Carey
Rudyard Kipling
Saint Augustine
Samuel B. Allison
Samuel Hopkins Adams
Sarah Bernhardt
Sarah C. Hallowell
Selma Lagerlof
Sherwood Anderson
Sigmund Freud
Standish O'Grady
Stanley Weyman
Stella Benson
Stella M. Francis

Stephen Crane
Stewart Edward White
Stijn Streuvels
Swami Abhedananda
Swami Parmananda
T. S. Ackland
T. S. Arthur
The Princess Der Ling
Thomas A. Janvier
Thomas A Kempis
Thomas Anderton
Thomas Bailey Aldrich
Thomas Bulfinch
Thomas De Quincey
Thomas Dixon
Thomas H. Huxley
Thomas Hardy
Thomas More
Thornton W. Burgess
U. S. Grant
Upton Sinclair
Valentine Williams
Various Authors
Vaughan Kester
Victor Appleton
Victor G. Durham
Victoria Cross
Virginia Woolf
Wadsworth Camp
Walter Camp
Walter Scott
Washington Irving
Wilbur Lawton
Wilkie Collins
Willa Cather
Willard F. Baker
William Dean Howells
William le Queux
W. Makepeace Thackeray
William W. Walter
William Shakespeare
Winston Churchill
Yei Theodora Ozaki
Yogi Ramacharaka
Young E. Allison
Zane Grey